In a vast
and untamed land,
true love comes
home at last....

Also by Jill Marie Landis

WILDFLOWER
SUNFLOWER

ROSE

JILL MARIE LANDIS

J

JOVE BOOKS, NEW YORK

ROSE

A Jove Book / published by arrangement with
the author

PRINTING HISTORY
Jove edition / September 1990

ISBN: 0-515-10346-2

Jove Books are published by The Berkley Publishing Group,
200 Madison Avenue, New York, New York 10016.
The name "JOVE" and the "J" logo
are trademarks belonging to Jove Publications, Inc.

PRINTED IN THE UNITED STATES OF AMERICA

10 9 8 7 6 5 4 3 2 1

Rose

*

Prologue

*

Italy, June 1887

The cluster of faded, slate-roofed buildings gathered beneath the Pennine Alps began to look like an ethereal fairy-tale setting as the roseate glow of the afternoon sun intensified. Row upon uneven row of houses in the village of Corio were bound between narrow cobblestone streets that had been laid over paths and byways once traveled by the foot soldiers of the Roman Empire. The worn streets intersected at the piazza that fronted the ancient church of San Genesio, a baroque edifice of brick and stone with tolling bells that marked the passage of time and lives. A yawning archway in a wall beside the church opened onto the narrow road that passed beneath and meandered its way downhill to the farming settlement of Crotte. There, on a gentle rise above the river Malone, amid fields stained emerald by summer crops and air pungent with the scent of new mown hay, stood a farmhouse nearly as old as the road itself.

A wild, unplanned garden bordered the yard that fronted the old stone house. Roses from deepest crimson to the delicate pinks of sunset grew alongside stark white calla lilies, rich violet hydrangeas, and fragrant multi-hued stocks. Garlic had been planted among the blushing roses to discourage pesky aphids while scattered basil, rosemary, thyme, and oregano plants grew among the ornamentals. A grapevine—the gnarled and twisted grandfather of them all—climbed a square-cornered trellis to frame the riotous colors below.

Within the kitchen of the old house pulsed heat and sound as intense as the vibrant colors of the summer garden. The cavernous room with its stone walls and earthen floor smelled of wood smoke, fried fish, and hot olive oil pungent with garlic. Laughter often interrupted the incessant chatter of women's voices to mingle with the familiar sounds of kitchen work: a knife that beat a tattoo on the wooden chopping block, the scrape of a spoon against the sides of a mixing bowl, the clatter of iron lids upon the stove top.

The racket and close, warm air in her aunt Rina's kitchen were nothing out of the ordinary, but as Rosa Audi paused to glance up from her pumping at the butter churn, she decided to seek relief from this symphony of routine. This was her last day in Corio, and nothing that occurred today should be taken for granted or seen as ordinary. Rosa was determined to hold each moment of this day in her heart. The hours of daylight were at their peak in June, the sun unwilling to slip behind the mountain until late in the evening. It would be light until after nine o'clock, and since the men used the extra hours to their advantage, it would be a while yet before they left the fields. There was still time for Rosa to escape the bustling activity in the kitchen.

Zia Rina stood over the frying pan, seasoning and turning the trout that sizzled in hot oil. Rosa's older, married sister, Angelina, could not relieve her of her duty at the churn, for she was busy taking bread from the oven. Rosa spied little Margarina standing in the doorway. When her niece glanced in her direction, Rosa waved her near. Within seconds, the dark-eyed, round-faced girl with bobbing braids and a ready, flashing smile had replaced Rosa at the churn.

As she slipped out of the kitchen into the warm summer evening, Rosa glanced around to be certain no one had seen her escape. Fortunately, her departure had gone unnoticed, and in the bustle of the kitchen, she would not be missed for a while. She used the hem of her apron to wipe her brow, then began walking up the path through the maze of white-barked birch, majestic elm and oak, and occasional deep green fir trees that grew on the hillside behind the house.

Rosa stopped near a stand of gentle birch trees and sat down

in the soft loam beside them. She gazed down on the men of
the village as they bundled and raked the early crop. Others
moved slowly across the field with their tall scythes swinging
to and fro, swiftly cutting off the slender stalks that rippled
before them much like waves on an emerald lake. The fecund
scent of new mown alfalfa lay heavy on the air.

She brushed aside a tendril that had escaped one of the two
thick braids of ebony hair she had wound about her head and
leaned back on her elbows with a gentle sigh. It was good to be
out of the kitchen, good to watch the shadows slip across the
ridges and fill the valleys beyond.

After a time, Rosa reached down into the deep pocket of the
much mended apron that covered her loose-fitting brown serge
gown and pulled out the folded page that was never far from
her these days. She held tightly to the letter from her husband,
Giovanni, as one holds on to a seed before it is planted, taking
care lest it blow away, carrying with it all hope for the future.

Carefully she opened the rumpled page. The creases along
each fold were nearly worn through, the edges frayed from
much handling. It did not matter that her fingers had nearly
rubbed the words away, for Rosa had committed them to
memory weeks ago.

"*Mia moglie*," Giovanni had written. My wife.

Rosa felt very little like a wife, but still, she thrilled at the
salutation. After all, she *was* his wife, even though Giovanni
had left for America barely a month after their wedding, even
though she still lived with her own raucous family and not his,
as a proper wife should do. She scanned the lines again and
tried to recall the sound of Giovanni's voice.

> *Mia moglie,*
>
> I have found a home. Not only a home, Rosa, but a place
> to live and work, in a store of our own. The village, Broken
> Shoe, is in the territory of Wyoming. It is small, perhaps not
> even as large as Corio, but I have seen the cities here, Rosa,
> and I know that you could not bear the darkness of the places
> where so many people from the old country have settled.
>
> Enclosed you will find a postal money order which you
> should change into American dollars. I send to you also a
> ticket for passage, Genoa to New York. When you arrive in
> Genoa, buy a train ticket there for the trip from New York to

Wyoming. No tariff is charged if you buy in Italy. Keep your money well hidden and tell no one how much you have. In New York, speak only to the Fathers of San Carlo Borromeo. They meet every ship and help those in need of assistance. Be careful of changing the train; be sure you are on the correct line. Find an American policeman, Rosa. They will help you if you need it.

I hope that you still practice your English with the contessa. Everyone here speaks only English. You must learn as much as you can, *cara,* for I wait for you and remain your own

Giovanni

"Cara, I wait for you," he had written.

As I wait for you, she thought.

Three years. It had been such a long, long time. How often had she despaired that the time to leave Corio would never come? Now, finally, when the sun rose tomorrow, it would be time to leave.

She sighed and folded the letter along the worn lines and slipped it back into her pocket. Tucking the loose strands of her abundant, waving ebony hair behind her ears, Rosa toyed with the rose-gold wedding band that encircled the third finger of her left hand. She tried to picture Giovanni as he had been three years ago, then refused to admit to herself that it was a difficult task.

Of course she remembered his warm brown eyes and the gentleness behind his smile. When Giovanni left Italy he had been slender, still boyish when compared to big men like her oldest brother, Guido. His nature was as gentle as his smile, his hopes and dreams for a future in America as high as the sky above Corio. She tried again to recall the sound of his voice, the touch of his hand, but sadly, her memories of him had become as faded as a sepia photograph. Rosa was certain, though, that when she saw him again, heard his voice, and felt his touch, the lonely years that had passed would become a memory.

Rosa stared down at the men moving across the field as they felled the alfalfa. Once bundled, it was hauled and hoisted into barns and stables to be used for winter feed for milk cows. Until the cold weather came, the animals were left to roam the low hills that surrounded the valley. She realized that when the first snowfall blanketed the land and frosted the trees, she would not be in Crotte to see it. She would not rush to greet the first flakes from the balcony that circled the upper floor of the stone house, nor would she lean out with her open palms to catch them. Did it snow in the place called Wyoming?

In the few precious letters Giovanni had sent to Italy, he had described his work and travels, but said nothing of the countryside where he had settled. She had learned little more than the cost of fruits and vegetables in America, the cost of land, the businesses Giovanni considered suitable—but of the land itself—she knew little. Whether it snowed or not, she was determined to love her new home. After all, it was the place her husband had chosen.

It was becoming harder to see the fields below, for the sun had slipped behind the hills. The valley had become cloaked in a gauzy blue-gray light. Fireflies capered around the tree trunks and hid in the tall grass, their flashing luminescent bodies reminding her of flickering votive candles in the church of San Genesio. She saw her three brothers—burly, heavyset men with dark flashing eyes and easy smiles—begin to move toward the house, their labors finished until the sun reappeared again in a few short hours. Rosa leapt to her feet and hastily brushed the grass and leaves from her skirt. With a glance toward the woods behind her, she hurried down the hillside, stepping carefully so as not to turn her ankle on a loose stone. It was enough that she had had the past few moments alone; it would not do to upset the men by being late to help with the meal. Not now, when there was so little time left with them, and especially not when Guido was so against her leaving.

When she reached the yard, the men were still out of sight, but Rosa could hear them splashing as they washed their hands and faces in the wooden kegs behind the house. Two large casks, cut in half and filled with spring water, served as the men's washroom during the warm months of the year. The cursory scrubbing was all they would permit themselves until week's end.

Her three brothers, accompanied by their brother-in-law Genesio, soon appeared around the corner of the house. They were dressed in the baggy woolen trousers that served as their work pants. The color of the pants had long ago faded beneath the sun and the beatings the fabrics had to withstand on wash day. Great perspiration stains encircled the armpits of the once-white shirts woven of thick, sturdy flax; water now soaked the front of them. Heavy leather work boots, so worn that the toes curled upward and the heels slanted with wear, completed their work attire.

During the summer, the evening meal was served outside at a long table set beneath the grape arbor. The hungry laborers made short work of the meal, and Rosa's last evening with her family passed all too quickly as she and the women scurried back and forth from the kitchen to the garden serving the many courses.

After everything was cleared away, the dishes washed, the kitchen tidied, Rosa returned to the garden to enjoy what was left of the warm evening. Zia Rina was already there, seated on a wooden swing suspended from the sturdy posts that shaped one end of the arbor. The old woman glanced up from where her nimble fingers, now gnarled with age, paused over the embroidery she was working. The piece of cloth she had woven herself; the initials she outlined read GAR for Giovanni and Rosa Audi. Thanks to her *zia*'s many contributions, Rosa's bride trunk was nearly filled with handwoven cloths, runners, and scarves. Crocheted lace to decorate table and chairs in her new home lay starched and ready between the larger pieces.

"*Zia*," Rosa warned, turning up the wick of the oil lamp that rested on a small round table her aunt had dragged out into the yard, "you must stop. This light is bad for your eyes."

Rina spoke in the same authoritative tone that her niece had used. "I know when it is time for me to stop. Go and get more wine for the men."

"Eh, Rosa, get another chair, too." Guido settled down in the rocking chair near Zia Rina's swing and issued orders much the way her papa used to before he died. Guido, at twenty-nine, was the oldest of the three sons, the head of the family now that both of their parents had died. Everyone deferred to his wishes. Rosa had the feeling they would have done so regardless of his age, for Guido had a way of commanding and cowing the others that came naturally to him. Taller than either Mario or Pino, Guido was built like a bull and was twice as nasty.

Unwilling to challenge him as she usually did, Rosa went to

get another straight-backed chair. She knew that if she refused to do his bidding, Zia Rina would jump up and fetch whatever Guido asked for. Even though it was the way of all men to order the women about, Rosa thought it unfair, especially when Guido was hale and hardy and Zia Rina so frail. Barely five feet tall, her *zia* reminded Rosa of a tiny gray field mouse with bright, shining black eyes that missed nothing. She was never idle. Rosa knew that if her *zia* could, she would devise a way to sew while she slept. A shadow crossed Rosa's brow and she wondered for the thousandth time how Zia Rina would fare alone with the household of men once she herself had gone to Giovanni in America.

Rina had been the only member of the family to offer encouragement to Rosa when she talked of leaving for America. As Rosa returned to the house and gathered more glasses and another bottle of wine for the men, she told herself that even her concern for Rina could not keep her from going to Giovanni.

The yard was cloaked in darkness now, illuminated only by the light that spilled out of the doorway and the soft glow of Zia Rina's lamp. The weak circle of light was easily swallowed up in the darkness. Stars dusted the heavens like seeds of new worlds scattered by the hand of God. The hills and distant mountain peaks loomed as giant silhouettes against the black sky.

Rosa passed out three glasses to the men and handed the tall, nearly opaque green bottle to Guido. As the men relaxed, seated on the mismatched straight-backed kitchen chairs, Rosa sat on the swing beside Rina. She remained silent, her hand resting against the pocket of her apron that contained Giovanni's letter. Suddenly exhausted, she hoped that in an hour or so the men would relax and nothing more would be required of her so that she could slip off to bed. Rosa envied Angelina. Her older sister had already gone, taking Margarina off to bed in their home down the lane.

The men talked among themselves for a time until Rosa, thinking they would surely be ready to retire soon, was about to stand and excuse herself. She had been lost in thought, reviewing each and every detail of her impending departure, when the heavy sound of Guido's deep voice interrupted her musing.

"So, Rosa, you're going after that lout, Giovanni, after all?"

They had had this same conversation many times; it was one Rosa had hoped to avoid on her last night at home. She refused to answer his insulting question and just stared back at him. The smirk that hooked his upper lip was not fully visible in the darkness, but she could sense its presence.

"Leave it alone, Guido." It was Pino who spoke. Now as always he was her defender. Not only were they the closest in age—he was three years older than her twenty—but they were alike in temperament and appearance as well. Except for the fact that Rosa's eyes were a strange blend of topaz with brown highlights and his were near black, Pino's eyes were as round and wide as hers. The shortest of her brothers, Pino was only a head taller than Rosa. His frame was thick and wide, his spine straight, his square hands capable of the tasks of the field.

Rosa stood, intent on leaving the brewing argument behind as she sought shelter in the house.

"Does Giovanni come to get her himself?" Guido persisted.

"No. He sends money and a letter. Three years, three letters." As if the others were incapable of counting, he held up a thumb and two fingers and shook them in Pino's face. He belched, a loud, rumbling sound that climbed upward from deep in his belly. "Three stinking letters and then the *command* for her to go to America alone. And what if I say she is not going?"

"Guido, *basta*," Zia Rina warned. She raised her hand as if her feeble show of strength could halt his argument.

Guido reached out and grabbed Rosa's arm. "Guido!" Rosa was startled by his physical assault.

"You are not as smart as you think you are, Rosa." He brought his face close to hers, and she could smell the wine on his breath. "You and your America. You know nothing." His grip tightened on her arm and she winced. "If you were so smart you would never have married a man who would run off and leave you. The man is a dreamer, a fool."

"Let go of my arm, Guido." Rosa held her temper in check as she tried to pull out of his punishing grip.

"Let her go, Guido." Pino stood so quickly that his chair toppled back with a soft thud as it hit the ground.

"Yes, let her go." Even Mario spoke up this time. Guido shot a dark look in his direction. Always a follower, Mario quickly slumped back down in his chair and poured himself another glass of wine.

"So, go, Rosa." Guido released her with a rough shove toward the house.

Rosa tilted her chin in defiance and spat the words back at him. "I will, Guido. And I'll be more than happy to see the last of you." She turned away from him and walked toward the door.

"You'll be back," Guido shouted after her. "You'll be back, begging to live here again."

Rosa halted inside the back door and hastily crossed herself. She hoped the harsh words she had fired at her brother would not call bad luck down upon her.

*

Chapter One

*

Wyoming, July 1887

A rickety oak table of unknown origin with a surface so scarred it might have been a chopping block functioned as a resting place for a pair of well-worn but comfortable boots coated with a fine layer of dust. From the scuffed leather of the boots emerged a pair of long, lean legs molded by muscle and enveloped in a pair of Levi's so worn that they shone at both knee and thigh.

Shifting his weight around in the swivel chair where he sat slouched behind his desk, Marshal Kase Storm swung first one and then the other booted foot to the floor. He folded back the front page of the *Cheyenne Leader*, then shook out a stubborn wrinkle along the fold. Scanning the page, Kase found nothing so noteworthy that it would change his life before sunset, and he tossed the newspaper on top of the clutter that already littered the table. Clasping his fingers behind his head, Kase spun the chair around in the opposite direction and tilted back, this time propping his feet up on the opposite corner of the table and stared out the window of the tiny room that served as his office.

The only sign of movement on the deserted street outside was a whirling dust devil. Kase watched it pass. Gazing out of the window, he was content to allow another hour of the day to slide by. A crooked smile crossed his face as he sat musing over his present circumstances. He'd heard Tombstone, Arizona, referred to as the town too tough to die and thought that if Busted Heel, Wyoming, were to have its own motto, it would surely be "Busted Heel, the town too dead to care."

The only danger he had faced in his six months as marshal of Busted Heel was breaking his neck as he hung over the roof of the local whorehouse trying to rescue a kitten that belonged to one of the girls. When the wooden rain gutter collapsed beneath his weight it gave Kase a heart-stopping scare while the four working girls and the local madam, all bedecked in sequins, satin, and feathers, squealed in fear from the muddy backyard below.

No, he thought, I'll be lucky if I run into any more danger than that.

Sometimes Kase wondered what he was doing wasting his days amid the clutter of the unkempt office or, when the spirit moved him, walking along the wood-plank sidewalk that fronted the few stores and shops that comprised the whistle-stop town of Busted Heel.

But then he would think back six months to the disclosure that had knocked him over with the swift, sure power of a mule's kick, and Kase Storm knew that it would be a while longer before he could go home again.

Three hollow knocks sounded on the door and without moving a muscle, Kase called out, "It's open! No use standing on the other side."

The door swung wide and Flossie Gibbs, the owner and madam of Busted Heel's Hospitality Parlor and Retreat, swept in on a gust of plains wind and cheap perfume, her flounced, chartreuse satin skirt rustling as she crossed the floor. The door banged shut behind her, and Kase knew without turning who had entered.

"Hey, Floss."

"Hey, Kase," she boomed in salutation. "How come you always know who it is without turnin' around?"

"I don't have to see folks to know who they are; I can smell 'em." He didn't tell her it was the overpowering scent of her perfume that gave her away.

Kase dropped his hands and spun the chair, then stood and stretched out to his full six-foot-three-inch height.

"All I have to do is peer into them crystal-ball blue eyes of yours and I forget you're part Indian at all," Flossie said.

"Well, as much as I'd like to forget it right now, I am." Because it was Flossie and she was his friend, he knew she meant no insult. Still, the reference hurt. "What can I do for you, ma'am?"

She reached up and straightened the collar of his brown cambric shirt and smoothed the seam along the shoulder. The fringed and beaded reticule that dangled from her wrist slapped gently against his chest with every move.

"Well, I jes' came over to invite you to supper with us, Marshal. It's been some time since we had us a dinner party, so I thought to cheer up the girls I'd order us a mess o' fried chicken over from Mrs. Matheson's boardin'house. That's about the only dish she can make without poisonin' us."

He nodded in agreement. "Sure, I'll be glad to come for dinner. What time?"

"Thought we'd start early. 'Bout five."

"Fine." He hooked his thumbs into his hip pockets and rocked back on the heels of his boots. "Things a little slow this time of year, Flossie?"

"No slower than any other time of the year in this four-whore town." She chuckled bawdily again, throwing back her head with a motion that set her ponderous bosom shaking. The lace that edged the low neckline of the shocking shade of green bobbed and fluttered as she laughed. "You noticed I don't count myself anymore, didn't ya, boy?"

Flossie peered at him out of the corner of her eye, and Kase could almost imagine her as she might have appeared forty years earlier. But now, at sixty, powder and rouge caked her skin, creating deeper creases in the lines around her eyes and mouth. He knew that beneath the brassy henna tint, her hair was no doubt frosted with silver. She told him once that she had begun whoring at sixteen. He guessed that she was probably quite a looker then.

"You've still got what it takes, Flossie, no doubt about that."

"Don't lie to a liar, boy. You know firsthand that I don't hold a candle to any of my girls."

He flushed at her words and was thankful that his earth-toned complexion hid his embarrassment. He had only befriended the youngest, Chicago Sue, but Flossie could not know that the young blonde who was only seventeen reminded him so much of his half sister, Annika, that he could not see himself making love to her. But it was true he'd sampled Felicity, Mira, and Satin. It would have been temptation enough for any man living in Busted Heel, but the fact that he rented a room in the Hospitality Parlor made his infrequent visits to them inevitable. Proximity was combined with the added incentive that the girls gave him free of charge what cost other cowboys cold hard cash.

"You think you ought to keep on calling the marshal 'boy'?" he teased.

"I figure since I was close to forty when you were a twinkle in your pappy's eye that I have the right to call you damn near anything I want."

A twinkle in your pappy's eye. The thought hit Kase like a winter gale and froze his high spirits. His fist clenched involuntarily. He walked away from Flossie before she could wonder how her words might have affected him. Shuffling through the posters, letters, and newspapers on the desk, Kase spoke to her over his shoulder. "I'll see you at five, then, Flossie."

As if she sensed his sudden need to be alone, Flossie Gibbs saw herself to the door. "See ya then, Kase," she called out before the door closed behind her with a bang.

He stood staring at the pile of papers on his desk for a moment as he tried to shake the dark thoughts that crowded in on him. A sigh was followed by a shudder that came from the toes of his boots and shook his entire frame. He had to get out. With a slight shake of his head, Kase made certain the gun rack was locked and then turned toward the bentwood hat rack on the wall near the door.

Grabbing his black Stetson, he opened the door with one hand and anchored the hat on his head with the other before he closed the door behind him. With a practiced hand, he nestled the band of the hat more securely around his forehead to shade his eyes. They were far too blue, much too visible, on the sunny street. Although there was no need to expect trouble, he knew that pinning the star of a lawman on his chest and wearing a Colt strapped low on his hip and tied at the thigh, issued an open invitation to any drifter looking to stir up trouble.

The street was nearly empty. Down the way, a farmer and his family loaded a wagon pulled up before Al-Ray's general store. Kase's boots rang hollow on the sidewalk that fronted the buildings on his side of the street. The main and only street in town boasted two distinct personalities. The west side housed the jail, the bath and barber shop, the Yee family's Chinese laundry, and Al-Ray's mercantile. A man could spend a night in the poke, have a bath and shave while his clothes were washed and pressed, then treat himself to a tin of tobacco before he crossed to the less reputable side of town.

Kase glanced across at the east side of the street. Two large buildings there housed Paddie O'Hallohan's Ruffled Garter Saloon and Flossie Gibbs's Hospitality Parlor and Retreat, where Flossie and the girls entertained long after Paddie's closed down for the night. The only other building on the east side was a tiny two-room store that had belonged to a wiry Italian immigrant until he was killed by a ricocheting bullet during a recent shoot-out between two drunken cowboys.

As Kase walked along, taking in the familiar sights and sound of Busted Heel, he thought about the circumstances that had led him to the remote Wyoming town. It seemed just yesterday that his stepfather had firmly taken him aside and asked him into the library for a serious discussion.

It had not taken long for word to reach Caleb Storm that his stepson, twenty-one and a junior lawyer with the prestigious firm of Rigby and Anderson, had attacked a client in the vestibule of the elegant offices overlooking the Charles River in Boston. That very afternoon, Caleb had ushered Kase into the library and impatiently motioned him toward one of the deep leather arm chairs near the fireplace.

Kase had stubbornly shaken his head and said, "I'd prefer to stand."

Caleb's tone had brooked no argument. "Sit! I'm not going to waste time beating around the bush, Kase. You have acted outrageously and I'd like to know why. This hasn't happened since you went to law school. I thought these undisciplined outbursts had ended."

Kase recalled brooding over an answer. No matter how hard he tried, he knew he could not emulate Caleb's even-tempered response to blatant insults to their mixed blood. Nor could Kase easily dismiss the whispers and sly glances that he had endured his entire life. His stepfather, Caleb Storm, was of mixed lineage; he, too, was half Sioux. But Caleb had always had the ability to maintain control of his emotions when confronted with outright bigotry. He was able to adapt to his surroundings, to work within the confines of white society. Kase, on the other hand, had learned to let his fists speak for him.

As he thought back to their confrontation, Kase could still feel the hurt emanating from Caleb as he waited for an explanation. But Kase had refused to give any excuse for his latest outburst. He knew his actions were indefensible. Through his own hard work at law school and through Caleb's influence in Washington, Kase had been granted a position with Rigby and Anderson, an old, well-established firm. Despite the stigma of his half-Sioux heritage, his reputation as an outstanding junior lawyer was growing. But in the library that day, Kase Storm had refused to defend himself. There was nothing he could say that might justify his physical attack on young Brandon Hamilton that morning. Nothing that Caleb would understand, for Caleb Storm would have handled the whole affair differently.

Kase thought he had put Brandon Hamilton and his other preparatory school classmates out of his mind until that morning when he stepped out of his office and overheard the young man speaking to Franklin Rigby, senior partner of the firm.

"I thought, Rigby, that a firm of your repute was beyond hiring anyone of mixed blood. I came seeking representation, not a sideshow medicine man. I won't have Kase Storm defend this suit. What's he prepared to do? A rain dance? Shake a few bones and feathers around the courtroom?"

Kase had watched Brandon straighten and look down his nose at Rigby. From the open doorway, he studied the aristocratic features that declared Brandon's Puritan heritage— a sharply defined nose, clear blue eyes, carefully combed wavy blond hair. He was a sterling example of Boston society's youth—wealthy, well educated, and able to trace his lineage back to the *Mayflower*. Brandon Hamilton had not changed all that much since their days together at the Bradford Preparatory

Academy outside Boston. Hamilton embodied all that Kase had learned to hate with a fury unnurtured by anything his parents ever taught him. Hamilton and his classmates had personally instructed him with their own brand of education.

Kase had been eight when Caleb Storm moved his family back to the Dakotas after a year in Boston. The boy had loved the open land and life on the plains. Then, after seven years, they re-settled in Boston, where Caleb and Analisa sent Kase off to school. Analisa Van Meeteren Storm did so reluctantly, for she had always kept Kase close to her, but she agreed with Caleb that an education would one day offer Kase more protection than her constant nurturing. And so, as in all things, they had decided together to send Kase away to school. "Education," Caleb had told him, "will make all the difference in your life. With it, doors will open that would otherwise remain closed. It will be your weapon and your strength." So although Kase hated the new hard shoes and starched collars, the bleak brick buildings of the city, he gave up the freedom he had known out west, left behind his Indian pony and comfortable clothes, and went off to school to please his parents.

At first, his new classmates had merely taunted him. But the teasing soon became anonymous letters of hate. When Kase had tried to follow Caleb's example and ignore them, his classmates changed their tactics. The taunts turned to jabs. He was tripped as he walked through the halls. A bucket of flour rigged above his door had doused him with its fine powdered whiteness when he entered the room. An accompanying note on his bed had assured him it was the whitest he would ever be. Finally, when some of the students surrounded him in the winter-barren woods that bordered the school and shaved his head in a symbolic scalping, Kase went to the headmaster.

When the culprits were let off with no more punishment than a verbal warning, the rage that had simmered inside him for so long reached the boiling point. From that very day, Kase Storm began to fight back, and did so thoroughly, employing all the fighting skills he had learned when he was just a youngster in the Dakotas.

At first he tried to keep the abuse he had suffered to himself, well aware that his mother was having a hard time of her own adjusting to city life. They had known the isolation of the prairie, the ceaseless wind and vast sea of open land, but it had not been as harsh as this human isolation. He thought it unjust that his mother had to suffer such a stigma. She was Dutch. She was white. Her husband was wealthy, and Caleb's family name still carried its own prestige in Boston. But even with all his advantages, Caleb was still half Sioux. Many doors were closed to him and, because of him, to Analisa. She had done the unspeakable by bearing a half-breed son, as well as Caleb's daughter, Annika. In the eyes of many, she was no longer fit to mingle in polite society.

Caleb has been careful to shield his Anja, as he called her, from insult. He surrounded her with his love and friends who stood beside him, friends he had made while serving the Bureau of Indian Affairs. But even as a child, Kase had been aware of the closed circle of friends they shared and the places they had never been because they were unwelcome.

He could still remember his life before Caleb Storm married his mother. They had lived in a one-room soddie outside Pella, Iowa, with his great-grandfather, the man he called Opa. As he grew older, the sly glances and whispers of the whites made him all too aware of the meaning of his mixed heritage. It became clear to him why his mother never went to town, why no children ever visited him when their own mothers placed sewing orders with Analisa. He came to realize that it was his mixed blood that set his mother apart from the Dutch community and forced her into the lonely existence she had known before Caleb came to them.

What he never fully understood, what his parents never completely explained, was what had become of the man, the Indian, who had fathered him and then left Analisa to face such isolation alone. How had Analisa met her Indian lover? Where had the man gone? What was his name?

Kase was certain he had inherited his fierce temper and intolerance from his true father. What else had he inherited from the mysterious man who had fathered him?

Caleb and Analisa had sent him to Bradford to make something of himself, and he wanted to please them above all else. He had tried to keep his problems at school from them. He fought with his growing rage, tried to become more like Caleb and to measure up to his stepfather's standards, but his dark looks and exotic features went against him. So, too, did his temper. Once he had decided to stand up for himself with his fists, once he had felt the satisfaction of using his size and growing prowess to keep his tormentors at bay, there was no turning back. He became proficient at fighting his own fights.

Despite how much his parents suffered whenever the letters from the school arrived, he never told them what had initiated the fights. Whenever Caleb asked him if his classmates had taunted him, he remained silent. But Analisa, anxiety etched upon her serenely beautiful features, knew what had happened.

"Kase," she often said, "*Laat het gaan*. Let it go. It is of no consequence. You must be bigger than they, more tolerant and forgiving."

But to Kase it was of consequence in its very unfairness. Injustice was something that Kase Storm could not abide.

Between his outbursts, Kase became sullen and withdrawn. He attended to his studies and, with the help of one caring teacher who had seen the potential in him, was able to excel. He looked forward to holidays when Caleb would take him hunting. They would spend days in the woods where his stepfather taught him to live off the land. Hunting, riding, and target practice helped ease the burden of his days at school.

When he signed on at Rigby and Anderson, he hoped he had put the past behind him. It had been three years since he had used his fists on any man, but his fury overwhelmed him the morning he overheard Brandon Hamilton's insults. He could not even recall moving across the room until he had held the man by the throat and pinned him against the wall. At six feet three, Kase towered over most men, and so Hamilton, a head shorter and pounds lighter had been easily grasped and thrust backward until he was pressed against the wall, fighting for breath.

Kase could still hear his own breath hissing between his teeth as he whispered close to the stunned face of the other man. "You want to see what an *Indian* can do, Hamilton? I'll show you firsthand. I can slit your balls off before you have a chance to feel the knife. Then you'll start choking on your own blood as I stuff them down your throat. But don't worry, before you black out I'll slit this reed-thin, lily-white throat of yours and put you out of your misery."

Hamilton sputtered as his complexion purpled, yet Kase did not loosen his grip until he felt Rigby pulling at his shoulder, shouting at him to let go.

Kase shook Brandon Hamilton like a dog and then released him. Weak-kneed, the man slid down the wall as Kase, without a word to anyone, reentered his office, packed up his personal papers, and went home. The confrontation had been worth the cost. At least, he had thought so until his own belligerence had pushed Caleb Storm to reveal a secret to the past that had sent Kase running from all he held dear.

He reached the end of the boardwalk, and his thoughts returned to the present. Time passed slowly in Busted Heel. For a man with nowhere to go and little to do except brood over his past, Kase felt no need to hurry. He sauntered across the street toward Paddie's Ruffled Garter Saloon.

He usually dropped in unannounced once every hour or so, just to be sure Paddie had everything under control. Pausing for a moment he rested against the door frame at the entrance to the saloon and gazed over the uneven swinging double doors into the darkened interior.

Slick Knox, owner of the bathhouse and barbershop, sat at a side table playing cards with a couple of drifters. Everything seemed quiet enough. Kase knew the man would leave the two drifters with enough money in their pockets to avoid trouble afterward. He was certain that Slick was a professional gambler turned businessman, but the man never admitted to as much. Since Knox seemed to be a fairly permanent fixture in town—one unwilling to cause trouble—Kase merely kept an eye on the games from time to time.

Paddie looked up and waved. Lamplight reflected off of his slick bald pate. His cheeks were red and his eyes twinkled as he stood behind the bar drying a beer glass. Black lace–edged garters of purple satin, the trademark of the Ruffled Garter Saloon, banded the man's upper arms. Kase thought that with the addition of a beard and a red cap, Paddie would be the perfect Sinter Klaas, the Dutch version of Saint Nicholas he had believed in as a child.

Kase waved back and crossed the street. Having a marshal around sometimes cramped the customers' style, so he rarely stayed in Paddie's very long. But maybe, he thought with a wry twist of his lips, he was not welcomed by the men who did not know him because he was a half-breed.

"Damn," he cursed under his breath. He'd never entertained such self-doubt before, so why start now?

A small body collided with his kneecaps, and Kase nearly toppled into the street. He reached out to grab the hitching post and straightened himself, but the hapless victim who'd careened into him was not so lucky. George Washington Davis sat sprawled in the dust beside Kase's booted feet, his ebony skin covered with the dust of Main Street.

"How's it goin' down there, G.W.?" Kase teased as he reached down to grab the boy's arm and hoist him to his feet.

G.W. was dressed as the urchin he was, shirtless and shoeless, with nothing beneath the overalls that hung from the boy's bony frame.

"Goin' jus' fine, Marshal. Pappy sent me to fetch you. Dat big old mule you call a hoss is all ready for you to collect."

The boy pointed toward Decatur Davis's blacksmith shop at the end of town in the event Kase had forgotten exactly where it was he'd left his horse.

"In that case, G.W., I'd better go get Sinbad." The two started down the middle of the empty street together, and Kase looked down at the nappy-headed boy who barely reached his gun belt.

"You think your pa would object to my giving you a treat for coming after me?" Kase inquired, his expression serious. He already knew the answer.

G.W.'s eyes lit up. "No, suh."

Kase flipped G.W. a nickel and watched the boy run off in the direction of Al-Ray's store. As Kase walked toward the blacksmith's shop, he pulled out the gold pocket watch that had once been Caleb Storm's father's and noted the hour. Deciding he had time for a ride before dinner, Kase snapped the timepiece shut and worked it down into the watch pocket of his denims with his forefinger. Maybe a long, hard ride would drive some of the confusion from his mind. He always had done some of his best thinking in the saddle.

*

Chapter
Two

*

The immigrant car of the Union Pacific bound for the end of the line at Promontory clattered and swayed as it rolled along the tracks. Part of a twenty-six-car caravan, the flat-roofed wooden box was sandwiched between a two-truck Shay locomotive and a jaunty red caboose. Rosa Audi swayed with the incessant motion of the train as she gazed out the window at the flowing landscape with the ever-changing colors of this raw new land. She had been staring for hours, at times aware of the passing grandeur, sometimes unaware of the scenery as she thought of home and family. Now that she was half a world away, Rosa knew her memories would have to last a lifetime.

Everyone had gathered to bid her farewell on the morning she left Crotte. Angelina had come with her husband Genesio who had dressed in his finest suit, his hair slicked and parted in the center. Mario had worn one of his long, dour expressions. Guido had sat in the rocking chair beneath the grape arbor. Even though it was still early in the day, he was already drinking too much wine. Zia Rina and Angelina's little Margarina had hovered about—questioning, straightening Rosa's dress and hat, checking and rechecking the trunk and valise until Rosa thought she would scream. Finally, it had been time to leave. Pino loaded her baggage into the rickety hay wagon and helped her into the high seat beside him.

Zia Rina had thrust a lush bouquet of carefully dethorned roses into her arms. Rosa buried her face in them, drinking in their heady fragrance while Pino flicked the reins over the horse's back. The wagon had lurched forward, nearly unseating her before beginning the journey out of Crotte.

Today, a month later, the memory of the parting was still vivid in Rosa's mind. She remembered that she had waved and waved to them all as the wagon creaked and groaned its way up the winding road to the village. Never before had the old stone house looked so warm and nurturing, the roses in the garden so vibrant, the twisted vines of the grape arbor so lush as they had on that last day. As Pino drove the old swayback nag up the road, Rosa promised herself that her new home would have a rose garden.

The old wagon labored up the hill and passed beneath the archway beside the church. When they reached the front of the church, Rosa asked him to stop. She climbed down and hurried across the piazza. The heavy wooden door of the church whined mournfully as she pushed it open just far enough to allow herself to slip inside. The interior of San Genesio's was cool and dark, an incense-scented retreat lit only by the colored shards of light that pierced the stained-glass windows to penetrate the gloom. Her gaze had been drawn upward to the vaulted ceiling that loomed above the darkened interior. There had been something ominous about leaving the church behind. How well she remembered kneeling on a hard wooded prie-dieu when she was barely tall enough to see over the top. At the end of the long aisle formed by neat rows of kneelers, shrouded in pristine white linen and dark mystery, the altar stood silent.

She could not help but think of how Giovanni might have looked as he celebrated his first mass here in the village church—but he had married her instead. God forgive me, she had prayed, for taking him from you. Then, unwilling to make Pino wait any longer, Rosa had whispered one final prayer, one for safe passage to America, crossed herself, and slipped out the door.

Now, as she stared out of the train window at the passing landscape, she thought of the flowers of Crotte, the empty church of San Genesio, and she wondered if she would find roses, or even a church, in this place called Wyoming.

As the train rattled down the line toward her destination, Rosa unconsciously smoothed the lush velvet of the black traveling dress her mentor, the Contessa de Raphael, had given her for the trek to America.

The contessa was a member of one of the many noble families that had chosen Corio as their summer residence. When the old count had died, the childless widow had decided to remain in the mountain retreat. The contessa, who could read and write both Italian and English, had been Rosa's only hope. Mustering her courage, Rosa had knocked at the great double doors of the contessa's villa and asked the woman for a position as a housemaid. Rosa then brazenly suggested that instead of paying her in coin, the contessa teach her to read and write English.

Rosa would not soon forget the relief she felt when the lady had laughed and shrugged, "Why not? It will be a challenge that will help fill the loneliness of my days." In time, the contessa had become more of a confidante than an employer. On Rosa's last visit to the villa the great lady had presented her with the velvet gown. "I am old, Rosa. I will never go to America. You must take my dress. At least that way it will be as if a part of me is there."

The train swayed on toward Wyoming. Rosa pressed her forehead against the windowpane seeking relief from the stifling heat in the long, narrow car that housed immigrant travelers. Other cars on the train were just as extreme in their plainness and designated for various groups of travelers. One was set aside for single men, another for Chinese and others of obvious exotic origins. Few windows were fully open, for the air outside was as hot as, or even hotter than, the air inside. What fresh air the passengers were afforded was no luxury, for it carried with it cinders and ash that poured from the locomotive's smokestack.

A barrel-chested conductor sporting a waxed mustache drew her attention as he walked along the passage between the wooden benches on either side of the aisle. The same man had been on duty the previous evening, and Rosa wondered how he managed to remain so cool and unruffled in the tailored midnight coat ornamented with its shining brass buttons, while she sat rumpled and overwarm in black velvet. The man's tie remained irritatingly straight and jauntily tied while his round, flat cap rode straight upon his head.

Last night he had offered to sell Rosa two hard lengths of

pine and three pillows stuffed with straw that would convert the stiff-backed, narrow benches into a bed. Rather than part with two dollars, she decided she would be quite as comfortable leaning against the window. It was not too long before the ache in her back and the crimp in her neck proved her wrong.

"Busted Heel, Wyoming, next stop!"

She nearly jumped out of her seat at the booming sound of the conductor's voice as he passed by her seat. Like every American she had encountered thus far, the man had a most peculiar habit of yelling as though he hoped to be heard by everyone within miles. He called out the same announcement twice more before he walked out of the rear door of the car. Rosa pressed her face against the window and tried to see down the tracks ahead. Anxious to stretch her legs, she reached up and unpinned the hat that matched her dress, another gift from the widowed contessa. Rosa smiled as she brushed the dust from the wide-brimmed hat that was unadorned except for a swag of netting draped across the front. Like her dress, the hat was black, and although Rosa had felt a slight, ominous stirring when she had donned the color relegated to widows, she thought the ensemble made her appear older and more sophisticated. The ebony did much to enhance the pure ivory tone of her skin and deepened the gold of her eyes to a darker brown.

Rosa glanced out the window again as she straightened her hat over the pile of unruly hair wound on the crown of her head. She secured the hat with a long, lethal-looking pin adorned with a pearl and wondered if Giovanni would still find her desirable. After all, she thought, he had not seen her for three years. Doubt assailed Rosa, and she fidgeted on the hard seat, tugging at her heavy, draped skirt. They had been married less than a month before he left for America in search of the dream he said he had for them both. It had been barely enough time to become used to the fact that she was married at all, hardly enough time to become versed in the ways of love between a man and his wife. The direction her thoughts had taken made her jumpy, and in the nervous way of all travelers, Rosa reached down for the hundredth time to reassure herself the bulging valise she had stored beneath the bench was still there.

"Busted Heel!"

As the conductor made a return trip through the car, she wondered if she would ever get used to the harsh sound of English. Everyone she had encountered spoke more rapidly, not to mention louder, than had the contessa.

Rosa frowned when she felt her hat list slowly toward her left ear. She planted her hand firmly in the center of it and hastily re-anchored the hat pin. Thankful that she had reached her stop at last, she remembered how the transfer station at Council Bluffs had nearly been her undoing. It was there Rosa had asked for a transfer to Broken Shoe, Wyoming. The station agent had informed her with very little sympathy that there was no such stop.

"Yes," Rosa had insisted in halting, heavily accented English. "There hasa to be. Is in Wyoming."

"No, there's not!" The man had leaned forward and yelled so loudly and distinctly that Rosa's face had flamed with color. Everyone on the loading dock had heard him. "There . . . is . . . no . . . such . . . place!" the man bellowed again, as if shouting at her would help her understand.

She had leaned toward him in retaliation, her face nearly pressed against the bars of the ticket window and shouted back. "Dare . . . hasa . . . to be . . . becausa . . . my husband . . . saysa . . . so!" Her nerves at the breaking point, she had pulled the letter from Giovanni out of her pocket and, without bothering to unfold it, waved it in his face.

The agent reached down and pulled a thick schedule book from a shelf below the counter. With an exaggerated sigh, he thumbed through it quickly and scanned the pages headed "Wyoming Territory."

"Egbert, Hillsdale, Busted Heel, Archer, Cheyenne." He leaned forward and shouted again. "Where?"

"Brokena Shoe." Rosa spoke through clenched teeth and wished for the first time ever that Guido was standing behind her.

The man threw back his head and howled with laughter.

"Lady, the only place I can find that might *remotely* be the place you want is this flyspeck on the map called Busted Heel." He pointed to the words she tried to read upside down. "I guess the closest your husband could come to that in Eye-talian is 'Broken Shoe.' You want a ticket?"

"To where?"

He began shouting again. "To . . . Busted . . . Heel!"

Rosa nodded, too angry to speak, and within moments the transaction had been made. The man had been more than insulting, the entire experience so wearing that Rosa had felt tears threaten. She longed to tell him that for all she cared, his stupid Union Pacific train could drive straight into the ocean once she disembarked.

Now she had reached the place called Busted Heel, which might or might not turn out to be the town of Broken Shoe that Giovanni had instructed her to find. As the train pulled into the station, her heart tripped faster as she realized that tonight she would sleep in a real bed. Beside Giovanni.

"You supposed to be the marshal o' this dirt hole?"

Kase hadn't heard anyone approach, nor had he heard the door open. The fact that he could have been a dead man by now did little to reassure him that the owner of the gruff voice did not mean to kill him. Sprawled out in his chair, his hands locked behind his head, Kase had his back to both the door and the intruder. His feet were propped up on the windowsill. There was no way he could reach for the Colt strapped to his thigh without the man in the doorway noticing, so he left his hands right where they were.

Resigned to the fact that his next move might just be his last, Kase drew a long, deep breath, lowered both feet slowly to the floor, and swiveled his chair, none too swiftly, toward the unexpected caller. As he turned, Kase became all too aware of the slow, steady beat of his heart, the breath that filled his lungs, and the still, hot July air that pressed down on him in the confined space of his office.

But when he recognized the unexpected caller, he relaxed and remained sprawled in the chair. "Yeah, I'm the marshal of this 'dirt hole.' What I want to know is what you're doing here?"

The one-eyed man stepped forward and closed the door behind him with a sun-stained brown hand.

"You might say I was just passin' through and heard this place had some young, two-bit marshal that couldn't tell a skunk from a house cat, so I came to have me a look-see."

"Or I might say that you were sent up here to find me. Mightn't I?" A frown marred Kase's strong features.

The old man looked around, searching for a place to spit, and then thought better of it. "Ya might," he agreed with a nod.

Kase stood and walked around the table. He extended a hand in greeting. "It's been a long time, Zach."

Zach Elliot reached out and pumped Kase's hand with a firm, steady handshake. "The last time I seen you, you was thirteen."

"How come you don't look any older?" Kase asked.

"Hell, boy, I was born old."

"I believe you were." Kase nodded in agreement as he assessed his old friend's appearance. Zach looked much the same as he'd been twenty years ago; even then, his strawlike hair had been snow white. The thick, shaggy mustache that hid his upper lip was the same shade except for the tobacco stains near the corners of his mouth. Where Zach's left eye should have been there was a patch of scar tissue. The trail of a knife wound traced a path through the wrinkles of his weather-beaten skin to the underside of his jawline. As Kase took in the beaked nose that twisted slightly to the left and the face shadowed by stubble, he fought against his feelings of hostility toward his old mentor. He was sure Caleb had sent Zach Elliot to talk him into going home.

Zach pulled his hand out of Kase's firm grip and pushed his turned-up shirtsleeves toward his elbows. Kase turned away, returned to his own side of the desk, and pulled open the bottom drawer. "I was just about to eat," Kase said as he fished through the drawer. He pulled out a can of beans and straightened up again. "Want to join me?"

"Cold beans?"

"You getting picky in your old age?" Kase wanted to know.

"Not me. An' sixty-five ain't nobody's old age. I was jes' thinkin' 'bout the kind of grub you must o' had livin' up there in Caleb's mansion." Zach walked to the corner of the room where he spit into the trash can, then lifted a bentwood chair and pulled it up to the front of the desk. Avoiding any comment on Boston, Kase sat down opposite him and shuffled through the top drawer for a can opener.

The marshal tossed a handful of papers out of the drawer, adding them to the confusion on top of the desk.

"This what you're a rootin' for?" Zach slipped his hand beneath the pile closest to him and withdrew a wickedly sharp blade Kase used to open his daily ration of cold beans.

"Thanks." Realizing he would need another bowl, Kase set down the can and started to rise.

"I'll eat outta the can," Zach volunteered, guessing the younger man's intentions.

Kase sat back down. The drawer was opened again, and this time Kase pulled out a bowl and two spoons.

"Ain't this the limit?" Zach watched while Kase unceremoniously dumped cold beans into the bowl.

"You want to eat or not?"

"I ain't sure at this point." Zach shook his head.

The meal was soon divided, and Kase eased back in his chair. They ate in silence until Kase set his empty bowl on the edge of the desk and looked across at Zach.

"If Caleb sent you to talk me into going back, you can let him know I'm not interested."

Zach held the empty bean can in one hand as he licked the spoon clean, then laid it on the desk. He leaned back, crossed a moccasined foot over his knee, and folded his arms across his chest. Zach stared at Kase with his faded brown eye.

"You growed taller, boy. Nastier, too. But I could still knock you from here to Sunday, kid."

"You think so?" Kase stared across the desk at the man who had taught him to ride when he was six and how to shoot a gun when he was not much older. Zach had a devil of a time convincing Analisa Storm that a ten-year-old needed to learn to handle a gun. "If the boy's gonna live out west he ought to know how not to blow his damn-fool head off," Zach had argued. By the time the Storms moved back to Boston, Kase was more proficient with a Colt than most grown men.

Pulling a wad of tobacco out of the pocket of his dust-coated Levi's, Zach tore off a plug and wedged it between his cheek and gum.

"Your ma's a might worried about ya, boy." The only sign of a change in Zach's expression was a crook of his brow. He seemed determined to take Kase's sullenness seriously.

Kase's gaze was drawn once more to the wood-framed

window set akilter in the right wall of the jail. His stomach tensed. An expert at slipping into stubborn silence, he still could not control his inner turmoil. He could do without this.

"It wouldn't harm you none to write to her, let her know you're still alive."

Kase could not hide the resentment in his tone. "How'd you find me?"

Zach shifted the tobacco and spit into the bean tin. "Didn't even have to look. The Rawlins fella that hired ya wrote and tol' your pa that he was as happy as a flea in a doghouse that he'd run into you in Kansas City. Then"—he spat again—"your pa sent a letter out to me, askin' quite politely, *if* it was convenient, and *if* I was between jobs, would I just happen on by a no-account town called Busted Heel and see how his boy was makin' out as marshal?"

His boy. Kase crossed his arms over his rib cage. He felt as if he'd just taken a punch to the gut. He wondered if Zach had known the truth all these years.

A fly buzzed in the stillness. While neither of them spoke, the hot air in the small room seemed to close in around them.

"You got trouble you can't handle, Kase?" Zach met his stare straight on.

"Nothing anyone can help me with, Zach."

Used to keeping his own council, Kase hesitated to open up to Zach, even though he knew the man as well as he did anyone. Zachariah Weston Elliot had been a scout for the army at Fort Sully in the Dakotas when Caleb Storm, then an undercover agent for the Bureau of Indian Affairs, moved Kase and Analisa there in 1871. But Kase knew the longer he kept silent, the more tension and anger would roil inside him. There was only one way to find out.

"Did you know who my real father was?"

Zach's answer was swift, his expression one of unveiled surprise. "No. I always thought it was Caleb."

Unable to sit any longer, Kase stood and began to slowly pace the confines of the small office. "My real father," he began, trailing his splayed fingers through his hair, "was a renegade Sioux who knifed and raped my mother when she was sixteen."

"Shit." Zach worked his tobacco plug and squinted up at Kase. "How'd you find that out?"

"Caleb told me." Kase shrugged and turned toward the window.

"What in the hell for?" Zach shook his head and asked the question more to himself than to Kase.

But Kase had heard, and turned on the old man with a vengeance. "Because I forced him to. I prodded and pried until he told me." He turned away again, unable to meet the old man's questioning stare, and wished to God he had never heard the truth.

Zach shook his head. "You and Caleb was always two peas in a pod. It was your ma I could never quite figure into the picture."

From the window where he stood, Kase watched a man cross the far end of the street, the image wavering like a specter in the heat waves that rose from the dry ground. Like the heat, the knot in his chest would not ease.

When they finally came, his words were soft-spoken. "My mother's family had just immigrated from Holland and were attacked as they crossed the plains. Her younger brother and sister were taken captive. Only Opa, my grandfather, and my mother survived. I still remember Opa, and living with him and Mother in a soddie in Iowa. I can even remember the day Caleb married my mother."

"Then you knew he wasn't your real pa."

As he recalled the years gone by, Kase smiled wistfully. "Sure, I knew. After they were married I always called him Papa. I remember wishing it to be true, but like any kid, I was always asking questions." His words brought little G.W. to mind. "Where's my real pa? What kind of an Indian is he? What happened to him?"

"And?"

"They gave me answers that didn't quite tally, so I kept it up. Why didn't we live in town after the Indian went away? What was his name? Where did he go? They said he was dead, that he had been a Sioux from the Pine Ridge Reservation, that my mother never knew his Indian name. She called him *mijn man*, a Dutch term for husband. She never used the more familiar, more endearing *echtgenoot*, which means husband, too. I used to wonder how they met, how they even communicated, because my mother only spoke Dutch before I was born. Finally, all the questions must have upset her, because one day

Caleb took me riding and he told me how sad it made my mother feel to remember the man, because he was dead. If I had any questions, I was to ask him, not Mother. So for a time I stopped asking. But it haunted me more and more."

"And in Boston?"

"They sent me to school." Unwilling to say more, unable to voice the bigotry and degradation he had faced, Kase returned to the chair behind his desk and stared at the scattered pages atop it.

But knowing the reception Kase would have met in the East, Zach quickly pieced together his own story. "So you got into a few scrapes?"

"It was more than a few. And the last one was in the law office where I worked."

"So Caleb told you the truth."

"Only after I forced him. I made him so damn mad he finally just blurted it all out."

It all came back to him, the inner turmoil, the seething fury he had felt as he sat in the library and refused to look up at Caleb. He knew his life would never change until he learned the truth about himself. His anger was stoked by fear of not knowing who or what he was, how he came to exist. Why couldn't he control himself?

In a rush of anger, Kase stood and faced Caleb toe to toe. "I'm not you, dammit! I never will be, because I'll never know who I really am. How can I when I've never gotten the truth out of you or my mother?"

Caleb had blanched. "What are you saying?"

"I don't see things the way you do. I don't fit in here and I never will."

"You don't want to."

"Not bad enough to be stepped on, to turn the other cheek time and time again," Kase had shouted.

"Have you ever tried?" Caleb shouted back.

"Do you really think I could? Maybe you don't. Maybe you've never tried to see my side or what trying to fit into this life is doing to me."

"Kase . . ." Caleb had reached out to him, put a hand on his shoulder, but Kase hit it away.

"I'm not like you. Maybe, just maybe, I'm like him. I'm like the man you and my mother could never bring yourselves to explain. That's what you think, isn't it?" Kase stepped close, backing Caleb toward the fireplace.

Caleb's expression became one of dark denial. "Never."

"Who was he?" Kase pressed.

"Forget it."

"Why? What are you hiding? Tell me!"

"I can't."

Kase reached out and grasped Caleb by the shoulders. "Who the hell was he? Who the hell am I?" he cried out.

Caleb shook him off. "All right," his eyes flashed with fury, "you want to know? Your father was a renegade Sioux who raped your mother and left her for dead."

As if he had taken a physical blow to the midsection, Kase tensed and stepped away. "Why didn't you tell me before now? Were you *truly* afraid I was like him?" he whispered.

Caleb shook his head, his eyes awash with unshed tears. "Never. I never thought that of you. Does it really matter so much that we wanted to keep this from you?"

"Yes, dammit, it matters. It explains a hell of a lot. My father was a savage, a murderer. He is the reason my mother has been forced to live in shame all these years. And I am, too."

Caleb's sad expression then darkened with a hint of returning anger.

"What do you mean, *all these years*?"

"If it hadn't been for me, her entire life could have been different. She could have lived a normal life, married a—" All too aware of what he had been about to say, Kase had become silent once again.

But in a tone as emotionless as a stone, Caleb had finished for him: "She could have married a white man. Is that what you were about to say?"

At the sound of a gasp from the open doorway, both men turned in unison and saw Analisa clinging to the door frame with one hand while she pressed the other against the base of her throat. Eyes wide with horror, she stood in stunned disbelief.

"Caleb? What is this?" Her gaze lingered on her husband an instant before she turned to Kase. "Kase? *Wat is er aan de hand?* What is going on?" Barely audible, her words reached him.

Kase turned away from Caleb, took a lingering look at his mother, and knew a blinding hurt that ached so badly, welled up from the depths of his soul with such ferocity, that he thought he might retch from the pain. He could not speak as he fought to control wave after wave of nausea.

Caleb crossed the room and took Analisa in his arms. She stared unmoving at her son as Caleb softly whispered, "Anja? Anja, it's all right, love."

Unable to meet their eyes, Kase had left the room. A few hours later without another word, without even a good-bye to his aunt or the half sister he adored, he left them. He had no plan other than to get through one day at a time. He crawled off alone like an injured wolf seeking its lair. He had no destination until he found himself accepting the job of marshal of Busted Heel.

Kase tried to put that terrible afternoon behind him as he looked at Zach Elliot. How could he explain what the truth had done to him? How could the old man know how he had felt when he learned he was the son of a murderer, a rapist? It was all too clear now why he had never been able to control his anger. He was certain he had inherited the blinding temper he fought so hard to keep on a tight rein, just as he was certain that he could never look his beautiful mother in the eye again without feeling all the shame she had been forced to endure because she chose to keep him.

Zach shifted uneasily on his chair. "That explains your aunt livin' on the Sioux reservation," he said half aloud.

"I grew up thinking my Aunt Meika had chosen the Sioux way of life. Now I find out she had been taken captive." He shook his head.

"What happened to the other one, the brother?"

"Pieter? No one knows. Caleb tried to track him through the BIA. But he seems to have disappeared."

"So after you found out about your mother, you just up and left home without a word?"

Unable to meet Zach's gaze, Kase stared at a point across the room.

"You ain't seen your ma?"

"Or my sister. Not since he told me the truth."

Zach's silence was accusation enough. Kase knew what his mother must be feeling, knew that his knowing would shame her further, but to keep from going insane, he had to heal his own wounds first.

The tension between the two men rode the hot air as close as the silence that surrounded them. Finally, to Kase's relief, Zach abruptly changed the subject. "Who's this Quentin Rawlins that hired you?"

"An old friend of Caleb's who knew him when he worked for the Bureau of Indian Affairs." Kase swiveled his chair back and forth, taking his time as he gave Zach an account of how he came to be marshal of Busted Heel. "I ran into him in a hotel in Kansas City and he asked straightaway if I'd consider coming out here to keep the peace. Seems he's worried about all the farmers moving in hereabouts, tends to think there's trouble brewing between the ranchers and the sodbusters."

"He might be right."

"He might be," Kase agreed, "but right now I'd say the biggest problem Quentin's got is how to keep his hands from dying of boredom and tearing up this place when they do get into town."

"Had some trouble already?"

"Nothing I couldn't handle." Kase finally smiled at Zach. "Just a few rowdies shooting up the town one night. Some poor little Italian fella was killed accidentally."

Kase paused long enough to stretch his hands high above his head and then lower them. "So," he began again in an effort to make up for his surly greeting, "you gonna stay around for a while, Zach? Or are you just here long enough to make sure I'm alive and then send a report back to Boston?"

"Well, I reckon I got no place to go for a while. 'Sides, what marshal couldn't use a deputy?"

"This one."

"Yeah?"

"There's nothing for me to do here, let alone a deputy, but you're welcome to stay."

"Where do ya bunk?"

Kase smiled again and waited for his old friend's reaction. "Got a room at the local pleasure palace."

"You such a good customer you need to call the place home?" Zach squinted his good eye and peered at Kase.

"Naw. It isn't like that, just not much else available in this one-horse town. The lady at the boardinghouse didn't take to having a 'breed' living under her roof. I have to admit, it's convenient living at Flossie's, although the decorating isn't exactly to my taste." He rolled up a Wanted poster lying atop the desk and used it to swat at a fly hovering above the empty bean bowl.

"If ya got an empty cell here in the jail, that's good enough for me for a spell."

Kase laughed. "Sure. Welcome to it. Nobody's been locked up in it for weeks."

"In that case, I think I'll go stretch out for a bit, 'cause I'm as tired as a tomcat that's been walkin' in mud. I'll jes' see to my horse and bring in my gear . . . Marshal."

"Go right ahead. It's about time I made the rounds anyway." Kase pulled on the gold chain that dangled from the watch pocket in his denims. He flipped open the lid of the timepiece and noted the time before he snapped it shut. He stood and shoved the watch back into his pocket. "Train's late. Must be on account of the big meeting in Cheyenne."

"What for?"

"It seems a lot of folks are pushing for Wyoming to become a state."

"Plan on things changin' a mite?" Zach wanted to know.

"Here?" Kase laughed and moved toward the door. "Not very likely." He nodded toward the solid plank door with a small barred window in the wall behind his desk. "Make yourself at home."

*

Chapter
Three

*

Rosa ran a shaking hand over her hair to make certain most of it was still upswept and in place and reached down to collect her valise. The small *Guide for Italian Immigrants* she had purchased in Genoa slipped from her lap to the floor, and she quickly rescued it, opened the valise, and shoved the pamphlet inside.

BEWARE OF OVERLY FRIENDLY PEOPLE.

THROW AWAY ALL WEAPONS YOU MAY HAVE.

SPEAK IN A LOW VOICE.

DO NOT GET EXCITED IN YOUR DISCUSSIONS.

DO NOT YELL OR WAVE YOUR HANDS ABOUT.

DO NOT SPIT ON THE SIDEWALK.

BEWARE OF STRANGE MEN OFFERING PROPOSALS OF MARRIAGE.

The list of admonitions in the *Guide* seemed endless. And silly. Still, Rosa had tried to memorize them all. She intended to make Giovanni proud of her. Had he changed very much over the past three years? Perhaps, she thought, he had become as outgoing and confident as the Americans she had seen on the streets of New York.

The train began to slow with a screech of brakes and a hiss

of steam, and through the window beside her, Rosa watched
the station at Busted Heel appear at last. A long platform
fronted a tiny building near the railroad tracks. Beyond the
depot, the town stood in profile against the empty landscape. A
few ramshackle wooden buildings stood in two straight lines
divided by a wide thoroughfare. As she stepped from the train
onto the firm footing of the wooden platform, she took a deep
breath and filled her lungs with the warm, dry air of Wyoming
in summer.

There was no sign of Giovanni on the platform.

Disappointment assailed her, doubt that was soon followed
by forgiveness as Rosa realized her husband had no way of
knowing exactly when she would arrive. His only alternative to
not meeting her would have been to greet every train that
stopped in Busted Heel.

The conductor stepped down to ask for the brass tag needed
to identify her trunk, which was stored in the baggage car.
Rosa reached inside the deep pocket of her dress until she
found it. Following the man's directions, she moved out of the
sun and stood alone beneath the overhang that fronted the small
building perched on the platform.

A slight movement to the right caught her eye and she
watched as the stationmaster opened the side door and stepped
out of the building that served as both ticket and telegraph
office. The look on his face was one of doubt, but his stride
was purposeful as he moved toward her.

"Have you got the right stop, miss?" His brows knit with
worry as he peered over spectacles that rode precariously near
the end of his nose.

"*Come dice*? Pardon?"

Realization dawned, and he bent down until they stood
nearly nose to nose. "Speakie English?" he yelled.

Rosa took a step backward and tried to enunciate as clearly
as she could. "*Sì*. This is Busted Heel?"

"Yes." He nodded officially. "Yes, it is."

The conductor interrupted as he set her trunk down with a
loud thud. Rose thanked him, then turned her attention back to
the stationmaster and waited for the hissing, chugging train to
depart before she spoke again.

"I come to meet my husband. Maybe you know him?" She
smiled hopefully. "Giovanni Audi?"

The man's open expression immediately fell, and he focused his attention on the ground. When he did raise his eyes, they failed to meet hers directly.

"Mrs. Audi, ma'am"—he cleared his throat—"I'm gonna send you along to see the town marshal, Kase Storm." He pointed in the direction of the group of buildings just beyond the platform.

"You walk down the left side o' Main Street till ya get to the jail and you'll most likely find Marshal Storm inside. If not, jes' wait there an' he'll be in shortly."

"Jail?" She'd never heard the word before.

Confusion must have etched itself upon her features, for he held up a hand, a signal for her to wait. The man hurried back into his office and returned a moment later with a small piece of paper on which he'd written the word "jail." Apologetically, he took Rosa by the elbow and turned her about before he walked her to the edge of the platform that faced the town. He pointed toward the wide street flanked by an assortment of false-fronted wooden buildings.

"You just stay on this side," he indicated the left, "until you come to the building with this word on it." He tapped the paper.

"But my husband said . . ."

He smiled a kindly, sympathetic smile that sent a wave of apprehension through Rosa. "Just go on along now, little lady, and I'll pull your trunk inside for you. No need to worry about that, too."

Although she continued to clutch the valise before her in both hands, she had forgotten about her trunk until the man mentioned it.

Slowly, moving as if in a daze, she made her way toward the group of buildings squatting on the open plain. *This* was Busted Heel? This small, dirty outpost standing unprotected from the elements by so much as a single tree? Even the village of Corio was far grander than *this*. Where were the green fields she had expected to see? The rich farmlands? In lieu of those, where was the thriving settlement of her dreams? *Dio*, she thought as she stared at the two straight rows of forlorn-looking buildings, where was the church?

But above all, *where* was Giovanni?

The heels of her high-button shoes rang loudly against the

boardwalk that rose above the dusty street. There was no one about, no sign of life other than a horse tied to a hitching rail farther along the way. A drop of perspiration trickled along her temple and started down her cheek before she swiped at it with her fingertips. The black velvet gown grew heavier with every step. The wide-brimmed hat, instead of affording some relief from the blazing sunshine, only added to her discomfort. She passed the first building, barely glancing at the various and sundry merchandise displayed in the windows.

The next shop was much smaller. The letters above the door spelled out "Laundry" in peeling white paint. A strange-sounding singsong language issued from inside the darkened interior. Curious, Rosa paused to listen for a moment before she hurried on.

"Barber, Baths and Dentistry." The words spread out in bold red, white, and blue across the next storefront. A striped pole stood against one corner of the building. Not only was the door closed, but the shades inside were drawn tight, so Rosa moved past without stopping to stare. Her attention was soon focused on the last building on the west side of the street.

"Jail." She compared the letters spelled out above the door with those on the paper in her hand. Hesitantly Rosa reached out and knocked.

When no one answered, she looked left and right. The street had been deserted since she arrived. The heat of the sun beat down on her mercilessly, and for a moment Rosa felt light-headed. Suddenly she wished she had eaten before she had given away her foodstuffs. She leaned forward and rested her forehead against the door frame, then tried the knob. It turned easily, and she pushed the door open.

It took only one glance around the tiny, cluttered room to see that this place called "jail" was unoccupied. A table heaped with loose papers, empty bowls, pens, an inkwell, and a pile of newspapers stood in the middle of the room. In the far corner, what appeared to be a new wood stove stood ready for winter. A safe, much like the one in the bank in Corio, only smaller, was positioned behind the table. Was this place a bank, then? She turned slowly, taking in the entire room, trying to determine the nature of the jail. Four rifles were chained together in a gun rack on the wall near another rack that was obviously for hats, although none hung there now. A broom stood in another corner. It was not until she noticed the sturdy wooden door on the back wall, a door with a small square window protected by bars, that she realized fully what the word "jail" meant.

Was Giovanni a prisoner? Could that fact explain the stationmaster's odd expression when she asked for her husband? Silently, she closed the outer door and crept toward the cell.

Dio! She swore silently. The little window was at least a head higher than she could stretch, even on tiptoe.

"Giovanni?" Her soft whisper was barely audible. There was no response from inside.

Quickly Rosa set her valise down beside the paper-strewn desk and rolled the chair that stood behind it over to the door. Just as she reached out to brace her hands on the arms of the chair, her hat slid forward over her eyes. Her temper got the best of her, and she fiercely shoved it back into place, unmindful of the damage to her hair until she heard a pin hit the floor. There was little time to waste, so she ignored the cascade of waving hair that brushed against her right cheek as she grasped the chair. She carefully placed one foot on the seat and crouched to maintain her balance before she lifted the other foot.

Too late, she discovered the chair could both swivel *and* tilt. As she reached up to grasp the bars of the window, the chair began to roll away from the door. As Rosa clung to the bars and fought for balance, she heard the front door open.

The chair continued to roll until Rosa found herself stretched full length, feet on the chair, hands clutching the bars of the cell window. Not until she hung nearly parallel with the floor did she hear the softly spoken words that issued from behind her.

"May I help you?"

The deep voice gave her little indication as to what type of man had entered the room. Still, she had no recourse but to accept his help.

"Take me down." She tried to swallow. "*Per piacere.* Please."

"My pleasure."

There was no mistaking the note of humor in the man's tone, nor could she dismiss the masculine strength in the sound of his deep voice. Rosa tried to peer over her shoulder but found her view of him hampered by her oversized hat. She heard him cross the room and stop directly behind her. Two strong hands grasped Rosa about the waist and steadied her on the chair.

"You can let go now." He spoke softly, gently now, his tone laced with humor.

Rosa released the death grip she held upon the bars and felt the man's warm hands tighten around her waist. He lifted her down as easily as if she were a child and set her on her feet. Taking a deep breath, Rosa straightened and turned to look up at her rescuer.

He was unlike anyone she'd ever seen before.

From the hint of amusement in his voice, she had expected him to be smiling. Instead, he was glowering at her. She wondered curiously what he would look like when he smiled. Her gaze drifted from his mouth, with the generous, sensual lips, to his eyes. There was a slight tilt to the corners of them, they were nearly almond in shape; large, wide, and startlingly blue. The warm brown tone of his skin made the color of his eyes more pronounced. His nose was wide, yet finely tapered, and as she stared at his exotic features, she was struck by the memory of the Roman statues she had seen adorning the fountains of Genoa.

But cold marble could not compare to this man who radiated such quiet strength. He stood silently awaiting an explanation.

"I . . . I'm a . . . I look for husband." She shook her head. Nervousness hampered the use of her newly acquired language. Before she could explain, he spoke again.

"You aren't going to find one in there. What kind do you need?"

"Kind?"

"Of husband."

"I have already one," she explained.

He crooked a brow. "Oh?"

"Yes." She nodded. "Giovanni. Giovanni Audi. I'm told by the train man to come here."

Rosa watched him turn away, and faced with the broad width of his shoulders, she suddenly realized how very tall he was. Much taller than Giovanni. Much taller than anyone she had ever seen. Were she to stand beside him, the top of her head would barely reach his shoulders.

She watched as he shoved his hands into the pockets of the close-fitting denim pants—pants more closely fitted than any of the men at home would have deigned to wear—and stared out the window.

"Sit down, ma'am."

A dry, metallic taste filled her mouth, and she realized her heart was pounding. Rosa started to protest. "But—"

Slowly the man turned around, and she felt his cool blue stare assessing her. He stretched out a hand.

"Please"—he indicated the empty chair—"sit down."

Except for the fact that she obviously possessed a pair of well-developed breasts beneath the unrelieved black velvet bodice, the woman poised stiffly on the edge of his chair might have been mistaken for a child. He guessed she was not much older than his half sister, Annika, who was only fourteen. Kase swallowed, glanced at the cluttered desktop, and then met her eyes once more. They were a rich golden topaz, as warm and sweet as dark honey. For a moment he forgot what he was going to say as he lost himself in her steady gaze. He swallowed again.

"Ma'am, I'm afraid I've got some bad news for you."

He cursed himself for having to be the one to tell her, wished there was an easy way, all the time knowing there wasn't. Not an hour ago as he spoke with Zach, he had casually mentioned the Italian bystander killed during a shooting spree. He had been so preoccupied with his own problems that not once since the accidental shooting had he stopped to think that the young man might have had family and friends somewhere. No one in town knew where the Italian had come from, or anything else about him except his name.

"*Signore?*"

Her soft question interrupted his thoughts, and Kase cursed himself again for making her wait, but damn, if this wasn't one of the hardest things he'd ever done.

The girl's heart was in her eyes, and she looked tired enough to drop right where she sat uncomfortably on the edge of his chair.

A soft mass of waving ebony hair had slipped out from beneath the huge hat on the crown of her head. He thought of his half sister again and was well aware that Annika would scoff at wearing anything so outdated as this girl's black velvet dress. Muttering a swear word under his breath, Kase wiped the palms of his hands on his thighs and hunkered down until his eyes were on a level with hers.

"Mrs. Audi . . ." He cleared his throat. "Your husband isn't here any longer."

"Not here?"

He would not have thought it possible for her to look any more wary, but suddenly her eyes widened and she reminded him of a wide-eyed rabbit frozen in fear. *Tell her.*

"He's dead, ma'am."

"Dead?" Her face paled.

"Dead," he repeated.

"How?"

"Shot."

"Shot?" When she repeated the word, her expression was blank, void of understanding.

"With a bullet." He pantomimed a shooting. "Gun. Shot." She choked on her husband's name. "Giovanni? Dead?" Kase nodded. "I'm afraid so."

"Who would want to shoot Giovanni?" she asked. "Why?" "It was an accident. He was standing out on the sidewalk and was hit by a stray bullet." Kase spoke slowly and watched the girl try to absorb all he was saying. "He died quickly," Kase added, hoping to offer some comfort, however small. "Probably didn't even know what hit him."

The honey-gold eyes suddenly flooded with tears that intensified their strange color. For a moment, he could only stare.

"Ma'am?"

A shudder racked her frame and the loosened lock of hair unfurled farther, cascading over her shoulder and down the bodice of her gown. He followed its fall, then looked away.

He could tell by her lost expression that she was having problems voicing her thoughts. When the pool of tears began to stream down her unmarred complexion, Kase stood up, suddenly uncomfortable at having to witness her sorrow.

"I'll get you a room at the boardinghouse for tonight," he quickly decided for her, "and you can be on the train again by tomorrow noon."

Kase stood, then turned away, but not before he caught a

glimpse of the girl wiping away tears with the sleeve of her gown. Should he offer her the comfort of an arm about her shoulder? Stymied, he stalled, toying with the edge of his desk. Would she want him touching her? He glanced over his shoulder. She was crying softly, her head bowed, her face hidden behind her hands.

Propriety be damned. If ever anyone was in need of a warm, sympathetic touch it was this slip of a girl in borrowed clothing.

Kase stepped over to her and reached out awkwardly, drew his hand away, then extended it again and gently patted her shoulder. He wished she would scream or cry. Anger he could deal with. Hysteria he could fight to calm. But these silent, pitiful tears left him feeling more than helpless.

"Ma'am?" He found himself moving to kneel before her again. "Mrs. Audi?"

She lowered her hands and stared at him as if suddenly remembering she was not alone.

"I . . . I am sorry. I am so . . . so . . ." She shook her head, searching for words. "I come from so far, wait so long to be with Giovanni."

He watched her wrap her arms protectively against her rib cage as if to shield herself from further pain. "Three years," she stopped to catch her breath, "three years I wait to come to America. When I am leaving, Guido said, 'You will be back, Rosa. You will see.'" She shook her head as if to deny this Guido's words. "I take the ship across the ocean and am sick all the time. I am afraid in New York. I ride the trains, always taking care to find the right one."

Unable to make much sense of her rambling, Kase offered silent comfort. The girl who had referred to herself as Rosa became increasingly upset as she spoke.

". . . There is no Broken Shoe, only Busted Heel. And the man says, You come the right place? I say yes. Then when I say . . . Giovanni's name . . . he says, go see the marshal."

She stood up so abruptly that she nearly knocked Kase off his feet. Stepping around him, she began to pace the room. Kase stood and watched, feeling helpless.

"What I am going to do?" Shouting now, she turned on him, her hands raised in appeal. "What?"

Kase stepped back and shrugged. "Go home."

"Home?" She looked as if he'd struck her.

He felt as if he had.

"Well, not right now, of course. For tonight you'll stay at Matheson's and tomorrow you'll go home." So saying, he rested his hands on the gun belt that rode at his hips.

The tears started again and she squared off to face him.

"Home?" She fairly shouted the word. "How?" With a desperate shake of her head, the velvet hat slid free of its precarious perch and floated to the floor like a dying black crow.

Kase bent to retrieve it and, as he straightened, saw her suddenly lean over his desk and support herself with the palms of her hands resting on top of the clutter. She wavered, about to collapse.

"Mrs. Audi, are you all right?"

As she turned to face him, the bulk of her hair fell free of its pins and tumbled past her shoulders to her waist. She shook her head. "No . . ."

Unsteady on her feet, she reached out for him. Kase stepped forward, tossed the hat on the desk, and slipped an arm about her waist. With a soft moan, the girl lost consciousness and crumpled against him, her head lolling against his shoulder. He stared down at her upturned face and noticed the thick, dark lashes wet with tears that lay unmoving against her porcelain skin. He scooped her up into his arms and moved the few steps to the chair. Holding her close, as a father might cradle a wounded child, he sat down and began to smooth back the strands of ebony that clung to her moist temple.

Kase jerked upright as Zach Elliot stuck his head around the half-open cell door.

"If you got everything under control now, I 'spect I can come on out."

Glaring in his direction, Kase once again took a firm hold on the girl in his arms and shifted in his seat.

"You nearly scared the life outta me, Zach. I forgot you were here."

"Well, I decided to lie low till you got this sorted out. I heard someone come in and creep up on the door kinda slow. Then I heard a woman's voice whisperin' something that sounded like 'Jee-vani' and I decided to wait to see what transpired.

That's when you came in, so I jes' treated myself to a listen."

"Yeah? Well, thanks for all your help with the bereaved widow. What'll I do with her now?" Kase shrugged and the girl moaned.

"If I had a looker like that stretched out in my arms, I guess I'd know what to do"—Zach shrugged—"but you'll probably end up doing jes' what you was tellin' her you would. Take her to the boardin'house."

"Like this?" Kase looked down at her again.

"Well, you could wait for her to wake up an' start yellin' again. Or you could give her over to the lady that runs the boardin'house—that is, assumin' there is one."

"Yeah. There is."

Kase thought of big Bertha Matheson and wondered if there was a gentle, caring bone in her obese body. He'd rather turn the girl over to Flossie, who would know for certain how to deal with her tears until the train pulled in tomorrow. But the widow Audi didn't look like the type who'd take to being left in a whorehouse. He shook his head and stood up, his mind set on carrying Rose to the boardinghouse at the end of the street. Zach was right. He didn't want to be around when she woke up again.

"Need any help?" Zach offered.

"No, just rest her hat on her stomach and put the valise in my hand." Kase thrust his fingertips forward from beneath the mound of velvet. "You might go on down to the depot for me and ask John Tuttle to store any other luggage she might have brought along. Tell him to hold tomorrow's noon train, 'cause she'll be getting on it."

Zach looked doubtful but held his tongue.

"Anything else?"

"Just open the door and stand out of the way."

Bertha Matheson was as uncaring as he had expected. She barely glanced at the girl in Kase's arms when she opened the door and asked, "What are you doing here? You know you ain't welcome."

The fact that he was marshal held little weight with Bertha. He was a half-breed, and in her eyes that made him an undesirable boarder. She had put him up for two nights because Quentin Rawlins had insisted she rent Kase a room when he first arrived in town. He had not been back since he took a room at Flossie's, preferring to live among people who did not glare at him every time they eyed him across a room.

He briefly explained the circumstances and then agreed when she told him he would have to pay for the girl's room in advance.

"Can't tell about these foreigners," she grumbled as she led him to one of the rooms at the top of the narrow stairs. As Kase carried the girl over the threshold and moved toward the iron-railed bed, Bertha warned, "I'll have no funny business here, mister. I run a good clean boardinghouse. You be down those steps in two minutes or I'll be up here with my broom."

He watched her huff out, his eyes following the motion of her ample hips and buttocks as they swayed along behind her. From the back she looked like a wide wall of calico banded by an apron bow.

Shifting the weight of the girl in his arms, he set her satchel on the floor and then gently laid her on the coverlet atop the narrow bed. The springs groaned in protest and he feared for a moment she might awaken, but it seemed shock and exhaustion had taken their toll. Kase set her hat on the bedside table, then smoothed her heavy skirt down, taking care to cover all signs of her ruffled white petticoats beneath. He straightened and for a moment stood staring down at her.

It was funny, he thought, how responsible he felt for this waiflike woman. He guessed that holding her in his arms as he carried her down Main Street accounted for this sudden feeling of protectiveness. That and the fact that she reminded him of his mother. At least Analisa had been accompanied by her family when she made the journey to America. This girl had traveled all the way alone. As he stared down at her, he became determined to see that she left Busted Heel and went back to Italy so that she would not have to endure any of the hardships his own mother had suffered.

No use getting all worked up, though, he told himself as he reached out to push her hair back off her face and spread it out on the pillow. After all, by tomorrow afternoon, she would be gone. He'd see her safely to the train and be done with it.

The room was nearly stifling. Kase was careful not to make a sound as he opened the windows to admit a cooling breeze, then returned to the bed. Perspiration glistened on her brow and dampened the wisps of hair near her face. He glanced back at the open door and hesitated. Bertha wouldn't take kindly to any request from him.

It took more than two minutes to remove her high-button shoes without a hook, but finally the task was accomplished. He listened intently, but still didn't hear Bertha making good on her threat, so he reached down and around the girl, gently slipped his hands under her, and began to unfasten the long line of round black buttons that ran down the back of her gown. At least she'd be a bit more comfortable, able to remove the gown alone when she awoke. The idea sounded logical enough until his fingers met with the soft silken feel of her skin and he felt a surge of warmth deep inside that didn't come from the heat in the room. At the same moment, he realized that his shirtfront was near enough to brush against the bodice of her gown and that it would only take the merest pressure from the palms of his hands at her back to press her against him. By the time he reached the last button at her waist, Kase had begun to sweat. Carefully he slipped his hands out from beneath her and straightened.

"*Damn*." The whispered word escaped him and his eyes narrowed as he stared down at the sleeping figure on the bed. What was there about the girl that just the sight of her, the slightest touch of his fingertips against her ivory skin, aroused him? What perverseness made him long to ignore her plight and take advantage of her unconsciousness?

Shaken by his thoughts, Kase quickly stepped back and walked away from her. Something inside made him stop at the threshold and turn to stare at her. She looked like a broken doll lying in the center of the bed, hair streaming out around her pale face, eyes closed, arms stretched out at her sides. He remembered her name and whispered it aloud. "Rose."

Without a sound, Kase stepped out into the hallway and closed the door behind him.

*

Chapter
Four

*

Rosa opened her eyes and found that she was still enshrouded in darkness. Startled, she sat up, her heart pounding as she looked about in confusion and tried to ease the panic that crowded in on her. Ghostly silver moonbeams streamed in through a side window to shed muted light on her surroundings. The moonlight illuminated a small, sparsely furnished room and as her vision adjusted to the weak light, she became aware of the ominous quiet that enveloped her. The quiet of death.

She realized suddenly that she was very much alone.

Now that the sun had set, the air was much cooler; the slight breeze lifted the translucent white curtains away from the windows. She was comforted somehow by the fluttering movement of the curtains; it seemed as if something were alive in the room beside herself. On shaking limbs, she rose and stood beside the bed, fighting the wave of dizziness that assailed her. The wooden floor was slick against her stockinged feet, and as she carefully crossed the room toward the window, she wondered who had removed her shoes. When her dress fell forward and slipped off her shoulders, she guessed that the same kind soul had unbuttoned it for her.

Brushing aside the curtain, she leaned against the window frame and stared out at the night. The window looked down upon the main street of Busted Heel, and from the height of the second story she could see the entire length of the street and the depot beyond. It was as deserted as she had last seen it, except that now the street and buildings were spared the glaring heat of the sun.

"*Giovanni è morto*." She whispered "Giovanni is dead," in Italian, hoping the familiar cadence of the words might make the truth real for her.

She knew with unwavering clarity that the marshal—the tall, dark man with the deep blue eyes—had not lied to her. His face had mirrored deep regret when he said the words. Giovanni *was* dead. He would not be meeting her at all. She would not be making a new home in this new land. She had nothing. And she was alone. Just as she had feared, God had finally claimed Giovanni for himself.

Her gaze moved up and away from the deserted street. As she stared skyward toward a million shining stars and tried to blink away a sudden rush of tears, the night sky served as a backdrop for the images her mind conjured. She had known of Giovanni all her life, for everyone knew everyone in Corio and Crotte, but until she was seventeen she had not met the young man who had been cloistered away with the priests since he was twelve years old. The first time she saw Giovanni, she had been in the piazza on market day. He had been walking between the market stalls with his sisters; they walked on either side of him as if to protect the young seminarian from the jostling and bustle of the Monday market.

He was home for a holiday, he said later when he came to call at the farmhouse in Crotte, home to visit his mother and sisters. For a week he found an excuse to visit the family—and in particular, Rosa—daily. Finally, as they walked through the quiet hillside above the house together, Giovanni told her he had begun thinking of leaving the seminary long before he met her. But once he met her, he had been certain a life in the priesthood was not for him.

She had never willfully done anything to tempt him away from the church, but doubt had caused her many sleepless nights in the beginning, when his family accused her of using every wile short of witchcraft to make him give up his calling. But at Giovanni's heated insistence, the protests ended and his family grew suddenly silent once the two were married. Coolly and unforgivingly silent.

Instead of being married in the church of San Genesio in Corio, Giovanni had taken her to Torino to state their vows before the very priests who had sought to claim him for the church. Fearful of meeting them at first, Rosa soon found the priests were happy that Giovanni had finally found peace, for his heart had long been unsettled. In reality, his vocation had been his mother's greatest wish, but not his own.

They had not been so warmly welcomed when they returned to Corio to face his family. Signora Audi took to ceaseless weeping and prayer and refused to speak to either of them. Giovanni's father threatened and shouted, and then he, too, wept as he offered them an old stone farmhouse that was little more than a pile of rubble on the side of a hill outside of the village.

For three weeks she tried, as only a seventeen-year-old bride would, to make a home of the drafty pile of rock that was not fit for use as a cow shed. In their living quarters above the barn, Rosa did her best to please Giovanni. By the time summer ended and the chill nights of October sent winds scuttling over the Alps to rattle the wooden doors and seep through the stone walls, Giovanni had made the decision to leave for America.

"You deserve more than this, Rosa," he had said. "I'll make a new life for us." His dark eyes had shone with the dream and determination he felt. "We will have everything in America."

Now she was in America and she had nothing. Not even a drafty home on the mountainside.

The memory of Guido's taunting words was a haunting reminder that Giovanni's death had irretrievably altered her life. Would she go back? There seemed to be no other choice. The big man, the marshal with the luminous eyes, had been adamant. Was it he who had brought her here? She wondered as she turned around and moved toward the bed again.

Her knees were trembling. An intense pain pounded against her temples. She remembered she had not eaten since early morning, but the thought of food choked her. Perhaps it was nearly morning again; perhaps the dawn was about to bring a day filled with more doubt and uncertainty about her future. Where would she sleep when night came again? How could she go on?

Rosa fought against the tears that threatened to overwhelm her. She shrugged helplessly, stared up at the ceiling, and swallowed. "You have him, God," she whispered aloud in the darkness. "I hope you are happy now." Then, thinking her words and thoughts must surely be blasphemous enough to call down more sorrow and bad luck, she crossed herself, sank to her knees, and sobbed out her sorrow.

It was a while before her tears subsided, but when they did, Rosa pulled herself to her feet. Glancing down, she stared at the black dress, a pool of darkness in the filtered moonlight. The color of widows. She would wear it for the rest of her life. With unsteady hands she drew the dress away from her shoulders and pushed it off until it fell around her ankles. Stepping out of the velvet that encircled her feet, Rosa turned back the coverlet and stretched out on the cool, crisp sheet, then closed her burning eyes against the uncertainty that would come with the rising sun.

A soft rapping at the door alerted Rosa to the fact that it was time to leave. The portal swung open to reveal the woman called Bertha Matheson, the proprietress of the boardinghouse who had curtly introduced herself earlier. The woman's bulk should have attested to her culinary skills, but if Rosa's early morning breakfast of runny eggs, burned biscuits, and ham slices so dry they resembled shoe leather was any indication of the rest of the fare, it would seem that only Bertha relished her own cooking.

"That man's at the door waiting to take you to the station." The woman boomed out the announcement and stared at Rosa as if she were the oddest of creatures.

"*Grazie.*" Rosa nodded in Bertha's direction and straightened the high collar of her dress. She stooped to pick up her valise and paused before the mirror above the washstand to appraise her appearance. This morning she'd braided her hair and wound the plaits around her head. There would be no more jaunty styles, for there was no one to try to impress. Giovanni was not here to appreciate her newly acquired sophistication. It was better to return to her old ways. Simple ways. Besides, there would be no loose pins or tumbling hair to battle. The style was practical, if not plain.

Her skin looked pale as alabaster against the dark ebony of her hair and the equally black sheen of the hat and dress. The weather outside was warming with each passing hour, and the heavy dress would soon become unbearably hot, but she was determined to wear black. Besides, she thought, her other dresses—gowns of more serviceable weight—were packed in her trunk at the station. The velvet would have to do. Muted purple shadows lay beneath the red-rimmed eyes that stared back at her from the mirror. Rosa decided she had never looked worse.

She shrugged at her image. What did it matter?

Silently she followed Mrs. Matheson down the stairs, stared at the woman's wide girth, and wondered if the landlady ever feared getting stuck between the wooden banister and the wall. Rosa tried to glance around Bertha, but did not see the man standing in the doorway until they reached the bottom of the stairs and the matron nodded and went back toward the kitchen. Rosa stood silent, staring up at Marshal Storm. Even in her sorrow, she noted that her memory of his striking good looks had not been exaggerated.

As he stood framed against the light in the open doorway, he towered over her, his hat in his hand. When he nodded politely in greeting, a thick shock of his straight black hair fell across his forehead. He shook his head and the stray lock fell back into place. His clothes were well fitted, almost too closely fitted against his wide shoulders and well-muscled arms. The soft fawn-brown material of his shirt appeared fragile and out of place on him, as if with a sudden movement, the seams would burst open and he would be freed of the encumbrance. He was wearing the sturdy blue denim pants that he had worn the day before.

"Ma'am." He nodded again and waited.

"*Buon giorno*, Marshal."

"Are you ready?"

She wanted to tell him that she would never be ready to walk out of this house and face the truth that waited beyond the door. Instead she whispered, "*Sì*."

He stepped aside and let her pass through the door before him. "Can I carry your bag, ma'am?"

"No. Is all right."

"I'd be happy to."

"I can do it."

"Fine."

The anger in his tone made her glance up at him from beneath the brim of her hat. His jaw was set and his eyes were trained on the street ahead of them. She wondered what had set his temper off, for surely she had done nothing to offend him. Rosa was thankful that he did not yell at her as if she were deaf, as had the other Americans she encountered.

This morning the thoroughfare seemed to bustle with life in comparison to yesterday's empty scene. A farmer was loading a wagon drawn up before the mercantile store, and farther down the street she could see two small Negro children darting back and forth along the boardwalk. As Rosa and Kase moved along in silence, neither of them bothered to use the walkway, but chose to continue down the middle of the dusty street. Determination lengthened their strides.

Rosa was hard put to keep up with him.

"That her, Kase?" A woman with bright red hair standing with both hands on her hips called out from the opposite side of the street. She stood before a gaily painted building, her skirt swaying from side to side like some huge magenta bell made of satin. Rosa glanced up at the evenly lettered words painted across the front of the building: Flossie Gibbs's Hospitality Parlor and Retreat. She did not understand a word of it.

She glanced up at the marshal in time to see him acknowledge the woman's greeting with a casual wave. Kase. The woman's words had nudged her memory. His name was Kase Storm.

"This is her, Flossie. On our way to the depot."

"You got time to stop and introduce her, now, don'tcha?"

He stopped dead still and Rosa followed suit. The marshal turned to look down at her for the first time since they had left the boardinghouse.

"Would you mind?" he asked. "Flossie's a friend."

She nodded. "*Va bene*."

They waited for the farm wagon to rumble by, and Rosa covered her mouth and nose against the swirl of rising dust kicked up by the horses' hooves. The man and woman seated upon the high bouncing seat of the wagon waved to Kase Storm as they rode past.

On the other side of the street Rosa and the marshal were greeted by Flossie Gibbs's wide welcoming smile.

"Howdy, ma'am." She reached down and grabbed Rosa's hand and began pumping it ferociously. "Kase here told me the sad news about your comin' in to town and havin' to leave again so quick. Too bad you can't stay a spell." She smiled down at Rosa, and the girl smiled back.

"I have no place here."

Rosa watched the other woman's smile fade.

"Only met your husband a few times, Miz Audi, but he seemed a real swell gent. Workin' so hard to set up that little store o' his. You can be right proud o' him. It's a real shame you can't stay and make a go of it."

"We gotta be moving, Flossie," Kase warned, his tone edgy.

"Don't be throwing that black look at me, Kase Storm. You got more than enough time to get this little gal to the depot."

"*Mi scusi*," Rosa interrupted, "you say my husband had a store, and this he wrote to me in a letter. Is all right I see it?"

"Don't see why not. Do you, Kase?"

Rosa thought she saw the woman's mouth twitch as if she was teasing the marshal in some way. His face showed no hint of a response.

"Sure."

Although he nodded in agreement, Rosa sensed he was none too happy with the outcome of their conversation with Flossie.

"Listen, Miz Audi, you decide not to leave town, you come to me and I'll see that you don't go hungry, hear? You can always work for me." With a boisterous laugh, the gaily dressed woman turned on her heel and waved them on.

"She is a nice woman," Rosa commented.

"Yeah."

"I can see the store?"

"Sure."

Used to men who were never at a loss for words, Rosa took the marshal's silence for anger, but curious to see the place Giovanni had hoped to turn into a store, she picked up her pace and kept up with him as he moved on down the street. They passed a large building with swinging double doors before the marshal stopped in front of a small, squat building with one large window that fronted Main Street. The door was of solid wood, the entire place whitewashed. No lettering adorned the front at all.

"That's it." He stood his ground in the street beneath the boardwalk and nodded toward the empty storefront.

Rosa ignored his coolness, gathered up her skirt, and

stepped up onto the walkway. She moved toward the building and tried the knob. The door swung inward.

In the eerie silence, she tried to feel her husband's former presence, but there was not a trace. In fact, there was nothing in the room except two bushel barrels, one filled with sprouted, overripe potatoes, the other half full of onions. A thick layer of dust from the street traffic covered the pine plank flooring, and beyond the empty front room, Rosa could see a smaller room through an open door.

Her footsteps rang out hollowly against the floorboards as she crossed the room and stood staring at the small place Giovanni must have called home. A greasy stove stood against one wall, the wood box yawning empty except for a few splinters of kindling. A cot, barely wide enough to accommodate a child, was pulled up against another wall. Hooks that she assumed once held Giovanni's things were lined up above it. The place was barren in its emptiness.

Rosa turned to leave and ran headlong into the solid wall of Marshal Storm's chest.

He stepped aside quickly, as if she had drenched him with boiling water. She, too, increased the space between them.

"I'm sorry, I—"

"*Mi scusi*, I—"

They both spoke at once and immediately fell silent.

Rosa put her hand against the crown of her hat, afraid it would come loose and fall off as she stood gazing up at him.

Neither of them moved. The stillness expanded and enveloped them in the dim interior of the small, stuffy rooms. Rosa wondered what kind of a wife she was that even now, only hours after hearing that her dear Giovanni was dead, she stood staring as if paralyzed into the fathomless blue eyes of this strange, silent man. A man who obviously held her in very little regard. She heard him clear his throat, and watched his lips as he parted them to speak.

"Ready?"

"*Sì*." She shook herself. "For what?"

"To go."

She started. And licked her dry lips. "Oh. *Sì*. To the train."

He turned away and began to move toward the door.

"Marshal . . . ?"

He stopped and turned back again to face her. "Ma'am?"

"Where is my husband . . . how do you say it?"

"Buried?" He made a swift motion with his hands.

"*Sì*. Buried." She looked at the floor and fought off a wave of dizziness.

"Outside of town, ma'am. In the graveyard."

"There is a church?"

He shook his head. "No."

"Oh." No priest to offer her consolation. No one to pray for Giovanni. No hallowed ground in which to bury him. Rosa sighed.

"Anything else, ma'am?" he asked after a pause.

"*Sì*. I would like to see it."

"The grave?"

"*Sì*. The grave." She nodded again. Didn't she owe Giovanni this much? As much as she did not want to see his grave, as much as she wanted to hold to the dream she once had, she knew she could not deny him this. Now when she told his family of his death, she could tell them honestly that she had seen Giovanni's grave and that she had prayed for him.

The marshal seemed hesitant to answer. She waited patiently as he made up his mind. He squinted into the sunshine and stared off down the street for a moment; then he sighed.

"You won't make the twelve o'clock," he said, disgruntled. "Have to take the two."

She assumed he was mumbling about the train. "Is all right for me."

He turned and stared down at her with a brow arched. "Is all right for you?" he repeated. He looked as if he was about to say more and then shrugged and said, "Then I guess is all right for me, too."

Rosa had the distinct impression he was mocking her in some way, but she was uncertain how or why he would do such a thing.

He turned on his heel and started walking down the street in the opposite direction. "Come on, then," he said over his shoulder without breaking his stride.

Rosa clasped her valise to her and hurried after him, afraid to ask him to slow down.

Fine, he thought as he led her back down Main Street. She demands I drive her out to the graveyard, but she won't let me touch her precious valise. He had caught her eyeing him over

and over and assumed she had never seen an Indian before. Let
her look. All white women did, although some were more
circumspect than others. He had been an exotic oddity in
Boston, someone the women speculated about, some with fear,
others with sexual curiosity. He had become aware of this
attraction as soon as he was old enough to view women with
the same regard.

No woman had ever piqued his interest romantically. His
law studies and subsequent career had taken precedence over
any lasting entanglements of the heart. He had had his share of
affairs in the East, but had never taken them seriously because
he could never rid himself of the notion that he was nothing
more to any of his partners than a taste of forbidden fruit.

Besides, he could never ask a woman to suffer the prejudice
that his mother had faced, and for that reason he never
imagined himself in a lasting relationship with any woman. For
the time being, Flossie's girls sufficed.

As they neared the livery, Kase checked the time and then
repocketed his watch, determined to have Rose Audi on the
two o'clock out of town. He glanced around the empty street.
This was no place for a girl like her. Not even with a husband.
Any man who brought a woman to live in a watering hole like
Busted Heel deserved to be shot. She would face nothing but
backbreaking work and unrelieved loneliness in a town whose
only luxury was a whorehouse. She deserved better and he took
it upon himself to make sure she was on the train at two, come
hell or high water.

They entered the cool darkness of a huge shed at the end of
the street. Rosa stared up at the sign that read G. Matheson's
Feed, Livery and Blacksmith. She recognized the name Matheson as the same as the owner of the boardinghouse and wanted
to ask the marshal about it, but thought better of it when he
ignored her and walked up to the blacksmith working over a
smoldering forge.

"I need to hire a rig, Decatur. Just for an hour or so." The
marshal tipped his hat back and looked around the shadowed
interior of the livery.

The burly, well-muscled black man was the first of his race
that Rosa had ever been so close to. She stared up at him,
mesmerized by the deep ebony of his sweat-sheened skin and
his tightly curled hair. He stared back.

"That her?" Decatur Davis spoke to Kase Storm as if she were not even present.

Kase nodded. "Yep."

"She speak English?" the man wanted to know.

"Yep." The marshal glanced at Rosa and then away.

The other man's curiosity seemed to be appeased, for he wiped his hands on a rag at the waistband of his apron and left Rosa and Kase to wait while he readied a rig.

Rosa looked around the huge barnlike structure as she waited patiently. Sunbeams cut through cracks between the wooden ceiling, highlighting the dust motes that drifted among the rafters. Occasionally a horse nickered or stamped. Flies buzzed lazily on the warm, close air. It reminded her very much of an Italian barn. Not so different from home, she thought.

She glanced up and found the marshal staring down at her with a thoughtful expression. When she met his gaze, he looked away.

"Hey! Marshal! Where ya goin'?"

The sharp, high-pitched call of a child's voice drew Rosa's attention. She watched a small boy, his skin as black as the smith's, run into the livery and pause beside Kase Storm.

The big man beside her squatted down on his haunches. "Taking the lady here out to the graveyard—and before you ask about it, no, you can't go."

"You bein' rude again, G.W.?" the blacksmith called out from the rear of the barn.

"No, suh," G.W. called back.

"Not at all, Decatur," the marshal assured the boy's father.

Rosa watched the exchange with interest.

The little boy squinted up at her. "You gonna live here?"

"No, she's not. She's leaving on the train right after we get back," Kase Storm informed the child before Rosa could answer for herself.

For some reason his assumption made her angry. The man was positively rude. She realized it felt good to feel something other than grief, but she did not voice her anger.

Decatur Davis led a horse with a shining black buggy up to the front of the stable and held the horse while Rosa set her valise on the floorboards. Kase Storm helped her board, and within minutes they were riding down Main Street, G.W.

Davis running along behind as fast as his spindly legs could carry him.

It was not a long ride, but the silence that hung between them made it an uncomfortable one. Rosa used the time to stare out at the surrounding landscape and try to acquaint herself with the place that might have been her home. The land to the west banked slowly upward toward the mountains in the distance. There was nothing to relieve the endless vista that stretched toward the east. Unlike the Alps that surrounded Corio by tenderly cupping the village amid their gentle peaks and valleys, the rugged mountains she saw in the distance looked as forbidding as the vast emptiness of the open plain.

Ahead of them Rosa saw what appeared to be a crooked fence standing on a barren rise in the land. Kase Storm must have seen it at the same time, for he nodded and flicked the reins over the horse's back. "That's the graveyard up ahead."

As the horse stepped lively, her mouth went dry. Rosa clutched her hands together in her lap and tried to keep her balance in the swaying rig lest she bump against him. What had appeared to be a tiny fence on the horizon was growing larger as they swiftly drew near.

The marshal pulled the rig up to the base of the rise and tugged back on the reins. He set the brake, tied the reins, and then jumped down. Rosa started to climb down alone, then stopped when she realized he was coming after her. Because of his earlier silence, she was a bit surprised by the polite offer of his hand. She grasped his fingers as he tightened his grip to help her down.

"I'll wait here, ma'am," he said softly, the usual harshness missing from his tone.

She wanted to say no, to tell him that she would rather have him walk with her, but unwilling to appear impolite or demanding, she held her silence. This was something she must do alone.

The few steps up the hill to the small plot of land surrounded by a wind-twisted fence of barbed wire and weathered stakes were the longest steps Rosa had ever taken. She stopped at the edge of the graveyard and stared down at the even rows of graves that dotted the hilltop. Some of the headstones stood askew, twisted by the settlement of the earth or by vandals, she knew not which. She tried to find Giovanni's grave, desperately made her mind focus on the foreign names and words that she did not understand.

Frustration quickly brought her to tears.

"Sorry to disturb you, ma'am, but I just remembered that you probably wouldn't know which one it was."

Rosa nearly fainted, he startled her so. She had not heard him approach. She glanced up to find him standing at her elbow, squinting at the graves. He pointed to a plot marked by a simple white cross without any ornamentation or markings at all.

"That's it," he said.

She thought he would leave her again, but instead, he remained standing beside her as she stared uncomprehendingly at her husband's grave.

It was all so final, so simple, and so sad. Rosa could not believe that Giovanni had come to such an end. What had his life been for? she wondered. Why had he come this far, only to die so suddenly and for nothing?

She shook her head and knew that she could not go any closer. Nor could she utter a prayer now that she stood face to face with the truth. The words would not come. Rosa turned away and stared at the rig at the bottom of the gentle slope. "I am ready now," she said simply.

The marshal stared down at her for a moment as if he had something to say. Then, without a word, he indicated with a wave of his hand that she should precede him down the hill.

*

Chapter
Five

*

All right, so the girl's not much older than your sister and she reminds you of your mother.

The thought tripped around in Kase Storm's mind and echoed with every heavy step he took as he made his way back down Main Street. He found himself comparing Rose Audi with Analisa Van Meeteren Storm, although Rose was quite opposite his mother in appearance. Analisa Storm was tall, blond, and Dutch; Rose was short, dark, and Italian. They were both beautiful. Just like his mother, Rose had suddenly found herself alone and grieving, abandoned in a foreign land, struggling with a new language, fighting to be brave. But there he wanted the similarities to end—before anything could happen to Rose, as it had to his mother. He took it upon himself to insist she leave Wyoming and return to her own people.

Rose Audi hadn't appeared very courageous a few moments ago when he left her sitting at the depot. She looked as forlorn and lost as an abandoned child, stubbornly fighting back tears as she waited for the train that would take her to San Francisco.

What he thought would be an easy task had instantly turned into a debate. He had insisted she go back to Italy and had offered to pay for her trip. Her eyes flashed as she stood firm and fought his suggestion.

"I will go to San Francisco," she had said. "There are many Italians in San Francisco. I will not go to Italy. No. Italy is no good for me now."

"Do you know anyone in San Francisco?"

When she hesitated before she nodded yes, he knew she was lying.

"Look, Mrs. Audi, go home."

"No. San Francisco."

Kase sighed. Time was running out. At least San Francisco was civilized and did have a large immigrant population. He hoped she could find people of her own kind who would take her in and a decent way to provide for herself. He glanced over and saw John Tuttle watching the exchange with interest from the ticket booth.

"Fine. San Francisco it is," Kase said, sliding the money beneath the window bars. He bought a one-way ticket and then handed it to her before he walked her to a nearby bench, tipped his hat, and quickly told her good-bye.

She had been unable to meet his gaze. Instead, she stared down at the ticket she held clutched in her hand. Coward that he was, afraid she was going to start crying again, Kase had left her there to wait alone.

The truth, he admitted to himself, was that he feared if he had stayed he might have sat down on the bench beside her and passed the time trying to ease her fears. He might have even gotten to know her. And for what? It was definitely better this way. He was sure of it.

"Marshal Kase?"

He felt a tug on his pant leg and glanced down.

"Hey, G.W.," he said in greeting.

"Hey, Marshal Kase." The boy looked up at him. "Anythin' you be needin' done this morning?"

Kase hated to squelch the hopeful expression in the child's glowing eyes. "Well," he began slowly, pressing himself to think of something, "you can go down to Al-Ray's store and tell them to send one of the boys around to my office to fill up the water barrel."

Intent upon his errand, George Washington Davis immediately started to run down the street, but Kase stopped him before the boy had gone ten steps.

"And, G.W., get yourself and Martha a sugarplum." Kase tossed a penny to the boy, who deftly caught it before he continued on his way, the light pink soles of his brown feet pounding against the boardwalk.

At Paddie's Ruffled Garter Saloon, Kase moved through the short double doors and set them swinging behind him.

"Mornin', Marshal." Paddie glanced up from behind the bar where he stood wiping glasses. Kase stared at Paddie's bald head and wondered if he shined that, too. Unlike most saloons, every inch of the Ruffled Garter was sparkling clean, even to the brass spittoons. With such an undeniable lack of patrons in Busted Heel, Paddie O'Hallohan had more than enough time to keep the place clean.

Kase walked up to the bar, rested his booted foot on the brass rail, and leaned forward.

"Whiskey, Paddie."

The diminutive bartender glanced at the clock on the wall near the end of the bar, then back at Kase.

"You sure, Marshal?"

"Why would I be asking if I wasn't sure?"

Paddie swiped at an invisible mark on the well-oiled surface of the bar. "It's only eleven-thirty."

"I can tell time."

The man shrugged and turned away without further argument. Kase avoided looking at himself in the long mirror behind the bar as he drew a dime out of his pocket and slapped it down.

Paddie set the drink before him, and Kase stared down into the rich amber liquid for a moment. Damn, if it didn't remind him of the color of the girl's eyes. He wrapped his long, slender fingers around the glass and lifted it to his lips.

Here's to you, Rose. Safe journey.

The whiskey was warm and smooth. It went down fast and easy.

He knew the bartender was watching him out of the corner of his eye and so Kase hid a smile. He had had his share of drinks here, but none at eleven-thirty in the morning, and never when he had the shining tin badge pinned on his chest. No wonder Paddie was ill at ease.

"Thanks," Kase nodded in the squat Irishman's direction. "One should do it."

He headed toward the door and wished he could dispatch Rose Audi from his mind as easily as he had the shot of whiskey.

* * *

The train tracks stretched away from the depot in both directions until they disappeared over the horizon. Rosa stared down at the ticket in her hand without really seeing it. She felt nothing. Kase Storm had insisted he purchase the ticket for her after she informed him, much to her humiliation, that she hadn't enough money left to buy one for herself. She shifted uncomfortably on the hard bench and swung her feet to and fro, the toes of her shoes scraping the rough wood of the platform.

You'll be back, Rosa.

Why was it she could not stop reminding herself of Guido's taunting prediction? She could just imagine her brother's face when she arrived back in Crotte. That was the reason she'd told the marshal she wanted to go west to San Francisco. Even in Corio Rosa had heard of the large settlement of Italians in San Francisco. It was second only to the one in New York. She might be able to find work in the city and make her way without having to return to Italy at all.

The thought did little to cheer her. Rosa tried to imagine herself moving through the bustling streets of San Francisco, a city she could not even picture. She shuddered and recalled how happy she had been that Giovanni had chosen to leave the crowded, dingy city of New York behind and move west. She remembered the tall, dark buildings and narrow streets that massed together on the shore of the Atlantic. It was impossible to think of herself making her way in any American city; she was a country girl, a simple girl. A farmer's daughter. In San Francisco she would be lost in the mass of humanity, a faceless specter moving through mobs of strangers.

If the marshal had had his way, she would be going back to Italy. She lied to him when he asked if she knew anyone in San Francisco, but there was no way she was going home before she had at least tried her luck here in America.

She brushed at a bothersome fly and thought about the desolate building Giovanni had rented. The secret of his dreams had died with him. She would never know why he had chosen this dusty little town for their home. Had he made any friends here? Perhaps the boisterous Mrs. Flossie had befriended him. Maybe he had envisioned fertile fields that stretched as far as the eye could see across the now barren land. Why here, Giovanni? What did you see in this place?

Rosa knew she would never know the answer if she got on

the train and left town as Marshal Kase Storm had so imperiously ordered her to do.

Who was he to decide the course of her life for her? The more she thought of him the angrier she became until finally she stood and stomped over to the barred ticket window.

"Yes, Mrs. Audi?" the man asked.

She looked in at the thin, nondescript man with glasses perched on the end of his nose and oiled-down brown hair and shoved the ticket toward him. "I want to change."

"Yes, ma'am. Where to now?" His brows knit in question.

"Nowhere."

"Ma'am?"

"I am not going."

"You're not? Not going?"

"No. I'm stay here." She felt vastly relieved just saying the words. It was not like her to hesitate. As she grew stronger in purpose and courage, Rosa drew herself up a little taller. "I want the money."

"But, Marshal Storm—"

"I am not going." She enunciated each word so that he would not mistake her meaning.

She could tell he was uncertain, so she stood silently staring up at him until the man moved to take the ticket she thrust toward him and opened the cash drawer below the window. He pushed a handful of bills and change across the counter. Rosa scooped them into her hand and quickly shoved them into her skirt pocket, afraid the man might change his mind and want it all back.

"I will leave the trunk here again, if is all right?"

He nodded. "Of course, ma'am, for as long as you like, but—"

"I will come for it when I have place to stay." She smiled at John Tuttle, hoping to ease some of the concern from his face. Was the man afraid of the marshal? Was that why he had been so hesitant to give her back the money?

"If you change your mind, ma'am, you hurry back and you can still make the train."

She shook her head. "I am certain. I stay here."

With that, Rosa stooped to lift her valise off the platform and, for the second time in two days, turned toward the town of Busted Heel. This time her shoulders were set with purpose.

* * *

"Looks like you got trouble."

Kase looked up at the sound of Zach Elliot's voice. "What?"

"I said, looks like—"

"I heard what you said," Kase snapped irritably. He was in no mood to be sociable. It had been easier to spend his time brooding before Zach came to town. He wished the old man would find something to do and leave him alone. "What kind of trouble?"

"Eye-talian. It's comin' this way."

Kase slammed the palms of his hands on the desk and stood up. He opened the door just as Rose was about to knock, watched her lower her hand and clear her throat. He knew one thing for certain; right now she was definitely a woman with a bee in her oversized bonnet.

"Why aren't you on the train?" he demanded.

"I am not going."

"What do you mean, you're not going?"

She did not look as if she was going to budge. "I am stay here. I will find work."

"Stay where? What work?"

Zach interrupted the exchange. "Why don't you two step inside and let me go out so you can settle this?"

Rose swept past Kase who continued to glare at her. She dropped her valise on the floor where it fell with a thud that echoed loudly in the stillness. Zach sauntered out, and Kase closed the door behind him without a sound. He extracted the gold watch from the depths of his pocket and quickly snapped it open, checked the time, then closed it. As he worked the timepiece back down into his denims, he met Rose's eyes again.

"You're going to miss the train if you aren't back there in ten minutes."

"I think you did not hear me. I am not going. I come here to say to you I will pay the money you give me for the ticket, but I am stay here. This is where Giovanni want me to live."

"Going to. It's *going to* stay here. But you're not. Giovanni isn't here anymore."

"But I am here."

Kase sighed. He had to make her understand that this was no place for a decent woman to live alone. It was hard, desperately lonely, and potentially dangerous for someone so vulnerable. Someone so young. Someone with eyes like melted honey. Someone so—

Kase started and shook himself out of the mesmerized stupor he was falling into. With his thumbs looped into his gun belt he said, "You have to leave."

"Why? You own the town?" She poked at his badge. What privileges was he entitled to as marshal? Could he make her leave?

"No." Irritated, he shook his head. "I don't own the town. But I do know what's good for a woman like you, and Busted Heel isn't it."

"You say to me, Marshal, what kind of woman I am?"

"What?"

She struggled to find the right words. "*Tell* me, what kind of a woman I am?"

He stepped closer. "Innocent. Alone. In need of protection. In need of a home and a means of support . . . a job," he explained further.

Rosa smiled, triumphant. "Your friend, Signora Flossie, she says I can have a job. I go to her next and say I take it."

"*Flossie?*"

She stepped back, amazed at the vehemence in his tone.

"Anyone *but* Flossie."

"But she is your friend . . ."

"She is. But she runs a whorehouse. And as far as I can tell, you aren't any whore."

"I do not understand."

Kase turned away, angry with himself for the sudden outburst. She had done little to deserve it, except irritate him. He refused to let his temper take over all reason. He tried cold detachment instead. "Of course you don't."

Silence lengthened between them. Finally she spoke again. "What is it?"

"I'm upset, that's what."

"No, I mean 'whore.' What is it?"

He groaned. He realized it was the kind of question his mother was continually asking Caleb. Kase felt his face flush with color as he met her unfaltering gaze. What in the hell was she doing to him? He was as skittish as a wild colt caught in a box canyon.

"A whore . . ." Kase cleared his throat and started over. "A whore is a woman who . . . who . . . gets paid for sharing her . . . pleasures."

"Ahh." She nodded, her eyes wide and serious. "*Prostituta.*" With three brothers in the house, she had heard that word before. "Signora Flossie, too?" Her tone was incredulous.

Kase pulled at the collar of his shirt and wondered exactly when it had become too tight. "No." He shook his head. "Not anymore. She just takes care of the girls who work for her. And"—he narrowed his eyes as he stared down at her—"*you* are not going to join them."

Rosa stuck out her chin. "*If* I want to, I will. But I *do not* want to, so I will not. But not because you say so," she added hastily.

"Of course not," Kase mumbled under his breath.

"I want Giovanni's store."

"What store? That empty building with a few rotten potatoes? How long do you think you can live on nothing? Besides, the place wasn't even his; he rented it." Those eyes, he thought, are going to do me in. Kase turned away from her and, with as much nonchalance as he could muster, began sorting through the mail and Wanted posters on the table.

"Whose is?"

"Whose is what?" He purposely baited her by pretending not to understand. It wasn't safe to turn around yet, for there was something about the flashing anger behind the topaz eyes that intrigued him. They reminded him of an electrical storm over the prairie. He wanted to watch the lightning flare a while longer, but refused to allow himself the pleasure.

"Whose is the building? Who owns it?" she shouted. Her limited patience was gone.

"Paddie."

Rosa folded her arms beneath her breasts, unwilling to be put off. Trying to calm herself, she asked in a more moderate tone, "Where is this Paddie?"

"Across the street. He owns the saloon, too."

"Ah. *Taverna.*"

She scooped up the valise and started toward the door. Without a sound and with uncannily graceful speed, Kase got there before her and leaned against it, arms crossed, lips set in a firm line.

"*Mi scusi*." Her request was polite but determined.

Kase shook his head in disbelief. The fool wasn't kidding. She intended to stay in Busted Heel. He knew a sudden urge to lift her up in his arms the way he had yesterday, carry her back to the depot, and shove her onto the train. The trouble was, yesterday she was unconscious. Today he was afraid to try it.

A shrill whistle sounded in the distance. He did not have to look at his watch to know that it was too late for him to take any action at all. Rose Audi smiled up all too smugly at him when he sighed in resignation.

He opened the door and watched her sweep past, head high, full skirt trailing across the dusty sidewalk, the wide, floppy hat giving her the appearance of a walking mushroom.

"Don't say I didn't warn you," he called out as the mushroom headed across the street toward the saloon.

Rosa did not need to turn around to see Kase Storm lounging against the door frame with his arms casually folded across his chest or the icy frigidity in his sky-blue eyes. She knew exactly what he was doing, for she could feel his gaze searing its way through her clothing. So she chose to think about her options instead. By concentrating on the glaring facts of harsh reality, Rosa was able to keep her mind off the man who watched her cross the street.

The facts were simple, the challenge great. She would use the ticket money to help herself get established. Before nightfall she must find a place to live, employment, and the hope of making enough money to pay Marshal Kase Storm back every last lira she owed him. *Dollar*, she reminded herself. Dollar.

With her newfound confidence undiminished, Rosa pushed open the doors of the Ruffled Garter Saloon and stepped just inside the large, nearly empty room. A tall, lanky man in a ruby satin vest and ruffle-fronted white shirt looked up from a deck of cards long enough to nod and smile at her from beneath a waxed handlebar mustache. He was seated across from the grizzled, strangely dressed man with the white hair and scarred face who had been in the marshal's office. The old man made no move. He just stared at her with his one good eye. There was no one else in the room except a short older man working behind the bar.

As she walked inside, determination in every step, the stout bartender hurried around the end of the long bar and met her before she could get more than a few feet inside the door. His face was shadowed with worry, his brows drooped, matching the downturned corners of his mouth.

"May I help you, ma'am?"

"*Sì*. Yes. I am Giovanni Audi's wife. I come to learn about his store."

The man did not ask her to step in farther or to sit down. Neither did he ask if she cared for any refreshment. Rosa thought it rude that he should not, but kept her thoughts to herself. She needed his help.

"His rent was all paid up, Mrs. Audi. Right up until he . . . well, till he died. Don't you be worrying none about that." So saying, Paddie O'Hallohan looked as if he expected her to leave.

Rosa took a deep breath. The man with the cards stopped pretending to shuffle them and leaned back, avidly watching their exchange.

"I want to pay for the store."

"Rent, you mean?"

"Yes," she said. "Rent. I like to rent Giovanni's store. How much is?"

Obviously flabbergasted by her request, Paddie sputtered. "Your husband paid five dollars a month."

"Five?" She paused and repeated the number to be certain she understood him correctly.

"Well, I could let you have it for four-fifty."

Rosa was silent for a moment, blinking once as she recalculated and stared. "Four-fifty?"

Paddie shifted uncomfortably from one foot to the other. "All right, four dollars a month. But that's as low as I can go."

Quattro. "*Bene.* I pay now."

Rosa set down her valise and reached into her pocket, withdrawing the crumpled wad of bills the ticket agent had given her. She counted out four dollars and paid Paddie O'Hallohan the rent on the building next door.

"You drive a hard bargain, Mrs. Audi. Now that you have it, what are you planning to do with the place?"

She shrugged. "A store."

"Busted Heel's got one store already. Al-Ray's. Why, Alice and Ray Wilkie have been here since the railroad came through and the town was laid out. It won't be easy to cut into their trade." He considered her for a moment. "Marshal Storm know you're staying on?"

She smiled. And lied. "But of course, Mr. Paddie. He is—how do you say it?—delighted." She heard the man with the eye patch begin to cough.

Paddie looked none too sure about her statement, but nodded and smiled in return. "I'll get you the key. Been leaving the place unlocked, seeing as how there's nothing in there. You'll be wanting to lock up, though." He spoke to her over his shoulder as he moved away. "I'm right here if you need anything."

Within moments Rosa was walking down the sidewalk again with her valise in one hand and the key to Giovanni's store tucked safely in her pocket with the rest of her borrowed funds. Her journey took her only a few steps before she stopped on the other side of the saloon at Flossie Gibbs's Hospitality Parlor and Retreat. After straightening her hat, Rosa rapped on the door and waited for someone to answer her knock. She did not wait long.

The door opened a mere crack, and a hushed voice informed her, "We're not open yet."

"*Mi scusi*," Rosa began. "I like to see Signora Flossie."

The door opened wider and a tall, lanky girl Rosa guessed could be no older than seventeen peered around it. Fine yellow hair stood out all around her head like scattered straw. The remnants of sleep puffed her eyelids.

"Flossie?" the blonde repeated.

"*Sì*. Tell the *signora* that Rosa Audi, who she met earlier this day, comes to see her."

The girl closed the door and left Rosa staring at the frosted-glass pane inches from her nose. Rosa began to tap her foot impatiently. Time was fleeting. There was much to do before nightfall.

Just as she heard the sound of approaching footsteps, Rosa saw behind the frosted glass the vibrant shade of magenta Flossie had been wearing earlier. She took a deep breath of the warm, dry air, and waited as the door opened.

"Miz Audi," Flossie said with a look of astonished curiosity on her face. "What can I do for you?"

Again, Rosa wondered at the rudeness of these Americans. Signora Flossie did not seem willing to invite her in out of the intense noonday heat. Rosa looked right and left before she voiced her request, but dared not turn around. *He* might still be watching. "I may come in to speak to you?" Rosa asked softly.

The older woman's surprise was evident, but she immediately stepped back into the cool, shadowed interior of the parlor. "Of course. Why, I didn't even think to ask a lady such as yourself if you'd like to come in. Then again, it's no wonder I forgot my manners. Haven't had a lady come to the door since I can remember." Flossie mumbled the last remark more to herself than to Rosa.

Rosa swept in and waited in the center of the room while her astonished hostess sent the young blonde off to fetch a pot of tea.

"*Tea?*" The blond girl's voice rose as she stared dumbstruck at Flossie.

"Tea," Flossie reiterated. "If you can't find some in the back cupboard, run over to the Yees' and ask for a pinch." She turned back to face Rosa. "Sit down, Miz Audi, and let me make up for my poor show o' manners."

Rosa sat, grateful to be in out of the sun's intense glare. She stared around the room, thinking it one of the loveliest she had ever seen, still amazed to think she was inside a bordello. The walls were covered with deep crimson paper gilded with an ornate design. Sconces that dripped with crystal teardrops and cradled oil lamps were scattered at intervals about the ruby-colored walls. Flossie sank down onto a mohair settee, its upholstered surface rubbed to shining with long wear.

"What can I do for you, Miz Audi. I thought you were leavin' town."

"I choose to stay."

Flossie Gibbs arched a brow. "I see."

"And now I need a job."

Flossie's eyes widened. "Here? I was only teasin' you when—"

"No!" Rosa said a little too quickly, then feared she might have insulted the *signora*. She smiled and lowered her voice. "No. I come to talk. Signor Paddie tells me about stores here in Busted Heel. He says if I open a store, everyone she's still going to buy from the old one."

"He's probably right." The madam nodded, her brow furrowed in concentration. "What do you know how to do?"

Before Rosa could respond, the blonde reentered the room with a pot of tea. Flossie pointed to the side table, then once more devoted her attention to Rosa. Leaning forward to accept a cup of tea from the blonde, Rosa considered Flossie's question. She blew on the steaming liquid, then looked up.

"You can go now, Chicago," Flossie Gibbs told the young girl. With a disgruntled look, the girl left the room.

Rosa listed her talents. "I can cook, clean, read, write . . . but not so good in English."

"Can you sew?"

Rosa made a face. "My aunt would say no."

Flossie laughed. "It was just a thought."

"I have now an empty store. I need to know what is possible to sell there."

"What people need and what they want are two different things. Folks around here are either farmers needin' seed and feed and calico, or they're cowboys needin' whiskey, a little tobacco, and comfortin'." She thought for a moment and then added, "But what they all want at one time or another when they come to town is good, decent vittles."

"Ahh," said Rosa sitting up a bit straighter. "Vittles!"

"Yep." Flossie nodded, obviously pleased with herself.

"What is vittles?"

Flossie threw back her head with hearty laughter that set her wide bosom jiggling. "Food, Miz Audi."

"The other store does not already sell food?"

"Not hot cooked meals. Why, the only way a body can get anything to eat here in Busted Heel is to cook it themselves or resort to eatin' Bertha Matheson's food, and her slop ain't fit for hogs."

Rosa thought back to the poor excuse for a meal that she'd pushed around her plate at breakfast and had to silently agree with Flossie's apt description.

"So," Flossie went on, "the way I see it is that you have two choices: you can work here, cookin' for me and my gals—seein' as how I been thinkin' of hirin' my own cook lately—or you could open up a café. Serve folks some vittles they wouldn't have to close their eyes and hold their noses to eat."

A *caffè*. A *ristorante*.

Rosa tried to imagine the musty, empty store filled with customers enjoying delicious meals, the likes of which she had not tasted since she left Corio. The Piedmont region of Italy was famous not only for its main course dishes but also for puddings, sweets, melted cheese *fondute*, and wines. Perhaps, she thought, with a lot of hard work and a little luck . . .

Flossie interrupted her musing. "O' course, it'll take you some time, not to mention money, to get set up. Why don't you take a job here with me until you get on your feet? With your husband dyin' and all . . . well, maybe you need a little time." Flossie eyed her carefully. "You might change your mind about leaving."

"Signora Flossie," Rosa began, confidently meeting the older woman's green-eyed stare, "my husband send for me. Now I am here. I must eat to live. To eat, I must make money." Rosa reached down for the valise at her feet. "I want to thank you. You are much help to me. I go now to my store and think about all you have said."

Flossie stood as Rosa did and walked her to the door. "I'll help you in any way I can, Miz Audi. You jes holler."

"Please call me Rosa, Signora Flossie."

"Sure thing, Rosie." The old woman looked pleased. "It'd be my pleasure."

"*Grazie*, Signora Flossie. *Buon giorno*."

"Bon-journey to you, too, Rosie, and good luck!"

Brushing her hands against the once-white dish towel tied around her waist, Rosa walked toward the shanty that stood behind the row of stores fronting Main Street. The yard around the place was littered with all manner of refuse. Broken wheels, lengths of wire, and empty cans and bottles were strewn about the ground around the clapboard shack with the vegetable garden beside it. As she took in the jumble of trash, the split-rail fence that housed a lazy sow and her shoats, and the chickens that scratched with futility in the well-packed earth about the yard, Rosa slowly became aware of the aches and pains that were beginning to settle into her limbs. It was late afternoon now, and the sun was moving all too quickly toward the west. Rosa gauged its progress and felt a sense of relief coupled with frustration. It would be good to stop work, but there was still so much to do.

The hours of the afternoon had flown by as she put her plan to open a café into effect. After her conversation with Flossie, Rosa had returned to Giovanni's store and assessed her situation. The place was knee deep in dirt. She took stock of the furnishings the rooms possessed. Aside from the dust, the cot, and the stove, there was an empty water barrel, a battered tin tub, and what was left of a straw broom.

What were you thinking of, Giovanni? she wondered as she glanced around the pitiful supply. What was your dream?

Shrugging off the questions that had plagued her since morning, Rosa had then sent for her trunk, making good the small Negro boy's offer to help. The child was the same one the marshal had spoken to earlier in the blacksmith's barn. He informed her his name was G. W. Davis and that he lived in the place just behind her store. It seemed that only pennies for candy were required to convert the small boy into an able-bodied co-worker. She welcomed G.W.'s company and put the boy to work immediately. Once he had carried a message to John Tuttle and her trunk was delivered, G.W. informed her that the Wilkies' sons—Robbie, Ritchie, Rudy, and Roy—took turns oiling the tall windmill at the edge of town and delivering water to the residents. She sent him along to the store with the message that she would like to pay for and receive her share of water as soon as possible.

While G.W. swept the floors from one end of the place to the other, Rosa changed into one of her familiar everyday dresses, tied on a makeshift apron, and took the stove to task. Her hands burned from the lye soap she used to polish the relic, and she promised to herself to keep the stove shining as long as it promised to turn out wondrous culinary delights in return.

Now, as she stopped outside the shanty, Rosa waited for the woman moving about inside to notice her. The door to the place was open, so Rosa could see nearly all of the one-room cabin. The place was crowded with a table and four chairs, a double bed in the corner, and the stove near the door. Rosa imagined the family seated about the rickety table and felt sad. It had been weeks since she had seen her own family, and now that Giovanni was gone, she would not know the luxury of having anyone to share her meals with. Determined not to cry, she fought back the tears that threatened and told herself that soon the café would be full of customers and she would not feel so alone.

The tall Negro woman she had seen only from afar was bent over an open oven door. The heat inside the small room must have been nearly overpowering. Rosa wondered how the very pregnant woman could stand it. Finally, the woman G.W. had informed her was his mother, Zetta, straightened. When she noticed Rosa standing outside, she smiled. She wiped her hands on her tightly stretched apron and reached up to be certain the scarf tied around her hair was straight.

"Yes?" Zetta Davis's smile was shy but welcoming.

"I am Rosa. Rosa Audi. Maybe you know my husband, Giovanni?"

"I did," Zetta said. "Spoke with him once or twice. Sorry about him gettin' hisself kilt." She looked Rosa up and down. "Decatur tol' me you was in town."

Rosa nodded, still ill at ease when offered condolences. "I am wondering. Can you tell me about the table?" She pointed toward the back of her store. "Was his?"

Zetta glanced toward the buildings. There was a weather-scarred table standing abandoned near the rear of Rosa's store.

"Yep. Used it to clean them vegetables he was settin' to sell."

"You know his ideas?" Anxious to hear more, Rosa raised a hand to shield her eyes from the sun.

"He was plannin' to cart in vegetables and fruits from Cheyenne. Seems a group of you folks was startin' up a colony there and been growin' all kinds of gardens. Why he thought anybody here in Busted Heel be needin' more than what we already had, I don't know. They already sellin' vegetables at Al-Ray's; most are mine, some the farmers bring in in trade. I got my own patch I used to make a little money now an' then. Weren't any need for any more vegetable sellers hereabouts." She squinted at Rosa. "You thinkin' on sellin' vegetables?"

"No. Cooking. I will start a café."

"Sho' nuf?"

"Sho' nuf?" Rosa had never heard the phrase, but thought it bore repeating. "Sho' nuf."

"Well, I'll be. A café, you say? Ain't this place turnin'

fancy, now?" Zetta laughed and called out to the children waiting for Rosa on the back step of the store. "You two childrens come on home right now! Time for dinner. Yore pappy'll be home shortly." Her attention on Rosa again, Zetta said, "My husband Decatur's the town blacksmith. You ever need anything fixed, you come to me, an' if G.W. and Martha get to pesterin' you too much, you jest shoo them on home."

"*Grazie.* You said you sell vegetables?"

"Sho' nuf."

"I want to buy. Tomorrow we will talk again."

"Nice meetin' you, Miz Audi." Zetta smiled.

"Rosa," she said over her shoulder. As she recrossed the yard, sidestepping the scattered chickens running to and fro, Rosa practiced the curious new phrase she had learned from Zetta Davis and looked forward to a bath.

*

Chapter
Six

*

As the sun moved on, easing its way across the plains until it disappeared beyond the horizon, dusk began to gather like fog about the town of Busted Heel. As the shadows between the buildings intensified, Kase Storm stood in his office and stared out of the dust-streaked window that fronted Main Street. With his hands shoved deep in his pockets and his feet spread wide against the pine plank floor, he let his expression mirror the growing shadows outside.

From where he stood he could not see into the small storefront across the street, and it irked him more than he liked to admit. He had a clear view of Flossie's place, a partial look into the well-lit saloon, but only a slant-eyed peek into the darkened interior of the shop Rosa Audi intended to call her own. Although darkness was rapidly settling in for the night, there was still no light visible through her front window. Kase wondered how long it would be before Rosa Audi decided it was time to light a lamp.

If she even owned one.

He shifted his weight to his left foot and ignored the sound of Zach Elliot entering the office.

"Still worryin' about the widow woman?"

Kase turned on his friend. "I'm not worrying. Not about her."

"No? Then why you been wanderin' around this place like a

pony with his bridle off? You got the worried look of a fish floppin' on a grassy bank wonderin' how he got there."

"You got a real way with words, Zach."

"No sense in shootin' straight and talkin' crooked." Zach frowned and rubbed the stubble of his beard with an open palm. "Been speculatin' on where a man might get a bite to eat tonight. What're you plannin' on? Cold beans in a dirty bowl again?"

"I was thinking of ordering a meal at Bertha's. Tonight's fried chicken night. It's the one thing she can't ruin." Kase shrugged.

"Yeah? I'll tag along."

Kase cleared his throat before he said, "I won't be eating there. Floss always brings me some when she picks up hers." He figured the old man might as well know where he stood with some of the townsfolk. "Bertha won't have a half-breed at her table."

Zach paused for a moment before he said, "Which doesn't sound like punishment from what you said a minute ago."

Kase cocked his head and half smiled. "I guess not, now that you mention it."

Kase reached up for the black hat slung over the rack near the open door and settled it on his head. "I think I'll just take one last walk around town and then meet you over there. If you run into Flossie Gibbs, introduce yourself. And be polite. She's a friend."

Zach rolled his eyes heavenward. "Already met her. Tough as an old hen. Wears so much paint she can't blush."

"She's got a heart as big as Wyoming, though. I'd appreciate it if you'd remember I told you that." Kase's voice was smooth as silk, emphasizing the strong warning behind the words.

"Defending old women, widows, and orphans seems to set real well with you, boy." Zach clapped Kase on the shoulder as he stepped outside. "I'll try and save you a drumstick."

Darkness quickly smothered the remaining sunlight. Kase sauntered down his side of the street, pausing long enough to thrust head and shoulders between the faded black drapes that hung in the doorway of the Yee family's laundry. The place was no bigger than his dressing room in the Storm mansion. It was filled with the eye-smarting smell of lye soap mixed with the cloying scent of incense. Flossie and the girls kept the family in business. So did Paddie, who wore a spanking white shirt every day, regardless of the fact that he had few customers who would even notice. As usual, the Chinese couple were arguing with each other while their daughter, a soulful twelve-year-old, looked up at Kase and smiled. He waved and ventured on.

One or two horses were tied up outside the saloon across the street. Cowboys from Mountain Shadows and other nearby ranches would be arriving now that the sun was down. But unless they got too liquored up, Kase did not expect any trouble. That was the reason he liked to sit unobtrusively at a corner table in the saloon until closing time. It helped pass the empty hours of an evening as well as curb the cow punchers' appetites for too much whiskey. After all, he reasoned, that was why Quentin Rawlins had hired him—to keep the peace in Busted Heel. The job kept him occupied while he tried to put his life back in order.

At first Kase had wondered why a man as wealthy and removed from the town as Rawlins even cared about Busted Heel's growth and reputation, but within a few hours of proposing the job to Kase, the man had explained. They had discussed the offer over dinner at the Grand Hotel in Kansas City just after they recognized each other on one of the city's main thoroughfares.

"The reason I want a good man out there, a man I can trust," Quentin said, leaning back on a thick rolled Havana cigar, "is because my spread's the biggest outfit near Busted Heel. I hire the most men, and I'll admit, running an operation as big as Mountain Shadows doesn't leave any room for getting to know the type of men I hire. I can only hope that I'm as good a judge of men as I am of cattle. But, times being what they are, with my investments spreading out over Wyoming and beyond, my foreman does most of the hiring these days. I guess what I'm trying to say"—he inhaled and set the tip of the cigar glowing—"is that I don't want to be responsible for any of my boys going hog wild and harming innocent townsfolk.

"I've known your father since we worked together for the Bureau. I'd trust him with my life, and I'd say the same for you, just knowing you've been raised by him. I won't tell you Busted Heel's not a lonesome, forlorn place right now, but I foresee the town growing in the next few years, right along with the rest of Wyoming. Statehood's just around the corner," the cattleman had predicted, "and that'll bring in all kinds of folks."

One of whom was a golden-eyed Italian girl with a head as hard as a mule could kick, Kase thought as he stood at the end of the sidewalk, staring at the dark interior of the empty shop across the street. He could pretend to Zach that he hadn't paid her any mind since she stalked away from the jail at midday, but he could not deny it to himself. That would make him twice the fool. Without wanting to, he had tracked her every move, tried not to notice when she left Paddie's with a smug look on her face and, he suspected, the key to the run-down store safely tucked in her pocket. He had only glanced up from the newspaper for a moment when he caught a glimpse of her leaving Flossie's. Then it took every ounce of fortitude he had not to walk over and ask Floss what the girl had wanted. He could just imagine the belly laugh Flossie Gibbs would enjoy over his uncalled-for curiosity.

He knew G.W. had spent the day running Rose's errands for her. Kase had watched the nappy-headed boy run from one end of town to the other, first to the depot and then down to Al-Ray's. She kept the youngster so busy G.W. hadn't pestered him all afternoon. Not that it bothered Kase. Not in the least. If the boy wanted to earn his penny candy elsewhere, good riddance.

By now she had probably unpacked the huge leather-strapped trunk he had seen John Tuttle haul out of his delivery wagon and slide across the sidewalk into the shop. He knew for a fact, after observing his mother and sister, that once a woman unpacked her goods she was ready to stay put, at least until she'd had the chance to wear everything she had hauled with her. That thought led him to speculate on whether the rest of Rose's clothes were too big for her, not to mention as old-fashioned as the black velvet dress.

Kase scuffed the sole of his boot against the edge of the sidewalk and stared at the darkened storefront. She was probably in the back room with the connecting door closed; that had to be the reason he could not see any light within. No need to stop by and see how she fared. None at all.

But he stepped off the boardwalk and crossed over to her side of the street anyway.

The front door to the little shop was locked. The faintest glow of light, a rectangle of golden yellow in the darkness, outlined the small door to the back room. The hum of low voices broken by the occasional high-pitched giggle of one of Flossie's girls issued from Paddie's next door. There was no one on the street. Deciding things were quieter than a hole in the ground and feeling not the least bit hungry yet, he moved toward the back of Rose's empty store.

Tired beyond exhaustion, Rosa had satisfied her hunger with a few slices of bread and a bowl of stew made of an unfamiliar meat that Zetta had brought over. After thanking her neighbor profusely, Rosa fell upon the food, remembering that just last night she had sworn she would never feel like eating again. Time and hard work seemed to have a way of healing all sorts of wounds.

Rosa glanced around the room, happy with the progress she'd made in just a few short hours. Her trunk stood against the back wall yawning open to reveal a few items still neatly stacked in the bottom. The few dresses she owned lined the wall above the cot, hanging on the very hooks that Giovanni had once used. The newly washed table stood in the center of the room and atop it were stacked the cups, saucers, bowls, and plates that had been safely wrapped in the linens packed in the trunk. Two small photographs, one of her mother and father and one of Giovanni, were on a crooked shelf near the stove.

The familiar sights and smells of Corio had been dredged up from the very depths of the trunk as Rosa unwrapped her precious possessions. The linen sheets had all been embroidered by her sister and Zia Rina. Handwoven runners and lace doilies had been lovingly wrapped and folded around each piece of china. Rose petals and spices were scattered among her belongings to keep them smelling sweet. Fragrant muslin packets of basil and oregano, anise, and thyme brought back bittersweet memories of Zia Rina. It was not difficult for Rosa to imagine the old woman sitting before the fire, bent over the squares of fabric as she sewed them together.

Rosa laughed aloud when she found two old iron keys at the bottom of the trunk. Ever cautious, Zia Rina had secretly sent them along for Rosa to use to guard against evil. Whenever a strong wind blew down a sapling or any other signs of misfortune materialized, Zia Rina would always cross two keys to drive away the bad luck that was sure to follow.

"*Grazie*, Zia Rina," Rosa whispered aloud in the empty room as she hung the keys on a nail beside the door where they would lock out bad luck. She looked at the collection of unpacked goods and smiled.

A single candle lit the room. There were four of them, each hand-dipped in scented wax and carried across the sea to be used during the first meal she served in her new home. But instead of sharing dinner with Giovanni, she had eaten alone in the semidarkness, leaning back against the now spotless stove. Aching for rest, she glanced over at the cot. She had beaten the dust off and covered the cot with a sheet so pristine in its whiteness it seemed a shame to use it on so humble a bed. The night was warm, balmy enough that she would need no other cover.

Slowly, in the dim light that cast tall, flickering shadows over the walls of the tiny room, Rosa began to unbutton the front of the brown dress that had faded to near beige. She drew it off her shoulders and let the bodice hang from the still buttoned waistband. The white camisole beneath clung to her damp skin, testimony to the heat. She unbuttoned the first three buttons. A pail of water on the unlit stove served as her wash basin as she dipped her cupped hands in again and again, splashing the refreshing liquid over her parched and dusty skin. Eyes closed, she reached out, searching for the linen towel she had looped over the oven door handle.

The slightest hint of a footfall outside caused Rosa to freeze just as her fingertips reached the towel. Holding her breath, she hastily dried her face and listened, head cocked to the side, for another sound. With one hand she held the towel pressed against the valley between her breasts, slim protection for whatever danger lurked outside. As she stood staring at the door, too afraid to move, she heard the sound again. There was definitely someone moving around out there.

G.W., she thought. Relieved, she started to step forward. Then she realized it was long past sunset and the child would be in bed.

When the door handle moved slightly to the right and then to the left, her heart began to pound so intensely that she thought she was going to faint. But as the door swung slowly open, she felt a strange, cool calm come over her. She would face the intruder and deal with him. Or die trying.

Determined to pick up the one remaining piece of wood and use it as a weapon, she moved toward the box just as the door opened completely.

Kase Storm stepped over the threshold.

Rosa did not know whether to grab the piece of wood and bring it down on the crown of his head or feel relieved at the sight of his familiar face. She did neither. Instead, she clutched the towel against her breasts and wondered at the reason for his intrusion.

"You left your door unlocked," he stated bluntly.

She nodded, unable to do more than stare and wonder what he wanted.

He returned her stare, determined to frighten her. She needed to learn what could easily happen to someone so vulnerable. "You don't realize there are all kinds of drifters who ride into town every night," he said, his eyes roving over her.

"Drifters?"

He stepped closer. "A woman like you shouldn't be living here alone at all, let alone with the door unlocked after sundown." He watched her slowly mounting panic and envisioned his mother's eyes wide with horror as she faced her attacker.

Rose reached up with her free hand to push aside a tendril of hair that had slipped free of her braids. It felt damp as she looped it behind her ear.

Kase could almost smell her fear. It was all too visible in the way she had begun to tremble. He knew he should stop what he was doing to her, but a cruel need to frighten some sense into her spurred him on. "What do you intend to do when some cowhand decides to walk in here the way I did? Have you thought about that?"

"No, I—"

"What if a man were to walk up to you like this?" In two strides he closed the space between them until they were standing toe to toe.

"I—" Rosa swallowed and tried to break the hold of his piercing gaze.

"What if some cowpoke were to put his hands on you, like this?" The sight of his dark fingers pressed into her white flesh shook him to the core. A man had roughly used his own mother once, forced his way into her flesh and left his seed inside her. That man's blood now surged through his veins.

He let go of Rose as if he had been scorched, but he did not back away.

Her mouth suddenly went dry, and Rosa licked her lips.

His voice was even softer now, huskier. He seemed a part of the shadows that snaked and twisted on the wall as the flame wavered on the slight evening breeze. "What would you do then, Rose? And if one of them decided to kiss you?" He put his hands on her again. "Pull you to him like this?"

He expected her to fight, but a gentle tug was all it took to bring her up against him. She was no longer staring into the depths of his eyes, but at the full lips so near her own. He smelled of dust and heat and leather. Her body acted on its own, and she raised herself up on tiptoe until their lips met.

If he was surprised by her spontaneous move, he did not show it as he pulled her against his hard length. One warm palm rested at the vulnerable point at the back of her neck while the other easily found a resting place at her waist. The towel, which she still clutched in her fingertips, was trapped between them, but it did not prevent Rosa from feeling the sharp pointed tin star he wore on his shirtfront press into the tender skin of her breast.

She was expecting a warm, undemanding kiss. The kind she had shared with Giovanni. Instead, Kase Storm's mouth swooped down to cover hers with a vengeance. His kiss was hard and demanding, unlike anything she had ever known or imagined. The pressure of his lips forced hers to part. His irreverent tongue teased the outline of her mouth for the slightest moment before it slipped inside, warming her to her toes as it explored, caressed, and tempted her to respond. Rosa was startled for a moment, afraid that this giant of a man was beyond her control. Frightened by the power of his kiss as well as her own startling reaction to it, Rosa sought to turn her head and draw her lips away. She was surprised when he easily complied and broke off just as suddenly as he had begun.

Releasing her abruptly, Kase stepped away. He had not expected her to allow him such liberties. Nor had he expected to be moved by her response. Rose had been frightened, but not enough to fight him. Had she been stunned into acquiescence, or was she so pliable out of mere curiosity? Whatever the reason, it seemed his crude attempt to persuade her to leave had backfired. He was the one shaken by the exchange.

Rosa was aware only of the swift beating of her heart, the mingled sounds of their uneven breathing, and his cold, assessing stare.

He reached for the top button of her camisole top. Rosa was not certain, but she thought she saw his fingers tremble slightly as he slipped the first, the second, and then the third button through the corresponding buttonholes. Then Kase Storm cleared his throat and straightened his already perfectly centered hat. "From now on, I suggest you keep that door locked."

As he left the room and silently closed the door, Rosa stood motionless and stared after him. The moment he was gone, she knew that she need not fear any strangers outside the unlocked door. No cowboy drifter could cause her any more shame than she had already brought upon herself by allowing Kase Storm to kiss her. With trembling fingertips, Rosa touched her lips. They still tingled from the pressure of his kiss. Was she no better than the women down the street? How could she have tarnished Giovanni's memory here in his very own store? Her reaction to the marshal's kiss frightened her more than the fact that he had kissed her. After all, what was the man to do when she'd practically thrown herself into his embrace?

She knew Kase Storm had only come to warn her, perhaps even frighten her into leaving town. Rosa shook her head, still clutching the towel to her breasts. If he meant to scare her, he had succeeded. But she was not afraid of him.

It was the wild, erratic beat of her heart and the warm arousal she had experienced in his arms that had scared her the most.

Alerted by the sound of revelry in the Ruffled Garter, Kase paused outside for a moment before he stepped through the swinging doors of the saloon. A few cowboys from Rawlins's Mountain Shadows Ranch were scattered about the room, some engaged in card games while others bellied up to the bar. In a far corner, Zach shared a table with Flossie and her girls. Intent on gnawing at a chicken leg, he glanced up as Kase crossed the room, then concentrated on his food once again.

"Hi, Kase. Pull up a chair and have some chicken. Zach brought you a plateful." Flossie scooted her chair aside to make room for him between herself and Chicago Sue.

Kase grabbed a chair from a nearby table and joined the group. Young Chicago Sue gave him a shy glance and a throaty "Hiya, Kase," as she handed him the plate of fried chicken, biscuits, and gravy that Zach pushed across the table.

Mira leaned back in her chair and took a long swallow of beer, then tossed her loose mane of riotous brown hair away from her face. "If you all don't mind, I'm gonna go back to the house and freshen up for tonight." She gave Kase a pouty, sensual smile and a look of open invitation before she stood and left the table.

Felicity, shortest of the four girls, a beauty with skin the color of a creamy white lily and bouncing hair as black as midnight, shook her head, disgusted by Mira's obvious advance.

Satin, with ruddy pink cheeks and a jovial smile that danced on her lips and lit her sparkling blue eyes, giggled. She returned her concentration to her dinner. Her plump frame attested to the fact that she, unlike everyone else in town, enjoyed Bertha Matheson's cooking. Kase thought the girl looked more like a milkmaid than a whore, but then all of Flossie's girls—except Mira—looked as if they belonged in a schoolroom.

"I thought you were going to eat at Bertha's, Zach," Kase said as he reached for a golden brown chicken thigh.

Before Zach could respond, Flossie explained. "This sweet man here was ordering your dinner when Chicago and I went to collect ours. Why, do you know, Kase, when I mentioned to Zach that I'm good enough to buy chicken from Bertha but that she don't consider me good enough to eat at her boardin'house, why, he up and brought his dinner over here so he could eat with us?"

Kase glanced across the table at Zach. The scout was inordinately preoccupied with his meal. "He's a real knight in shining armor," Kase said.

"Speakin' of knights in shining armor," Zach shot back, "what's the widow woman up to?"

"That Italian girl?" Felicity asked. "I'm dying to see her."

Floss nodded. "She's a beauty. Don't you think so, Kase?"

"I saw her. She came over today—" Chicago Sue began, but Flossie cut her off with a quick shake of her head.

"Hell if I know what she's going to do," Kase said, answering Zach while ignoring Flossie's obvious attempt to get him to comment on Rosa's looks.

Zach dipped a biscuit into his gravy. "Didn't you find out anything?"

"No."

"Zach here tried to get me to bet two bits that you'd have her talked into leavin' town tomorrow," Flossie said between bites.

Kase frowned. Since when was any of this their business?

"Shoot, you was gone long enough." Zach bit into the biscuit and then tried to tear at it with his teeth. "Damn!"

Satin began giggling again, her round cheeks pinkening as she watched Zach's antics.

"Watch it," Paddie called out from behind the bar. "A fella was damn near killed in here one night when Mira threw one of Bertha's biscuits at him!"

Kase listened to the laughter that filled the room and smiled, but held back from entering the round of easy banter that followed. With his thoughts centered on the building next door, he failed to notice the knowing looks that passed between Floss and Zach. Try as he might, he could not dismiss the memory of Rose Audi, half dressed and doe eyed, as she clutched her damp chemise to her breasts.

He had not meant to enjoy kissing her. It was the furthest thing from his mind when he entered the near empty store, but when she brushed aside the stray lock of hair and looked up at him, wide-eyed and trembling, he could not help but step closer. Her soft, pale skin, cast in golden candlelight, had begged to be touched. Once his fingertips connected with her warm flesh, he felt as if he had been jolted by lightning. But when he pulled her closer, when she raised herself up to meet his lips instead of pushing him away . . .

Kase shifted uncomfortably in his chair and tried to forget the way she'd felt in his arms. He had an idea it would be just as difficult as ignoring the insistent ache in his loins. It wouldn't do to let his thoughts keep riding roughshod down the trail they were taking. Not at all. Not here in public.

Let her sleep there all alone tonight, he thought. The place was dismal enough in the daytime, but in the dim light, the dark, empty corners would soon close in on her. He silently bet himself she would move out in the morning without any coaxing at all.

Zetta's rooster woke Rosa at dawn. The morning passed all too quickly as she continued her cleaning assault on the empty store. At noon, she washed and changed into her black traveling dress and prepared to visit Al-Ray's general store. She decided to forgo wearing the velvet hat, afraid that trying to keep it anchored on her head while carrying a basket of groceries might prove too complicated a task. She straightened the overlarge gown once more, picked up her reticule and empty basket, and opened the front door.

Kase Storm blocked her exit.

The man seemed to fill the doorway, his powerful build and height overwhelming her once again. Rosa stepped back and tried to speak but was at a loss for words. She realized she was thinking in Italian again and fought for command of the English she knew. For some reason, Kase Storm drove all rational thought from her mind.

He folded his arms across his chest and appeared all too smug as he said, "Leaving?"

She paused for a moment while she collected her thoughts. "Yes. To the store."

"Oh."

Rosa wondered if his shuttered expression hid disappointment or relief.

"Mind if I walk with you?"

A sudden picture of herself half dressed and leaning into his embrace flashed through her mind. She stared at the badge on his striped shirtfront, traced the line of buttons up to his white collar, and then tried to see around him to the street beyond. "*Va bene*." She nodded.

They walked in silence, Kase matching his long stride to her short quick one. They stepped off the boardwalk and crossed the street. They were on the other side before Kase spoke.

"What are you planning to do?"

"I will open a place to sell vittles. A café. A *ristorante*."

"Why?"

She shrugged and finally looked up at him. "Because there is no good food here. I can cook." She held her hands wide, unmindful of the basket, and shrugged again. "Why not?" Rosa stepped up on the boardwalk.

Kase stood his ground in the street. They were nearly eye to eye. "I'm not going to be responsible for you if you stay."

"Responsible?" The word was new to her.

"Yeah. I'm not going to worry about you or watch out for you—any more than I do for anyone else in this town."

"And why should you do this for me, Marshal?"

"Just in case you had any notions after last night—"

"I think maybe we forget last night." Rosa felt her cheeks burning. She turned away, set on escaping Marshal Kase Storm.

He reached out and grabbed her arm. Rosa glanced in both directions before she turned around to face him again.

"Why don't you just leave town?" he persisted.

Her reserve snapped. "*Dio!* Why? I tell you why." She set the basket on the walk beside her and planted one fist on her hip. Rosa held up her other hand and, thumb first, began to count off the reasons for him. "My brother, he say I'll be back, so I'm not go back. *You* keep say I must go back. Signora Flossie say I can cook and make money here. Giovanni choose this place for me—" she raised her voice to emphasize her determination and opened both arms wide, appealing to him as she made her final argument—"and I want stay!"

At the end of her tirade, she calmed enough to notice that a stony silence was his only response.

Speak in a low voice.

Do not yell or wave your hands about.

Do not get excited in your discussions.

Dio! She realized every time she saw this man she broke the rules in the *Guide for Italian Immigrants*. Chagrined, Rosa reached down for her basket and in a more subdued tone informed him, "So that is why I stay. Sho' nuf."

She heard him sigh. It was the long, slow sigh of a man who had reached the end of his patience. Rosa waited to see what Kase would say. When he finally spoke, his voice was so low she barely heard the words he uttered.

"This isn't the kind of place where you're likely to find another husband."

Confused, Rosa feared she had mistranslated his words. "*Scusi?*" The boldface words of the immigrant's guide flashed before her eyes: "Beware of strange men offering proposals of marriage."

"A woman can live here without marry, yes?"

"Look." He pushed his hat back off his forehead and frowned. "Of course. But will you be content living alone forever?" He thought of the kiss they had shared. She was sensual, vibrant, a woman with plenty of love to give the right man. "The only candidates you'll find around here are no-account drifters who haven't the slightest intention of taking up with a decent woman."

"And you?" she threw back at him.

"I don't count."

"No?"

"No. Most definitely not."

"Because you hate Italians? You are too good for me?"

Was she so naive that she did not think the color of his skin mattered? "I'm afraid you've got that backwards."

"Then it is because you think so little of yourself?"

Frustrated, Kase glared at her. "Look, Rose, I'm trying to tell you that for your own good you need to be wary. If you're so set on staying, just don't take up with the first man who comes along."

She looked at him as if he had lost his mind. "In Italy," she began, "the man visits the woman, brings flowers, meets the family of the woman. In Italy"—Rosa drew herself up as far as her diminutive height would allow and straightened her shoulders—"a man asks to marry when he is in love. It must be proper, correct. The flowers, the family. I'm not marry anybody I'm not knowing, or a man who does not know such things. And *I'm not leave here.*"

Rosa took a deep breath. After one look at his dark expression, she decided she had said enough. "*Scusi*, Signor Marshal," she said stepping around him. "*Buon giorno.*"

The interior of Al-Ray's was crowded floor to ceiling with goods. Rosa wove her way around the boxes and barrels stacked about the room, trying to keep her mind on the contents of display cases and shelves, but it was as hard to dismiss Kase Storm and his sudden proposal as it was to stop the angry trembling that had overtaken her the moment she stalked away from the infuriating man. She stopped, lost in thought, and stared at a cracker barrel near the counter. He had looked so surprised when he proposed that she could only surmise that his declaration was as sudden and innocent as it seemed. What *had* he been thinking of? Surely not love. They barely knew each other, and except for the kiss they had exchanged last night, she doubted that he even *liked* her.

There was the kiss to take into account. A kiss the likes of which she had never received before, even from Giovanni. Especially from Giovanni.

Rosa wished there was someone she could talk to about the strange doubts and feelings she had experienced in Kase Storm's arms—feelings that should never have overcome a woman who was mourning her husband. Maybe Signora Flossie, she thought. If anyone would know anything about men, it would be someone in the *signora*'s business. If things got more confusing, perhaps the woman could help. Rosa decided to wait and see.

"May I help you?"

Rosa looked up at a dark-haired woman whose face was wreathed in smiles. "*Sì, signora.* I need vegetables, chicken, some eggs, farina, flour, corn . . . corn flour, oil, garlic."

"Cornmeal?" The woman made a grinding motion with her hands.

"*Sì.* Cornmeal."

In no time at all, Alice Wilkie filled what she could of Rosa's order. The chicken, she said, must be purchased from Zetta Davis, for she was "fresh out." Rosa stared at the canned goods that lined the shelves, but found them out of her price range.

"Anything else?" Alice asked.

"You sell wine?"

For a moment, Alice Wilkie frowned, then leaned close and whispered confidentially, "I hear tell you folks drink wine breakfast, dinner, and supper. That true?"

Rosa nodded.

"Well, Ray don't sell wine here. Some of the folks in these parts don't hold to liquor drinking. But if you need a smidgen,

Paddie's always good for a bottle of it, for cooking purposes, of course. I hear you plan on stayin' here in Busted Heel."

"Yes. I will open a small *trattoria*, a *ristorante*. I will serve the wine there."

Alice Wilkie's eyes widened. "I see."

"You come by sometime."

"When do you plan on openin' the place?"

"Tonight."

"*Tonight*!" Alice looked astounded. "*This* tonight?"

"*Sì.*" Rosa hid a smile. The woman's face could not hide her amazement. She thanked Alice and started for the door.

"Miss . . ."

"Rosa."

"Miss Rosa," Alice crossed the room and opened the door for her, "don't set your heart on drummin' up a lot of business here in Busted Heel. The few farmers hereabouts can't afford restaurant food, an' the big ranchers go on into Cheyenne. As far as any other business you might have, well, folks don't hold much store in things foreign around these parts."

Rosa nodded, not quite sure she understood all Alice Wilkie was saying. As she thanked the woman again and stepped out into the sunlight, she was certain of one thing. She would "set her heart" as Alice said, on having a lot of business. How else could it come about if she did not hold the dream in her heart?

*

Chapter
Seven

*

"What's she doing now?"

Kase ignored Zach's question and stalked away from the window. He rolled the chair out from behind his desk, sat down, and shook out the latest edition of the *Cheyenne Leader*. With problems of his own to sort out, the last thing he needed to be concerned with was the widow Audi. Besides, Zach knew as well as he did what she was doing now. She was carrying chairs, one a time, from Paddie's saloon to her store.

"Why, it looks like she's carryin' chairs down the street." Zach answered his own question with such an innocent tone that Kase was tempted to throw the inkwell at him.

Kase turned the page and the paper crackled.

Zach would not let up. " 'Pears she's bound to open up tonight, just like Paddie said."

"It's a free country," Kase grunted.

"All the more reason why I'd be eatin' there if I had a dollar to my name," Zach said.

Unable to concentrate, Kase frowned at the printed page.

Zach continued to share his wealth of unsolicited knowledge. "You know, Floss and the girls went into Cheyenne for the day. Won't be back till around nine tonight. Back too late to have dinner at the widow's."

Kase shifted the paper toward the window, then glanced outside. The sun would set soon. His stomach growled.

"Paddie can't leave the bar, and you can bet that no one else is gonna take a chance and eat Eye-talian food."

Slamming the paper down on the desk, Kase stared at Zach. "So?"

"So if someone would loan me a couple o' dollars, I'd be willin' to go over to the new café and have supper. I hate to see the little widow work this hard only to have no one show up on her first day of business. Unless o' course you been plannin' to go over."

"Not on your life."

Everything was ready. With hands on hips, Rosa surveyed the room and decided she was pleased with her work. Two tables along with an assortment of borrowed chairs were situated opposite each other in the center of the room. Covered with handwoven cloths from her trunk, set with silverware and glasses, complete with a candle and a small vase of black-eyed Susans, the tables only needed patrons to make them come alive.

Commingled scents of garlic and herbs wafted on air already thick with the aroma of fresh-baked bread. Rosa paused long enough to light each candle, reach up to be certain her hair was still neatly combed and twisted up on the crown of her head, then brushed at the front of her spotless white apron. She opened the front door and let the cool night air carry the fragrance of her labors out onto Main Street. Busted Heel had never smelled so good.

Rosa walked back into the kitchen, mentally reviewing the menu she planned to serve as she lifted the lids of pots and saucepans. She opened the oven door and sniffed with satisfaction at the cipolle ripiene, onions stuffed with butter and bread crumbs, that were lined up like soldiers in a pan. Chicken was simmering in tomatoes and wine; potato gnocchi sat warming on the back of the stove. Warm, thick-crusted bread waited on her worktable. For dessert, she had piled a platter with fruits and a few precious nuts purchased at Al-Ray's. All she needed now was a customer.

An hour went by without so much as a shadow passing her door. Worried that the food might go to waste, Rosa was tempted to walk next door to Paddie's and personally invite the cowhands who were regular customers to a special introductory meal. After all, she had spread the word about town that she would be opening her *ristorante* tonight. By now someone surely would have come in to eat. Perhaps if they were given a free sample, the men would realize what they were missing. Perhaps she should have waited until Flossie and the girls were back from Cheyenne.

Just as she straightened a perfectly smooth tablecloth once more and debated whether or not to blow out the candles, the one-eyed man named Zach Elliot walked through the doorway. Rosa stiffened as nervousness assailed her. She forced a welcoming smile to her lips and personally escorted him to a table. She wondered if the marshal had sent him to spy on her.

"Welcome, *signore*. Sit. Relax."

"Howdy, ma'am." He sat.

She waited for him to remove his hat. When he did not, she began to explain the menu, then ended with, "And for dessert, *frutta*."

Rosa felt a bead of sweat trickle down her temple. She would not allow herself to brush it aside until he said, "I'm not rightly sure I understood all you said, ma'am, but I'm as hungry as a bear just outta hibernation, so you bring it on."

She hovered over him while he ate, watched as he stared at the steaming potato dumplings before he dipped into the gnocchi. The chicken disappeared in the blink of an eye, and he asked for a second onion. Rosa gave him two more. He ate nearly an entire loaf of bread smothered in butter and drank two glasses of wine from a bottle she had bought at Paddie's. When she brought out the fruit platter, Zach got to his feet.

He reached for an apple, shined it on his buckskin shirt, and smiled. "Ma'am, that was, without a doubt, one of the best meals I ever sat down to. Now, how much do I owe you?"

"Seventy-five cents," she said, half afraid of his reaction, but Zetta had claimed the price fair enough, especially since Rosa insisted on including the wine.

"Seventy-five it is, ma'am." He put a silver dollar on the table and started to leave.

"*Signore*, wait, I give you change."

"The rest is for you, ma'am. Put it in a safe place."

"Well?" Kase pushed away from the bar and handed his empty water glass back to Paddie. He never drank anything stronger in the evenings when trouble was likely to occur. Liquor never agreed with him anyway. He had a low tolerance for it.

"More water?" the bartender asked.

Kase nodded. Paddie lingered at the end of the bar long enough to hear what Zach had to say about his meal.

"Best damned food I ever ate."

Much to Kase's chagrin, the old scout announced it loud and clear enough for every man in Paddie's to hear. "Melt in your mouth. Bread better'n what Ma used to make. Chicken so tender it won't hardly stay on the fork. Some sort o' floatin' potato dumplin's that make a grown man want to cry. Not to mention one of the prettiest little cooks in the country."

By now every cowboy in the room was hanging on his every word.

"Where's this, old-timer?" one asked.

"Zach—" Kase's voice was low and laced with warning.

"Right next door, son."

Kase watched a virtual stampede of cowhands move through the swinging doors. Paddie pushed a glass of water along the bar toward him. "Could you two watch the place while I go over and see if she'll make up a covered dish for me?" Without waiting for a reply, the bald man took off his apron and hurried toward the door.

Zach leaned back against the bar and crossed his arms. In a casual tone that Kase knew spelled trouble, Zach asked, "Was that you I saw sneakin' past the front door of the widow's while I was eatin'?" When Kase refused to answer, the scout chuckled deep in his throat and wanted to know, "How were your beans, boy?"

It took more than the first night's rush of customers to make Rosa's Ristorante a success. In need of funds to purchase more staples from Al-Ray's, Rosa went back to Flossie and told her she was willing to clean for her. Delighted, Flossie asked her to come in early every morning so that she could work downstairs while the rest of the household was sleeping. Floss excluded the upper floor from Rosa's duties by explaining that the girls cleaned their own rooms. The plan agreed with Rosa, who would then be finished well before noon and able to prepare the evening meal at the restaurant.

For her first day on the job at the pleasure palace, Rosa donned her faded brown work dress and wrapped a muslin dishcloth turban style about her head. The house was as quiet as a tomb when she let herself in with the key Flossie had given her. The house smelled of cigar smoke and stale air. Rosa longed to open the heavy velvet drapes and raise the windows, but Floss had already given her instructions that the drapes were to remain closed. Rosa lit the lamps about the room and set to work.

The place still amazed Rosa. The elegant furnishings and wine-red walls, side tables covered with keepsakes and gilded sconces, were unlike anything she had ever seen. Floss had said the items were things she'd been collecting all her life. Rosa straightened fringed pillows, swept the floors, and then dusted the various tables and bric-a-brac in the crowded room.

With a rag moistened with kerosene oil, she dampened any scratches she found on the furniture and then used the same treatment on the gilt-edged picture frames. The task accomplished, she paused and looked around. Her mind strayed to the women who slept upstairs, and she tried to forget the nature of their business and the reason why they slept so late into the day.

When everything had been cleaned to her satisfaction, she moved on to the kitchen where she tidied up the cups and glasses that had been used the night before and then set out to clean the firebox in the range. A goose-wing duster hung on the wall beside the stove, and she used it to brush the ashes out of the box. Just as she bent over, the back door opened and Kase Storm walked in as if he owned the place. He stopped suddenly at the sight of her and frowned.

Rosa looked up, her face smudged with ashes, her turban dipping low over one brow. "What are you doing here?" She set the bucket down and as she straightened, brushed the ashes from her hands. It was the second time she had seen Kase Storm since the night he had kissed her. She still assumed he had done it to frighten her away, and she wanted to let him know she did not fear him.

She watched him as he tensed, his hostility clearly visible in his unnaturally rigid stance and piercing stare. She straightened, ready to meet the challenge of his temper, surprised to find herself relishing the thought of a good argument. Not since she left Corio and Guido behind had she taken part in a real door-slamming, dish-throwing argument. Spoiling for just such an exchange, she welcomed the marshal's antagonistic attitude.

"I live here," he said. "What are you doing here?"

Astonished, Rosa was speechless for a second before she replied, "You live *here*?"

He crooked a brow, his sardonic expression daring her to question him further. When she did not, he said, "I asked what you were doing here."

"I work here."

Myriad emotions flickered across his dark expression, not the least of which was impatience. Then he shuttered his gaze and merely stared. The slight flare of his nostrils gave his anger away.

Used to dealing with Guido, as well of the rest of her volatile family, she refused to let him intimidate her. With them, the tears, the shouting, and the anger came and went as quickly as the easy laughter and binding love that they shared; their emotions gathered and dispersed as easily as storm clouds before and after a summer shower. But Marshal Kase Storm was becoming more and more a puzzle to her. Each time she saw him, he either remained willfully silent or demanded that she leave Wyoming. She could not forgive the way he had tried to instill fear in her by using his touch to frighten her and by kissing her so roughly. But she could not understand why he still seemed so upset. If only he would tell her why he objected so to her staying in Busted Heel. What was it about her that maddened him? What did he want from her? Until she knew why he was so hostile toward her, Rosa felt she would never understand him.

Kase Storm watched her stand up to him and wondered why Rose's every act seemed to goad his temper to the limit. Her stubborn determination to put herself into harm's way was becoming more of a strain on his self-control. He was so angry he did not stop to weigh her words, nor did he take in the rag tied about her head or her worn clothing. When she admitted she worked at Flossie's he immediately assumed the worst— that her circumstances had forced her to give up her respectability—and he knew if she had only listened to him and gone home, none of this would have happened.

He had come in late last night, after he made one last tour of the town, checked locked doors, paused outside her place, and then moved on. Had she been here at Flossie's all that time? Had she been lying beneath some cowhand under the very roof where he slept? "Since when have you been working here?"

"Since now. Today."

As if that settled the matter, he reached out without warning and grabbed her wrist. Before she could do more than sputter her outrage in an attempt to twist away, Kase yanked her along behind him. He pulled her out the door, down the step, and into the yard out back.

The bright morning sunlight shook Rosa out of her astonishment and she jerked her wrist away from his grasp. "*Basta!*" She yelled at him to stop, startling him with her outburst. He immediately let her go.

Instead of fleeing, she advanced, sick of his manhandling. She forced him back as she marched over the dusty ground. Her turban rode precariously over one eye, but she did not falter.

When Kase halted, more than curious to see what she would do, she threw up her hands dramatically and continued shouting. "What'sa matter with you?"

His voice was so low that she could barely hear him. "Nothing's wrong with me. *I'm* not the one who took a job in a whorehouse. If you needed money, I'd have given you some—"

"For a ticket to Italy! Why you want me gone, eh, Marshal? You hate Italians so much?"

Befuddled, Kase shook his head. "You're crazy."

Furiously, Rosa prodded him, poking a finger between the two top buttons of his shirt. "*You* are the crazy one, *signore*. You come into my place to scare me to leave. You come here to tell me to quit the job I just get." She jabbed him again. "Why?"

His expression darkened. Kase clenched his fists and turned away from her with a softly murmured "Forget it." He had not taken three long strides before Rosa caught up with him and grabbed his arm. With a hearty tug, she forced him to face her again.

"I'm not forget it! Why you hate me so much? Why?" Determined to break through his silence and learn why he wanted her away from Busted Heel so badly, she pressed him for an answer.

His tone was bitter when he replied, "If you want to be a whore, go to it." He pulled away from her, too upset to even look at her for fear he would reach out and try and shake some sense into her. She infuriated him as no woman ever had. The idea that she had been forced to whore for Floss shook him deeply. The thought of her servicing men in one of the gaudy rooms upstairs sickened him. Was it because now anyone who could pay the price could have her for a tumble? Or was it because she was now available to him as well?

He chanced a glance in her direction and found her staring up at him, her face ashen, her expression one of shock.

"Whore? *Whore*? Again and again this word. I tell you I am not a whore. I am, how do you say it? A *cameriera* for Signora Flossie. I clean the house."

"You're a *maid*?" His scowl deepened.

She shrugged her shoulders, hands outstretched. "I don't know. I clean the front room. I clean the dishes. This is a maid?"

He watched her straighten her ridiculous turban. It seemed she had a penchant for wearing unsightly headgear. Suddenly feeling foolish, Kase felt the beginnings of a blush suffuse his face. "A maid."

"So?" she said, her tone more subdued as she waited expectantly.

"So what?"

"So why you want me to go back to Italy? Maybe you tell me now so I'm not always have to guess, okay? Maybe then I know why you try to make me afraid." She decided that mentioning the kiss would not be wise. It would not do to slip and let him know that it had affected her in any way at all.

A window rattled behind them. Kase and Rosa turned in time to see Floss struggling, pounding the warped corners of the frame until she had raised it far enough to thrust head and shoulders outside and glare down at them. She rubbed her eyes and squinted, trying to bring the world into focus. In a hoarse whisper that carried well past them, she called down. "Could you two keep the ruckus down to a mild roar? People are tryin' to get some shut-eye up here." With that, she slammed the window shut and pulled the draperies together so vigorously that it set them swaying.

Rosa was concerned that her new job might be at stake. Kase wondered what he could say to her that might explain the reasons behind his hostility. He was sure most of his insistence that she leave stemmed from the fact that he did not consider Busted Heel a safe haven for a beautiful, respectable woman alone. But how could he explain the loneliness of the prairie to her? The wide open reaches of vast emptiness could pull the life right out of a person. Should he tell her that some newcomers never learned to love the freedom and beauty in the wild wind and rain that swept the plains, the deep snow that hugged the land in winter, or the fierce sun that baked it dry in summer?

Busted Heel was a fit place for Flossie and the girls, a fine place for local cowhands. Except for an occasional rancher and his family who did not have the time to make the trip to Cheyenne, Busted Heel was a watering hole for drifters, lost souls who had no more attachments than a passel of tumbleweeds; folks like Slick the gambler and Zach Elliot, folks who did not belong anywhere; men like himself, who didn't know who or what they were.

Busted Heel was definitely not meant for someone as young and beautiful as Rose Audi. Aside from her husband's untimely death, he guessed she was still relatively innocent of the harsh realities of the world. She deserved better. But she did not seem convinced.

He looked down into her upturned face, saw the honey-colored eyes that searched his for an answer, and knew in an instant a deeper reason for the way she always set him on edge.

He wanted her.

Kase Storm wanted Rose the way he had never wanted a woman before, and the realization scared the hell out of him because he knew he couldn't have her. Not ever. Not after what he had learned about his father. Not with all the doubts he still harbored about what he might become. She was from another world. He doubted if she even knew what his being half Indian meant as far as society was concerned, but he sure as hell wasn't going to give her a chance to find out. Besides, he hadn't given her any reason to care for him in the least.

"Well?" she said, quite cocky now that she had backed him halfway across the yard.

There were plenty of reasons why he wanted her out of town and out of his life. But judging by the determined set of his jaw and the challenge sparkling in her eyes, he knew she would not pay heed to any of them. Kase tucked his thumbs into the gun belt that rode his hips as casually as if he'd been born wearing it and ground out, "If you're dead set on staying here for the rest of your life, be my guest."

She watched him stalk away and found herself left without an explanation for his surly manner once again. Rosa felt like chasing him down and planting a fist against his chin. It infuriated her further to realize she probably couldn't even reach it. Still itching for a good fight she stomped back to Flossie's, paused long enough to kick the step on her way in, then slammed the door.

Between Flossie and her girls, the Mountain Shadows cowhands, Paddie's covered dish orders, and Zach's walking testimonials, Rosa soon had more business than she could handle alone. Within one week she had hired Hung Yee's daughter, Chin, to help out in the kitchen when things were busy. George and Martha Washington swept the floors and replaced the candles every morning while Zetta helped out by supplying eggs and freshly dressed chickens.

Rosa found time to paint a sign, boldly lettered in red and white, that proclaimed Rosa's Ristorante, Fine Foods of Italy. Paddie, as owner of the building, felt it was his duty to hang the sign properly above the door.

By the end of the month, Rosa had saved enough money to choose wine-red material from Al-Ray's for long red table runners to top her white cloths. She worked by candlelight late into the night to hem the runners. When she discovered Floss discarding an armload of well-worn gowns, Rosa cut them apart and fashioned colorful mismatched curtains for the front window. As she looked around the café at the end of her third week in business, Rosa could safely assure herself that her establishment was a success. Almost.

The one person she wanted most to walk through the door had not yet done so. She wanted Kase Storm to witness her success, but he had not said so much as a curt hello since their argument in Flossie's yard. Rosa was beginning to think she had imagined the kiss that had passed between them that first night in the empty store. She had seen him nearly every morning as she crossed the street on her way to shop at Al-Ray's, but he tended to stay near the jail at his end of the street rather than come anywhere near the restaurant.

She thought that perhaps he was angered by her success but could find no reason for him to wish her such ill will. Then last night, while she worked side by side with Chin Yee, drying dishes and stacking them on the sideboard, Rosa had remembered the money he had paid for her train fare to California, the money she had used to start the restaurant instead. This morning she had awakened determined to return every penny to him.

Rosa dressed with care, choosing a high-collared white blouse with fitted sleeves and a wine skirt of henrietta that fit close to her hips and fell gracefully to the ankles of her high-button shoes. She donned her wide-brimmed velvet hat, took up her reticule, shooed G.W. and his sister out the back door, and set out to repay her debt.

Quentin Rawlins rarely came to Busted Heel, so when Kase saw him ride into town well before noon, he stepped outside the office to greet his father's old friend. He watched the man ride up on a thoroughbred golden palomino and realized that even though Quentin was in his early forties, he was still fit. His thick chestnut hair was shot with silver, his wide shoulders erect, his muscular frame trim. He sat his horse with the grace of a man who had spent his life in the saddle. Impeccably dressed, Rawlins casually exuded the wealth and success achieved by many cattlemen of the region.

He rode up to the hitching rail outside the jail and dismounted. Three of the men who rode with him went on past and stopped at Al-Ray's. A flicker of white drew Kase's attention to the end of the street. He felt himself grit his teeth as he watched the cowboys tip their hats and then stop to stare at Rose Audi as she crossed the street. She smiled in greeting and spoke to the three men for a moment before she moved on. Since she appeared to be moving in his direction, he paused for a moment to wonder what she was up to.

He watched her walk along the boardwalk. The broad-brimmed hat cast her face in shadow. The demure high-collared blouse only accentuated her full breasts, while the slim, tapered skirt called attention to her narrow hips and tiny waist. He thought he saw her smile in his direction, but before he knew for sure, Quentin interrupted his perusal.

"That wouldn't by any chance be the widow Audi I've been hearing so much about, would it?" Quentin asked.

"It would and it is." Kase turned, suddenly curious. "What have you heard?"

Quentin smiled. "Only good things. That she's the best cook west of the Mississippi and that Busted Heel's lucky to have her. No one took the time to tell me she was a beauty, but from the way the boys go on about her, I should have guessed as much."

Kase felt something inexplicable tighten in his gut. For some reason it irked him to think "the boys" spent any time at all talking about Rose Audi.

He could hear her footsteps approaching. As she drew near, Quentin leaned closer and asked Kase to introduce him. Kase knew without looking when Rose was standing beside him on the boardwalk. He turned and found her smiling down at Quentin who had not yet stepped up out of the street.

Although he had not meant them to be, Kase's words of introduction were terse. "Rose Audi, this is Quentin Rawlins, owner of Mountain Shadows Ranch. Quentin, Mrs. Audi."

Quentin reached out for Rose's hand and in a grand gesture, drew it to his lips. "My pleasure, ma'am."

"*Grazie, signore.*"

When she blushed and bestowed a sparkling smile on Rawlins, Kase felt his jaw clench involuntarily. But when she turned her smile on him, the clench moved to his midsection. It had been three long weeks since he'd been this close to her, and to his dismay, Kase found her far lovelier than he remembered.

"Signor Marshal, I come to discuss business with you," she said as soberly as she could with her heart beating in her ears and the blood suffusing her cheeks.

"In that case, Mrs. Audi," Quentin interrupted, "I'll make myself scarce for a few moments while you two take care of business." He turned and headed toward Al-Ray's before either Kase or Rose could protest.

Kase stood wondering what she might want with him before he remembered his manners and asked her into his office.

Rose entered before him and Kase closed the door. He watched her open the drawstrings of her small black bag. She took out a roll of bills and held them toward him. "The money I owe to you, Marshal, is here. All of it."

He hesitated, then reached out and took the wad of bills, then handed them back. "Keep it."

"No," she shook her head. "I have no need." She thrust it toward him. "Is yours. You keep."

"You might need it." He pushed her hand away.

She threw the money on the desk.

He didn't know what else to say. For some inexplicable reason he felt as if he should keep talking so that she would not leave. He didn't exactly want her thinking he hated her, but she was just so damned determined. His own stubborn pride kept him silent. He couldn't bring himself to congratulate her on her success. Gathering up the bills, he toyed with the money for a moment before he shoved it into his back pocket.

"I should go . . ." she said.

"Thanks for paying me back so soon. You're sure you don't need—"

"No. I've no need."

"Well, then, I guess . . ."

"*Buon giorno*, Marshal." She put her hand on the door handle, then paused and turned around. "I will give you one dinner gratis, no money, if you like, because you are my— investor."

"That's kind of you, Mrs. Audi, but no, thanks."

"Rosa," she corrected.

"Rose," he amended.

"*Va bene.*"

He saw her frown as she started out the door again and felt an overwhelming need to apologize for the way he had treated her. But it wouldn't do to start anything he knew would be better off left alone. He didn't have to remind himself he was still a half-breed, not to mention a man whose questionable heritage made him unfit for the likes of Rose Audi. But there was something about the disappointment in her stance that made him speak.

"Thanks anyway, Rose."

She turned on him, eyes bright, a smile back in place. "Not Rose. Rosa."

"So you have business with the widow Audi, eh, Kase?" Laugh lines radiated from the sun-browned skin around Quentin Rawlins's blue eyes as he pulled a chair up to Kase's desk.

"Not anymore."

"A misunderstanding?"

Kase shook his head. "No, not at all. I loaned her some money when she first came to town and found out her husband was dead. Paid for her train ticket out of here, but she used the fare to stake her business instead."

"Nothing like good old Yankee ingenuity." Rawlins laughed heartily. "Why's that bother you, Kase?"

"To be honest, I don't know. It just does. The fact is, she's just so damned stubborn. I told her to get on the train and head home and she refused."

"It seems to have turned out all right."

"For now. I just don't think a decent woman living alone belongs here in Busted Heel."

Quentin stretched and then fingered a silver button on his shirt. "She's quite a looker. I doubt if you'll have to worry about her being alone very long." He looked around the jailhouse office and then back at Kase. "You must have guessed I didn't ride into town just to get a glimpse of the widow Audi."

I hope not. Kase waited patiently. Sooner or later Quentin would get around to having his say.

"You ever heard of the Dawson gang?"

Kase settled back in his chair, glad to have his mind on something besides Rose Audi. "Can't say as I have."

"Four of the meanest sons of bitches ever born."

"Brothers?"

"Yep. Bad blood runs in their veins."

Kase suddenly wondered if there was any truth to that old saying. If so, what of his own bad blood? Suddenly he didn't want to hear what Quentin had to say. It seemed there wasn't any subject that was safe for him to think about anymore. Not bloodlines, not Rose Audi. Maybe, he thought, it was time to move on.

Quentin took his silence for attention. "The Dawsons started out as petty thieves bothering farmers on small spreads without the manpower to stand up to them. They moved up to shootin' up towns and riding roughshod over places like Busted Heel. Done some horse-thieving."

"Have they been spotted around here?"

"South of Cheyenne last month. Who knows where they are now? Just keep your eye out for four or more men riding together, strangers you might not recognize. Are you familiar with most of my men by now?"

"Most of them. You keep adding new ones, which makes it tough, but they always come into town together, so it's easy to pick 'em out."

"I've had a run of good luck lately, hired a good crew. Just sold off a herd of beef for the highest price yet. I'm thinking it's about time I did a little celebrating."

Kase looked doubtful. "So you came to Busted Heel instead of heading into Cheyenne?"

Quentin laughed. "No, I came to Busted Heel to tell you about the Dawsons and to eat at Rosa's place. I'll tell you how I plan to celebrate over dinner." He stood up and walked to the hat rack beside the door. Quentin reached for his gray felt Stetson and waited for Kase to join him. "Come on, Kase. I'll buy."

Except for Slick Knox, who sat slowly savoring a cup of coffee, the restaurant was empty. Rosa bustled about in the kitchen and wondered whether or not to deep-fry any more uova alla torinese when she heard the front door open. She leaned away from the stove and peered around the door frame. Her breath caught in her throat.

Kase Storm and the big man he had introduced her to earlier were standing in the dining room, waiting to be seated.

She dropped the spoon and pressed her palms against her cheeks and then her forehead. The kitchen was sweltering, her face flushed. The hairstyle she'd taken such pains with that morning rode nearer the nape of her neck than the crown of her head.

And Kase Storm was standing in her restaurant.

The day's menu suddenly seemed inadequate. She glanced at the vegetable soup, breaded eggs, spinach tossed with garlic, the sautéed rabbit and polenta and silently scoffed, "Peasant fare."

She peered around the door frame again. The Rawlins man exchanged greetings with Slick Knox while Kase Storm stood silent, his hands shoved deep in his back pockets. His hooded eyes took in every detail of the room.

There was no time to change the menu. They were waiting.

Rosa took a deep breath and smiled. Then she stepped into the dining room.

"*Benvenuto*, gentlemen. Please, sit. Sit." She drew a chair away from the empty table and waited while Kase indicated that Quentin should be seated first.

"Well, Rosa," Quentin began, "I've heard nothing but good things about your cooking, so I decided to try it for myself. We'll have two of whatever you're serving today."

She wanted to keep her gaze from straying to Kase, tried to concentrate on Quentin Rawlins's words, but was finding it nearly impossible. "*Grazie, signore*. I hope you like it. *Un momento*. I'll bring the soup first."

Without another glance in Kase Storm's direction, she returned to the kitchen. Once inside the smaller room, Rosa leaned against the wall and tried to catch her breath. Her hand shook as she ladled the soup into two bowls. What had come over her? She wanted to speak to Kase, but each time she started to say anything directly to him, she was overwhelmed by fear.

What if she said something wrong?

What if she made him angry again without knowing why?

What if the soup got cold before she carried it out to them?

She scolded herself for her foolishness and served the soup. Rosa set Quentin's down without mishap, then walked around the table and reached out to set Kase's bowl at his place. Her breast accidentally brushed his shoulder. She was close enough to hear his swift in-drawn breath. As Rosa set the bowl down, a spoonful of soup sloshed over the lip.

"*Scusi*."

"It's all right," he mumbled.

Quentin silently watched the exchange. "Can you sit with us, Miss Rosa, while we eat?"

Rosa glanced toward the door and then to Slick Knox's deserted chair. The barber had put his money beside his empty plate and left while she was serving the other men. Since there was no reason why she should not join them, Rosa pulled out a chair and sat down.

"This is delicious," Quentin said. "What do you think, Kase?"

Kase glanced up at Rosa long enough to mumble "Great." He dipped his head again and concentrated on the soup.

As he grew silent, Rosa's apprehension mounted. She turned her attention to Quentin. "Yours is the ranch where the cowmen work?"

Quentin laughed easily. "Yep, but around here the men who own the cattle are called cowmen and the men who work for them are called cowhands, or cowboys. I hear they're some of your best customers." He leaned forward conspiratorially. "You just let me know if you have trouble with any of 'em and I'll see they don't bother you any more."

Kase shifted uncomfortably in his chair.

Rosa glanced in his direction, then back at the older man. "*Grazie,* Signore Quentin, but they have been gentlemen."

"Well, that's a relief. I don't see how they could be anything but gentlemen around a lady such as yourself." After one look at the marshal's face, Quentin finished his soup in silence.

Rosa waited for Kase to speak, but he continued to stare at her without saying a word. She chanced a glance in his direction and was assaulted by his blue-eyed gaze. When she caught herself staring back at him, she nearly jumped out of her chair and grabbed his empty bowl.

"I will get the rest."

Kase followed her with his eyes. Her wine-colored skirt twitched provocatively from side to side with each step. He hoped he could make it through the next course.

"Never took you for a coward, boy."

Quentin's soft words drew his full attention. "What do you mean by that?" Kase's voice was low, the words carefully drawn out.

Quentin leaned back in his chair and stretched his legs out beneath the table. "I know your pa, that's all, and I figured you to be more like him. He'd never let a woman make a stone statue out of him." The older man frowned and straightened. "What's eatin' at you, son?"

Everything was eating at him. Since the moment he walked

in the door, Rose had met his eyes only once; then she had run from the room like a skittish colt. Each time she spoke to Quentin, Kase felt his stomach knot as tight as wet rawhide drying in the sun. For all he knew, the food she had served him tasted like the bottom of an old shoe; his mouth had gone dry at the sight of her. Now Quentin Rawlins was calling him a coward and he couldn't come up with an argument. He didn't know why in the hell he was feeling the way he was, but he did know things hadn't been right since the day Rose Audi stepped off the train.

"Nothing's eating me." He went silent again when Rose entered and set down their plates.

"Can you stay, Rosa?" Quentin asked again.

"I must check on the pudding, *signore*. Perhaps later."

Kase watched her smile down on Quentin and then picked up his knife and fork. He attacked the succulent portion of rabbit on his plate and listened to the sound of her receding footsteps.

"I'm having a big shindig out at the ranch, Kase. Whole town's invited, all my men, some of the farmers close to town. Might even ask some of the folks I know in Cheyenne to come out to stay the night."

"When?"

"Two weeks. I'd like to have you there, of course."

"Sure."

There was a long pause. Quentin looked thoughtful before he added, "Thought you might drive Rosa out to the party." He took a bite of food, chewed, swallowed, and then continued. "Don't think she could very well ride out with Flossie and the girls. The Wilkies' wagon will be full of Wilkies."

Kase looked skeptical. "You're inviting Floss and the girls?"

"Floss and I go way back. Wouldn't want the boys to be disappointed. There's not enough women to go around at a dance anyway, and after all, this is a party for the boys."

Kase felt Quentin watching him intently. He kept eating.

"Guess if you don't want to bring her out, I could send one of the boys after her. One I know to be a real gentleman, that is."

Kase nearly choked. He swallowed and then ground out, "I'll take her."

*

Chapter Eight

*

With her head bent in concentration, Rosa tugged a shawl tight about her shoulders and carefully walked across the uneven ground. An autumn chill rode the ever-present wind as the morning sun shone bright in a cloudless blue sky. Stealing a few precious hours away from the endless tasks in the kitchen as well as the close stuffiness that pervaded Flossie's parlor, Rosa made her way across the open landscape, intent on visiting Giovanni's grave.

She had awakened with a deep longing for home and family coupled with a need to escape the daily routine she had established in her new surroundings. After a brief visit to Flossie's to quickly dust and set the kitchen to rights, Rosa set out to find the graveyard, traveling in the direction she and Kase Storm had taken the day she arrived in Busted Heel.

She paused for a moment to look back at the two even rows of wooden structures that comprised the town and shook her head. The place looked more like a child's set of wooden blocks than a true village. From a distance it appeared fragile enough to be toppled by a storm. Rosa sighed, shook her head, then turned northwest and continued on. She judged the gravesite to be on a knoll just ahead and was soon reassured when she spied a lone gnarled sage that had managed to gain stature in the twisted form of a tree. They had passed by the same landmark in the buggy that first day.

For a moment she wondered if it was a good idea to be so far from the town all alone, then put the thought aside before it became an unlucky one. She did not intend to stay long, and judging from the emptiness of the landscape, she did not expect to see another living soul.

Marching on with stalwart determination, she skirted the largest of the countless rocks embedded in the dry soil. Tufts of thick sun-yellowed grass along with scattered animal dung and the dry remnants of spring wildflowers littered the ground. Bordered by the mountains on the northwest, the landscape was deceptive. It had appeared flat when she gazed at it from her kitchen window, but once she started out on foot, she discovered that the land had been molded into gentle waves that rose gradually toward the mountains. It was vast, wind-swept, and seemingly barren and did little to relieve the sense of loss she had experienced all morning.

Within half an hour's time, Rosa reached the graveyard. She walked inside the dilapidated stake-and-wire fence before she paused to look back at Busted Heel. The town had become a speck on the horizon. As she walked past the few scattered graves, Rosa wondered who might be buried here and how they came to die in such a place. When she reached the crude wooden cross that marked Giovanni's grave, she tossed aside a few loose rocks and sat down on the ground beside it.

Alone on the prairie, Rosa thought about all the times in Corio when she had wished for a moment's peace. Now her wish had come true and she found that the countless quiet hours she spent alone were wearing on her. Flossie Gibbs had befriended her and she felt she could go to her for advice and companionship, but the kindhearted woman was not *famiglia*, not of her blood or background. There was no one here who really knew Rosa, her likes, her dislikes, her own personal history. She missed the close bond that came with such knowledge.

She had written to Zia Rina, but it was far too soon to expect an answer. It would be weeks before her letter reached Corio and perhaps months before Zia Rina sent one in return. Smiling, she imagined her aunt carrying the letter to the village and showing it to everyone. She shook her head and wondered how many arguments would arise as the family sat around the table deciding what to include in their response.

Using the corner of her shawl, she wiped away the fine dust

that lingered on the cross and wondered if her own stubborn determination would force her to spend her life alone on the prairie. Would the years slip by as quickly as the past few weeks until she was as gnarled and bent as the twisted sage? Would she dry up and blow away like the tumbleweeds?

As much as she hated to admit it, Rosa began to wonder if Kase Storm had not been correct in insisting that she leave Busted Heel. At the very least she could have gone to San Francisco to live among other Italians. There she could have spoken her own language and lived among people whose customs and manners were familiar to her. Here she was so lonely that not a day passed when she did not think of her former home and family.

Her thoughts led her to wonder what sort of a man Kase Storm was. Why was he so bitter? So intolerant? She knew he was as determined as she, a man who, once having decided upon a course of action, did not like to change his mind. But why was he afraid to show any emotion other than anger? And even that he often tried to hide behind a cold stare.

Rosa tried to remember if she had ever seen the man smile. She did not think so. Nor had she heard him laugh. It would be a challenge to try to make him laugh. It would be a pleasant change to see his eyes shine with happiness. Could he ever be anything but upset with her? Her thoughts wandered until she found herself thinking it might be nice to experience his kiss again, and then suddenly, remembering where she was, she quickly crossed herself and glanced at Giovanni's grave. Apologetically she shrugged and said aloud, "What harm is there now, Giovanni? It is because you left me alone that I think such thoughts."

Deciding that she had spent enough time away from her tasks, Rosa stood and shook the loose soil from her skirt. She looked up at the rugged mountains in the distance and then out across the land. When she noticed a lone rider coming from the direction of town, she chided herself for not having seen him sooner. He was still too far away for her to make out what manner of a man he was, and she knew a moment of fear. All of Kase Storm's warnings came to mind. Should she run or crouch behind a grave marker and hope he passed by without noticing her?

She glanced around and knew immediately that both ideas

were ridiculous. The rider stood between her and town. The headstones were far too narrow to conceal more than a very small child. The man was approaching rapidly now. From a distance he appeared to be part of the horse he was riding. The scene reminded her of the mythical creature, the centaur, half man, half beast. Her heart began a rapid beat.

Stupida, stupida. She had no one but herself to blame for the consequences of her own carelessness.

As the rider approached, his horse's hooves churning up the dry soil as it closed the space between them, Rosa strained to see this man who rode so gracefully. He had indeed become a part of the animal beneath him. It was not long before she recognized the man's face beneath the shadow cast by the wide brim of his hat, but even so, her pulse did not return to normal. She noticed a cloth bag tied to his saddle horn, its contents clinking and chiming together.

Kase Storm drew his horse to a halt just outside the rickety fence, and Rosa prepared herself for an onslaught of disapproval.

Kase dismounted and quickly tied Sinbad's reins to a fence post before he strode through the graveyard gate. Without a word he glanced first at Rose and then at the deserted landscape as if to emphasize their isolation. Anyone could have come along and raped her, murdered her, or even carried her away, and no one in town would ever have known what had become of her. He was too furious to speak as he watched her expression change from one of open welcome to one of familiar obstinacy. He knew he was in for another argument.

Mad enough to toss her over his saddle and carry her back to town, he took a step toward her. Rose stepped back and nearly tripped over the cross at the head of her husband's grave. Kase reached out and grabbed her by the wrist to right her before she pulled away.

"I know what you will say to me," she said before he had a chance to speak. "I am stupid to be here alone."

"Exactly."

"And you will say that someone might come and hurt me."

"Right."

"Maybe kill me."

"Yep."

"And so you are once again angry with me."

"That's right." He folded his arms across his chest and waited for her to go on, admitting to himself that she was doing a fine job without his having to say anything.

Unexpectedly, she began to laugh.

He scowled. "What's so funny?" he asked.

"You, Marshal. You are always the same. So big and strong and angry. Do you never smile?"

Taken aback, he felt his frown deepen. "No."

She crossed her arms and looked at him skeptically "Pooh. I don't believe it."

He smiled then, unable to resist.

Her own smile widened as her eyes sparkled up at him. "You do smile! A handsome smile, too."

At that he felt a strange constriction about his heart. He felt safer when she was yelling at him. He resumed what he hoped was an unreadable stare, and then without another word he walked back to his horse.

Feeling relieved and at the same time disappointed, Rosa thought he was going to leave her in peace until she watched him untie the bag on his saddle. The rattling and clinking began again as he carried the bag many yards distance. She watched curiously as he opened the drawstring and started pulling out bottles and cans of all shapes and sizes and proceeded to set them upright on the ground all around him. He placed some in a line, others he stood on rocks, still others he scattered about at random. He left a few bottles in the bag and walked back away in the opposite direction.

She clapped her hands over her ears when he drew his gun and began to blow the bottles to smithereens. The cans bounced and sailed in all directions. He paused long enough to reload when necessary, but kept on firing until he had broken all the bottles and the cans had flown out of range.

She did not think he had missed a shot. Rosa was so impressed by the display that she nearly called out a compliment. He continued to ignore her as he reloaded and holstered his gun and then picked up the bag again. It appeared the show had not ended.

Rosa waited as Kase reopened the bag and drew out another bottle. He held it by the neck, tossed it high in the air, drew his gun, and fired, all in a matter of seconds. The glass shattered and fell like amber hail a few yards away.

He repeated the movement four times, each time holstering his gun and drawing after he had thrown the bottle. Each time he hit the target. Finally, just when she thought he was finished and had begun to walk toward her, Kase tossed one last bottle high in the air, spun, crouched, and blew it apart. He reloaded again.

With an attitude of practiced nonchalance he entered the graveyard and stood before her. He glanced toward town again, then back to Rosa. "Are you ever going to get it into your head what kind of danger you're in here?"

"I am not afraid of you, Marshal, even if you are a big man who shoots at little cans and bottles."

"I'm not talking about me. Did you ever stop to think that you could scream your head off out here and no one would hear you?"

"Do you only think of the bad things, Marshal? Do you not think of the good?" With a wide sweep of her arm she made him look out past the graveyard. "The day is beautiful. The air is clean. It is good to walk in the sun. Do you not think of these things, too?"

He looked around. How long had it been since he had really taken the time to appreciate the simple things Rose spoke of? It was a glorious day. Summer was ending, but the days were still sunny and warm. The land was barren, but its very emptiness gave him a sense of freedom. He certainly did not feel hemmed in, as he had back east. Maybe he had forgotten how to think of the good, as Rose suggested.

She stood there smiling up at him with her hands on her hips, her cheeks pinkened by the sun, her eyes aglow. She looked fresh and clean, innocent and inviting. Expectant.

He had to get her back to town before he did something he would regret. "Come on. I'm taking you back." Without waiting for a reply, he took her by the arm and headed toward Sinbad. She hurried to keep up with him and nearly tripped over a grave. She crossed herself. He tugged her forward. When they reached the massive black horse, she refused to let him help her up into the saddle.

"I will walk."

"I need to get back to town," he said.

"I walk here. I will walk back."

"Not on my time. Come on."

She turned her back on him, and Kase watched her rich ebony braid as it swayed with every step. He mounted up.

Sinbad sidestepped and shook his head, eager to break stride and race across the open ground, but Kase kept him reined in as he rode up behind Rose. She quickened her pace, but refused to stop walking. Kase rode behind her in silence.

"You might as well save your shoes."

"My shoes are old. You go."

He pushed Sinbad as close to her heels as was safe. Rose glanced over her shoulder when the big horse nudged her with his nose. She scowled and walked faster. The strange procession lasted for nearly a half-mile before Kase was certain that Rose would not change her mind and accept a ride. Nor did it seem he would be able to goad her into it. Finally, granting her a minor victory, he dismounted. Leading Sinbad, Kase walked beside Rose.

"You are a fine shooter," she said finally, trying to think of something to ease the tension between them.

"Shot. You would say I am a good shot. Not shooter."

"Ah. *Grazie.*"

"You're welcome."

They continued on, Rosa swinging her arms, taking deep breaths of the fresh air, enjoying the scenery. Happy to be out of the confines of the kitchen, she refused to let Kase's dour attitude ruin her excursion. When she thought he was not paying attention, she glanced up at him. His expression was unreadable, impassive. Rosa wondered how he managed to maintain such a cool exterior.

Neither of them spoke until Rosa tried again. "I have been thinking of my family. I miss them very much. It is hard because I have no one to tell these things to."

He did not really want to hear about her loneliness. It reminded him too much of his own. He had, after all, tried to tell her to go home, so she had no one but herself to thank for her situation. Still, the eager way she waited for him to comment made him respond. "Do you have a big family?"

"Not so big as some. I have three brothers and a sister who has a child. I have an aunt and many cousins."

"What about your parents?"

She shrugged. "Both dead, many years now. One day the wagon turned over and fell down the mountain." Hardly able to believe they were truly conversing civilly, Rosa decided to ask him about his own family. "Your parents are alive?"

He wiped his brow, shoved his hat to the crown of his head, and realized he was clenching his teeth. Kase let his gaze follow the horizon line. "My mother and stepfather live in Boston. So does my sister." He found talking about his family more painful than he had anticipated.

"Your sister is older than you?"

"Younger. Seven years younger. She's fourteen."

"Ah. My sister is older. My brothers are older, too."

Kase realized with relief that they were nearly back to town. As if she sensed he was hesitant to talk about his home, Rosa chatted on about Italy, the village, and the mountains that she had left behind. Half listening, Kase let her talk until they reached the back door of her café. He took in the squalor spilling out around the Davises' shanty and caught sight of G.W. jumping up and down inside the open doorway of the shack. It was a painful reminder of his life in the sod house until he noticed the smile on the boy's face and realized that young children were often blissfully unaware of their circumstances. The shanty was, after all, G.W.'s home.

Rosa hesitated to go inside now that a truce of sorts existed between them. She reached out and placed a hand on his shirtsleeve to draw his attention back to her.

"I must say *grazie*, Marshal, for you did not tell me again how I was stupid to go out to the grave alone. I will not do it again."

"I hope not." He would have added that he was sorry for the pompous way he had acted and that his attitude only stemmed from concern. But there was still something disturbing about the way she was smiling up at him, and he thought it best to say as little as possible.

"I thank you for the smile," she said cheerfully. "Maybe one day I will see it again." With that she released his arm and started to leave.

"Rose?" Her name was on his lips before he realized he had spoken.

"*Si?*"

Kase searched for something to say. "I'll pick you up tomorrow at three-thirty for the barbecue."

He did not think it possible, but her smile brightened.

"*Grazie*, Marshal. *Buon giorno*."

After she stepped inside and closed the door, Kase was surprised to find that he, too, was smiling.

"Is this proper dress for Signor Quentin's party?" Rosa waited for Flossie's verdict. It came immediately and left no room for doubt.

"Honey, you look as good as one of them dumplin's you make—and that's mighty good!" Flossie walked around Rosa once more, surveying her from head to toe.

More nervous than she had been the day the restaurant opened, Rosa had come to show Flossie the black floral-patterned skirt and matching jacket she had donned for the party at Quentin Rawlins's ranch. Rosa smiled, relieved that the woman found the outfit suitable; it was her only choice besides the black velvet dress the contessa had given her.

"Those pink roses against that black background fabric make a pretty picture. They match the roses on your cheeks," Flossie added.

"*Grazie*." Rosa's blush deepened as she fingered the material lovingly. It was a matching two-piece outfit; the jacket sported long sleeves and a fitted bodice. A narrow band of lace adorned the high-banded collar and cuffs; a row of jet-black buttons ran from her throat to the hem of the blouse. The skirt was simply cut and styled without bustle or train. "My sister, Angelina, made it for me before I come to America. When she bought the cloth, she said, roses for Rosa."

"I'd say she has a good eye for choosing material. You look wonderful, honey, so just calm down an' try to have a good time. What time is Kase s'posed to be pickin' you up?"

"Three-thirty."

Flossie glanced down at the brooch watch pinned to her ample bosom. "He'll be comin' back pretty quick, then."

"Then I must go." Rosa did not want him to find her here waiting for him; it was bad enough that she was so excited at the prospect of riding to Mountain Shadows alone with him. She thanked Flossie once again for the encouragement, then stopped before she opened the front door. "*Signora*, may I ask

you something that is—I don't know how to say the words—
about my feelings?"

"Something personal?" Flossie glanced at the door to the
back room as well as the stairway to be sure none of the girls
were nearby. "Ask away. It won't get any farther than this
room."

Rosa took a deep breath. She had to talk to someone about
her feelings for Kase Storm. In the weeks since she'd been in
Busted Heel, Flossie had become not only one of Rosa's best
customers, but a friend. Now she would become her confidante. "I try to be a good widow and think of Giovanni"—she
was uncertain of the correct words to express the turmoil
building inside her—"but sometimes I am very mixed up when
I see Kase Storm." She felt herself redden, but continued to
meet Flossie's understanding gaze. "Sometimes, when I think
about the marshal I have feelings that a woman should only
have for her husband.

"I know so little of this man, and I think he does not even
like me so much, but I cannot seem to stop thinking about him.
Then I think I am bad because I am a widow and Giovanni
wanted so much that I be here with him. I am confused." She
shrugged, unsure of how to proceed.

Flossie took her hand and led her to one of the settees in the
parlor. "Look, honey, what you're feelin' is perfectly normal.
How long were you married to this Giovanni?"

"A little bit more than three years. I am married at seventeen."

"How long since you seen him?"

"Three years. He left Italy one month after we are married."

Flossie sniffed, obviously thinking little of Rosa's husband's
actions. "So you been without him nearly the whole time you
been married?"

"*Sì.*"

"I don't mean to get personal, but have you slept with a man
in all that time?"

Rosa's face flamed. She looked at her hands instead of at
Flossie. Rosa shook her head. "No," she whispered. She could
not bring herself to tell Flossie about the night Kase Storm had
kissed her.

Floss slapped her hands against her thighs. "Then my
professional opinion tells me you're long overdue. If you've

got feelin's for Kase Storm, you make 'em known. Any fool can see he's got a hankerin' for you."

Hopeful, Rosa glanced up again. "But he does not come to the restaurant. When I see him, he does not talk to me. He is always angry, and I do not know why this is."

"He's backed hisself into a corner, that's why, and he doesn't know how to get out. He doesn't think a nice gal like you has any business out here alone, and when he told you to leave town, you didn't take his advice. He 'spected you to give up and high-tail it back home."

"I like it here. I am happy."

"I'll tell you one thing: Kase hasn't been with any of my girls since you showed up. For a red-blooded man livin' under the same roof with four fine young fillies ready to run, I'd say he had a major change of mind, and I think you are responsible for it. If you feel the same about him, I say you should tell him."

"In Italy we let the man speak of love. A woman should not have to tell a man how she feels. He should know."

"You're not in Italy, Rosie honey, that's the first thing you have to remember. Some men are too proud to bend. You just might have to prod that stubborn cuss along."

"But I know so little of men. Giovanni was so different. Kase Storm is like his name—a storm that is cold and fierce. What if I say the wrong words? What if you make a mistake and he does not think of me in this way?"

Flossie studied her intently before she answered. "There is a part of Kase he keeps locked away, I've seen that from the first—but out here you'd be hard-pressed to find a man without some sort of past. Knowin' what I do of Kase, I imagine it's something he'll work out in time. As for you worryin' about lettin' him know how you feel—what if you never said anything? What if that's all it takes to get you two together? You owe it to yourself to try." She reached out and straightened the shoulder of Rosa's blouse. "You've been knockin' yourself out day and night in that restaurant of yours. You go out tonight and have yourself some fun. Do what comes natural and don't worry about what might or might not happen."

Rosa reached out and hugged Flossie. It was a quick, sure gesture intended to seal their friendship and express her gratitude. "I will see you at the party?" she asked.

"All gussied up. Whole town's invited. Quentin doesn't let propriety stand in his way. 'Sides, folks aren't gonna tell one of the richest cattlemen in the country they want to rearrange his guest list." Flossie thought for a moment before she added, "Listen, Rosie, you'll be meetin' the upstandin' folk at the party, decent, respectable women like yourself. Take my advice and don't let on that we know one another. Me 'n' the girls will be leavin' early on anyway—probably takin' some of the men with us. There's one thing to be said for livin' in the West; there's more 'n enough men to go around."

Rosa drew herself up, affronted by her friend's suggestion. "I would never pretend that you are not my friend, *signora*. Never. A true friend is not just a friend sometimes and not others."

"Now, don't go gettin' that Italian temper up." Flossie's grateful smile belied her teasing tone. She glanced at her watch again. "You better go on home now, girl, 'cause I expect Kase will be stompin' through here any time now." Flossie stood and Rosa followed suit. "You take care and think about what I said, you hear?"

"*Grazie, signora*. I will."

Rosa stepped into the afternoon sunlight and closed the door behind her. How could she *not* think of all Flossie had said? She waved at Paddie as she passed by the Ruffled Garter, took a deep breath, and quickened her stride. It was nearly time to go.

Kase glared at his reflection in the mirror and then reached for the button at his collar. His fingers fumbled their way down the front of the striped long-sleeved shirt before he shrugged it off and cast it aside. He glanced around his room and shook his head before he reached inside the tall armoire for another shirt.

Mira leaned against the door frame, scantily dressed in a silk camisole top and pantaloons, a paisley shawl carelessly draped across one shoulder. Chicago Sue lay sprawled on her stomach across his bed, knees bent, ankles crossed behind her, as she watched him toss aside another shirt and reach for a third.

"There's no damned privacy around this place," he mumbled to himself as he rebuttoned and then shoved his shirttail into his open trousers. He turned back to the mirror to survey the results of this final choice. Better. The sky-blue shirt complemented his eyes—even he could see that—while the color softened the deep cinnamon hue of his complexion. He looked at his nose; it was too wide, too long, too straight. There was nothing, he decided, he could do about that. Nor could he change his lips; as far as he was concerned, they were too full. Smiling might help, but he'd be damned if he would practice with Chicago and Mira hanging on his every move.

"Show's over, girls. Everyone out."

"Can't expect much privacy livin' in a whorehouse," Mira drawled.

"I pay rent here, ladies. Out." He thumbed toward the door and crooked a brow at Chicago Sue. The girl groaned and rolled over. She pulled the edges of her robe together in a weak gesture of modesty before she stood.

"See ya later, Kase," she said with a smile as she shook her wild blond mane.

Because she reminded him of his half sister, Annika, Kase had befriended Chicago and often allowed her in his room when she wanted to talk—a privilege he did not extend to the others. Lately he'd been careful to keep the door open during her innocent visits.

"Later, Sue. Out, Mira." He stepped closer, then gave the long, lean, green-eyed beauty a nod and a look that told her he meant the dismissal. Whenever Mira saw him, she made it all too clear she would not mind having him in her bed again. He didn't want her to think he was willing to oblige.

He closed the door and then picked up his gun belt and holster. He had debated wearing it, then reckoned it would not be out of place for the local lawman to wear his weapon to a party. He strapped on the holster and fingered the ivory grip of his forty-four. Caleb had given him the gun the year he entered law school along with advice on when and how to use it. He allowed himself a moment to think about his stepfather. He wondered how Caleb was and when he would be able to face his stepfather again to apologize for the things he had said and done. He knew he should write, but decided mere words on paper could never explain the sorrow he'd felt from the moment he had goaded Caleb into revealing the truth about his real father. The emptiness he felt inside was overwhelming. He needed time, that was all. Time to let the truth become reality.

Time! Kase reached for the pocket watch on his dresser and

glanced at the time. He was late. He still had to go down to the livery and pick up the buggy he had hired from Decatur. He crossed back to the armoire and took out the suit coat that matched his fine tailored wool trousers. As he pulled it on and smoothed the lapels he thought that there was something to be said for having money after all. His mother had picked out the suit; the rich brown fabric and cut were the finest Boston had to offer. He pocketed the watch, ran his hand over his hair and brushed it away from his forehead. It fell back naturally, dipping nearly over one eye, but there was no time to worry about it.

He had to get Rose.

Rosa unsuccessfully tried to ignore the feel of Kase Storm's strong hands about her waist as he lifted her down from the carriage. Her attempts to dismiss him failed as he set her down between him and the shining black vehicle. It was a moment before he moved. There was no way she could disregard the man who towered over her, the heat that radiated from him, or the mingled scents of wool, leather, and bay rum that enveloped him. Instead of wearing his usual garb, he was dressed like a gentleman in a stylish suit of striped, warm brown wool. Beneath the brim of his dark Stetson, his eyes seemed bluer than ever. Although his taunting half-smile had made few appearances while they were on the road to Mountain Shadows, his manners had been faultless, his demeanor polite. They had barely exchanged ten words.

"After you." He stepped aside to allow her to pass.

Rosa remained all too aware of him as he followed close behind her, his hand occasionally reaching out to her waist as she sidestepped the buckboards and buggies drawn up together just inside the network of fences that surrounded Quentin Rawlins's sprawling ranch house. They walked in silence across a dry, grassy expanse. The sound of laughter and frivolity drifted around them on the late afternoon breeze.

The house, an imposing two-story, molded itself to the flowing landscape. The violet-shadowed mountains behind it provided a dramatic backdrop for the brick and wood structure, which boasted two enormous chimneys and leaded-glass windows. The house stood well away from the outbuildings beyond. Rosa tried to concentrate on their names—tack room, bunkhouse, chuck house—as Kase explained the uses for them, but somehow she was more aware of his hand gently riding at her waist.

Quentin's house reflected Wyoming's openness. In Corio, his home would have been considered a castle. It was far grander than the contessa's villa, but dwarfed as it was by the mountains and the land that spread out all around it, the impressive size of the house seemed only natural.

The area between the house and the outbuildings bustled with activity. Unlike the bare, treeless main street in town, Quentin's yard was alive with trees, stately oaks and maples, their branches adorned with leaves that were beginning to hint at the arrival of autumn. Rosa realized for the first time that summer was nearly through. By now, Zia Rina's flowers would have died, and the roses would have finished blooming for another year.

Beneath colorful paper lanterns strung from tree to tree, three men worked to stake a wide canvas tarp. They pulled it tight and smoothed it over the dusty ground. A man with a fiddle sat on a nearby stump tuning his instrument. Trestle tables and benches were set up near long serving tables lined with various bowls and covered dishes. A few women labored near the tables, arranging and then rearranging the bowls. To one side of the house, a cook in an oilcloth apron turned huge slabs of beef on a grill above an open pit.

Rosa reached out to Kase without thinking and rested her hand on his coatsleeve. "What is this called?"

"He's barbecuing. Ranchers like to cook the meat over the open fire. The smoke flavors the beef. Would you like to watch?"

She nodded and then realized her hand was still on his arm. She felt him stiffen. Rosa turned away quickly, moving in the direction of the huge pit. The smell of roasting beef drifted on the smoky air. She wondered how the charred meat could possibly taste good, although she was intrigued by the delicious scent. As they drew near, she recognized Quentin Rawlins when he called out to them.

"Welcome, you two. Did you have a good ride out? How're things in town?"

Rosa assured him their ride had been pleasant and listened while Kase told him things in town were as uneventful as ever.

"I'm glad to see you here." Rawlins looked from one silent figure to the other. "Both of you." He took Rosa's hand and led her away from Kase. "Come on, Rosa, I'd like you to meet some of the other ladies here. I figure it won't hurt to do a little advertising. They just might be able to convince their husbands they need a night off from cookin' once in a while."

She glanced back over her shoulder. Kase made no effort to follow. He watched them for a moment before he walked toward a group of men talking near the canvas dance floor.

Rosa caught sight of Kase only from a distance as the late afternoon drifted into evening. Quentin Rawlins kept her by his side throughout the introductions to the other women in attendance. They were a varied group of ranchers' wives, townsfolk from Cheyenne, and a few farmers and their families. All of them were cordial, eager to learn about her restaurant. All of them wanted to know how she managed alone. When the buffet dinner began, Quentin returned to her side and then sat beside her at one of the long trestle tables. He monopolized her time so thoroughly that she could not spare Flossie more than a brief hello and a smile.

Unobtrusively, she tried to locate Kase among the crowd of townsmen, women, and cowhands who crowded into the yard to partake of the feast. He was seated at the table farthest from her with Flossie, Slick Knox, and three women she assumed were Flossie's employees. Rosa wanted to study the three women without appearing curious, so she stole sly glances in their direction. Flamboyantly dressed in vibrant silk and satin, the women were by far the most attractive at the party. It was no wonder the marshal had chosen to enjoy their company rather than hers.

Rosa forced herself to look away and study the scene around her. The sun was setting behind the mountains in the distance, the sky streaked with vibrant pinks and reds against the darker shadows of high clouds. Lanterns placed along the length of the tables were lit, casting the faces that lined each side in light and shadow. The language was far different, the faces unfamiliar, but Rosa was reminded all the same of late summer nights in Crotte. She glanced down the table to her left, and found her gaze arrested by Kase Storm's stare. In the gilding of lamplight, his features appeared cast in bronze; his eyes were startling blue in contrast. He was seated between Flossie Gibbs

and the youngest of her girls, Chicago Sue. The blonde with
the riotous frizzy hair was chatting amiably to Kase as she ate,
totally unaware that his attention was elsewhere.

Rosa smiled across the distance, happy to note Kase Storm
was at least aware of her presence, then turned to answer a
question put to her by Quentin.

"Yes, I have danced," she said, "but not often."

"Well, you'll have all the practice you'll ever need tonight,
little lady, because after we eat, the dancing starts. I'd be
obliged if you'd have the first dance with me."

She tried to steal another glance at Kase and found his
attention on Chicago Sue. "I would be happy to dance with
you, Signor Quentin."

Quentin Rawlins was not the only man she danced with that
night. A long succession of rowdy cowhands demanded a turn,
as did mild-mannered bachelors from Cheyenne. By the end of
the first hour of dancing, the soles of her feet ached and the
tops had been bruised by overzealous partners. By the end of
the second hour, she had received four proposals of marriage.
By eleven o'clock, as she watched Flossie and the girls—
surrounded by at least ten cowboys—walk toward their wagon,
Rosa wished she could go home with them. She was exhausted, not to mention disappointed. Kase Storm had not
asked her to dance with him even once.

She had tried not to focus her attention on him as he whirled
by with one after another of Flossie's girls on his arm, tried not
to stare into the darkened yard and watch him as he stood
beneath the trees drinking with the other men. Whether he
watched her with such interest she could not say. She never
caught him looking in her direction.

The lively music never stopped as one fiddler relieved the
next. Rosa asked the name of every new dance she learned—
lancers, Newports, schottisches, polkas—but try as she might
to perfect her steps, most of her partners were as inept as she.
But what they lacked in finesse they more than made up for in
enthusiasm. Finally, near midnight, Quentin announced the
last dance would be followed by dessert and coffee. Rosa stood
on the edge of the makeshift dance floor, determined not to let
herself look for Kase, certain he would end the evening
dancing with Chicago Sue, the girl he seemed to choose most
often. She watched Quentin as he smiled and nodded to his

guests. Her host was crossing the canvas, moving in her direction.

Kase watched Rose from the shadows that shrouded the area beyond the perimeter of the glowing lamplight. He had caught her watching him all evening, but so far had resisted the temptation of the veiled invitation in her eyes. He had not set himself an easy task—not when her apparent interest in him only helped stir up the growing need he felt whenever she was about.

Tonight had only proved to him that becoming involved with Rose Audi in any way would be all wrong. He knew that as surely as he knew the sun would come up tomorrow morning. All evening he had watched as Quentin danced attendance on Rose, introduced her to Cheyenne's society matrons, seated her beside him at dinner, and carefully kept her too occupied to have time for Flossie or him. Quentin had helped Rose slip into the good graces of polite society, kept her reputation intact by steering her away from her acquaintances and by emphasizing the fact that he found her entrepreneurial talents quite amazing.

Kase could not blame Quentin for his protectiveness toward Rose. Nor, he guessed, could Floss—Kase could tell as much from the woman's own careful avoidance of Rose Audi. But he could not help but wonder how Rose would react if she realized what the three of them had been up to.

The last dance was about to begin. Kase shifted and straightened his collar as he glanced around the dance floor. Most of the couples from Cheyenne had taken their leave. He wondered if it would do any harm for him to ask Rose to dance.

He had found himself thinking of her all evening—perhaps because each time he glanced in her direction, she had quickly looked away. Although her stubborn determination angered him, he had to admit that she had so far proved herself both capable and independent. He remembered the way her honey-colored eyes had danced when she tried to make him smile the day before and slowly found he was convincing himself that one dance would not ruin her reputation beyond repair.

He knew if he hesitated a moment longer that Quentin was bound to step in and dance with Rose, who was standing near the edge of the dance floor, her gaze searching the shadows.

* * *

"May I have this dance?"

The words were softly spoken near her ear. She held her breath, turned around, and found herself face to face with Kase. Rosa had to swallow before she could answer. Suddenly the incessant throbbing in her toes was forgotten. Her exhaustion vanished with each rapidly accelerating beat of her heart.

She nodded.

He reached down for her hand as the strains of a waltz began to drift on the crisp September night air that surrounded them. She knew she was staring up helplessly into his eyes, but found she could not move. He placed her fingers on his shoulder and reached for her other hand and held it captive in his own. She was forced to tip her head back to accommodate his height, but she was unwilling to tear her eyes away from his gaze. He pulled her close as he took control and whirled them onto the dance floor.

His steps were smooth and sure, his movements perfectly timed. As they began to glide and twirl to the music, Rosa caught glimpses of the starry sky above them. Kase did not speak, nor did he smile down at her as he had his other partners. Instead, he studied her intently, his expression closed and serious. Midnight blue in the semidarkness, his eyes showed little emotion. He looked down at her with the hooded, watchful gaze of a hunter.

He stopped dancing even though the haunting waltz played on. Without a word, without releasing the hand he held so tightly in his own, he glanced around and then led her off the dance floor. Rosa let him pull her into the darkness. He stalked toward the wagons, his long stride no match for her shorter steps. She began to run to keep up with him. The hand that held hers squeezed her fingers tighter as she stopped to ease a stitch in her side. He turned and looked back at her.

"Please . . ."

He halted, a look of surprise on his face, as if he realized for the first time what he had done. They were near the hired carriage, far from the lights swinging in the yard, and hidden by darkness from the view of the revelers. He stepped close to her, let go of her hand long enough to reach out and grasp her shoulders as he had before. Her breath was coming faster now, her eyes wide in anticipation.

Kase pulled her up hard against his length, one arm moving to encircle her shoulders while he draped the other across her hips to press her against him. His breath was warm and whiskey-scented, the rough material of his suit a sharp contrast to the soft sensual feel of his lips against hers. His kiss, as before, was not gentle, and yet she felt no fear as his lips played against hers. As if he might devour her with his kiss, Kase ground his lips against hers, slanted his mouth and slid his tongue between her teeth.

Rosa uttered a muffled groan and pulled him closer, as she strained upward, clasping him to her as the exchange deepened. The arm he held across her hips lowered until his hand cupped her derriere. He fit her to him. She could feel the hard length of his manhood burgeoning beneath the heavy suit material.

The kiss ended—not abruptly as it had the night he kissed her in the store—but slowly as he drew his lips away from hers until they stood breathing heavily, still clasped in each other's arms. He kissed her temple, then her cheek. She felt his breath whisper past her ear as he sighed.

"Let's go."

*

Chapter Nine

*

"Should we not tell Signor Quentin good-bye?"

"No." He held her elbow as she climbed up into the carriage.

"We should tell him *grazie*," she tried again.

"He'll think I had to get back because of all the cowhands who followed Flossie and the girls to town."

"Do you?"

"I think you know why I want to leave. Besides, Zach stayed in town to look after things."

She watched him pick up the reins and signal the horse to move forward. "Why we are leaving before the party is ended?"

He was hungry for the taste of her, aching with need, and out of patience. It was evident in his tone. "You're playing with fire, Rose. You know it, though, don't you?"

Surprised by the harshness in his voice, she looked away. What he said was true and she knew it. He was as volatile as a powder keg. What she did not understand was why.

"Look, Rose. We have to get something straight."

"Rosa."

He ignored the correction. "Ever since the first day you came to Busted Heel, I've felt responsible for you."

Puzzled, she shook her head. "Why?"

He shrugged. "I'm the marshal. I feel responsible for you the way I feel responsible for everyone in town." The next reason was harder to put into words. After a pause he continued, "You remind me a lot of my mother."

"Your *mother?*" Her heart sank. Just when she was marveling that this usually angry, brooding man was beginning to share some of his thoughts and feelings with her, he tells her she reminds him of his mother. Rosa sighed. A woman does not want to remind a man of his mother.

Kase went on, unmindful of her disappointment. "She came to this country from Europe, too." He paused, collecting his thoughts, carefully choosing his words. "Things weren't easy for her, either."

Rosa watched as he flexed and unflexed his fingers and then rubbed his palms on his thighs unwilling to say any more.

"But I am not your mother."

"No, definitely not." He relaxed a little and leaned back against the seat.

Jealous of the attention he had paid Flossie's women all evening, especially one in particular, she could not resist saying, "The girls from Flossie's house do not remind you of your mother. Perhaps you do not care for me because your hands are already loaded."

"*What?*"

"Your hands are loaded with the others."

After straining to comprehend, Kase suddenly laughed out loud. "Do you mean *full?* My hands are full?"

His laughter riled her. "Full, loaded, is no difference." She pictured his hands, dark and sure, occupied with Chicago's more glamorous attributes.

"Floss's girls are friends."

"The blond one, too?"

"Especially the blond one. She's like a sister to me."

Suspicious, Rosa arched a brow. Her skepticism was evident, even in the moonlight.

"Don't give me that look," he said.

"Don't give me the lie."

"I'm not lying. She's a friend."

Rosa shrugged. "If you say so."

"I do say so. There's no need to get huffy." Kase sat in stony silence as the carriage moved down the road. The horse's dark mane shone blue-black in the moonlight. The road was a white ribbon against the black earth; the moonlit sky hovered close above them. Rosa shivered in the crisp air; it seemed much cooler than it had been before sunset. She rubbed her arms to warm them as, more confused than ever by his actions, she tried to ignore the man beside her.

As the carriage rolled on toward Busted Heel, the strained silence lengthened between them. She shifted as the jolting ride became more uncomfortable, the night air more chilled as the moments passed. When a back wheel hit a rock, Rosa bounced upward and lost her balance. She nearly landed atop Kase's thigh. He drove the carriage off the main road for a few yards, then stopped. After looping the reins around the brake, he reached under the seat and brought forth a thick striped blanket.

"Stand up," he directed.

When Rosa stood, he wrapped the blanket around her and, when she sat back down, tucked it end over end about her legs. He started to reach for the reins again, then stopped. He took off his hat, set it on his knee, and leaned back against the leather seat. Kase stared out at the dark flat land that stretched endlessly before them.

"I don't see how you have any call to ask me about Chicago when I spent the night watching every damned man in the place dance with you—"

"Not every one."

"Close to it. You have Quentin Rawlins eating out of your hand. I found out something about myself tonight, Rose. I don't like to see other men put their hands on you. I don't like to watch you smile up into other men's eyes, either." He turned toward her and moved his arm, resting it on the seat behind her. His fingertips toyed with the material of her jacket sleeve.

His admission filled every corner of her heart with joy, but she did not know how to respond to it. She met his eyes as he continued.

"I've never been jealous in my life, and I don't like feeling the way I do."

"Because you do not like feeling anything, Marshal."

His eyes roamed over her face. "Meaning?"

Moonlight gleamed against his raven-black hair. His lips were full and inviting. She took a deep breath, thankful that he could not see the way her fingers were clasped together beneath the blanket. She was afraid to push him too far, afraid to try to make him put into words all that he was feeling. From what she had experienced of Kase Storm, she knew he was a man who kept all he felt hidden behind one of two masks—silence or anger. It might take a lifetime to learn what was hidden behind them. At this moment Rosa only cared about tonight. Flossie's advice was still fresh in her mind: *If you've got feelin's for Kase Storm, you make 'em known. . . . Do what comes natural.*

"Kiss me," she said.

"Dammit!" he said softly. There was only so much a man could withstand. He pulled her roughly into his hard embrace and did as she asked. His kiss was long, slow, and thorough. Rosa felt trapped in the cocoon he'd made of the blanket. She longed to hold him, to slide her fingers through his thick straight hair.

As their lips finally parted and Rosa took a deep breath, Kase settled back against the seat. They stared up at the moon that rode the sky and silhouetted the distant mountains with its silver light.

Things had progressed further than he had intended, but somehow, sitting alone with Rose in the cool night air under a wide star-filled sky, he found himself unwilling to leave. He felt a quiet peace that he had not known in months. He hated to end the moment, but refused to lead her on.

"You deserve the best life has to offer, Rose." In a tone that held no self-pity, only certainty, he added, "And that doesn't include me."

"You think little of yourself, Marshal. Why?" How could a man who was so strong and determined have such a weak opinion of himself?

"There's a lot you don't know about me, Rose. A lot I don't know about myself."

"I will never know unless you tell me."

"What if I say it's something I can't talk about?"

"I say a man must unburden his heart before he can open it to another."

He kissed the soft flesh of her neck, ran his tongue around the edge of her ear, then drew her earlobe between his teeth. She shivered and nestled closer. He thought about her simple statement: *A man must unburden his heart before he can open it to another.* Could he tell her that after twenty-one years he had finally learned the truth about his father—and that that truth explained the way he saw himself? How could he tell her of the confusion, the guilt, of knowing his very life began with an act of violence and violation?

It would take hours to tell the girl in his arms about his mother and of the way she had been forced to scrape out a living on the prairie, of the shame she endured because she kept him by her side. He would have to tell Rose of Caleb Storm, his stepfather, the man who had adopted and loved him as a father loves his own flesh and blood. And what would he say of the man whose blood ran in his veins? The man who was responsible for his unmistakable Indian features and coloring.

"Do you ever wonder who I am? Where I come from?" he asked.

She drew back and studied his features, then smiled. "I think you are a Gypsy. We have many in Europe."

He shook his head in wonder. Was she so naive that she did not know what he was? Part of him wanted to believe she was sincere, but his more cynical nature wondered if she was toying with him. As he concentrated on her tempting lips, he found it impossible to resist, no matter what her motives. Kase smiled slowly. "For tonight, then, I'll be your Gypsy." He traced the smile on her lips with his tongue.

"I want to touch you," she whispered and his breath caught in his throat. Swiftly he folded back the blanket. It fell around her hips.

Rosa reached up and encircled his neck with her arms. Able to slip her fingers into his hair, she raked them through the silken mass and then pulled his head down until his lips touched hers.

His fingers found the buttons that closed the front of her jacket. Unerringly, he worked them free one by one. As his lips moved against hers, as their tongues met and explored each other, his hands brushed aside the rose-patterned material and reached inside. The cold night air slipped between them as his hands began to massage the full, rounded breasts he found beneath her camisole top. Her nipples flowered into hardened peaks at his touch. Blood pulsed through her veins, rushing to further heighten the tortured nerve endings that made her breasts tingle as the ivory skin over them stretched taut.

"Please," she begged and tried to draw him back when he

pulled away. A rush of night air kissed her heated flesh. Reaching up, he pulled the pins from her hair and let the mass of raven tresses fall until they reached her hips and flowed around the seat. He laid her back against the carriage seat and knelt on the floor beside her.

Rosa held her breath, thankful for the darkness that hid the riotous red blush that she could feel suffusing her cheeks. She knew she should close her eyes for modesty's sake, thought it was a sin to watch what she was allowing him to do to her—but she was already a sinner. She could not bear to shut him out of her vision.

If this is a sin, Rosa thought, then let me die a sinner. Kase Storm had already aroused more passion in her than Giovanni ever had, touched her as her husband never dared. Giovanni was a man of God, a man who would have been a priest if not for his sudden decision to marry her. But as Kase Storm nuzzled her ear, enticing her with his lips, she released all thought of Giovanni.

Kase smoothed her flowing hair and watched it fall to the floor. He knew he was stepping beyond the boundaries he had set for himself, but he could not stop what she had begun when she requested a kiss.

She was breathing rapidly in anticipation of his next move. He leaned down and carefully slipped his fingers beneath the lace edge of her camisole. The feminine feel of the soft lace itself excited him. Her skin was warm and pliant beneath it. Slowly he drew the edge of the cotton batiste downward, careful not to tear it, until her breasts were exposed to his gaze. They burgeoned up and over the top of her undergarment, the dark peaks with their crowning nipples beckoned him to taste them. He dipped his head and ran the tip of his tongue around a swollen bud before he gently drew it between his teeth.

She moaned aloud, a sound that echoed mingled feelings of release and intensified longing. Her fingers dug into the material stretched taut across his wide shoulders. She clung, afraid to let go and find herself spinning free, flung out into a universe of sensation.

He suckled one breast and released it, then ministered to the other. Again she experienced an overwhelming need and again she moaned. As he sucked and gently nibbled at her breasts, she thrashed her head from side to side, giving in to the exquisite torture, wondering if she could stand more even as she prayed he would never stop.

Lost in the taste of her silken skin, surrounded by the sound of her heavy breathing and the incessant throbbing of his own blood as it pounded through his veins, Kase was oblivious to the sound of an approaching wagon as it moved along the road behind them. Finally, as the other vehicle drew near, the jingle of the harness and rattle of the wooden floorboards penetrated his thoughts.

"Hallo! Everything all right?" a man's voice called out across the distance that separated the two vehicles.

Rosa gasped and tried to sit up. She clutched the front of her jacket together, a futile attempt, since her breasts were unleashed and straining over the top of her camisole.

Kase drew a ragged breath. "Stay down," he whispered. His tone brooked no argument.

She complied, finding it all too easy to close her eyes against the embarrassment of her situation. Her awkward position left her little to do except cross her arms over her breasts as Kase stood to look over the back of the carriage.

He cupped his hands around his mouth and called back, "Everything's fine. Just watching the moonrise."

"Good night, then," the man called back. They could hear the sound of laughter and happy chatter as the wagon moved on down the road.

Kase took Rosa's hand and drew her to a sitting position. Gently he brushed her hair back over her shoulders and then reached out for her hands. He uncrossed her arms and then slipped his fingers beneath her breasts. The weight of them rested against his knuckles. Carefully he pulled her camisole up until she was covered once again, then drew the sides of her jacket together. With painstaking care, he rebuttoned the jet buttons and then grabbed the hem of her fitted jacket and tugged it down over her waist until it rested on her hips.

Reminded of the night he had first kissed her, Kase wondered if he was doomed to spend all of their stolen moments buttoning Rose's clothes. He offered a silent prayer of thanks for the interruption that had allowed him enough time to cool off and think about the ramifications of his actions. Until he could come to terms with his past, there was no way he could involve Rosa Audi with his future. She was too vulnerable, and far too willing.

He leaned forward and placed a chaste kiss on her forehead. "They weren't close enough to see us." He brushed her lips with his, then drew the blanket up over her shoulders again. "Are you all right?"

"*Sì.*"

"Good. It's time we head back to town."

Still shaking, as much from unfulfilled desire as from fear, Rosa nodded.

Rosa moved through the following morning in a daze, her thoughts centered on the night before. No matter how she tried, she could not forget her wanton disregard for propriety. Standing over a steaming pot of chicken stock, she closed her eyes against the memory of Kase Storm leaning over her as she lay sprawled against the cold leather seat of the hired buggy. Even now she could recall the scratch of the heavy blanket against her back, the sharp night air that added to the erotic sensation of his lips against her bare skin, the rush of heat that seared her as he laved her breasts with his tongue.

An insistent pounding at the back door startled her into awareness. Rosa left the stock to simmer and went to answer the summons. It was G.W. Davis, come to sweep the floor.

Relieved to see that it was only the child and not Kase, Rosa forced a smile. She would have to come to terms with herself and her actions of the previous evening before diners arrived for the midday meal. She set the boy to his task, crossed the dining room to survey the three tables that now served the customers, and unlocked the front door. She paused on the walk for a moment and glanced toward the jailhouse. There was no sign of Kase, although the door to the building stood open. Quickly she stepped back inside.

What shall I do when I see him? she wondered. What shall I say? She thought perhaps she should apologize for her actions, then remembered the long silent ride back to town and knew that the opportunity for an apology had passed. Kase had not touched her again, except to help her from the carriage. He had walked her to the door, said good night with a nod, and waited while she turned the key. In her mind, she dreaded coming face to face with him again. In her heart, she could not wait to see him.

He did not come in for the midday meal. In a way, she was not surprised—he had yet to return for a meal since the day he ate with Quentin Rawlins—but she had half expected him to come today. Instead, it was his friend Zach, along with Paddie O'Hallohan, who arrived a short while after noon.

"Howdy, Miz Rosie."

He studied her for so long with his one-eyed stare that she colored. Surely Kase had not told the man what had passed between them?

"Signor Zach, Signor Paddie. Please, sit."

Flossie, they explained, was tending bar so that Paddie could experience eating at the café instead of standing behind the bar, shoveling down food they carried in to him. Since it was his first visit, and he the provider of most of her chairs and all of the tables, Rosa took extra care with their meal. Hovering attentively over the men, she served them chicken soup with tender, fragrant vegetables, roast chicken, potatoes boiled and tossed with butter and garlic, bread, and finally dessert.

Not once did Zach Elliot mention Kase.

Not once did she ask about him.

Rosa retreated to the kitchen and slid the soiled dishes into a dishpan of water. She reached up to the windowsill where she kept an earthenware pitcher wrapped in towels to chill the drinking water. Returning to the dining room, she filled Paddie's water glass, then Zach's, all the while trying to summon her courage.

They both spoke at once.

"How is—"

"Kase said to—"

"*Scusi*," she said, blushing furiously.

Zach scratched at the perpetual white stubble that silvered his face, leaned back in the chair, and stretched his legs under the table. Then he hiked his waistband up. "Kase said to tell you good-bye."

Her heart sank and she felt her breath leave her. "Good-bye?" She could barely say the word. Rosa turned away and left the men alone at the table. She did not hear Zach's chair scrape across the floor.

"Miz Rosie?" He had followed her into the kitchen.

Rosa rewrapped the pitcher and set it back on the window-sill. She blinked furiously, fighting tears, before she turned around to face Zach Elliot.

"I thought rather than fish around for some decorated words to tell you he rode outta town this mornin', I'd just tell ya what he said. I didn't mean to hurt you none by bein' so blunt."

She could see he was trying to make amends for the shock his news had wrought, but could make no comment.

"Come to think on it, he did say more'n good-bye. Not much, but as I can recall, Kase said . . . well, he said . . ."

It was Zach's turn to color from embarrassment. Rosa came to his aid.

"It is all right, *signor*. You need not lie to me. He told you to tell me good-bye, *si*? You have done that. *Va bene*."

She turned away, pretending to fuss with the cutlery lined up on her worktable.

"There's a lot you don't know about Kase, Miz Rosa. He didn't even tell me where he went, but I got a hunch. Left me in charge and said he'd be back jest as soon as he could." He lifted the brim of his hat and reached up to scratch beneath his hat band.

Kase's own words echoed in her mind: *There's a lot you don't know about me, Rose. A lot I don't know about myself*.

As Zach Elliot stood in the middle of her kitchen looking worried, Rosa tried to smile. She failed miserably.

The Pine Ridge Reservation was a good two hundred miles from Cheyenne. Kase traversed the land slowly as he followed Horse Creek and continued northward across a section of Nebraska's open land to the White River, the one the Sioux called the Smoky Earth River. From there it was a short distance to the reservation. He found it healing to spend the days alone. The open space of the Badlands afforded him time to listen to the meadowlark's last song of the season and watch the prairie dogs at play.

The Badlands were not entirely wasteland torn by wind and water, as the name suggested. In the spring and summer the land had been alive with grasses now turned brown and gone to seed. Coyote shared the landscape with badgers and ferrets as well as the playful prairie dogs. But not once on his journey eastward did he see a buffalo. As Kase looked across the land that once easily supported vast herds of buffalo on its natural bounty of grasses, it seemed a valuable piece of the whole was missing.

The reservation land was dry and nearly barren. The grass in the higher elevations had survived the harsh drought of summer, but here, where the plain spread out and the wind raked the land night and day, barely a weed survived. Ramshackle houses made of scraps of wood, twisted boughs of cottonwood, and various pieces of hides dotted the landscape. Many of the shacks appeared deserted; others were obviously still occupied. Futile attempts at farming were evident near some of the patchwork houses. Forlorn, half-grown cornstalks that had been bleached nearly white by the heat stood alongside other shriveled crops like skeletons against the prairie landscape.

As he traveled across the reservation he was able to communicate with the people living there, and was thankful that Caleb had insisted he learn the language. Kase and Caleb had sometimes communicated in Sioux when they were alone together. Kase often used Dutch when he spoke to his mother, but Annika, his half sister, refused to use either. As stubborn as the rest of her family, she insisted on speaking English all the time.

Studying the harsh conditions and the poverty the Pine Ridge dwellers faced, Kase realized for the first time exactly what it meant for him to have been spared a life there. He would never be fully accepted by the whites, but Caleb's moneyed position and Kase's law degree ensured that he would never be forced to experience the hunger and poverty that was a way of life on the reservation. He would never be forced to scratch a living out of worthless soil or be dependent on government handouts of beef, coffee, and sugar to keep his family from starvation.

As he made his way across the land he gained much needed information that would help him in his quest. He was advised to go to the agency distribution center the Sioux called Wakpamni and seek out the shaman, Running Elk, an elder who knew everything about the People. Robert Shield, a young man about his own age, advised Kase to leave his white man's clothing, saddle, and guns in his care, for if Kase took them to the agency, he would be forced to surrender his arms to the agency police. Shield told him it would be dangerous to go about armed, since it was against the law for the Sioux to do so. The man feared Kase would surely become a target for the Indian police. Shield seemed like a man he could trust, and having no alternative, Kase gave over his possessions for safekeeping.

Kase remembered the police, or Metal Badges, as they were called, who were hired by the agents to keep the peace among the People. As a boy he had admired the shining buttons and insignia on their dark uniforms. Now he had a badge himself tucked into his saddlebag. He had been lucky not to have run into the Indian police thus far.

The day after he met Robert Shield, Kase rode into the Pine Ridge Agency dressed in a pair of the man's faded woolen trousers and a buckskin shirt. He wondered—as he had each and every day since he left Busted Heel—how Rose fared and what she might be doing. He had left Zach instructions to watch over her and had taken the old man's ribbing when he did. He thought of Rose and Zach, of Floss and the girls. All of them were misfits of one kind or another who had been brought together by the hand of fate.

He found himself anxious to return to Busted Heel, and to Rose, but knew he could not go back until he had faced and dealt with his past.

*

Chapter
Ten

*

As the sun slipped behind the mountains earlier each evening, the nights grew increasingly cooler and the days shorter. Rosa's Ristorante continued to serve cowhands, townsfolk, and visitors to Busted Heel alike. As the weeks passed with no word at all from Kase Storm, Rosa spent every waking hour hard at work cooking, painting, organizing, shopping, smiling. But more often than not, her smiles were forced.

There were days when she grew impatient with herself. Didn't she have everything she had hoped for? Her *ristorante* was a success; she had made enough money not only to whitewash the inside of the place but to pay for wineglasses and a special shipment of red wine from New York. It gave her great satisfaction to look around and admire all she had accomplished. Through tragedy she had become independent, far more so than she would have ever been in Corio. Surely her hard-won success would prove to Kase Storm that she did belong in Busted Heel.

There were days during his absence when she grew impatient with him. Where was he? If he was coming back, when would that be? She vacillated between hate and love. Sometimes she itched to slap him for the worry he had caused; at other times, all she wanted was to feel his arms about her. More often than not, she wondered if there was anything between them except a night of stolen kisses and fondling. She did not really know him, for he had never really opened his heart to her. Why should she hope there ever might be anything more? He was a brooding, silent man who became angry with her as easily as he drew a breath. Would he ever change?

It was mid-September and Rosa was in her usual state of confusion over Kase Storm when Quentin Rawlins strode into the café. He had the same self-assured aura that Kase exuded, that of a large man in a small room. He was tall, strong-shouldered, confident. Quentin bestowed a wide, warm smile upon her as he worked his way past the crowded tables and stopped just inside the kitchen door.

"Rose"—he took in her cheeks flushed from the warmth of the stove, her neat, upswept hairstyle, her spotless apron— "how are you?"

"*Bene*. Fine." Before she turned to him, she bent to lift a loaf of bread from the oven. "You come to eat, Signor Quentin? There is room at the table near the window." Rosa saw no need to seat customers alone when there was room at an occupied table. Everyone seemed to enjoy the family-style atmosphere as farmers ate with ranch hands and storekeepers with travelers.

He shook his head, "Not yet. I want to talk to you alone first. Am I in the way?" He reached for an olive in a dish on the worktable and popped it in his mouth.

"No," she shook her head as she kept on working.

She felt his eyes on her but was able to accomplish her tasks with an ease she would never have known if it had been Kase Storm watching her bustle about the kitchen. Quentin came to town often, usually on the way to or from Cheyenne, and Rosa enjoyed his visits. While most cattlemen preferred to live in Cheyenne and visit their ranches occasionally, Quentin wanted to live in the sprawling ranch house at the base of the mountains. Rosa could well understand his choice of residence, for the land around Mountain Shadows reminded her of Corio.

Between his sojourns he often stopped in to eat, and when she had time to listen, Quentin regaled her with descriptions of Cheyenne. The Cheyenne Club, his home away from home, was an imposing two-story building complete with a restaurant and bar, billiard room, library, and six rooms for cattlemen like himself who found a need to stay in town for the night. He told

Rosa with a laugh that the members had voted long ago not to provide a separate dining room for women. The place was a haven for men only.

From Quentin she learned that Cheyenne had an opera house, three grand hotels, variety theaters, and, he said, with a smile, all the comforts of Busted Heel, except on a far grander scale.

"You had a good trip?" she asked.

"Yep, but I have to go back at the end of the week to sign some deeds."

She sliced some bread and placed the heavenly fragrant pieces on a side dish with a slab of butter. This she handed to Quentin before she lifted two dinner plates heaped with egg noodles smothered in cream sauce. "Come. You carry that for me," she said over her shoulder with a smile. She led him into the dining room, and since her customers seemed content for the moment, she sat down across from him.

"It's amazing what you've done with this place, Rosa."

As he looked the place over, she felt herself glow with pride. "Next I will have lights on the walls," she told him confidently.

"Rosa, I wouldn't doubt that you can do anything, but there's no electricity in Busted Heel and I don't foresee any coming for a few years. How do you propose to accomplish that?"

She shook her head. "I will have the kind like Flossie. They hold the candles."

He looked aghast. "*You've* been to Flossie's?"

"Yes," she said truthfully. "She is my friend. Sometimes in the early morning I still clean the downstairs of her house. And she gives me tea. But," she added, "she does not often get up before afternoon."

"I wouldn't think so," he said, half to himself. "What else do you have in store for the illustrious diners of Busted Heel?"

Rosa laughed, and realized that for the first time in days, she was enjoying herself.

"You know, Rosa, I'll loan you anything you need if you want to expand your business. I know a good thing when I see it."

"*Grazie, signor*, but my *ristorante* is big enough for Busted Heel and for me. Any more would be too much too soon."

"Are you happy here, Rosa? Do you see yourself working forever?"

She frowned, wondering why he might think her unhappy. "I have not thought—"

"I just wondered, a fine-looking woman like yourself. I know you needed time to mourn your husband. My own wife passed away fifteen years ago. Don't you ever think of sharing your life with a man? Of letting someone take care of you for a change?"

How could she tell him she would not allow herself to dwell on such thoughts? They only led her to think of Kase Storm.

"Don't tell me no one's proposed to you yet?"

Rosa laughed. "Many of your workers."

"And you turned them down?"

"*Sì.*"

"Then I guess there's no use in me trying to persuade you to marry me, is there?"

She took a deep breath and wished he had not complicated their relationship with his proposal. She valued him as a friend, nothing more. "No, Signor Quentin. I have no wish to marry."

"Yet," he added.

"Not yet."

"You won't crush an old man by telling him he shouldn't keep trying, will you?"

She stared down at her hands as she twisted her apron. "I am happy that we are friends, Signor Quentin, but"—she forced herself to meet his gaze—"I do not want you to think that maybe some day we will marry. You are my friend, *signore*, but nothing more. I hope we will remain friends." She released a pent-up breath and waited nervously for him to reply. He looked down at her for a moment. Then, to her relief, Quentin Rawlins smiled.

"I'm glad you told me, Rosa. I admire honesty in a person more than any other trait." His blue eyes took on their mischievous twinkle. "Now humor an old man, would you? Is there someone else?"

She felt the heat of embarrassment suffuse her face, but did not look away from him. "I think maybe the marshal."

For the first time ever, she saw him frown. "Kase?"

She nodded.

"I see."

"I thought he is your friend, *signore*."

Quentin lowered his fork and leaned toward her with his elbows resting on the table. "He is; don't get me wrong. He's a well-educated man from a fine family—"

"*Si?*"

"Rosa, you know he is part Sioux."

"Oh."

"Do you know what that means?"

"No."

He sighed before he added, "He is half Indian."

She drew back, leaning against the back of the chair. "And this makes a difference for you?"

Quentin's expression was one of concern. He shook his head and said, "No, not really," but his tone belied the response. "Well, not in an everyday sense. But, Rosa, I don't think you realize what other people would think of you taking up with a man of Indian blood."

She watched him closely, trying to weigh his words against his expression. He said that Kase's bloodlines made no difference to him, and yet his concern told her otherwise.

"I am Italian," she said.

"I know that, but—"

"I, too, am different."

He looked as if he were carrying a heavy weight as he said, "But you're still white."

She knew her displeasure was mirrored in her eyes. She shrugged. "White, brown. Is no difference to me."

"To you, perhaps not, but you have no idea what people will think, or how you would be treated if you married a half-breed."

"The people here are my friends."

"I'm not talking about Busted Heel, Rosa. I'm talking about the rest of the world."

As the tension between them increased, her stomach tied itself in knots. Hoping to relieve the strain she smiled. "You think the rest of the world will be mad with Rosa?"

"This is not a laughing matter. Kase is a half-breed. That's something you have to face if you care about your future or your children's future, if you should have any. I consider him a friend, just as his father is my friend, but as *your* friend I'm trying to spare you a lot of heartache. Of course, if you've

made up your mind that you have to have him, I'll back you."
He reached out and took her hand. "But I'd advise you to think
long and hard about this."

His warning was all she needed to make her dig in her heels.
With a stubborn tilt of her chin she told him frankly, "I listen
to my heart, *signore*."

"But hearts are blind."

Rosa studied him until he began to eat again and then
excused herself. She returned to the table to offer him more
wine, which he declined. After the bill was all settled, she
walked him to the door.

A sudden thought struck her. What if Quentin Rawlins told
Kase what she had just admitted? First Flossie, now Quentin.
She might just as well put a sign in the window announcing her
attraction to Kase to the entire town.

"*Signore*, I must ask you as a friend not to speak about this,
most especially, do not tell the marshal. Maybe I should not
have spoken."

"I won't say anything to Kase. Besides, if the man has half
a brain in his head he's already in love with you. But I want
you to think about what I've said and just remember, if you
ever need a loan to help you expand the business, Rosa, you
come to me and you've got it. I know a good investment when
I see one."

"I will, *signore*," she promised.

She stood in the open doorway for a moment and watched
him walk away. His words gave her much to consider.

It was near the end of September, the Moon of the Black
Calf, when Kase reached Wakpamni, the distribution center at
Pine Ridge. White-faced buttes covered with yellow pine were
scattered across the open prairie surrounding the area. He
dismounted and walked amid the groupings of tipis that
dotted the open plain. No tree or ridge protected the Wakpamni
or the dwellings there from the onslaught of the prairie winds.
The ground was windswept and barren, but the inhabitants
of the village seemed not to notice as they moved about.

Flatbed wagons were pulled up alongside many of the
dwellings, and beside them sat men and women huddled in
striped woolen blankets. They watched him as he passed. He

stopped a smiling young woman with a wide-eyed child beside her to ask where he could find Running Elk, the shaman.

A group of older women walked past just as the girl was about to answer. He merely glanced at the women before he turned his attention back to the comely young mother. Before she could speak, a woman disengaged herself from the group and hesitantly approached Kase. She could have been no more than forty, but her face showed years of hardship. She stared at him as if she were entranced. But as she drew nearer, her eyes widened in fear and horror. Kase looked around for help when she cast aside her robe and fell on her knees before him. Screaming and crying, she began to tear at her hair.

Her startled companions drew away and the young woman's child began howling, adding to the general hysteria. Kase stood immobilized by the scene as others came running. Men and women crowded close as children tried to break into the circle that quickly formed about Kase and the wailing woman. A touch upon his sleeve caused Kase to start and reach for the gun that usually rode his hip. His hand came away empty. Shaken by the episode, he turned to see who had touched him and found himself gazing down into the clear dark eyes of a wizened old man. He knew without being told that the man could be none other than Running Elk.

The old man walked past Kase and knelt beside the woman. He spoke to her softly, whispering words that only she could hear. As the man tried to calm the woman, Kase stared at the buffalo robe the shaman wore. It was painted with colorful yellow spots and stars. Weasel skins and squirrel tails along with pendants of feathers and assorted bells hung from the robe. A rawhide medicine bag painted with a symbol of a running elk and decorated with feathers and beads hung from the waistband of his buckskin pants.

Running Elk drew a wand made of chicken and magpie feathers. He shook the wand and waved it back and forth over the sobbing woman and began to chant. As he did, she slowly regained control. Running Elk stood and motioned some of the other women near. At a sharp word from the shaman, they hesitantly approached and knelt beside her. As they whispered softly among themselves, Running Elk stood and returned to Kase's side.

When Kase began to speak, Running Elk shook his head,

warning him to be silent. He took hold of Kase and led him away from the disturbing scene. Kase followed without question, grateful to leave the others staring after him. When they reached a large dwelling covered with faded symbols, the old man disappeared inside.

Kase removed his hat and ran his fingers through his hair. He wiped his palms on his thighs and then scratched on the tipi near the entrance. When the shaman bade him enter, Kase drew aside the door flap and stooped to step into the dim interior of the tipi. Once inside, he paused, trying to recall all Caleb had taught him about Sioux etiquette. He stepped to the right, the way a man should do when entering a tipi, and then sat down before the old shaman. The place smelled of smoke and sweat, of hides and close, warm air.

The man's skin was as creased as an eroded hillside. When he hunched over a small fire, Kase saw that his face was not only lined but still faintly streaked with grime. The old man clutched a blanket about his shoulders. His hair was as white as snow, parted into two braids that hung past his shoulders. He was thin to the point of emaciation, but his eyes shone like the coals burning in the fire ring in the center of the tipi.

"Sit down, my son," he said, his strong voice at odds with his frail appearance.

Kase sat, laid his hat beside him, and waited for the old one to speak. He did not have to wait long.

"So, you have come."

"You *know* me?" Kase swallowed. For the first time in his life he felt afraid enough to run.

"I know you." The old one stared and waited for Kase to speak again.

"How? And what was wrong with that woman? Did she know me?"

"She thought you were a ghost—the ghost of her husband. She saw his face in yours."

Kase frowned. Could it be? "Who was her husband?"

The old man's gaze was hooded. "Why have you come?"

"I am Kase Storm. I want to know of a man of the Oglala, a man who once traveled into the Iowa land." *A man who raped my mother.*

"Many men have traveled past the edges of the reservation, but none for many years."

"This would have been over twenty-one years ago."

The shaman closed his eyes and nodded. He was silent for so long Kase was certain he had fallen asleep. Then, without opening his eyes, Running Elk said, "Why do you seek the name of such a man?"

Angry, certain the old man was toying with him, Kase answered sullenly, "I think you know why. And I think you know the man I speak of."

"You are angry because you are afraid. What is it you fear?"

Startled, Kase dropped his gaze and stared into the fire. He did feel fear. Heart-stopping fear that had pervaded his being since the woman outside had fallen at his feet. He sensed that before he left Pine Ridge he would know all he had come to learn.

He spoke slowly, piecing the story together for the shaman. "The man and his band attacked a family of immigrants traveling through Iowa. They carried off my mother's younger brother and sister. They killed everyone but an old man, and after raping my mother, they left her for dead."

Running Elk stared hard at Kase. "I see many things in your eyes besides fear. Anger and hatred are there, too."

"He raped my mother."

"The man left his seed in her."

Kase nodded. "I am his son."

The old man said nothing.

Kase gave him more information. "My mother's brother and sister were taken during the raid. The sister chose to remain with the Sioux after she married a man called Swift Otter. The boy, Pieter, we have received no word of in many years."

Running Elk took a deep breath and mumbled a prayer chant that Kase could not hear. Then he spoke. "I know of the woman who is Swift Otter's first wife, just as I know of the men who brought her to live among us. You now claim as your father the man named Caleb Storm who is known among the People as Raven's Shadow, do you not?"

"Yes."

"He is the agent who brought Red Dog's band back to the reservation. He was at the fort, Sully, many years ago."

"Yes."

"Why has he not told you of your father? Why has your mother remained silent?"

"My mother remembers nothing of the attack, and so she could not identify the man. Caleb told me what happened, but nothing about the man except that he was a murderer and a rapist." Ashamed, Kase looked away.

"The man who gave you life was named Red Dog. He was a subchief, a leader of a small band of Oglala that refused to accept reservation life. His ways were wild. As a youth of only sixteen summers, Red Dog went with eight others to raid the settled Iowa lands. They returned with the captives. Years later, he left the reservation again. His followers deserted him. He died a broken man, killed in a minor skirmish with the white soldiers."

Kase tried to digest all Running Elk told him. Nothing he heard surprised him, except that the man who had fathered him had been so young. The rest was much as he expected. His true father had been a renegade, a rapist, a man who rebelled until the end of his life.

"You have the look of Red Dog about you," the shaman said. "To his wife, you are his ghost."

The thought did little to ease Kase's mind. Not only did the man's blood run through his veins, but Red Dog's image was mirrored in his own features. He thanked God that Analisa did not remember the man's face.

The shaman was studying him intently. "Now that you know who fathered you, tell me what it is that you still fear, and why you have come so far."

Kase struggled with himself, with the very fear the old man could easily see. He leaned forward and rested his arms on his knees. Interlacing his fingers, he stared at his hands and slowly put his fears into words.

"I'm scared I am like him. I had to learn about this man, to know whether he might have led a good life later on. I don't know who I am or what I'm capable of and it scares the hell out of me."

"And so you strike out at others. Who you are, Kase Storm, is within your own heart. You are not your father, nor are you your mother. You are an individual, a soul unto yourself. Look to the sacred center of yourself and you will have the answers you seek. Do not look to the past or to the future."

"And just how am I to find this sacred center of myself?" He could not keep the sarcasm from his tone.

A frown further creased Running Elk's brow. "Have you never experienced *hanbleceya*, never cried for a vision?"

"Vision quests aren't all that popular in Boston right now."

"It is time you sought the truth that lies within."

"Perhaps it's too late," Kase admitted. "I thought only young boys went on vision quests."

"*Hanbleceya* can be undertaken at any age. I will help you to prepare."

*

Chapter
Eleven

*

"*Dio*!" Rosa cried out and released the pan handle she had unthinkingly grabbed without a pot holder. She shook her stinging fingers and then inspected them. They did not appear about to blister, so she contented herself with dipping them in the dishwater.

Nothing seemed to be going right. The fire she kept burning in the stove had gone out sometime in the middle of the night. She had arisen with a neck stiff from sleeping on her narrow cot in the cold kitchen. Chin Yee had arrived late, tearfully apologetic, but late nonetheless. A farmer and his wife, in town to buy supplies, were waiting impatiently in the dining room for their midday meal.

She heard the front door open and close. Wiping her hands on a dish towel hanging from the waistband of her apron, Rosa went out to greet her customers. Two men in dark woolen suits and brown bowler hats seated themselves near the window. She was arrested by their appearance. Although their clothing was of fine materials cut in the latest style, the shirts they wore beneath the suits were wrinkled, not to mention soiled with grease stains and frayed at the collar. Both men wore holstered guns strapped to their thighs. They appeared to be near the same age, and from the likeness of their features, she guessed they were related.

They smiled and nodded, ordered complete meals, and then,

stretching out in their chairs, they alternately leered in her direction and stared out the window.

"Miss Rosa, we got to get back out to the ranch," the farmer seated with his frowning wife reminded her.

"I'm sorry, Signor Shaw. I will bring your plates out."

She hurried into the kitchen where she dished up generous portions of noodles and roast beef, then sent Chin scurrying into the dining room with the orders while she boiled more noodles for the newcomers.

When the Yee girl reentered the kitchen, Rosa noted bright tears sparkling in her dark almond-shaped eyes. "Chin? What's the matter?"

Chin shook her head.

"What?" Rosa demanded.

"Nothing," the young girl whispered.

"You tell Rosa what's the matter or I'm lose my temper." Rosa reached out and put her hands on Chin's shoulders, forcing the girl to meet her stare.

"The man pulled my hair." She drew her queue over her shoulder. The long single braid hung past her waist.

"*Basta*!" Rosa stormed into the dining room and faced the two strangers at the window table. "How come you tease the girl?" she demanded. Her usual attempts to perfect her English were forgotten in her anger.

Without bothering to straighten himself up, the heavier of the two men indolently stared up at her. A smirk curled his lips. The younger spoke. "Didn't mean any harm, ma'am." His tone was far from apologetic.

"I been wonderin'," the other said, "what else you serve besides food?"

"Wine," Rosa said.

"Well." He rubbed his hand across his jaw and slowly stared her up and down. His eyes returned to her breasts. "I was thinkin' of somethin' a little tastier. Something imported."

Slowly becoming aware that he was insulting her, Rosa felt the flush rise to her cheeks. The younger of two men watched the exchange and then spit into the corner.

Rosa's temper snapped.

"Get out," she said, fighting to keep her voice low so as not to disturb the farmer and his wife.

"Out? I don't think you mean that, spitfire. Do you think she means it, Bart?" The heavyset man looked to the younger for confirmation.

"Hell no, Bert. I hear tell when most women say no, what they mean is yes."

"I heard that somewheres, too, now that I think on it." Bert stood up and took a step toward her.

"I said get out," Rosa repeated. "Nobody spits on my floor."

The second man stood. Rosa held her breath.

"I'm not plannin' on going anyplace," Bert said before he reached out and grabbed Rosa by the shoulders. She tried to pull out of his grasp and heard the shoulder seam of her white blouse give way.

"Look here, mister." The farmer attempted to push away from the table and come to Rosa's aid.

"Don't move, old man," Bart said. His hand flicked to his side and whisked his gun out of his holster.

Rosa heard the kitchen door slam.

Bert pulled her up against him. "Now, tell me," he said, leering down into Rosa's face, "what's for dinner?"

"Let me go." She refused to cry. Nor would she scream. Fully aware of the farmer held at gunpoint, conscious of the soft sobbing of his wife, Rosa fought to remain calm.

"I don't think so," Bert said. "I kinda like the feel of this hot little Italian in my arms. Watch the door, Bart." He turned, pressed Rosa against him, and began to back out of the dining room toward the kitchen.

"Watch the door, Bart. Watch the door, Bart. That's all I ever hear," Bart complained as his gaze moved swiftly away from the subdued farmer who stood with his napkin hanging over the front of his overalls.

"This won't take long at all, Bart. Just keep lookin' out that door," Bert warned.

Suddenly Rosa felt the man stiffen. He halted just outside the kitchen doorway. She heard Zach Elliot's voice behind him.

"That's the cold barrel of a forty-four you feel pressin' into your back, mister. Now, if I was you, I'd have your friend drop his gun and I'd let go of the girl."

Bert let go of Rosa, and she stepped away from him. When Zach stepped out into the dining room, his gun trained on Bert, she moved past them and into the kitchen. Chin Yee stood beside the stove trembling, but trying to smile. Rosa quickly slipped an arm about the girl.

"Put your gun back, Bart," Bert warned.

The other young gunman hesitated, and Zach cocked his gun.

"Do it," Bert demanded.

"Put it on the table and step away from it," Zach clarified.

When Paddie O'Hallohan stepped through the front door carrying the sawed-off shotgun he kept behind the bar, Bart complied. He laid his gun on the table and raised his hands.

Zach reached out and relieved the man called Bert of his own hardware. "Now I'd like you two to get on your horses and start ridin' out of town. And I don't want to see either of you around here again."

"You know who you're talkin' to, old man?" Bart asked, one eye on Paddie, who hovered behind him.

"Yeah. I'm talkin' to a coward that has to hold a gun to a woman's head to get what he wants. That don't make you much of a man in my book." Zach prodded the man forward. Rosa, her arm around Chin for support as much as for comfort, followed Zach into the dining room. She couldn't hold back a smile when she saw Paddie in the doorway, the sunlight shining off his bald pate.

"You'll be sorry, old man," Bert warned.

"I'll be the judge of that," Zach mumbled.

"You can't keep our guns," Bart protested as Paddie moved aside to let them through the doorway.

"You write to me from wherever you end up and I'll mail 'em to ya."

The back door slammed and Rosa jumped. Slick Knox walked into the dining room, a gun in each hand. "You got troubles, Miss Rosa?" he wanted to know.

Rosa had never seen the usually jovial gambler so serious. His lips were set beneath his waxed mustache, his brows drawn together. Suddenly the unusually silent gambler was a man she would not want to cross.

"The *signori* Zach and Paddie came to help. I thank you, Signor Slick, for your help, too."

Slick moved past her and stepped out onto the walk with the others. Within moments the two strangers were out of sight.

The shaken farmer sat back down, and Rosa released Chin long enough to apologize to the Shaws.

"It weren't your fault, Miss Rosa. Don't you pay it no mind." Although his hand was still shaking, the man reached for his fork and proceeded to finish his meal. His wife sniffed loudly, blew her nose into the napkin, and stared at her plate.

Within moments, Zach, Paddie, and Slick returned.

"You all right now, Miz Rosie?" Zach wanted to know; his grizzled hair was wild beneath his slouching hat, his brow knit in a frown.

She smiled tremulously at each of them in turn. Paddie mopped his head with a handkerchief, his ruddy cheeks aflame. Slick looked as unruffled as ever as he casually shoved his guns into the waistband of his gaily striped pants.

Rosa felt her eyes mist with tears.

"Such good friends," she whispered. "I thank you all." She straightened the front of her apron and blinked back tears. "Now sit." Businesslike, she pulled out a chair with a flourish. "Sit. Eat. *Mangia*. Today everyone at Rosa's eats free!"

On a wind-beaten bluff, lying in a pit covered with brush and leaves, Kase awoke and stared out of the narrow opening at the panoramic landscape that stretched toward the horizon. The morning sun was about to rise, to break through the clouds and melt away the shroud of tenacious fog that clung to the streams and riverbeds in the flatlands below. He crawled out of the pit and began the ritual prayer to Anpo Wichpi, the morning star, by standing in turn beside each of four sapling poles thrust into the earth at the directional points, north, south, east, and west. Decorative colored rags fluttered from each pole, their incessant rustling the only sound in the silence of dawn. The sacred pipe, *cannunpa wakan*, he kept with him every moment, just as Running Elk had directed. The colorfully decorated pipe had been filled with *cansasa*, a native tobacco made of redwood, and then sealed with tallow. It would protect him from evil as long as he held it.

Once his prayers were over, he returned to the pit, his energy all but depleted after three days of fasting. As he sat in the brisk morning air waiting for the vision Running Elk had assured him would come, he wondered what in the hell he was doing. The shaman had taken him to the sacred hill, instructed him in the digging of the pit, and said he would return in four days. During that time Kase was to stay in the pit and listen carefully to the birds and animals that would bring him messages.

The morning lengthened and the shadows shortened as the sun reached the midday sky. Kase decided he had no business sitting nearly naked in the middle of nowhere waiting for something that he only half believed would happen. For all he knew, the shaman's work was merely hocus-pocus. Caleb had taught him the rudimentary facts of Sioux religion and lore, but aside from having interesting discussions, they had never practiced any of the rituals. Now, instead of feeling enthusiasm for what the shaman predicted would happen to him, Kase only experienced doubt.

He did not belong here; that much had been evident from the beginning. Conditioned to ride for miles, not walk, he was exhausted after an hour of the slow, easy jog Running Elk had suggested he maintain as he accompanied the shaman, who rode on horseback, to the bluff. His feet, encased in low-cut moccasins, ached where they had become bruised. There was something to be said for a good pair of boots, especially when a man faced a long walk over rocky terrain. He was bone-tired, his calves and thigh muscles ached from the strain of overuse, and he was filthy with dust. No, he thought with a wry smile and a shake of his head, he did not belong here.

If the old man had not seemed so certain that a vision quest was the only way to settle his unanswered questions, Kase would have ended the farce after thirty minutes of running and returned to the settlement near the agency. But Running Elk's eyes had held such promise, his softly spoken instructions had been so firm with belief, that Kase agreed to try. The old man was certain a vision would come after he had fasted, prayed, waited in the pit, and opened his spirit to the knowledge that would surely come to him.

But so far he had heard nothing.

I'm too old for this. Youths go on vision quests. This, he decided, is a waste of time.

Cramped from sitting cross-legged, Kase stretched his legs out before him, lifted his face toward the sun, and sighed. Tomorrow, when Running Elk returned, he would tell the shaman that the quest had been a failure. He had wasted enough time and felt an overwhelming urge to return to Busted

Heel. He told himself it was because Zach needed to be relieved of his voluntary job as marshal, but he knew that was a lie. He thought of Rose Audi more with every passing day.

As the sun hovered above him, he tried to forget the hunger gnawing at his innards and wrestled with the question of Rose's place in his life. He picked up a small stone near his thigh and tossed it out over the precipice. At first she had infuriated him with her stubborn refusal to leave Busted Heel. But it was evident she wasn't going anywhere. Even he had to admit he admired her tenacity. She had managed to turn the dreary store her husband left behind into a growing business and at the same time befriended everyone she met. What would happen to those ties if he followed his own heart and asked her to share his future? Would people think less of her for loving a half-breed?

There were so many things in his heart he had never revealed to her—things she had tried to get him to speak of—and upon his return to town he intended to tell her about his past as well as the place she now held in his heart. He had never cared for a woman before the way he cared for Rose. With a shrug he admitted to himself that what he felt could very well be love. But if he loved her, should he subject her to the prejudice she would surely face if she shared his love and his life? He knew without a doubt that if any woman could face the challenge, it was Rose.

Quiet hours passed and the shadows began to lengthen as he wrestled with his thoughts. Kase heard a ground squirrel scuffling through the nearby brush in search of food for winter storage. It turned bright brown eyes his way and paused long enough to watch him for a moment before it hurried on without a word. He shook his head, closed his eyes, and let the last warm rays of the sun drive away the autumn chill. Was he losing his mind? He was actually listening for talking animals.

Before it became dark, he lay down again and covered himself with the thick buffalo robe the old man had given him. He found his body slowing down, conserving movement now that it found itself in a state of semistarvation. Kase stared into the darkness and welcomed the night; Running Elk would return at dawn.

Sleep finally came and then, uncertain of how much time had elapsed, a slight sound brought him upright and alert.

Suddenly wary, he was startled by the sight of an old man he had never seen before sitting near the pit.

Silver moonlight highlighted the man's wrinkled features. He wore his hair long, parted in the middle, and plaited into two braids that hung over his shoulders. The braids swayed slightly with his every breath. He was large and, unlike Running Elk, still well built and obviously well fed. He was Sioux, of that Kase was certain, for his coloring was as dark a bronze as any of the men he had met at Pine Ridge, and like many of them, he appeared to be tall. The man sat cross-legged, unafraid, waiting for Kase to speak.

There was something vaguely and oddly familiar about the man. Startled by the direction his thoughts had suddenly taken, Kase became wary and asked his strange visitor outright, "Are you Red Dog?"

The old man shook his head, and a crooked smile teased his full lips.

"No," he said softly. "I am not Red Dog. I am not your father."

"Who, then, are you?" Kase said, continuing in the language of the Sioux.

"Someone you should know well."

"I've never seen you before." Kase shook his head and stared into the man's clear eyes. In the darkness, he could not make out their color, but he could feel a sense of overwhelming tranquillity and love that emanated from them. "How did you get here?"

"I have come the same way as you."

"Why are you here?" He knew he should be uneasy, knew he should look for any companions the man might have, but for some inexplicable reason, Kase knew the old man meant him no harm.

"I have come to help you find the answers you seek."

"How? Did you know Red Dog?"

"No."

"Are you a friend of Caleb Storm?"

"No."

"Then how—"

"I know you. That is all you need to know. It is enough. Close your eyes, Kase Storm, and see what I already know."

Kase did as the old man bade and closed his eyes. Images

began to take shape in his mind's eye, scenes of times long past. He saw the old soddie where he had lived with his mother, watched himself as a small boy with raven-black hair and shining eyes as he climbed up on her lap and let her rock him to sleep. He could feel her love as she kissed the crown of his head and snuggled him close to her. The familiar loving sound of his mother singing an old Dutch lullaby seemed to float on the very air about him.

"I see myself as a child," he whispered to the old man.

"Now see what you have forgotten."

Kase studied the tranquil scene in the vision and watched his mother look up. At that very instant he could feel the love she felt for him reflected in her eyes. She had loved him above all else. Unconditionally. How he had been conceived mattered not one whit to her.

Scenes from the past began to flood upon him faster and faster. He saw himself—still a child—leading his grandfather by the hand around the yard outside their soddie. Opa laughed gaily at his antics and stooped to ruffle his hair. Caleb entered the dream scene and laughed, lifting Kase high in the air, tossing him about as he always had when he was a boy. Then Kase had suddenly grown a few years older and was seated in the kitchen of the Boston mansion with his Aunt Ruth, Caleb's stepmother. The scene was reminiscent of the quiet times and talks the two of them often shared. His sister, Annika, danced into his thoughts and began to follow a slightly older version of himself. He saw her clearly, as he never had before, with hero worship and love reflected in her eyes.

It went on and on. He saw himself in many stages of growth throughout his life, saw those around him, both at home and in Busted Heel, people who had been his teachers and his friends—and always he saw their innermost feelings reflected in their eyes. He saw none of the prejudice or injustice he had suffered as he returned through time to his school years. Instead he was shown memories of the teachers who had not let his mixed blood matter to them. One such man, Professor Daniel Exeter, he had long ago forgotten. The man had seen the potential in him and had worked with him long hours after class. He saw that his former employer, Franklin Rigby, had valued him for his own expertise and had not hired him because of Caleb's influence. Kase realized for the first time that if he had not let his defensive anger cloud his thinking he might have seen many things clearly.

He was shown scenes of his early years with Zach Elliot; the man had tutored him the way he would have taught his own son. And last he had a glimpse of Rose as she had appeared the night of Quentin's party, waiting for him to come to her, asking him to unburden his heart.

When the visions faded, he found himself alone with the old man, overwhelmed by the sense of peace and well-being brought on by all he had seen.

"What have you learned, now that you have seen your world through eyes of love and not anger?" The old man spoke softly, leading him like a child through his thoughts.

Frowning, Kase tried to put his feelings into words. "More important than seeing myself, I have seen the way others see me." He shrugged. "I have seen that it does not matter who or what my father was. My mother loved me without regret, as did all of my family."

"And the fear you have of your father's blood? The anger and hatred you have for those who mistreated you?"

"I am still uncertain. How do I know I will not become like him? How do I know I am not capable of the same crimes?"

"You are your own man, Kase Storm. Your life is your own. Go from this place and begin to look at the world through eyes of love, as you have just done. Let go of your hate. Be your own shaman and walk without fear."

The old man stared at Kase across the fire. Dizziness assailed Kase along with an eerie sinking sensation. The stranger's image began to waver in the moonlight, to expand and contract until it began to fade. As Kase watched in amazement, the old one's eyes became clearer. Kase held them in his gaze until they were all that was left of the image. Finally even the eerie sight of the man's glowing eyes disappeared.

Kase pulled the robe closer and tried to stop the shudders that rocked through him. He tried to understand the strange dream, if indeed it was a dream, that had seemed all too real. He could not stop thinking about the eyes of the mysterious old man. They were large, clear, and blue, as blue as the prairie skies on a summer day, the blue of the seas around Holland—as blue as his own.

Kase knew then, just as surely as he knew his own name, that he had just peered into his own soul.

The buffalo hide wrapped about his shoulder stank, but it did not matter; the end of his ordeal had come. Kase Storm broke the tallow seal on the sacred pipe and handed it to the shaman, who lit the pipe and drew deeply on it. He passed the pipe to Kase who was finally warm and feeling languid after time spent in the sweat lodge. His purification was the last step in the *hanbleceya*.

A low fire glowed directly beneath the smoke hole of Running Elk's tipi. The old man had insisted Kase relate his experience before they shared the pipe. Running Elk sat in silence until the tobacco was gone, then set the pipe on the blanket before him. Then the shaman spoke.

"What meaning does the vision hold for you?" he asked.

Kase shook his head and stared into the fire. "It might have been a vision," he said, still wondering what had happened out on the plain. "It was a dream unlike any other dream I've ever had."

"A dream. A vision. There is no difference."

Kase remembered how disturbed he had felt when the dream ended, for the color of the images he had seen had been so vibrant—the dream more real than life.

Running Elk leaned forward, his gaze intense, his eyes reflecting the shining embers of the fire as he interpreted the vision. "Red Dog was not in the dream. It was a dream about you and the ones who love you. He was not important enough for you to dream of. He gave you life. His blood is your blood, but what you are, what you have become, has nothing to do with him.

"He spilled his seed, nothing more. It was your mother, who, like the mother earth that nurtures every seed that falls onto her soil, nurtured you. It was she who gave you life. Just as your true father was not in your dreams, so he has never had a claim on your life. He only has the power over you that you give him. Your mother accepts you because you were a gift to her in a time of great need. Without you, her life would not have been complete. Your stepfather gave you the knowledge and the power you need to live in the white world. It was his purpose in life to find and raise you. But do not forget your

Sioux heritage. See your world as a place of love. Focus not on the hate that will always surround you. Accept it as part of your world, just as love is part of your world, for love and hate, like good and bad, are in balance. Do not cling to the shadows of the past."

The old man reached into a leather pouch at his waist. Sprinkling a handful of pungent herbs on the fire, he closed his eyes and began to chant softly as the fragrant scent of sage rose heavenward.

Kase closed his eyes and began to rock slowly back and forth, lulled by the rhythm of the ancient shaman's chant. He concentrated on the words repeated in lilting Sioux:

> *We are safe from harm.*
> *We are safe from harm.*
> *Dreamers who have dreamed.*
> *We are safe from harm.*

*

Chapter
Twelve

*

The golden glow from the hanging chandelier in the Ruffled Garter could not match the radiant gleam in Flossie Gibbs's eyes as she gazed at the crowd that had assembled at Paddie's to celebrate her birthday. Laughter and applause followed shouts of surprise as hoots and hollers fairly shook the walls of the saloon. Rosa joined in the celebration, clapping as wildly as the others, while Flossie beamed and preened, a riotous vision of flaming hennaed hair, chartreuse satin, and black lace.

"Thank you, one and all!" Floss yelled above the ruckus. With a flourish, Paddie handed her a tumbler full of his finest whiskey, and she held the glass aloft in a toast to the crowd. "I don't know how you all found out about my birthday"—her eyes sparkled with innocent mischief—"but damned if I'm not glad you did! Here's to me, here's to you, and here's to more birthdays!"

Despite Flossie's feigned surprise, Rosa knew that everyone in the room—aside from a few cowboys new to the surrounding ranches—had known for weeks about the birthday. The madam herself had let the "secret" slip at least once a day for the last three months.

The morning of the big event, as she had done in previous years, Flossie purposely kept herself occupied in her room while Chicago Sue, Mira, Felicity, and Satin oversaw preparations for the gala at Paddie's. Rosa volunteered to bake

Flossie's favorite birthday cake—chocolate with berry filling—when she learned about the annual celebration undertaken every October twenty-third. What amazed her the most was the expression of absolute astonishment Flossie enacted when she entered the saloon on Slick Knox's arm and found them all gathered and shouting "Surprise!"

The melodic notes Slick now milked out of the little-used piano standing against the far wall added a festive touch to the atmosphere, and moved by the contagious revelry, Rosa found herself enjoying everyone's antics. Flossie insisted there be games, and so, like obedient children, even the roughest cowhands lined up to bob for apples. Between the bobbing and the drinking, the cowhands became pleasantly tipsy, and Rosa, dressed once again in the rose-patterned skirt and jacket she had worn to the barbecue at Mountain Shadows, soon found herself the object of their more amorous attention. Firm but patient, Rosa brushed aside a squeeze here, a pinch there, and found herself grateful for Zach, who always seemed to be hovering somewhere nearby. His quelling one-eyed stare served her well that evening whenever any of the men became too forward.

Paddie put Rosa to work behind the bar after a brief discussion between him and Zach in which they determined it was the safest place for her. Sheltered by the stout barricade of the long bar, Rosa observed the goings on in relative safety. She could not help but admire the ease with which Flossie's girls handled the advances of the men. Where she had blushed and skirted shy of wandering hands, she noticed that even young Chicago Sue was adept at swatting the men playfully aside.

An hour or two into the party, Rosa studied Felicity as she openly flirted with a rugged, bowlegged cowboy. When the man leaned close and whispered in her ear, Felicity's black eyes flashed up at him in approval. Within minutes the couple stood and left the saloon. Rosa watched them walk in the direction of Flossie's and was torn between feelings of righteousness and envy. When she caught Zach Elliot watching her closely she busied herself with the task of arranging glasses on a shelf behind the bar and tried to dismiss the feeling that he knew good and well what she had been thinking.

It did not matter to her in the least that, aside from Flossie and the girls from the Hospitality Parlor, she was the only woman in the place. In the last few months Rosa had come to realize the particular place she held among the citizens of Busted Heel. As a widow, she was afforded far more freedom than an unmarried young woman would have had. As a single woman who had established a legitimate business, she was an oddity. But although she had befriended whore and housewife alike, Rosa had never given the upstanding citizens of the town—folks like the Wilkies, John Tuttle and his wife, and the Shaws who farmed nearby—reason to gossip.

Everyone knew Rosa slept alone on the cot in the kitchen of her restaurant; they had it straight from Zetta Davis, who made daily deliveries of eggs and vegetables to Alice and Ray Wilkie's store. Everyone knew, too, that if Alice ever heard any different, she would not hesitate to tell it. Above all, Rosa knew what having a good name in a small town meant. In that respect, Busted Heel was no different from Corio.

That was why she was appalled at what she caught herself thinking when Felicity walked out of the saloon on the arm of the smiling blond cowboy. She found herself wondering what they would do in Felicity's room, wondered if their exchange would compare at all to the brief but searing passion she had known the night Kase Storm caressed her in the moonlight. Would the cowboy's hands be as gentle or as sure? Would he elicit the same response from Felicity as Kase had from her when his lips touched her breasts? Or would the exchange be as tepid as those she had experienced with Giovanni?

She jumped when Paddie interrupted her wayward thoughts. "Like a glass of wine, Rosa?" Without waiting for her reply, he reached down behind the bar and drew forth a bottle of ruby red cabernet he saved for special occasions.

"*Grazie, signore.*" She raised her glass with a smile. It was a night to celebrate. Time to put her curious thoughts aside.

"It's time to cut the cake, Rosa!" Flossie called out from across the room. Her cheeks were stained a bright red that clashed with her chartreuse gown, but her excitement did not deter her from orchestrating her own party. "Everybody start singin'!"

The wind was howling off the Laramies and beating its way across the open range by the time Kase rode back into Busted

Heel. He made straight for Rose's, ready for a hot meal, a glass
of wine, and a good look at the woman whose image had
dogged his trail for the last hundred miles.

Happier than he had felt in months, ready to face one day at
a time, he rode head down, collar up against the increasing
onslaught of the wind. He passed the depot and, out of habit,
drew close enough to see that the station house was locked up
tight for the night. The train would not come through again
until eight-ten in the morning. With some surprise, he noticed
how good it felt to look down the wide, empty expanse of Main
Street. An inordinate number of horses were tied to the
hitching rails along the Ruffled Garter side of the street. The
animals crowded together as they sought shelter from the wind.
Light from the saloon spilled out into the night. The sound of
singing filled the air, and beneath the caterwauling he could
detect the tinny notes of the piano that was generally ignored
by Paddie's patrons. He wondered what was going on, but
decided he could wait to find out. Let Zach have one more
night on duty. Tonight was his.

It was not until he neared the end of the street that Kase
noticed that the restaurant was dark. By his reckoning—his
heirloom watch had long since stopped, and he had yet to reset
it—it was barely after eight o'clock. Even if her trade for the
evening had been light, she would certainly still be cleaning
up. He knew her routine by heart, for even though he had failed
to eat at the restaurant more than once, he had spent plenty of
nights walking by, watching, checking to be sure she was safe.

Kase began to wonder if Zach had taken the time to do the
same. He had asked the old man specifically to see to Rose's
safety while he was away, but suppose Zach had been lax in his
duty? As he nudged Sinbad to a faster pace, he hesitated to
think of what could have happened to Rose in his absence.

What if she had taken his advice and left town?

By the time he reached the front of her place and dismounted, by the time he knotted his reins about the hitching
post, the uncertainty that gnawed at his gut was all too real. He
tried to ignore the foot-stomping and whistling next door as he
leaned forward, cupped his hands around his eyes, and pressed
his nose against the wide glass window of the restaurant. The
darkened interior revealed the ghostly shapes of cloth-draped

tables and empty chairs. There was no light shining in the kitchen, not even the soft glow of a single oil lamp.

His heart pounded as anger and a feeling he refused to recognize as fear welled up inside him. He tried to remind himself of his vision and remain calm, tried to stem the tide of frustration he was feeling. In seconds he was off the walk and moving around to the back of the café.

A shoat squealed in fright and Kase cursed aloud as he tripped over it in the pitch darkness. One of Decatur Davis's hounds howled out a brief warning, but there was no sign of movement inside the ramshackle cabin behind the restaurant.

When he finally reached the back door to Rose's place, Kase did not hesitate long enough to knock. He tried the knob, and the door slowly swung open. He stepped on the crooked wooden stoop and then into the dark kitchen. Unerringly, he crossed to the stove and felt along the wall until he touched the match holder hanging nearby. The flame flared and the acrid smell of sulfur singed the air. He held the match aloft long enough to swing his gaze about the room. Fresh loaves of bread lined the worktable. Her familiar white apron and other articles of clothing hung neatly on the nails above the cot. Rose's trunk still stood in the far corner of the tidy room. Kase felt the knot around his heart ease as he took in the visible signs that she had not left town.

The match burned down and singed his fingertips, but he barely felt the pain as an overwhelming sense of relief flooded through him. Shrouded in darkness, surrounded by the pleasant, homey scent of fresh bread and vanilla, he inhaled deeply and realized that had he relied on his sense of smell alone, he would have known immediately that Rose was still in Busted Heel. When his stomach growled, he made his way through the darkness to the worktable and picked up a loaf of bread. He tore the crusty heel off one end and took a bite.

With the bread in one hand, he pulled up his coat collar and stepped back out into the windy night. Rather than traipse around in the dark behind the buildings, he walked back to the boardwalk and headed next door to Paddie's. From the sound of it, every single man within riding distance was celebrating inside. If Zach Elliot was doing his duty, he would be there, too. And he had damned well better know where Rose was, Kase thought.

The raucous singing had calmed to boisterous catcalls and whistles, the off-key piano notes still drifted above the noise. He stepped inside the swinging doors and let his gaze move over the revelers. The chocolate cake crumbs on empty plates scattered about the tables instantly reminded him that it was Flossie's birthday. She had hinted of the event often enough before he left town.

In the far corner near the piano, Satin stood on a table surrounded by hooting cowhands. Slowly, surely, inch by deliberate inch, she raised the flounced hem of her gown until it revealed her plump, dimpled knee. Cheers shook the rafters as shouts of encouragement filled the air. Flossie and Zach sat at a nearby table, engaged in deep conversation. Kase knew he would have to warn the usually wary Zach against sitting with his back to the door of the saloon while he was acting lawman.

Mira had not noticed his entrance yet, nor had Chicago Sue. He was thankful that both had their hands full of amorous men contending for favors. Paddie, as usual, was cleaning up the place; he hurried about collecting empty plates and glasses.

Out of habit, Kase swung his gaze to the bar and was suddenly arrested by the sight of Rose standing motionless, poised with a dish towel and a glass in her hands. She was staring at him.

As he crossed the room, his eyes never once left her face. No one as yet had noticed his entrance, but in his mind, the cacophony in the room seemed to have decreased to a distant roar. He stopped, unable to get any closer because of the bar that separated them, but continued to hold her gaze with his.

His voice was low, yet the words reached her easily. "I didn't know where you were."

"I am here. For the surprise." She continued to stare up at him, her strange golden-brown eyes aglow with unusual brightness. "I did not know where *you* were."

"You might say I was lost," he said. When he saw her look of concern, he amended his statement. "Not really. At least, not anymore."

Rosa silently regretted the polished width of mahogany that separated them. She had an overwhelming urge to reach out and touch Kase Storm, just to be certain that she was not dreaming. She glanced over at Paddie and found him suddenly preoccupied with lining up the already perfectly straight whiskey bottles along the back shelf. When she caught him staring in the mirror over the bar, he quickly looked away.

She set down the glass and dish towel. Her fingers trembling, Rosa untied the towel she had wrapped about her waist and unconsciously folded the white cotton material before she laid it on the bar. The shouts and cheers died down after Satin finally displayed not only her knees but also ample thighs adorned with scarlet garters. Slick Knox toned down the keyboard melody until the slow, lilting strains of a waltz filled the air. The group around Satin disbanded, and as a few of the men began to shuffle toward the bar, Kase reached across it to take Rosa's hand.

Astounded by the happiness she experienced at just the sight of him, but powerless to speak, Rosa merely stared. She had been aware of his presence since the moment he pushed through the doors and walked into the crowded room. It had taken her a moment to be sure, but when Kase stood and took in the crowd, Rosa was certain it was him. She drank in the sight of him; he was taller, more vibrant, and definitely more powerful than any other man in the room.

Seeing him again moved her in ways she'd never expected. Elation, curiosity, and most surprising, a longing warmth suffused her, swept through her, and left her nearly breathless at the sight of him. As she stared up at Kase she realized that, for the first time, there was not even a hint of hostility in his eyes.

"May I have this dance?" he asked.

She looked around and noticed that no one else was dancing. She looked back at Kase; he was waiting patiently for her answer. Her mouth gone suddenly dry, she licked her lips and placed her fingertips against his palm. He held her hand high as they walked the length of the bar, he on one side, she on the other, until they reached the end and Rosa stepped into his arms.

The brisk chill carried on the night wind still claimed his dark skin. She felt the winter's cold on his fingertips and knew his cheeks would feel the same. He was still bundled inside a heavy coat he had buttoned to the neck. His collar stood high, drawn up for protection against the wind. As they moved through the first tentative steps together, she reached up to fold back his coat collar and let her fingers brush his cheek. As she had expected, his skin was smooth and cool to the touch. Still shadowed by his hat, his deep blue eyes were dark, but not fathomless. They seemed to mirror everything she was feeling.

Rosa felt her heart take wing and soar.

Go slowly, go softly, she warned herself, unavoidably thinking of all that had transpired the last time they had danced together. She could feel his open palm where it rested against the small of her back, felt the pressure of it increase until he held her so close the bodice of her jacket pressed against his coat.

Mesmerized, she could not take her eyes from his face and so she indulged herself with the sight of him. She took her lead from his actions, and when his gaze dropped to her lips, she concentrated on his. She was rewarded by the appearance of the slow, endearing half-smile she had come to know. As they moved through the steps of the waltz, totally unaware of the others around them, they became the focus of the attention of everyone in the room.

A cowboy near the bar broke the spell when, in a voice loud enough for everyone to hear, he asked, "Hey, Marshal, how come you get to dance with Miss Rosa and we don't?"

Simultaneously, Satin called his name as Chicago Sue squealed "Kase is home!" from her perch on a cowhand's knee. She quickly disengaged herself and flew across the room to his side as Satin hurried away from her own bevy of admirers.

Flossie, having downed one drink too many, slapped her palms on the top of the table and levered herself to a standing position. Surprised by Kase's sudden appearance, Zach stood and then stepped aside to allow Flossie to pass by—not out of any gentlemanly habit but out of fear that she might mow him down in her haste to reach Kase.

Rosa stepped aside as the three women surrounded him much like a mother hen and her brood, all clucking and chirping.

"What're you doin' all bundled up, boy?" Flossie asked, weaving precariously. "Didn't pay you any mind when you walked in. Thought you were just another cowboy come to m' party!"

Reluctantly, Kase glanced over their heads at Rosa and shrugged. When she watched him greet an overexuberant

Chicago Sue with a quick kiss, she controlled a wave of jealousy by reminding herself of Flossie's words: *He hasn't been with any of my girls since you showed up*.

When Mira slowly, provocatively made her way toward Kase with a smooth, calculated smile on her lips, Rosa could not bear to watch. Instead, she rejoined Paddie behind the bar. Her glorious reunion with Kase was over. The women led Kase back to Flossie's table where he took a seat facing her. Rosa kept her trembling hands occupied as she dried a few more glasses and lined them up on a shelf behind the bar. When she allowed herself a glance in his direction, Kase caught her eye across the room. With a nod, he indicated that she should join him. Before she left the bar, she cut a large portion of cake and asked Paddie for two more glasses of wine.

Rosa worked her way through the crowded room until she stood behind Kase, then leaned over his shoulder and placed the cake and a glass of wine before him. She stepped back and stood on the fringe of the circle that surrounded him.

Kase reached back around and grabbed her wrist. "Sit by me." His tone was sure without being commanding.

Zach stood, intending to give up his chair. Rosa motioned him down. "I will stay here," she said, content to stand behind Kase's right shoulder, near enough to reach out and touch him if she wished, far enough away to maintain some vestige of composure. From her vantage point Rosa could watch the expression of everyone assembled about the table. Flossie sat listening to Kase with a glazed but happy look in her eyes. Chicago Sue was once again giggling with her cowboy while Satin sat perched on the edge of her chair as if she was ready to jump in Kase's lap at any given moment. Kase ignored Satin as he asked Zach and Flossie for news. A feeling of unease settled over Rosa. She looked over at Mira and found the brunette glaring openly in her direction.

Rosa squared her shoulders and held her ground. Let the woman glare. It was she, Rosa, whom Kase had asked to join him.

"Anything happen I should know about?" Kase asked Zach.

"Nothin', just the usual, except for one thing—"

Quickly Rosa caught Zach's eye and shook her head. She did not want Kase to know about the men who had been rude to her in the restaurant; the incident had passed without mishap. She did not wish to call attention to the confrontation again. It would only give Kase an excuse to say "I told you so."

"Nothin' that I need to tell you about tonight."

Thankful for his silence, Rosa smiled down at Zach.

"Kase, you're back!" The interruption came from Felicity this time, her male companion all but forgotten when she reentered the saloon and spied Kase. If anything had transpired in her room at the bordello, the effects of the exchange were not evident, for not even a lock of her intricate hairstyle was out of place. High color spotted the girl's usually ivory skin and she appeared unruffled as she brushed past Rosa to give Kase a welcoming hug and a kiss on the cheek.

Glancing across the room, Rosa caught her own reflection in the mirror behind the bar. She had done nothing boisterous to warrant it, but her hair, coiled in a loose bun atop her head, had slipped off center. As she looked at Mira again, she felt like a farm girl playing at sophistication while the other girls were as bright and shining as a handful of new coins. Surreptitiously she studied each girl in turn: Mira, with her riotous head of curling brunette hair and snapping green eyes; Felicity, a woman of contrast with her ivory skin and short, waving blue-black tresses; Satin, who might have been a ruddy-cheeked peasant with her round cheeks and equally round blue eyes; and finally, Chicago Sue, still so young with her frizzy mane of white-blond hair and well-rouged cheeks.

None of them wore their hair as long as she did; Rosa had never cut hers in her life. Perhaps, she thought, she should see about trimming it, at least to her shoulders. After all, she was not a farm girl anymore. Beside the others, Rosa felt like a *lavandaia,* a washerwoman, a drudge. The fact that Kase had singled her out first when he walked into the saloon, that he had asked her to stay by his side, did little to erase the knowledge that he had known most, if not all, of the other women intimately. He had put his hands on them, perhaps even made them moan with delight the way he had her.

Jealousy claimed her again. She lifted her glass and drank half of the ruby wine. Despite Quentin's warnings, it seemed Flossie's girls had no reservations about Kase's mixed blood. Mira's fiery glances made her desires all too clear. Rosa knew that if she wanted to experience Kase Storm's affectionate embrace, the heated kisses he so expertly gave her the night of the barbecue, she would have to make her wishes known. She finished the wine and poured herself another glass.

Slick began to play again, softly this time, and Kase dismissed all their questions regarding his absence with a smile and a brief "I went hunting." Slowly the group disbanded and the girls began moving among the men, encouraging them to buy more of Paddie's liquor, singling out those they would entertain personally. When Satin gave up her chair beside Kase, Rosa slid into it. He turned to her with his slight smile and reached for her hand beneath the table. A warm current of excitement moved through her and she dropped her gaze.

"Did you find what you were huntin' for?" Zach leaned close, a knowing look in his eyes.

Kase smiled. "I think so."

"I'd say that's cause for another drink."

Paddie, who was at Zach's elbow, acknowledged the deputy's words and brought back more whiskey along with a bottle of wine. He filled their glasses and left the bottle.

"I 'spect, then, everythin's pretty well settled in your mind?" Zach asked, tossing back the whiskey and wiping his mouth on the back of his hand.

Kase glanced at Rose before he answered. "A lot of things."

"Glad to hear it," Zach said, his attention drawn to Flossie, who stood long enough to yell "Drinks on the house!" before she sank none too gracefully back into her chair and nearly tipped over backward. Zach bit his cheeks to hide his smile.

Kase turned to his mentor and friend once more. "Zach, I left Sinbad in front of the café. Do you think—"

Without waiting for Kase to finish his request, Zach got to his feet. "I'll take care of him," he said. Within moments he left the saloon.

Kase drained his second glass of wine and noticed Rose had already done the same. Knowing how the least bit of alcohol affected him, he decided he'd had enough, but he refilled Rose's glass again. They sat in silence for a time as she sipped her wine. Then he leaned close and whispered, "We need to talk. Alone."

"We can go to the restaurant. You are hungry?" Mentally she went over the list of foodstuffs she had on hand and what she could cook for him should he require dinner.

He shook his head. "No, after the cake and wine, I'm not that hungry."

He thought of her cold, dark kitchen with its austere narrow cot. The place might still hold too many memories of her husband. They definitely could not go to the restaurant.

As if she sensed his hesitation, Rose whispered, "We can go to your room. Is all right?"

Quickly he took in the crowd and noticed with relief that all the girls were still in the saloon. Flossie sagged forward with her nose on the table, alternately hiccuping and sipping from the watered-down whiskey in her glass. Kase suspected that Paddie had taken to lightening her drinks for the last hour or so, but the measure seemed to have come too late to stave off the effects of the alcohol. No one was paying them any mind, and there would be no one at the Hospitality Parlor to see them enter. He would make damn sure no one saw Rose leave.

"Let's go, then." He let go of her hand and stood, then stepped aside to let her precede him. As an afterthought, Kase reached back and grabbed the wine. Just before they passed through the swinging doors, he stopped her. "Do you have a coat?"

"*Sì*. In the café." It had been warmer when she walked over, the wind not yet whipped to a frenzy.

He slipped out of his thick jacket and draped it across her shoulders, then drew it tight, bunching the heavy wool in his hands. Using the grip he held on the coat, he pulled her close and bent forward, intent upon kissing her. A loud guffaw from the back of the room instantly reminded Kase of where they were. He straightened and turned her to face the doors.

With one hand riding at the small of her back, he led her outside.

Rosa shivered in anticipation as much as from the cold blast of air that whipped some of the pins from her hair. The heavy mass began to slide even farther off the crown of her head.

"The wind!" she groaned aloud without thinking.

His blood was running so hot that he could not feel the effects of the chilling wind. In one fluid movement, he scooped her up into his arms and held her against his chest until they reached the building next door. Handing her the bottle, Kase shifted her weight and turned the knob with his free hand. Kicking the door closed behind him, he crossed the parlor, passed through a doorway hung with swagged red velvet drapes dripping with tassels, and mounted the stairs to the second floor.

Rosa clung, wordless, with her arms about his neck. All of her senses were attuned to him. She heard the soft tread of his boots on the carpet runner, felt him shift his weight for balance as he reached the top of the stairs, and smelled wood smoke mingled with the scent of sage upon his skin. She held on tighter.

Kase quickly made his way along the dimly lit hallway and wondered if the woman in his arms was as totally absorbed in him as he was in her.

He carried her down the hall past evenly spaced doors that lined the hallway. Each one sported a small sign embellished with gilded scrollwork that spelled out the name of the girl who occupied the room. When they reached a door marked Private, Kase halted and fumbled in his pocket for a key.

"You can put me down," she said, her voice wavering.

"Not on your life." The key slipped into his fingers and then just as easily slid into the lock. Once more Kase kicked a door closed behind them, but this time he turned and locked it. Only then, cloaked in darkness, did he set Rosa on her feet.

It was pitch black in the room. Rosa stood still and listened to the sounds he made as he lit a lamp. The flame flared, and as Kase replaced the red glass globe, the room was bathed in a muted rose glow. Crystal teardrops hung from the globe and chimed together with a soft tinkling sound as he reached beneath them to turn the knob that raised the lamp wick.

As Rosa stood in the center of the room, still clutching his coat and the wine, Kase took off his hat and hung it on the bedpost. Unbuckling his gun belt, he slung it across the back of a chair near the door, then turned to see how Rosa fared. She was looking around in awe, her gaze taking in every facet of his room. He had always found it cheap and gaudy. Living in a whorehouse did have its drawbacks.

"Flossie decorated it," he said in explanation.

Rosa stared around the room. It was more elaborate than any place she had ever seen. Crystal teardrops dangled from every lamp globe. A fringed paisley shawl was draped over the top of his bureau; another was swagged from the dressing screen in the corner. Thick tasseled curtains of crimson velvet hung over the windows. She did not have to look down to be aware of the equally plush carpet beneath her feet. Ornate flocked wall covering, in the same pattern that adorned the parlor downstairs, was repeated in the room.

When she finally allowed herself a glance at the tall bed near the windows, Rosa could not help but stare. It was covered with a spread of ruby satin that was trimmed with a darker burgundy lace. A dozen pillows, also swathed in satin and lace, were piled against the carved headboard.

"Listen, I know it's pretty awful. I— We can go to your place . . ."

She turned to him again. "It is beautiful."

If her tone had not been one of undisguised wonder, he might have laughed. Instead, he considered the room from her point of view—that of a young woman from a small village somewhere in Italy. Perhaps to her the room *was* beautiful. He had never thought of the place as anything but brassy and overwhelming. But tonight, with Rose standing as innocent as a Madonna in the middle of it all, the room did take on a certain luster he had never noticed before.

An awkward moment stretched between them until, driven by the lack of any better idea of where to begin, he crossed the room and took the wine from her, set it on a bedside table, and then pulled her toward him.

She continued to clutch the jacket closed. Gently he eased it from her shoulders and tossed it on the chair.

"Still cold?" he asked.

She shook her head.

"I want to tell you where I've been, to explain . . ." He felt awkward, tongue-tied in a way he had never been with a woman.

Lulled by the wine, her senses attuned to the man standing tall and proud before her, Rosa realized Kase was about to open his heart to her. Wherever he had gone, whatever he had experienced, had changed him. She could see that much in his eyes.

"Make love to me," she said.

He wondered if she knew what she was doing to him. He clasped her to him, held her so close he thought he would die from the need that surged through him, hardening him more

than he had already hardened, making him ache to take her
without preamble.

"Are you sure, Rose?" He held her face between his palms
and searched her eyes.

"Yes. I am sure."

"There are things you haven't considered. Things you still
don't know."

"There is no need. I know my heart."

"Rose, I want you more than you'll ever know."

"Show me."

"But—"

Stubbornly she pulled away. "Then I will go."

He knew he should let her walk away. His newfound peace
of mind was all too fresh, too fragile to gamble against Rose's
trust. What if he was not able to keep his temper at bay?
Besides, the fact remained that he was still a half-breed. Kase
told himself that for her own good he should let her go, even
if she went in anger. He held himself back and watched her
cross the room, determined not to call her back. But when she
paused at the door and turned to him with tears in her eyes, his
heart melted and he was lost.

"Aw, Rose." In two strides he crossed the room and swept
her back into his arms.

He covered her lips with his. Unwilling to wait to invade
some part of her, Kase thrust his tongue into her mouth, where
it met and sparred against her own. When Rose moaned low in
her throat and clung to him, he knew a feeling of release.
Everything suddenly seemed right with himself and the world.
For tonight, with his Rose in his arms, Kase Storm had finally
found a place where he belonged.

Slowly, the kiss ended, but the maddening longing lingered.
He reached up and imprisoned her face between his hands
again.

"I have no flowers," he whispered. "And I have not met
your family, but if it's what you want, I intend to make love to
you, Rose Audi. And I intend to do it tonight."

He pulled out what remained of the pins in her hair and
carelessly tossed them aside, then ran his splayed fingers
through the long, silken length of the rippling midnight skeins
until it fell around her hips.

"I love your hair," he whispered against her ear as he

continued to gently finger-comb handfuls and watch it fall back into place.

All her notions of cutting it fled.

He reached for the top button on her jacket and she held her breath. As he worked it free, he said softly, "You do what I do."

She reached for the button that held his shirt collar closed. When his collar was free of the shirt, she dropped it to the floor, just as he had her pins.

He unfastened the row of buttons along the bodice of her two-piece dress.

She unfastened his shirtfront.

When he drew her blouse open and began to slip it from her shoulders, she suddenly looked up, her expression one of bewilderment.

"You are not going to put out the light?" she asked.

"No," he said. "I'm not."

Chapter
Thirteen

✳

"No?" Her eyes widened in astonishment.

Kase shook his head. "No," he whispered.

Her jacket fell to the floor with a hush of sound when he slid it off her shoulders. Her skin was bathed in the luminous roseate glow, her camisole stained pink in the pastel light.

Suddenly embarrassed, Rosa felt exposed, as indeed she was, to his raw gaze. Kase took full advantage of that exposure. She did not know how to react; Giovanni never had suggested that she undress before him. She had always changed first and then climbed into bed, well hidden from neck to ankle by one of her voluminous white nightgowns. Their lovemaking, an awkward, fumbling affair carried on beneath blankets and nightclothes, had always taken place in the dark.

Somehow she knew instinctively that tonight would be different. Still, she wished Kase would take her in his arms rather than leave her standing so vulnerably exposed. She peered up at him from beneath lowered lashes and found him smiling his tantalizing half-smile. Her embarrassment forgotten, she knew then that she would do anything he asked.

His warm breath grazed her cheek as he bent to whisper in her ear. "It's your turn now."

Rosa stared at his unbuttoned shirtfront and the inviting slash of dark, satin-smooth skin that showed behind the gaping linen. Entranced by the mystery of all that was not yet exposed to her view, she gathered her courage and reached out impulsively, grabbed the sides of his shirt, and yanked the linen out of his waistband.

His smile widened.

Inspired by his reaction to her forwardness, Rosa stretched upward and tried to push the shirt off of his shoulders. He helped by shrugging himself free. The shirt fell to the floor.

Rosa smiled in triumph. It was his turn.

He reached around behind her and fought to release the stubborn hooks and eyes that held her waistband closed. She assisted by taking a step toward him, but discovered the move only placed her a breath away from his broad, smooth-skinned chest. She watched his breast rise and fall with each breath, felt the magnetic heat that radiated from him. Nothing in the world could have kept her from pressing her lips to the place where his heart was pounding as wildly as her own.

The hook and eye finally gave. Rosa felt the waistband sag before it draped her hips. Kase slipped his thumbs inside the skirt and pushed the fabric past her hips to the floor. She stood in a puddle of rose-patterned wool.

He took her hand like a courtier, and she stepped out of her skirt like a queen. Kase led her to the bed. The mound of lace and fringe-edged pillows lay scattered about the bed; he swept them out of the way with a wave of his arm. Then, before he directed her to sit, he tossed back the satin spread.

Rosa sat on the edge of the bed, and Kase knelt before her, his capable hands working the buttons of her shoes free. He threw the shoes aside, then rolled down her ribbed woolen stockings. A frown creased his brow, and he looked up at her questioningly.

"Have you ever had a pair of silk stockings?" He thought of his sister, who had probably not worn wool stockings since she was eleven. Caleb always teased Annika that she must have been appointed to the post of national clothes collector without the family's knowledge. Her room was usually cluttered with petticoats and shoes, hats, and all manner of women's gee-gaws. Now that he thought of it, he'd seen more than one pair of expensive embroidered stockings hanging from her bureau drawer.

Rosa shook her head, worried that she had somehow proved unworthy.

Kase made a mental note to ask his mother to send him a few

pairs of stylish silk stockings when he wrote to her tomorrow. He noticed Rosa's apprehensive expression. "Would you like some wine?" he asked.

The wine she had already consumed had warmed her, made her feel more relaxed than she ever imagined she could under the circumstances. Though she was far from intoxicated, Rosa knew the wine was helping her ease into this new experience of sitting half naked with her dark-skinned Gypsy kneeling at her feet. She visibly started when he reached beneath her petticoat and rested his heated palms against her thighs.

"No, *grazie*, no wine." She was barely able to speak.

Kase stared up at her, took in the sight of her hair falling about her shoulders, saw it piled up about her hips, midnight black against the sheets. Her eyes were round with anticipation and wonder; her lips, already swollen from his kisses, appeared moist and inviting.

He slid his hands higher, reveling in the feel of her silken thighs. Leaning forward, he pressed his upper body against her knees and slowly slid his hands up to her hips. He reached for the waistband of her petticoat. The bow that held the under-garment closed slipped open easily. He hooked his thumbs into her petticoat and pantalets. When he tried to remove them, she balked.

Rosa leaned forward and cupped his face in her hands. She kissed him gently, her hair falling forward to tease him where it grazed his bare chest. She whispered against his lips. "Please. I cannot. Not with the light." She held her breath, hoping he would not be angered by her request.

"The lamp stays on, but I'm going to try to stand up"—he gave her a wry smile—"and I'm going to pour two glasses of wine. Then I'm going to get out of these pants and join you. If you hurry, you should have just enough time to get all that off"—he pointed to her underclothes—"and get under the sheet before I get back."

He was up and moving before she translated all he had said. When understanding dawned, Rosa stood and scrambled to the other side of the bed hoping it might afford her some modesty. She shucked off her pantalets and petticoat, then slid beneath the sheet. The camisole was still on when he crossed the room, stark naked, a wineglass in either hand.

Rosa stared at him, at the lean, long look of him in his

nudity, at the unleashed strength in his torso and his erection. Then she looked at the fragile wineglasses in his hands and started to giggle.

"Thanks." He feigned a frown. "What's so funny?"

She took the glass he offered. "I am thinking, such a very interesting waiter you would make at Rosa's in that . . . that . . ."

"Getup?"

"*Sì.*"

He slid beneath the sheet and used two pillows to prop himself up against the headboard. "A toast," he said, raising his glass high, "to beginnings."

"*Salute.*"

Kase drained his wine and set the glass aside.

"That is not the way one should drink fine wine."

He noted her slightly trembling hand. "That's the way you had better drink it or you'll end up wearing it." As he leaned toward her, the bed dipped with his weight.

Rosa took a sip, then another, but found her fingers trembling so that she could not drink any more. As it was, ruby drops of cabernet stained her camisole and ran slowly down her breast.

Kase took her glass and turned away long enough to place it beside his own. Then he stretched across the bed and leaned over to slide his tongue down the slick trail of wine on her breast until the camisole prevented further exploration.

"I thought you were going to undress."

"I did—most."

"Oh, now I have to do the rest?"

"Sho' nuf." There was a hint of mischief in her eyes.

The hearty sound of his laughter filled the room and Rosa's heart swelled. She had made him laugh at last.

His laughter subsided, but a smile played about his lips. "Easy enough," he obliged as he slipped the straps down her arms.

"That's not the way."

"No?"

"No. Over the head. Up."

He sighed. When she raised her arms willingly, he grabbed the hem of the camisole and drew it off. With a flick of his wrist the cotton top went flying.

He drew the sheet back exposing the full lushness of her breasts. Before she could protest, Kase traced one of her peaked nipples with his tongue, then drew it between his teeth and tenderly toyed with the ripened bud until Rosa began to writhe in passionate agony. As his own excitement steadily increased, he ministered to the other dusky brown peak. Breathless, she clung to him, dazed by the sensations he plumbed from a wellspring deep within her. Consumed by overwhelming need, Rosa held him close, afraid to move lest he stop.

Their limbs entwined. Kase pinned her beneath his heavier frame as she undulated against him and sought release from the pent-up desire that threatened to explode at any moment. He knew he would have to move slowly for her sake as well as his own lest he bring them both to the brink of completion too quickly. Trying to ignore the aching pressure in his loins, he pulled away and gazed down at the woman in his arms. Her cheeks were flushed, her eyes dazed, her lips parted.

"Please . . ." she implored in a whisper.

His lips plundered hers, his tongue searched and demanded as it heightened their mutual pleasure. His hand slipped over the indentation of her waist, the lush curve of her hip. He brushed the silken nest at the apex of her thighs and then, without hesitation, his fingers found the enticingly moist entrance hidden there.

Instinctively, she raised her hips at his touch. As he delved deeper, as he ministered to her with sure, quick strokes, Rosa shuddered, clasped him tighter, and strained against him. His hands were magic, confident, and expert. Her every thought became focused on the man who plied her with such care, such finesse. His tongue circled slowly, tantalizing her own as his fingers duplicated the movement inside her. Soon her hips were sensuously imitating the same motions.

A sound was torn from her throat; a low, agonized moan that gave voice to the intense fire he had stoked inside her. As he muttered encouragement against her lips, his breath was hot and sweetly scented with wine. Rosa was lost in a world of sensation, a world scented with sage, wood smoke, and the maleness of him. She tasted the salt on his skin and the wine on his lips that mingled with the essence that was Kase alone.

His skin was hot, moist with a sheen of perspiration. His hair fell forward with a feather-light caress to tease her cheek.

He continued to urge her to the brink of climax with his hand until he knew she was on the verge of release; then he pulled away and tried to still his own labored breathing. The sound of laughter echoed hollowly through the hallway outside, but Rosa was oblivious to the intrusion. Kase drew her into his arms and held her close as she continued to undulate against his hips with slow, rhythmic movements.

Raising himself on an elbow, Kase stared down at Rosa, gauged the hunger he saw reflected in her eyes, and knew that he could not wait any longer to give her what they both craved. He reached out and his hand came in contact with one of the satin pillows shoved against the headboard. He pulled it close, then, slipping one hand beneath her, silently urged her to raise her hips.

Consumed with want, Rosa complied, and Kase deftly slid the pillow beneath her. Positioned thus, her hips tilted to receive him, her heart beating with anticipation that only intensified with each passing second, Rosa held her breath.

He slid his hand along her thigh, gave her a silent signal that begged admittance, and she complied by spreading her legs to accommodate him. Gently, careful to keep his heavier weight from taxing her too greatly, Kase moved over her until he rested between her thighs.

She was grateful that he had insisted the lamp remain lit, for the lamplight enabled her to see the desire mirrored in his deep blue eyes. He smiled his slow, easy smile, then dipped his head to tug once more at her nipples before he groaned aloud. It was a rough sound, a totally male sound that made Rosa instantly aware of the power he held leashed inside.

Then suddenly he pressed the tip of his heated shaft to the entrance of her womanhood. There was no hesitant searching, no wavering indecisiveness. As Kase buried himself within her, the angle of her hips allowed him full access to her heated depths. Slowly, surely, he began to plunge and withdraw until Rosa cried out, not in pain, but in joy, until she was convulsed with waves of passion that only intensified until Kase clasped her to him. He cried out hoarsely as his own passion culminated in release.

As her climax radiated upward and outward in ever-

widening circles of sensation, as she felt him spew his seed
deep inside her, Rosa realized a fulfillment she had never
experienced with Giovanni, one she never even knew was
possible. Shaken by her response to Kase, she closed her mind
to such haunting thoughts and reveled in the moment.

Sweat-sheened and slippery, they lay replete in each other's
arms as the violence of their passion quieted to a joyous
blending of heartbeats. Kase gently eased the pillow from
beneath her hips as he rolled to his back, pulling her against his
side. Despite the heat that emanated from him, Rosa snuggled
beside Kase and rested her cheek against his collarbone. She
kissed the hollow of his throat and let her fingers trail over the
hard plane of his well-defined chest, then spread her palm over
his lower abdomen.

He pulled the sheet over them both and lay content, stared up
at the ceiling, and rested his cheek against her hair.

A door slammed somewhere down the hall, followed by the
echo of booted feet pounding down the stairs. One of the girls
giggled; it sounded like Satin. Within a few moments, another
moaned. It could have been any one of them.

Rosa shifted slightly and Kase glanced down at her. She had
covered her eyes with her hand.

"What are you thinking?" Kase whispered, hoping she was
not suddenly experiencing regret.

Her tone was hesitant. Unsure. "I try not to think."

Rosa reached for Kase and laid her palm against his smooth
chest. His skin was hot, his heartbeat slowing to a more even
tempo. She tried to banish the sinful admission that plagued
her. In the few weeks time she had lived with Giovanni, their
lovemaking had never brought her close to the complete
satisfaction and fulfillment she had just experienced in Kase
Storm's arms.

She had been Giovanni's spouse. His wife before God and
man. Now she had to face what her lustful need for Kase Storm
had led her to become. His lover. His whore. Moments ago she
had been so hungry for his touch that she had begged him to
make love to her.

Would he have taken her had she not asked him? He had
only invited her to talk, to hear him out. She had suggested he
bring her here. She wanted to cover her face in shame and
weep when she realized that in her eagerness to have him she

had not even let him speak. She knew him no better than she had before they had made love; but she knew for certain that he had the ability to carry her to heights undreamed of—to touch her very soul in ways she never knew existed.

She closed her eyes and tried to calm her own racing heart. She felt Kase stretch toward the lamp on the bedside table and touch the key to the wick. Carefully, he lowered it until the room was bathed in darkness.

Even the darkness did not enable Rosa to hide her confusion and mounting shame. With every passing second she became more determined to slip away once Kase fell asleep.

Unaware of her turmoil, Kase smiled into the darkness. For the first time in a long while things felt right. He pulled Rose close and snuggled beside her, determined to hold her throughout the night. He planned to wake long before dawn and be certain he got her out of his room and the building before anyone was up and about. He kissed the top of her head and let his hand slide down the satin length of her hair until she relaxed and her breathing became deep and even.

The gray light of dawn muted the brash color of the walls in Kase's room. He stretched slowly, careful not to awaken the woman sleeping beside him. Determined to have her up and dressed before anyone else was awake, he decided it would not hurt to let Rose sleep another quarter-hour. If they left by the outside back stairs and walked behind the buildings to the restaurant, she could get home without arousing suspicion.

Asleep on her stomach, Rose stirred slightly, snuggled deeper beneath the blankets, and hugged the pillow closer. Left alone, she would probably sleep until noon and the fault would be his.

Feeling quite smug in his happiness, Kase laced his fingers together behind his head and stared at the ceiling. There was a lot to take care of today. His first order of business would be to write his parents. A letter of apology was long overdue; his mother deserved better than this separation and silence. Silk stockings for Rose were the next order of business, along with roses. He would give her more roses than she had ever seen. Right after he proposed. Then he would alert Quentin to the fact that the position of marshal was open. Kase would be going home soon—taking his new bride home, he amended.

Rawlins needed to start looking for a new marshal for Busted Heel.

Someone scratched the door and he straightened, afraid it was Chicago or one of the other girls come to visit. One glance toward the window ruled out the idea. It was still far too early for any of them to be up.

He finger-combed his hair as he crossed the room to answer the summons. Nude, he opened the door a crack and grumbled, "Come back later."

A worn, sun-baked hand tried to push the door open wider. Kase held firm and peered around the edge. It was Zach Elliot.

"What do you want?" Kase whispered, afraid of waking Rose.

"Get your gun."

It was all his old friend needed to say. Kase shut the door and rummaged through the pile of clothing on the floor until he found his pants. He shook them out and slid them on, shoved his feet in his boots, then grabbed his gun belt and slung it around his waist. Shirtless, he donned his jacket. Opening the door just wide enough to slip out, he joined Zach in the hallway. The old man frowned at the closed door, but did not volunteer any advice.

"What's going on?" Kase led the way down the back stairs.

"While you were gone, two ugly cusses rode into town and tried to rough up Miz Rosa."

Kase stopped dead still and turned on Zach. "What!"

"Like I said, two ugly—"

"What happened to Rose? Why didn't anybody say anything about this last night?"

"One day two ruffians went into the café and wanted a little more than food. The Chinee girl came runnin' to me, and I got there before anythin' happened, but I can tell you they weren't none too happy when they rode outta town gunless. Alice Wilkie was up early this mornin', and she said she saw them hangin' around down by the depot. I thought maybe you might want to add to the firepower if trouble starts." His brow creased again before he added, "If I'da known you was occupied, I'da never come a-callin'."

Afraid Zach would somehow guess that it was Rose in his room, he tried to lighten the mood. "That's what happens when you live in a whorehouse, I guess."

"I guess, but knowin' a real woman might take a notion to get upset over it might make me think more'n twice about foolin' around."

"Meaning?"

"If I have to explain it to ya, boy, I'm wastin' my breath."

Zach turned and led the way down the street. The ruse had worked, for he obviously thought the woman in the room upstairs was someone other than Rose. Kase was about to smile, but the expression was short-lived when a gunshot rang out at the far end of the street.

Rosa awoke with a start and, disoriented, sat up. She took in the strange surroundings, and as realization came flooding back, she groaned aloud, hastily pulling the sheet over her bare breasts. Tangled in her own hair, she tried to extricate herself, thankful that Kase was not in the room. Before she could wonder where he was, the sound of gunshots reverberated on the cold morning air.

There was movement in the hallway. She half expected Kase to walk through the door, but when more shots rang out, she was certain he was somehow involved. Black fear, fear as cold as death, swept over her. She glanced at the pile of clothing on the floor. Realizing it would take far too long to dress, she scrambled across the bed toward the tall wardrobe on the other side of the room. Frantic, she pulled out and tossed aside one shirt, then another. Finally, she came upon a quilted satin robe and slipped it on. Nearly able to wrap it around herself twice, Rosa knotted the belt at the waist, raced across the room, and flung the door open.

She nearly ran into Flossie, who stood rooted to the floor outside Kase's room, pressing a thick, dampened towel to her forehead. Her face was slathered with cucumber cream; the concoction gave her the look of a ghost prowling the hall. Rosa nearly jumped out of her skin at the sight, but the sound of gunfire shocked her into action.

"What is happening?" she demanded of Flossie.

"Sounds like someone's bustin' up the town. Probably nothin' Kase can't handle."

Rosa pushed past the madam and began running toward the stairs. She had lost her husband to a stray bullet. She refused to think that she might lose Kase Storm the same way. *Dio!* Not Kase.

"Stop!" Flossie's hushed voice held such authoritative command that Rosa froze at the top of the stairs and turned around. "Not that way. Lordy, girl, you want the whole town to see you run outta here like that? Go the back way." Flossie pointed down the hall in the opposite direction.

Rosa tore along the hall and down the outside stairs, her bare feet pounding, her hair flying out around her. The sleeves of the oversized robe flapped like crows' wings as she ran out the back door and over the hard, frozen ground. The deserted back lot behind the buildings smelled of fecund earth and pigs. She ran over uneven clods of dirt, the remains of Zetta's summer garden. Her feet stung with cold. Clutching the robe, Rosa ran past the back of Paddie's saloon, past the Davises' shanty, which stood empty, its door gaping wide, past her own back door, and then around the end of the row of buildings.

Without pause, she stepped up on the wooden walk that fronted the shops. The shooting had ended, but her breath caught in her throat when she saw the crowd gathered outside her restaurant window. She could not see over the backs of the men who huddled around a figure lying on the walk, but she recognized Slick Knox and Paddie, as well as two cowboys from Flossie's party. The wranglers were not dressed much better than she; they sported B.V.D.'s, boots, and Stetsons. As he hung on to his father's legs, G.W. Davis stared into the circle of onlookers. Martha cried and clung to her mother's skirts. The sight of Zach Elliot's stern expression as he pushed back his hat and casually spat out a stream of tobacco did little to lessen her fear.

Rosa began shoving men aside, fully expecting to find Kase Storm lying in a pool of blood, his unseeing eyes staring heavenward, his face ashen. Instead, she found him squatting down on his haunches, his suit coat open to reveal his naked upper body as he leaned down to close a dead man's eyes. In a glance she recognized the dead man as Bert, the one who had tried to drag her into her own kitchen in broad daylight. He appeared even younger in death, his features softened, his beard a light scattering of golden hair. The plaid suit he had worn on the day he accosted her was no longer new. It appeared to have been in steady use since she had seen him

last. It was rumpled, as if he had slept in it. She looked around
for his companion, the one he had called Bart, but the other
man was nowhere in sight.

As she stared down at the body, then the trail of blood that
disappeared into the street, she became all too aware of the
attention her disheveled appearance had attracted. Rosa
straightened and pulled the robe tighter.

Kase unfolded to his full height. His eyes never left her face.
Frantically, she searched for any sign of harm, but saw there
was not even a scratch on him. Overwhelming relief was
followed closely by all-consuming anger. It very well might
have been Kase lying dead in the street instead of the other
man. The thought unnerved her. She looked past him and for
the first time noticed that the front window of her restaurant no
longer contained glass. The entire pane had been blown to
smithereens.

No one in the crowd uttered a sound. Some continued to
stare in awe at the bullet-riddled body while the rest watched
the silent exchange between Kase and Rosa. She stared at the
shattered glass on the sidewalk, at Kase, outwardly calm and
unharmed, and then down at herself. Her hair hung free, the
robe did little to cover her ankles and bare feet. What in the
world had she become?

The sight of Rose standing on the street in his robe startled
Kase Storm out of the shock he had experienced when he
realized he had killed a man. Any thoughts he had entertained
about inheriting his blood father's murderous ways were wiped
out the moment he realized a man had died by his hand. It was
all he could do to keep from vomiting in front of the gathering
crowd. If it had not been for Zach's steady hand on his shoulder
he felt he might run from the scene.

Somehow he calmly issued orders to Zach and two others to
carry the body down to his office and lay it out. An undertaker
would have to be called from Cheyenne. He sent Decatur Davis
to Mountain Shadows for Quentin. The man had to be told that
he wanted out of this job as soon as possible. Then, his nerves
still on edge, he realized he would have to get Rose out of the
way. Assuming a casual tone, he stepped over the man on the
ground and said, "I'm real sorry about your window, Mrs.
Audi, ma'am."

Unaware that he was only trying to protect her, Rosa

blanched at his nonchalance. *Mrs. Audi? Ma'am?* Before she could stop herself, she raised her hand and slapped him with all the gusto she could muster.

"What in the hell was that for?" he shouted.

She leaned forward and glared up at him. "The window!" she screamed back, then turned and marched off the way she had come. When she reached the back door of the restaurant, she went inside and slammed the door so hard the noise easily carried out onto the street.

Fuming, Rosa locked the back door and shoved the work-table in front of the entrance that led to the dining room, successfully barricading herself in the kitchen. She refused to think of the dead man on the other side of the dining room window, the crowd, or most of all, Kase Storm. Trying to calm herself, she boiled a kettleful of water and mixed it with water from the barrel out back until she had filled a tin tub. Then she bathed, standing in the washtub in the middle of the floor.

She knew it would take her more than one sponge bath to wash away the memory of the night she had spent in Kase Storm's arms.

And what of Giovanni's memory? Giovanni. She closed her eyes and tried to conjure up his image. It was nearly impossible now. Only the image of Kase Storm came clearly to mind. Kase standing nude beside the bed, Kase kneeling before her. It did not take much imagination to recall the feel of his flesh against her flesh or his hard length sheathed fully inside her.

Suddenly ashamed, she berated herself for her easily fallen widowhood. Giovanni was six months gone, and she had already given herself to another man, even begged him to take her. She had never been a proper widow, never worn black, never even written to his parents. Had she been living in Corio, Rosa knew she would be clothed in black from head to toe for years. What a widow. What a horrid way to treat her husband's memory.

When she thought of the night past and of the casual disregard she had shown for propriety and her good name, Rosa almost wept. When Kase returned last night, the mere sight of him had made her forget that she was not one of Flossie's fancy women. She prayed that no one had seen her rush out of Flossie's place half dressed. Most of the townsfolk knew she cleaned for Flossie, and they knew that was all she did. She hoped everyone thought she had been hiding in the café, waiting for the gunfire to end, that she had run out of her own back door when it was over. Only Flossie knew her secret and she knew Flossie would keep it for her.

As she scrubbed herself dry with a towel and then dressed as hastily as possible before braiding her hair and twisting the coils around her head, Rosa repeated a litany of prayers. God would forgive her this one transgression. He would not let one moment of passion outweigh a lifetime of good behavior. Would he? No, she had to believe that he would forgive her last night.

She had to see Kase soon; she needed her shoes. Rosa promised herself that when she did see Kase Storm again, she would tell him that she'd never forget herself again. Not once more. Not ever.

She tossed the dirty bathwater out the back door and then pushed the table away from the other. As she laid wood in the stove, Rosa tried to ignore the sound of someone sweeping up broken glass from the walk outside the dining room.

*

Chapter
Fourteen

*

G.W. Davis licked his fingers with loud smacking sounds that usually alerted Rosa to the fact that he had finished with his treat and was ready for another. She did not immediately respond, so the licking and smacking grew louder. Using a far more direct approach, Martha Washington Davis tugged on Rosa's skirt with her sticky fingers. "I want more."

Rosa shook off her preoccupation, sighed, and glanced down at the dark-skinned child hovering near her knees. She took another cinnamon bun off the oven, divided it, and gave the halves to the children, then licked the sugary sweetness from her own fingers. A knock sounded at the back door. Rosa's hand trembled slightly as she opened the door. The intuition that had rattled her nerves proved to be correct; Kase Storm stood just outside, a well-wrapped bundle under his arm.

Rosa pulled her scattered nerves together. "G.W., take your sister home now. Come back tomorrow."

"Aw, Miz Rosa, we won't get in the way none. 'Sides, you got lots more buns left."

Kase stepped inside the back door. "Get, G.W."

The boy scuffed out, dejected, but paused long enough to be sure Martha was toddling after him.

"Smells like sticky buns." Kase sniffed the air.

"What do you want?" She tried to still the inner quaking that threatened to become visible.

His expression was one of concern. He frowned and said, "Among other things, I came to return your clothes."

He held the bundle out to her, and she accepted it without looking at it. She put the clothes on her cot and took his robe from a hook on the wall. Without bothering to fold it, she handed it to him.

He tossed it on her cot with the rest of her things. "Keep it. I came to tell you that I telegraphed Cheyenne. Walkers is putting the glass on the next train through. It should be here before tonight."

"*Grazie*." Silent, she waited for him to leave.

He didn't move.

Instead, Kase took a deep breath. Frustrated, he shifted his weight and continued to stare down at her. He noticed her bare toes sticking out from beneath the hem of her skirt and realized he had just returned her only pair of shoes. Her toes were not all he noticed. Her arms were crossed protectively across her breasts and she appeared to be glowering at him.

"Look, Rosa, I don't know why you're still so upset. I'm sorry about what happened this morning. I wanted to get you out of Flossie's before the dawn; then Zach came for me and—"

"And you ran out into the street to maybe be killed."

"—and as a man sworn to uphold the law, I had to do my duty."

She didn't appear to be placated.

He tried again. "I said, I ordered your window."

She pointed toward the door. "Go now."

"What in the hell's wrong with you?"

She emphasized every word, pronouncing it distinctly. "What in hell is wrong with me?" Hands on hips, she stepped toward him until she dared go no closer. "I wake up alone in a bordello, and I am wondering why I am alone. Then I hear the guns, and I think you are dead. So, stupid Rosa, I grab the robe. I run outside—no shoes, no stockings, no dress. I run and run and my heart is beating so hard I think I will die myself. All the time I am thinking you are dead. Then I run to the street and you are alive and I am a fool."

He tried to follow the logic of her complaint, but failed. "*You* suggested my place. Would you rather I had died?" His first mistake was making the joke. The second was that he smiled.

"No! But I do not want to feel this fear again. And I am ashamed."

"Ashamed?" Kase nearly spit out the word.

His face instantly darkened with a fury she had never seen before. Instinctively Rosa raised her hand in her own defense. His hand swung past her and slammed against the wall beside them. Rosa flinched, truly afraid of him for the first time ever.

"Ashamed?" He leaned close and forced her to try to escape him.

There was nowhere to run.

"So you've had second thoughts about sleeping with an Indian. Is that it?"

Frightened beyond belief, she managed to whisper, "No."

"No?"

She shook her head with a frantic glance toward the door.

He echoed her words of the night before. " 'Make love to me, Kase.' " His tone was bitter, his eyes haunted. "Did you do it to find out what it's like to sleep with a half-breed? Was it *savage* enough for you, Rose?"

She covered her face with her hands as a sob escaped her. He grabbed her wrists and jerked her hands away from her face. "Look at me! Or can't you stand to now?"

"You do not understand." She struggled to speak as she gasped for breath. "I am ashamed for myself. Of what I did with you in the night, what I am become. It is not *you* that causes my shame. Never you. It is those things I have done. I do not wish to think of it, and to see you makes me remember it all."

He let go of her wrists and tried to understand what she was trying to say. He took a deep breath and struggled to bring his temper under control. Regretting the outburst that had frightened her so, he waited a moment until he could almost think rationally again. He stepped forward, intent upon taking her in his arms.

Rosa stepped away. "Don't touch me!"

"Rose, please."

She shook her head violently. "No. I have done things I do not wish to think of, and to see you makes me think of them."

"Things?" His brow arched suggestively as he recalled the night they had spent together.

"*Sì*. Things." She began to count on her fingers, holding them up for his benefit. "I disgrace Giovanni. He is not dead six months and I disgrace him. I become a fool this morning in the street. When you are near me I have not the power to think. Go away. Please."

"You're the one who begged me for it last night, Rose." He stepped toward her.

Rosa stepped back again.

Kase smiled a slow half-smile. "You're going to end up on the stove if you don't stop backing away from me."

The sight of his easy smile was nearly her undoing. She was shaking all over, but stood her ground. "Please go."

Kase stared at her and tried to understand what she was trying to say. "Tell me the truth." With a gentle shake, he forced her to look at him again. "You're not upset because I might have been killed—"

"*Sì*, I—"

"And you're certainly not sorry you betrayed Saint Giovanni's memory last night."

She took a swift breath when she realized what he'd said. Undaunted, Kase pressed her. "You're afraid of what happened between us last night. My guess is that you felt things you never imagined you could feel. Do you know how I know that, Rose?"

She shook her head.

"Do you?" He bent closer.

"No." She licked her lips.

"Because *I* felt things last night that I've never felt before, feelings that might scare a person if that person wasn't sure, *really sure*, of what she wanted. I'm not going to pretend I don't go along with whatever mixed-up feelings you're entertaining right now. Don't you think I'm mixed up, too? But I'm not going to beg, either. You asked me once to share my feelings with you, but I'd kept things bottled up inside for so long I didn't know how. Don't you start doing the same thing, Rose. Face what you're feeling and get used to it. When you're through fooling yourself, when you're ready to talk about this, you let me know. But don't hide what you're feeling for too long, Rose. You certainly didn't last night."

Abruptly he released her and walked away. He stopped and, just as he opened the back door, paused long enough to say "Your window will be in by nightfall."

The door slammed shut behind him.

Rosa stared at the door for a moment, then marched toward it, turned the knob, and yanked it open. Pulling the door open as far as possible, she swung it forward and listened in acute satisfaction as it slammed again. Twice as hard.

Nearly a week had passed without repercussions from her appearance on the street the morning of the shooting. Just as she had hoped, everyone thought she was asleep in her kitchen when the shooting started. Far from being accused of having loose morals, she was lauded as the poor widow woman who lived alone, unprotected, easy prey to ruffians like the Dawsons. A reporter from the *Cheyenne Leader* was sent out to Busted Heel to cover the story, but on Flossie's advice, Rosa refused to talk to him. Poor thing is too distraught, everyone said. No one mentioned that she had recovered enough from the ordeal to open the restaurant the very evening of the shooting. But the entire town noticed the new window, and everyone was talking about how the good marshal had paid for it himself.

Afraid of running into Kase on the street, Rosa had sent the Yee girl for the grocery orders all week. But this morning, after two gray, overcast days, Rosa could not stand being cooped up in the restaurant. She wrapped herself warmly in her winter coat, donned her new hat, and hung her market basket over her arm. The hat was a man's black Stetson, one that had been forgotten months ago by one of Floss's customers. Knowing Rosa's penchant for utilizing castoffs, Floss had offered it to her one morning and Rosa had gladly accepted. It would keep her velvet hat from suffering during the harsh winter snows. Floss had donated a long striped pheasant feather, which Rosa stuck into the hatband. She had rounded out the crown and loved to stuff her hair inside it and pull the hat low on her forehead.

Ready for her first outing in days, she stepped outside. Without being obvious, Rosa looked up and down Main before she continued on her way. There was no sign of Kase Storm, so she walked toward Al-Ray's.

Zach Elliot and Bertha Matheson's husband, who had taken to sitting around the potbellied stove in the middle of the room, were absent today. Alice Wilkie, obviously starved for company in the usually busy store, wiped her hands on her apron and climbed down from the tall ladder where she was stocking goods. She proceeded to follow Rosa from one end of the store to the other, chattering away without pause. Rosa requested a cut of ham and Alice lowered one from where it hung from the ceiling.

"John Tuttle said Marshal Kase sent a telegram to some woman in Boston name of Analisa Storm."

Rosa's stomach suddenly lurched. What was Alice Wilkie trying to tell her? Was Kase preparing to go away? She tried to sound disinterested, but her voice shook. "*Si*? Boston?"

"It's back east."

"Slick heard it from Paddie that Zach told him Kase was something fierce to see when he faced down that Bert Dawson. Said it wasn't only that the man was wanted in three states, but that the marshal saw red when Zach told him about that man having accosted you right there in your own restaurant."

Rosa scooped flour out of the bin beneath the counter, listening intently as Alice prattled on.

"I would love to have seen that." Alice cackled. "What with the marshal being a 'breed an' all, I guess that accounts for his terrible temper—not that I've ever seen it. Ray was there. Said the marshal's eyes was blazin' as hot as his gun." She sawed off one slab of ham after another, weighing them as she talked. "I hear he's part Sioux, and God knows they're mean. I read the government's always havin' trouble with them. Not all that far from here, either, just up to Pine Ridge Reservation. Did you hear the marshal wants to up and quit now? I declare. I would've thought things were just gettin' interesting for him."

"Pardon? What did you say?" Rosa handed Alice the sack of flour and waited for the woman to explain.

"The marshal intends to quit, soon as Rawlins can find a new man."

"No," Rosa interrupted, "before. You use a word I do not understand. About the marshal."

Alice wrinkled her brow as she tried to remember all she'd said. " 'Breed? What did you think he was? Clearly the man ain't all white, not that it makes no never mind to me. His money's as good here as the next man's." She thumbed over her shoulder in the general direction of the boardinghouse. "I hear tell"—Alice leaned forward and began to whisper, although the place was still empty—"that's why he moved out of Bertha's right after he first got here. Far as I'm concerned, he's a good enough sort, but I'd have to think about it before I let him live under my roof. You never know when one of them might take it into his head to attack a white woman." Alice leaned forward and waved Rosa closer. "The sight of a woman's white skin really riles some of them bucks up."

Rosa fought to keep her expression bland. She could hardly believe this woman was serious. "You believe this?"

"Well, I hear tell—"

"Do white women never marry these men of mixed blood? Did not a white woman marry an Indian to make such a child?"

"Well, sure, honey, but no decent woman would do such a thing."

"And if one did so? What if this happened?"

"Well, I guess that would be food for speculation." Alice glanced slyly at Rosa. "I can't imagine any decent woman from around these parts considerin' such a thing—beddin' down with a half-breed—but if one did, why, I reckon she'd have to put up with whatever folks thought of her. Don't you think so?"

Rosa felt sorry for this woman who judged others so easily. Had Alice Wilkie never loved enough to overcome her prejudice? Kase Storm's mixed blood had never mattered to Rosa, and it did not now, but Alice's views helped clarify the burden of hatred he had been forced to bear his entire life. He had reason to be angry. She was becoming angry herself.

Rosa stared, no longer listening, as Alice wrapped up the ham and then totaled her items.

"Want to pay for your week's water delivery now? Roy'll be bringin' it around regular till the pump freezes up." Moving as if in a trance, Rosa paid for her goods. She thanked Alice, then walked outside.

The shopkeeper's words had deepened her already dismal mood until her spirit was as low as the day was gray. There was no denying that she missed Kase terribly. After what she had just heard, she longed to go to him and offer him comfort for all he had ever suffered.

But she knew what that comfort would lead to, and until he had expressed his own words of love, until she knew that he truly wanted her as much as she did him, Rosa refused to make a fool of herself. She shifted the heavy basket she carried and purposely refused to glance toward the jail. Now that she had barred him from her life, she missed him as sorely as if he had been part of it forever.

The clouds seemed to lower as she walked down Main. Even her jaunty Stetson with its perky feather did not cheer her as it usually did. At the moment life seemed incredibly unfair.

The huge black safe behind Kase Storm's desk had not been opened once since he took over as marshal. Luckily no one had wanted him to put anything away for safekeeping. It seemed Quentin did not have the combination, nor did he have any inkling as to who might. For some reason, this morning had seemed like as good a time as any for Kase to fool with the blasted thing. Besides, sitting on the floor in front of the safe kept him from staring out the window waiting for some sign of Rose.

But it did not keep Zach Elliot from reporting her every move.

"There she goes, back up the street toward the restaurant." Zach paused long enough to spit into the spittoon Kase insisted he use, stare over at Kase, then continue. "She's wearin' a man's Stetson with some kind of feather stuck in the band."

Kase was determined not to respond, and he succeeded. But the image of Rose in another oversized hat came instantly to mind. He spun the lock and squinted at the safe.

"I still can't figure out what you did to make her so danged mad. Why, she's even taken to glarin' at me when I go in the café. Seems like you'd be good enough to go over and tell her I ain't to be blamed for your transgressions."

"I guess she's still mad because of her broken window."

Zach spit again. "Well, now, I guess some folks would believe that's the cause o' your troubles, but I don't."

Kase stared at the painting on the front of the safe. Tall cypress trees lined an avenue that led to a shimmering pond. It reminded him of pictures he'd seen of Rome, Italy.

He sighed.

"Could be," Zach was saying, "she found out about the girl in your room the night of the party."

Kase spun around on the seat of his Levi's to face Zach. "What?"

"Maybe she found out you had a girl that night."

"What are you talking about?" He stood up and brushed at his pants, trying to appear offhanded as he questioned Zach.

"After Flossie's party. When I had to wake you that mornin', it was all too clear to me there was a girl in your room. You made a big enough show of not lettin' me see past you. If I know it, what's to say Rosa don't know it? After all, Floss is a friend of hers."

Kase smiled. "Floss is a friend of mine, too."

"Well, be that as it may, if it was me, I'd be tryin' my damnedest to make it up to her."

"If there was something to make up," Kase said.

Zach looked at him sideways. "If there was."

"Open the door, Miz Rosa. We got somethin' for ya."

"Wait, wait, wait. *Un momento*." Rosa shook out a clean tablecloth and let it settle over a table before she hurried to the front door. She could see the top of G.W.'s head and what looked like—she opened the door to be sure—roses.

"For you!" G.W.'s smile was a mile wide as she took the armful of red roses from him.

"Where did you get such a wonderful gift?" She stared down at the huge bouquet of perfect red rosebuds, then beyond the child. There was no one standing behind him.

"The marshal tol' me to bring 'em to you. He said I was to stay and then tell him what you said when I gave 'em to you."

It had been three weeks since she had even spoken to Kase Storm.

Rosa tried to hide any reaction to the gift, but a smile teased the corners of her mouth. "*Grazie*, G.W.," was all she said, but as she closed the door behind Kase's willing messenger, she buried her face in the ruby-red blooms and inhaled their precious scent.

Ten minutes had not passed before Flossie came knocking on the front window carrying a tall vase. When Rosa opened the door, Flossie bustled past her and scanned the room.

"So," she said, her bosom heaving as she tried to catch her breath, "where are they?"

"Who?" Rosa asked, fully aware of the purpose of her friend's sudden visit.

"Not who, what. Where are the roses?"

"You know about the roses?"

"Honey, there's probably not a soul in town that doesn't know about the roses. It's the end of November and there's not a rose bloomin' in Busted Heel. Besides, John Tuttle just delivered them to Kase from the station. Seems the marshal sent all the way to California for 'em from some fancy hothouse. Anyway, Kase had G.W. bring 'em over, and you know that child couldn't keep a secret to save his life."

"And as soon as Signora Wilkie hears of my roses, all of America will know," Rosa laughed.

Floss laughed, too. "You're right there, Rosa. Now, let's see 'em."

Rosa led her to the kitchen where she had put the roses in the water pitcher.

"Here," Flossie offered the tall porcelain vase, "I thought you might need this."

"Thank you, *signora*. I will take care with it."

"Forget it. What I want to know is, are you plannin' to speak to the marshal now? That boy's sufferin', you know."

Rosa held up her hand in defense, "Please . . ."

"I know it ain't none of my business, Rosa, really it ain't, but I know since you spent the night with Kase you ain't seen fit to talk to him. I don't want to know why; all I want you to do is think about talkin' this out with him."

"Did he ask you to say these things to me?"

"Lordy, no. Up until this passel of roses arrived, he's been actin' like you don't even exist."

Rosa hugged the vase tighter and fought down the lump in her throat. "Has he . . ." She turned away from Flossie, her face aflame with embarrassment, but she had to know. "Has he—"

"Slept with one of the girls?" Flossie finished for her. "No, honey, you don't need to concern yourself with that. He's havin' himself a good sulk. He don't know any of 'em exist." Her penciled brows arched as if she'd just had a revelation.

"Not yet, at least. But if I were you, I wouldn't be puttin' him off too long. A man's dry spells usually don't last too long."

So many of her neighbors wandered by to see the roses that Rosa put them in the center of the window table where everyone could enjoy them. The bouquet had become such a topic of conversation that G.W. insisted he had to have a rose for his mother. Rosa gave away two when Martha came running in on his heels demanding one for herself.

The rosebuds opened to full bloom and soon filled the air with their heady fragrance. Rosa found herself looking at them a thousand times a day. With each glance, she thought of Kase. Still, she could not convince herself that it would help to go and talk with him. If anything, as vulnerable as she felt, she knew she would probably fall into his arms again. And then his bed. He had to come to her. To profess his love. To propose in a proper manner.

One afternoon, just after the sun had burst through the clouds, Quentin Rawlins walked into Rosa's, dressed for cold weather in a fleece-lined wool jacket. His smile further lit up the day, and she found herself crossing the room to greet him.

"Signor Quentin! It has been a long time since you came to Rosa's!"

He gave her a warm hug. "It was roundup. The boys took off right after Flossie's party and just got back. I thought you might like to come out to the ranch for Sunday dinner."

She started to refuse, then thought the change of scenery might just lift her spirits. "I will come and cook a special dinner for you," she offered.

"Hell, no. The idea is for you to have the day off. My cook can do the honors." He took her hands in his. "I'll send one of the boys to get you, Rosa. You be ready by two, and dress warm, you hear?"

"Thank you, Quentin. I will be ready."

As he started out the door he caught sight of the roses, but left the café without saying a word about them. At first Rosa thought it odd that the flowers, which were such a topic of conversation with the townsfolk, had failed to earn even a comment from Quentin, but then, she thought, why would a man of wealth and prominence think to ask about a bouquet of roses?

*

Chapter Fifteen

*

On Wednesday morning Rosa dressed with care. Her black skirt with its simple lines fit her well; her crisp white blouse complemented her dark hair. As she surveyed her effort in the small square of mirror hanging near her cot, she decided she made a presentable guest for dinner at Quentin's. If only she felt as good as she looked. Not even the idea of dining with one of the richest, most eligible widowers in Wyoming cheered her.

Promptly at two o'clock she heard a knock on the door and went to answer it, fully expecting one of Quentin's ranch hands to be there waiting for her.

Instead, she opened the door to Zach Elliot.

He tipped his hat to her. "Miz Rosa. I come to carry you out to the Rawlins ranch."

For a moment she was taken aback. "You? The *signore* said he is sending one of his own men." For a fleeting moment she wondered if Kase Storm might be behind Zach's appearance.

"It seems he don't trust any of his own boys to drive you, ma'am. He asked me to do it."

"I—" She hesitated.

"You comin' or not?"

"Signor Rawlins sent you?"

"I said he did. I ain't been called a liar for some time."

She could see his patience was ebbing. A buckboard stood behind him in the street, the horses shaking their heads impatiently. She recognized the brand on them as the same symbol she had seen hanging over the gate at Mountain Shadows.

"*Va bene*. I go." Rosa went inside and donned her coat, then locked the door behind her and let Zach help her up onto the wagon seat.

The ride was as chilly with silence as it was with cold. The clouds that had gathered low threatened rain, and the temperature seemed to plummet as they neared the base of the mountains. Zach Elliot slouched forward, his arms resting on his knees, and drove the team in silence. As he peered out from beneath the brim of his hat, he kept his eyes on the heavily grooved wagon wheel ruts in the road.

Rosa could think of no comfortable way to start a conversation with the old man. She wanted to ask Zach about Kase, how he was, if he ever mentioned her. Instead, she rode in huddled silence, her arms wrapped about her against the cold. Hatless, she bemoaned the fact that she had forgotten to bring along her Stetson.

Relieved when they finally turned up the drive to the ranch house, anxious to be inside and out of the cold, Rosa stared at the two-story ranch house. Smoke spiraled out of the chimneys and hugged the roofline. As they passed the barn she recognized Zach's horse tied at the hitching rail in front of it. He drew the buckboard alongside the wide veranda before he jumped down to help her to the ground.

Wondering if he would drive her back to town, she asked, "You will be eating here?"

"Naw, I'll be headin' on back to town. You have a good dinner, Miz Rosa."

She frowned. "How am I to go back?"

He paused for a fraction of a second before he answered. "Quentin said he's got a ride all arranged for you."

"Then, *grazie*, Signor Zach."

"Have yourself a good dinner, Miz Rosa."

The inside of Quentin Rawlins's house was far different from Flossie's place, but it was equally awe-inspiring. She had seen it only once before, the night of the barbecue, when guests had moved about freely. She was looking forward to seeing every detail of the exquisite rooms downstairs. With his usual exuberance, Quentin ushered her into the entrance hall, a room nearly as large as Flossie's entire parlor. Rosa stared at a piano covered with a fringed paisley shawl. The instrument shared one wall with a gigantic spread of antlers. Chairs of assorted styles were grouped at random about the room while an imposing clock stood near an arched doorway that led to the rooms beyond. Impressively large paintings hung near the ceilings; lamps and candelabra graced cloth-draped tables. There were more furnishings in the room than she had ever seen assembled in one place in her life. Quentin took her arm and led her into a side parlor that was even larger than the entry. Its plump-cushioned chairs and deep couch were arranged around an imposing fireplace. A crackling fire that drove the November chill from the room beckoned Rosa nearer.

"Your home is wonderful, *signore,* full of many fine things." She crossed the room and stood before the mantel above the massive stone fireplace. A collection of cloisonné vases and covered dishes lined the black walnut mantel. The delicate objects bespoke a woman's touch.

"I really haven't done much to it since my wife died."

Quentin mentioned his wife infrequently. All Rosa really knew of the woman was that she had borne Quentin a son who was currently traveling in Europe. Fearing his silence came from pain, Rosa decided not to question him further.

Drawn to a wicker rocking chair padded with crazy-quilt cushions, Rosa touched its high back and set it rocking.

"Have a seat," Quentin invited. "I thought you might like a little sherry before dinner. My housekeeper, Mrs. Benton, said the meal won't be ready for a while yet."

"*Grazie.*" Rosa sat down to wait while he crossed the room to pour the drinks.

Quentin sat across from her and began to regale her with tales of the years he had spent as a cowhand driving cattle along the Chisholm Trail. For some inexplicable reason, Rosa thought she sensed a new nervousness about the usually confident man. As she watched him talk, seated as he was on the edge of the sofa, she prayed silently that he was not about to propose marriage to her again. Not now. Not with her heart still in turmoil over Kase Storm.

"Damn," he mumbled as he stood and walked to the window, "it's starting to sleet."

"Sleet?" She was unfamiliar with the word.

"Frozen rain. Like ice." Quentin pantomimed falling rain, then shrugged.

"I am thankful it is not the falling ice balls," Rosa said, relieved.

Quentin tried to look serious, but Rosa could see his lips twitching. "Ice balls?" He arched a brow.

"*Sì*," she nodded. "When they fall, you must cross the keys against bad luck."

"Ahh," he said seriously. Then, despite his efforts, he laughed aloud and shook his head. "I have no idea what you're talking about, Rosa."

Rosa began to explain, then thought better of it. "It is just a custom of my country, to keep away the *male*, the evil."

The tall clock in the hallway chimed the half-hour and Quentin's smile changed to a frown. He exhaled deeply and excused himself. "I need to talk to Mrs. Benton."

Quentin returned in a few moments and offered her another glass of sherry. "It will be a while before dinner is ready," he explained offhandedly.

He reached for a large wooden box that contained a stereopticon and carefully removed it with a stack of double-sided pictures that he said had recently arrived from Paris where his son, Quentin Junior, was staying. They viewed each of the pictures twice. Imagining some disaster in the kitchen, Rosa began to wonder whether she should ask if the cook needed her help.

Before she could decide, booted feet sounded on the veranda followed by the sound of a determined knock at the door. Quentin was on his feet at the first footfall. From the rocking chair before the fire, Rosa could not see the newcomer, nor could she hear what Quentin said in low muffled tones. Curious, she stood and shook out her skirt. Just then Quentin walked back into the room followed by a tall man covered by an oilcloth slicker. His dark hat was pulled low enough to shield his face from both the weather and her perusal. Water slowly dripped from his slicker onto Quentin's Oriental carpet.

"Get out of that coat and I'll hang it by the fire," Quentin advised.

Rosa watched as the visitor removed his gloves. At the sight of deep brown skin and well-shaped hands, the strong fingers with their evenly trimmed nails, she blanched. Kase Storm removed his hat and brushed water from its crown. When his eyes met hers across the room, he arched a finely tapered brow and nodded a silent greeting.

"Let me have your coat." Quentin studiously avoided Rosa's eyes as he hung the wet slicker over the back of a chair near the fireplace.

At first she was too stunned to speak as she stared at the imposing figure in a starched white shirt, black dress pants, and matching coat. Then Rosa's simmering anger began to boil. She had been tricked, duped by a man she had considered her good friend. "I must go," she announced.

"Rosa, please, we haven't even had dinner yet," Quentin said.

"No. I must go." She looked straight at Kase. "Now."

Quentin looked at Kase, who merely shrugged. "I told you she'd be mad," Quentin said. "Listen, Rosa, this whole thing was his idea. When Kase told me—"

Rosa's gaze swung back to Kase. "You *told* him?" she asked, disbelieving.

"I told him we had an argument," Kase explained.

Quentin cut in again. "He told me you were mad at him for shooting out your window, and he asked for my help." He no longer sounded as sure as he had at the beginning of his statement.

Knowing his feelings about Kase's desirability as a husband, Rosa was surprised that Quentin had agreed to become part of this scheme to get them together. Rosa took a deep breath, determined to make Quentin understand. "There is more wrong here than a broken window, *signore,* and the marshal, he knows this. I am surprised to find that you are a part of this . . . this deception. Now I want my coat. I want to go."

Mrs. Benton, the ranch foreman's wife who worked as Quentin's housekeeper and cook, chose just that moment to step into the parlor. "Dinner's been sittin' so long the roast elk's gonna taste like jerky if somebody don't come on and eat right quick."

Quentin had the decency to look embarrassed as he shrugged. "For Mrs. Benton's sake, do you think you could consider staying long enough to eat? I'm downright starving and I promise to take you home just as soon as we're through."

Ignoring Kase, who was occupied with pouring himself some sherry, Rosa watched the drizzling sleet and hesitated to answer. She did have to eat. It might as well be here. "*Va bene*," she said. "I will eat. Then, *you* will take me back."

Quentin bowed his acquiescence, and Rosa led the way to the dining room.

Kase had not looked directly at her since they left the parlor. It was good, Rosa decided, that he had not. She did not need his startlingly blue eyes boring into hers. Nor did she need to speak to him to know that he was as fully aware of her as she was of him.

Even though she was still furious at being duped, Rosa admitted to herself that she was enjoying both the meal and the conversation. During her self-imposed silence, she listened to the men talk about the future of Wyoming. Many nights after closing the restaurant, she had struggled to read the *Cheyenne Leader* to learn what was going on in this new country she had adopted as her own, but listening to them talk of the changes that would come with impending statehood made the news all that much clearer. She also became aware of how well educated Kase was.

"Why wouldn't a rash of families move into Wyoming when we become a state?" Quentin asked, following a statement he'd made previously. "It will be the only state where women have the vote. The territorial government won't agree to go into the union without the women's vote. I can foresee trainloads of new folks moving in after that. Not that I'm happy about it. Most of them'll be farmers, and you know what they're doing to the open rangeland."

Kase nodded, intent on cutting a slice of roast elk.

Rosa watched him from beneath half-lowered lashes.

Quentin finished and set his cutlery down. He pushed back his chair and stared at the two silent figures consciously ignoring each other. He shook his head. "So, Kase," he said abruptly, "what have you heard of the rest of the Dawson gang?"

Rosa put down her fork as the image of Bert Dawson, sprawled dead on her sidewalk, came to mind.

Kase glanced hesitantly at Rosa. "Not much."

Quentin persisted. "I hope to God we've seen the last of them. What happened after the shooting?"

"The usual, I guess. A reporter came out from the *Leader* and took the story. Brought along a photographer."

"I always thought that was a particularly disgusting habit," Quentin commented. "I don't know why anyone would want to buy souvenir pictures of a dead bandit shot full of holes, but I've sure seen my share. First ones I ever saw were taken of some of the James gang after the shoot-out in Northfield, Minnesota, back in 'seventy-six."

Rosa put her napkin down alongside her plate.

Kase shifted in his seat. "Quentin," he said softly.

Rawlins cleared his throat, suddenly aware of his lack of sensitivity. "So, everything else in town's been quiet?"

"Real quiet," Kase said. Finally he looked directly at Rose. "Too quiet." His attention drifted to Quentin again. "Have you found someone to take my place yet?"

"To tell you the truth, I haven't had time to look. I was hoping you would consent to stay on until spring."

Kase studied Rose, who kept her eyes on her empty plate. "I don't know what my plans are for certain, but I want out."

"Killing doesn't sit well with you?"

"Not at all."

Quentin changed the subject by asking for Kase's advice on a land contract he was about to enter into, and Rosa saw a facet of Kase Storm's life she had not known existed. It seemed he was well versed in the law and able to give Quentin advice on many matters.

When they finished their meal, Quentin asked the cook to serve dessert and coffee immediately. He ate in silence, his mood mirroring the one shared by his two silent companions. He frowned down at his apple cobbler. The weak sunlight had faded into darkness, and now the room was aglow with lamplight. His expression thoughtful, Quentin glanced at the tall side window. He took a deep breath and sighed, then looked at Rosa.

"Rosa, it's started to snow. There's no way I'm letting any of the men take you back with the chance of a big storm hitting."

"I will not go back with him," she said, indicating Kase with a nod.

"I'm not letting him go, either," Quentin said emphatically. "Nobody's going out in this." He waved a hand toward the window. "Have to be a fool to try it."

"But—" Faced with the temptation of spending the night under the same roof with Kase, she could only protest. "But, *signore*—"

"No buts. I'll have Mrs. Benton make up the guest room. Kase, you can have Quent's room for tonight. I won't hear anything else about it from either of you."

Rosa stared at Quentin. Kase stared at Rosa. Quentin suddenly became intent on staring at the bottom of his cobbler bowl.

Rosa's tone was soft, yet laced with accusation. "I thought you were my friend, *signore*."

Abruptly the rancher pushed his chair back and rounded the table to stand behind her. "Come with me," he said.

Quentin walked her to the entry hall and opened the front door. A cold blast of air swept into the cheery warmth of the room. Rosa saw little beyond the lamplight that spilled out into the night, but she could see a thick curtain of snow falling just beyond the veranda, the flakes both thick and silent as they quickly piled up on the ground.

She stepped back and Quentin closed the door. "Satisfied?" he asked, before he added softly, "Rosa, I am your friend. If I wasn't, I might think about letting you go out in that, but as it is, I want to see you safe. I'm sorry."

"I am sorry, too. I am sorry you trick me." Rosa sighed, resigned to her fate, and glanced toward Kase, who was still seated at the dining table. "I stay," she said, "until tomorrow."

Mrs. Benton, a kindly woman with weathered skin and a harried expression, ushered Rosa to a room that was warm and welcoming. A huge bed framed with rough-hewn logs, striped rugs, and simple furnishings presented a soothing contrast to the crowded parlor. The graying cook gave Rosa one of her own nightgowns and explained reassuringly that she had agreed to stay in a room near the kitchen on the first floor for the night. The woman lit the lamps and banked the fire before she left Rosa alone.

Nearly lost in the voluminous folds of Mrs. Benton's prim muslin nightgown, Rosa perched on the side of the bed, her dark hair drawn over one shoulder as she rhythmically brushed the ebony skeins. The task occupied her hands, but not her mind, as she periodically glanced toward the door, alert to every sound in the hallway. Finally she heard the men's heavily booted feet mount the stairs, listened as Quentin bid Kase good night, then heard the closing doors.

The house settled into silence, but Rosa could not sleep. She walked to the window and tried to see outside. The heat from within had frosted the panes, so she cleared a small circle in the condensation and tried to see out into the darkness. Her own golden eyes along with the flames in the lamps were mirrored in the windowpane. Snowflakes swirled past gracefully, the closest illuminated by the light behind her.

Though no sound alerted her, she felt a slight draft of cool air and stiffened, suddenly aware of a presence in the room. Before she turned toward the door, Rosa saw a flicker of movement reflected in the window beside her own image. She caught her breath and spun around.

Kase Storm was carefully closing the door behind him.

"Go away," she whispered.

Bootless, he silently crossed the room on stockinged feet. Her terse command had no effect on him.

Rosa stared at him mutely and wondered how such a large man could move so gracefully without making a sound. Her heart was pounding, but not from fear—and that thought alone frightened her. She heard the soft whisper of his clothing just before he stepped up to her, a dark shadow in the lamplight. The fathomless depths of his eyes were lost in the semidarkness. She tried to swallow, but found her throat exceedingly dry. She licked her lips.

He reached out until he held her by the shoulders. His eyes searched hers intently before he drew her close.

"You're as stubborn as I am, Rose," he whispered.

With her cheek pressed against his shirtfront, she could hear the strong, steady beat of his heart and the sound of his voice as the words echoed through him.

"I've missed you, Rose." He held her away and looked down into her eyes once more.

She tried to shake her head, tried to dismiss his words and to deny her own need, but found it impossible to do so.

"You do not understand," she interrupted.

His hands tightened on her shoulders. "I do understand. I had no right to take you to my room the night of Flossie's party. I should not have made love to you, no matter what you said that night. If I hadn't, you wouldn't have had to go through what you did the next morning. I'm sorry for the way it turned out"—he slid his palms down her arms until he held her hands in his—"but I won't lie to you, Rose. I'm not sorry that you were safe at Flossie's when Bert Dawson tried to break into your place. And I'm not sorry about what happened in my room. I'm not sorry about the way I feel when you're in my arms. I love you."

"Kase—"

"I do." He admitted it with a smile. "And this time I want to do this right. My being here for dinner was all my idea. Quentin told me it wouldn't work, but now it seems that even the weather is on my side."

She tried to pull away, afraid of being lulled by his husky whisper and the touch of his warm fingers against her skin. When he continued to hold her hands, she stopped struggling and found herself almost afraid he would let go, yet equally afraid of what would surely happen if he did not. She tried to make sense of what he was saying, but all she could concentrate on was his declaration of love. He loved her. The words played over and over in her mind like a litany.

"Rose, that night I wanted to tell you everything about myself. I wanted to explain the way I treated you when you first came to Busted Heel. Will you hear me out now?"

Her heart melted as she stared up at him. Rosa nodded and indicated that he should sit on a leather chair near the window. She crossed the room to sit on the bed.

Slowly, choosing his words carefully so that she would understand fully, he told her the story of his life from the very beginning. He talked of his background in Boston and the West. When he spoke of his mother's rape, she cried. He spoke with detachment as if he were telling someone else's story. There was no pity or self-loathing in his tone. He told her of his argument with Caleb, his stepfather, and of his self-doubt.

As he spoke, Rosa drew up her knees beneath the wide folds

of the gown and hugged them to her. She became mesmerized by the story and was able to picture it all. She found herself longing to know his courageous mother, Analisa. There was much she could learn from such a woman.

He concluded with the tale of his visit to the old Indian wise man. She smiled when he told how the man suggested he see the world through eyes of love. When he finished, he sat without moving, awaiting her reaction.

She never dreamed there was so much to this man's life. Given what had happened to his mother, Rosa understood why he had feared for her own safety and tried to get her to give up and go home. She understood his fears of becoming a man like his blood father. Wouldn't anyone be afraid of such an uncertainty?

Most of all she realized that he had finally opened his heart to her. It was an indication of how much he did trust and care for her, and Rosa's heart sang with joy.

In the dim, lamplit room, it was hard for them to see each other clearly. Their faces were muted planes of light and shadow. Afraid of what her reaction to his revelations might be, Kase asked softly, "You haven't said anything."

Rose stood, trying to find the words that would express her joy. He mistook her lengthy silence for anger, her hesitation for rejection, and swiftly crossed the room to tower over her. "Listen, Rose," he said, his lips taut, his features set, "I've faced up to what I feel. I know you're as hardheaded as I am, and I figured that if we were going to get anywhere at all, I'd have to speak up. I guess I was wrong." He turned away and stalked across the room.

She did not have to see his expression to know that he was truly angry now. The knowledge spurred her into action, and she ran across the room after him. She reached out for his hand. When her fingers touched his, he stopped immediately, but he did not turn to face her.

"Kase." Her voice was hesitant, uncertain. She hoped he was not so angry that he would not forgive her. Slowly he turned to look down at her again, his face still expressionless, his emotions well hidden. "*Io te amo,*" Rosa whispered, then realized he might not understand. "I love you. For everything you tell to me this night, thank you."

Without a moment's hesitation, he drew her roughly into his

embrace and nearly knocked the breath from her as he pulled her against the unyielding hardness of his chest. His lips captured hers in a kiss that was punishing in its demand. She returned it full measure until, breathless, she pulled away. When she looked up at him, Kase's eyes were warm and alive again, his lips softly curved in a smile.

"God, you scared me, Rose," he said with a shake of his head.

She shrugged and smiled. "You surprise me, that is all."

"I guess I surprised myself." He bent low and kissed her again. "You never told me how you liked the roses."

"*Molto bene.* I liked."

"Good. I'll send for more."

"There is no need." She shook her head. "They are expensive, no?"

"No. Nothing's too expensive for you." He held her close and rocked her slowly. "Nothing."

A door closed somewhere on the first floor, and Rosa tried to step out of his embrace. "You must go now," she warned.

"Go?" he whispered.

"*Sì.*"

He kissed her again. It was a slow, lingering kiss that held both a question and a promise. As his lips plied hers, Rosa felt a moist warmth spread through her until it concentrated itself in the throbbing pearl between her legs. When she leaned close and pressed against him, his arms tightened around her.

When the kiss finally ended, he whispered again, "You want me to go now?"

"*Sì.*" She would not give in again.

This time he nuzzled the sensitive skin beneath her ear. A shiver ran down her spine.

"Rose?"

"Umm?"

"If you want me to leave, you'll have to let go."

Rosa looked down and was surprised to find his shirtfront clutched in her hands. She was even more surprised when Kase scooped her into his arms and carried her to the bed.

He set her on the edge of the bed and knelt before her. Tenderly he tugged down the hem of her nightgown until it reached her ankles, then reached up and brushed the riotous fall of thick ebony hair behind her. Rosa cupped his face in her hands.

"I intend to do this right this time. I sent you flowers. I'm on my knees. Will you marry me?" He had never thought to say the words, never dreamed he would find a woman able to face the challenge that marriage to him would entail.

"*Sì*. Yes." She bent to kiss him and he straightened, his warm, sure hands resting on her thighs.

His lips played against hers with a feather-light touch before his tongue teased them open. As the kiss deepened, she drew him near. He pressed closer. He was still on his knees when his hands began to explore, and soon, before she was even aware of what he was doing, he drew her nightgown up until the hem rested on her thighs.

"So much for propriety," he whispered against her lips when the kiss ended. He shrugged. "I tried."

She clung to him as though she would be lost if she let go and reveled in the feel of his gentle touch. Kase ran his hands along the smooth, satin length of her inner thighs until his fingertips rested against the warm nest of their apex. Rosa gasped in surprise and straightened. She pulled back and found him staring into her eyes.

"Relax, Rose," he whispered, his voice husky and filled with longing. "I won't hurt you." He gently nudged her legs apart and began to explore her inner recesses with his fingertips.

"The door . . ." she protested weakly.

"Is closed. Everyone's asleep by now."

With her hands resting on his shoulders, she closed her eyes, unwilling to submit to the intensity of his stare. She heard him clear his throat, felt him lean closer and then touch his lips to hers.

"Look at me," he said.

She opened her eyes.

She slid his fingers farther inside her, and she felt her inner flesh melt around him.

"I love you, Rose."

"I, too, love you," she managed to gasp before she lost herself to the pleasure of the incessant thrust of his hand. Her fingertips dug into his shoulders and she leaned back, opening herself further to his explorations. Lost in sensation, she closed her eyes and tossed her head from side to side as he teased her until she felt about to burst into bloom.

When he withdrew his hand, she moaned in frustration and opened her eyes. Kase stood where a second before he had knelt, between her knees at the bedside. His eyes never left hers as he unbuttoned his shirt and stripped it off, then reached for his belt. He tossed his pants aside and then shrugged off the long wool underwear that did little to hide the evidence of his desire.

He bent over her, but instead of taking her in his arms, as she expected, he reached for the abundant white lawn of the borrowed nightgown and began to draw the material upward. She assisted by raising her hips off the bed and then her shoulders until she was free of the cumbersome nightdress. Kase tossed it aside. Rosa fought back the urge to grasp the bedspread and draw it over her.

She expected him to join her on the bed, to take her in his arms and end his silent perusal of her body. Instead, he reached for her, grasped her by the waist and pulled her toward him until her hips rested against the edge of the bed and her legs dangled toward the floor. She held her breath, expectant, yet uncertain of exactly what to expect. Focusing on the burning intensity of his gaze as he stared down at her, she tried to avoid blatantly staring at his throbbing arousal.

He leaned down and carefully lowered himself into her. With his hands beside her head, he took the bulk of his weight on his arms. His skin was on fire where it touched her, his breath warm against her cheek. Kase slowly eased into her, deliberate in his movements, careful to hold back lest he bring himself to fulfillment before her. Finally, when he was fully sheathed inside her, he paused long enough to sigh and tenderly kiss her cheek.

"You feel so good," he said.

Her heart clamored against his. "You, too."

"I've never loved anyone this way, Rose. No one."

"Not for me, either."

He searched her eyes for the truth. "You don't have to say that, Rose. I know you loved your husband."

Her eyes flooded with unshed tears, and then as he watched one trickle down across her temple he regretted having mentioned her husband at a time like this.

"I'm sorry," he began to apologize but she stopped him with a shake of her head.

"No. I loved Giovanni, but not this way. Never the way I love you."

"God, Rose."

It was all he said, all he could say before he began to move inside her, to ride and thrust and press full length against the shuddering wall of her inner core.

She clasped him to her, clinging with her arms about his neck and her legs wrapped about his waist. She rode out the storm of their heated exchange, rose to meet his thrusts and urge him on until she moaned with the pleasurable pain of his frenzied movements.

"Come, Rose," he invited. "Come with me."

She gave herself over to the insistent throbbing that had built inside her, lost herself in every pulsing wave after wave of rapture that shook her as she felt him burst forth inside her.

They drifted back to reality with the same gentle settling as the snowflakes outside the window, and like the snowflakes, they lay side by side, each uniquely different from the other, and yet the same. Replete, comfortable in each other's arms, they rested while their ragged breathing calmed and their heartbeats slowed to normal. Kase held her close until he felt Rose shiver, then let her go long enough to help her rise, pull back the covers, and see her safely tucked beneath them.

He put a log on the fire and stirred it back to life, turned down the lamp, then crawled into bed beside her.

They slept as they had but once before; she nestled against him, her head resting near his collarbone, her hip-length hair a veil that draped them both.

Chapter
Sixteen

*

They talked of everything and nothing, of likes and dislikes, of families and friends, as they shared the quiet hours before the dawn spread its light across the plain. Their whispered exchanges were silenced by stolen kisses and caresses until Kase drew Rosa close and placed a kiss against her temple.

"I have to get back to my room before Quentin gets up."

The thought startled her back to the reality of their situation. Rosa glanced toward the darkened window. The sun was not yet up.

"I'll take you back to town with me today," he went on, planning aloud, "and tonight we'll have supper together. Alone," he amended. "We'll celebrate."

"After the restaurant is closed," she added. "I have a special surprise for the celebration, I think."

He turned toward her. "Oh?"

"*Sí.*"

"What is it?"

"If I say what it is, it is no longer a surprise." A special shipment of cabernet she had ordered from Cheyenne was due to arrive on the afternoon train.

She reached out for him and smoothed his hair back away from his face. "Is true that soon you will not be the marshal?"

"*Sí*, is true. I never planned on staying here, and now that we're to be married, I hope Quentin finds a replacement soon."

Impulsively, she hugged him close. "Then we go to visit

your family in . . ." She tried to remember the name of the city where his people lived.

"Boston. We can be married there. Wait until you see the house." The "house" was a mansion, but Kase decided to withhold some surprises of his own. Now that things were settled, he could not wait to introduce Rose to Analisa and Caleb. He could hardly wait to see the two women together. He knew instinctively that Caleb would love Rose and welcome her into the family.

"We will not marry here?"

She sounded so disappointed that Kase found himself frowning into the darkness. "I just assumed we'd be married in Boston. If you'd rather not—"

"No." She shook her head.

He straightened against the headboard. "I forgot about your family. Do you want to go back to Italy to get married?"

"No!" She was emphatic. "No Italy." In the eyes of her family she was barely a widow. Five months alone in America and already she had fallen wildly in love with a man they would never approve of, not with his dark Gypsy looks. They would have nothing in common; he was not even a farmer. Her relatives, though she loved them, were as prejudiced as the rest of her countrymen. Every province claimed superiority over the others, and so suspicion was cast on anyone not of the Piedmont. No. She did not desire a wedding in Italy. "I thought here," she said hesitantly, "with my new friends."

He smiled into the darkness and hugged her close. There was no doubt in his mind that, given the chance, she would invite all of Busted Heel to the wedding. He wondered how many of them would actually attend and not object to their marriage. Kase was looking forward to telling Floss and Zach that his plan had not only succeeded in unruffling Rosa's feathers, but that she had even agreed to marry him. Both Flossie and Zach felt they'd had a hand in the matchmaking.

"If that's what you want, we'll be married here. As soon as possible. My parents can give us a reception in Boston."

"Reception?"

"A party. A fiesta." He used one of the few Spanish words he knew.

"Ah. Festa."

"Do you think it is possible, a priest?"

He could not resist teasing her. "What's a possible priest?"

She poked him in the ribs with an elbow. "Is a priest in Cheyenne? Is possible he can marry us?"

"I don't see why not. I'll go into Cheyenne and find out tomorrow."

She shook her head in protest. "Not tomorrow. You will stay with me tomorrow. For now I keep you with me."

"Fine with me. I'll be in your custody as long as you like, but I don't want to wait too long." Determined not to harm Rosa's reputation, Kase put off thinking about their living arrangements. She would face enough change once they were married. He prayed silently that he was doing the right thing.

They fell silent, each lost in thought. Rosa hoped she would meet his family's approval far more than she had Giovanni's. Kase knew how proud and happy his mother would be to meet the woman he had finally chosen for his wife.

"I'm going back to my room now." He sighed regretfully and gave her a final parting kiss, one he hoped would leave her thinking of him all day long. "I'll see you downstairs at breakfast."

It was near noon, but still so cold in the marshal's office that Kase had his coat on. He added more wood to the cast-iron stove in the corner before he returned to his desk. The usual disheveled pile of newspapers and notices had been sorted into neat stacks or tossed into the stove until the desktop had taken on an entirely new appearance. His pen and inkwell had made acquaintance with each other after months of separation amid the clutter. Kase sealed the letter he had just written to his family and looked up when Zach Elliot entered the office.

"It's about time you showed up." Kase looked down at the letter in his hands.

"I didn't know I was 'sposed to be here at any given time." Zach sauntered toward the stove and rested his foot on its nickeled footrail.

"Where you been?" Kase asked, trying to hide his excitement. He had expected Zach to be in the office when he arrived; Kase wanted him to be the first to know that Rosa had agreed to marry him.

"I been out tryin' to stay warm in this godforsaken hole. Where you been?"

"I spent the night at Quentin's."

Zach arched a brow. "Oh? And the widow?"

Kase shrugged. "It started snowing and Quentin insisted we both stay on."

"Didn't think she was even gonna get in the rig with me yesterday. I expected her to hightail it out o' there the minute she laid eyes on you. Now I owe O'Hallohan two bits."

"You should know better than to bet against a sure thing."

Zach scratched at his stubbled beard. "You're sure a mite more confident today than you was yesterday." He pointed to the neat arrangement of papers on the desktop. "What's the occasion?"

Kase smiled. "It's not every day a man gets engaged."

"Congratulations." Zach spit into the wastebasket. Straight-faced, he asked, "To who?"

"Who do you think?" Kase countered with a teasing twist to his smile.

"Hell, then, I just lost another two bits." Zach smiled despite the outcome of his gambling.

"Paddie again?"

"Naw, Floss this time."

"You should know better than—"

"—to bet on a sure thing," Zach finished for him. He crossed the room and formally offered Kase his hand. "Congratulations again, boy. I wish you years of happiness. By the way, I saw your bride-to-be headin' for the depot a few minutes back. She appeared to be a woman with a purpose."

"The depot?"

"Yeah, bundled up to the eyeballs with a head scarf under her hat and a coat, but I could tell it was her just the same."

Kase stood, set his letter aside, and stretched. He smoothed the pleated front of his blue madras shirt and adjusted the collar, then brushed back his hair with the palm of his hand. The room was getting warmer. He crossed to the coat hook intent on shedding his jacket when Zach said, "Here comes Tuttle, tearin' up the street in an all-fired hurry. Ain't even got on a coat."

Kase glanced out the window at the harried ticket agent and met him at the door. John Tuttle entered the office at a run and sputtered to a halt, wheezing and gasping for air. His wild eyes looked like two beacons in the gray pallor of his skin.

"Marshal, you gotta come quick, there's trouble on the train."

Kase strapped on his gun belt as Zach snapped to attention across the room. "Calm down, John. What's happening?"

Gasping for breath between sentences, Tuttle began to explain. "It's the Dawsons. They're here again and they're on the train. Took it over a few miles back and rode it on in. When the engineer refused to go on, they shot him. Threw him out on the platform right in front of me."

Kase grabbed a rifle from the gun rack and charged out the door. Zach, equally well armed, followed close behind the two men.

"I never saw anything like it, Marshal. Never." John Tuttle talked incessantly as the three hurried along Main Street.

"How many men?"

"I don't know." Tuttle shook his head. "Seems like I saw rifle barrels aimin' out of every window."

"What do they want, did they say?"

"Yeah. Somehow they must have found out this is the least crowded run out of Cheyenne, but it carries the railroad payroll. They want another engineer, demand to be taken as far as Denver. Somewhere before Denver they want horses waitin' for them and a clear shot to the south. They wanted me to telegraph Cheyenne for another engineer, but the lines are down, have been since the snow last night. I thought I was gonna take a bullet when I told 'em. They didn't believe it. Then the ornery one got off—the one that's been here before— and checked the telegraph key. Finally he believed me. That's when he rounded up the folks they were holdin' on the platform and put them aboard, too."

Zach cut in immediately. "What folks on the platform?"

"The ones waitin' on the three o'clock."

Kase halted in mid-stride and grabbed John Tuttle by the front of his shirt. The small man dangled in Kase's grip, his toes scraping the ground.

"*What* people on the platform?" Cold, spine-chilling fear crawled down Kase's backbone and then up again until he felt the hair stand up at the nape of his neck.

John Tuttle tried to swallow, but Kase's desperate hold was cutting into his windpipe. "A couple of cowhands headin' east and"—Tuttle's eyes bulged—"Miss Rosa." He gasped out her name.

Kase let go and John Tuttle crumpled to the snow-covered street. Zach pulled him up and dragged him along as they hurried toward the station.

By the time they had traveled the length of Main Street, Paddie O'Hallohan and Slick Knox were right behind them, armed and ready to face whatever had the other three men on the move.

"What in the hell was Rose doing here?" Kase rounded on the helpless agent when they finally reached the shelter of the station.

Tuttle ran a shaking hand across his eyes and shrugged. "She had a special shipment of wine comin' in—been waitin' on it for days—and today of all days she comes to see if it's on the three o'clock. They rounded her up with the rest. Lord, Marshal, there was nothin' I could do."

Kase looked past the man, studying what he could see of the stranded train. His temper had simmered to a steady boil. His major concern now was to get Rosa and the rest of the hostages off the train. Then he would deal with the Dawsons. "What can you tell me about this train, John?"

"Things could be worse. Not that many cars on this run, not even a first-class coach. Couple of freight cars, two day coaches, the caboose. That's why it's the gold run. No fuss, no bother. They put out a dummy train all armed and guarded that's supposed to handle the Denver payroll."

"But if you know that, so do a lot of other people."

Tuttle nodded. "I guess so."

"How many of the gang are on board?"

"I think they have a man on each car."

"Any way of uncoupling the engine from the rest?"

John shook his head. "Not from here. With the lines down there's no way to signal ahead to the dispatcher. We could have a real problem 'long about dark. No way to warn off the six o'clock."

Kase turned to Zach. "Get down to Al-Ray's and have Ray ride into Cheyenne on the fastest horse Decatur has in his stable. Have him warn them at the depot that our lines are down and that we've got a train standing here at the station. Tell him to bring back an engineer and as many men as the marshal can spare. If they come by train, be sure they stop far enough away to be out of sight of town. Have Ray send his oldest boy to Mountain Shadows. Tell him to have Quentin round up his best shots and get down here."

"Right." Zach was off and running, one hand holding his hat on.

"What other crewmen are on the train?" Kase asked Tuttle.

"Couple o' brakemen, a fireman, the conductor. One of the brakemen tried to jump off the top of the car, but a gunman signaled him back."

"Are the railroad men armed?"

"I don't know. Might have been a rifle up in the engine. Could be the reason the engineer's dead now."

"Damn." Kase shook his head as he stared at the train. There had to be a way to get aboard without any of the gunmen being aware of the intrusion. If there was no way in, he would have to find a way to get everyone out.

He refused to let himself think of Rose. It was the only way he could suppress the rage coupled with fear that roiled inside him. He pulled out his watch and checked the time, then flicked the piece closed. Three-thirty.

"Tell me again exactly what they wanted you to do." Kase spoke to John Tuttle in hushed tones as the men crouched behind the station.

"They told me to come get you. To tell you they were demanding another engineer and they wanted horses left for them just outside of Denver."

"Wait here."

John Tuttle was happy to oblige as Kase laid his rifle on the ground and stepped out from behind the building. He held his hands high, in plain sight of anyone on the train.

"Bart Dawson!" he called out. "Dawson, I'm the marshal here. What do you want?"

A shot rang out and Kase lunged behind the building. "Damn!" he said again.

"What I want," Dawson called out, "is your hide. You're the one that killed my brother, ain'tcha, Marshal 'Breed?"

"That's right," Kase yelled back. "If I'm the one you want, why don't you come on down off the train and we'll settle this between us."

"Not on your life," Bart sneered back. "'Sides, I brought

the rest o' the boys with me. I don't think even you can stand up to all of us, Marshal."

"All of you?"

"Yeah. All of us. I got five good men ridin' with me now."

Kase turned to John Tuttle, who was squatting on the ground with his hands over his ears. "There's six of them," Kase whispered, then looked over his shoulder. Zach was running back up the street. Paddie and Slick Knox remained silent, willing to let Kase handle the situation.

"Hey, Marshal," Bart Dawson called out again. "What you gonna do about gettin' us an engineer?"

Kase looked at a huffing, puffing Zach who nodded confirmation; then he shouted back, "We sent to Cheyenne. It'll take some time. Why don't you let the women and children off?"

"Not on your life."

"Shit!" Zach cursed and spit. Slick Knox reached down and pulled a shivering John Tuttle to his feet. Paddie was sweating despite the cold.

"What are we going to do?" Zach wanted to know. "You got any bright ideas?"

"Until one of us can come up with something, we'll wait for the engineer and reinforcements." A muscle jumped along Kase's jaw as he clenched his teeth. He wanted to call out to Rose, to tell her not to panic, that he'd see her to safety, but he knew that drawing attention to her would only put her in greater jeopardy. There were two things he could do now: hope the engineer from Cheyenne arrived soon, and pray that Bart Dawson would keep his hands off Rose.

Somewhere behind her, the only other woman aboard whimpered softly. Rosa tried to turn around to see.

"Eyes forward, little lady." The guard who paced the aisle swung his rifle in her direction, and Rosa immediately cast her eyes to the floor and turned around.

There were no more than half a dozen passengers in the railroad car, all of them male except the woman who continued to sob. Rosa had recognized Bart Dawson when he stepped out onto the platform to round her up along with the two men waiting to board the train, and although she had donned a shawl and wrapped it about her head and shoulders before she put on her hat, he immediately recognized her. Dawson had grabbed her upper arm and personally dragged her aboard the railroad car. Once they were inside, he thrust Rosa into a seat and warned her with a scowl that she had to stay put or else.

"You're the bitch that got Bert killed, but don't think I'm as stupid as he was," he warned. Bart Dawson leaned close to her and Rosa tried to turn her head, but he grasped her chin and forced her to look at his face. "Don't think you'll be gettin' off easy, either. You're one of my aces in the hole, and I plan to play you. And jest 'cause you're a woman don't mean I won't kill ya." He gave her a last hard look and then stalked away.

The guard assigned to the coach was unfamiliar to her, and she suspected he was not a Dawson; he was much shorter and darker than the two men who had been in her restaurant.

The other hostages, a varied lot, were herded together in the forward passenger car. Two young cowboys who had been waiting on the platform with Rosa had been forced to turn over their weapons and leave their belongings outside. They complied willingly with their captors' demands, but not the railroad men, who showed their anger by arguing and scowling. After many threats and much shouting, they, too, had complied with the gang and were seated separately in the passenger car.

The wood-paneled day car held only two other passengers— a man and the crying woman whom Rosa had spared only a cursory glance after the guard warned her to keep her eyes to herself.

She tried to see out the window, but it was fogged. A few moments before, she had heard Kase call out to Bart Dawson and heard the answering gunshots. Her hands were balled in her lap, her fingers intertwined as she tried to still their trembling. It seemed an eternity before she heard Kase's voice again and was able to breathe freely.

Prayer was an alternative to her fright. Prayer and silence. She closed her eyes and tried hard to imagine what it would feel like when she stepped off the train into Kase Storm's arms.

A woman's cry for help shattered the vision Rosa had conjured. The lady who had been crying was now frantic. "My husband needs help!"

Rosa was afraid to turn around again, but as the guard moved to the back of the car, she chanced a peek over her shoulder. The woman, who was well dressed and sporting a stylish hat, was fanning her husband, who had slumped against her. His face was mottled; his hands furiously clutched at his collar.

"Please help him," the woman cried out again.

A railroad man in overalls stood up.

The uniformed conductor swore.

The guard fired the gun toward the ceiling. The sound of the shot reverberated through the close confines of the coach. Rosa pressed her hands over her ears.

"Everybody stay put," the guard warned. His eyes narrowed until they were barely visible beneath the brim of his hat. "I ain't fallin' for no tricks."

The rear door of the car burst open and a second gunman entered. "What's goin' on?"

The first man pointed his rifle barrel at the now gasping, obviously ailing passenger. "Could be a trick."

"It's no trick," the now frantic woman stood and pleaded. "My husband has a bad heart."

"It don't look like it's gettin' no better," the second gunman said as the sick man slumped forward and fell against the seat in front of him. The woman screamed.

The first guard unceremoniously shoved her aside and threw the unconscious passenger back against the seat. He felt the man's neck, searching for a pulse. From the look of satisfaction on the gunman's face, Rosa knew there was no response.

"He's dead," the man announced to the second guard.

The woman began to sob. Rosa longed to comfort her, but fear held her immobile.

When Bart Dawson came through the door, Rosa pulled her shawl farther forward and listened intently, trying to understand the men's conversation.

"What in the hell was you shootin' at?" Dawson demanded.

The guard smiled sadistically. "Just keepin' everybody in their places. We got a dead one here, boss." He swung his gun barrel back toward the body. "Seems he couldn't take the excitement."

Dawson stared at the dead man for a while; then he smiled. "Drag him out of there. I've got an idea."

The guard obeyed. Rosa watched while Dawson began to pace the aisle. "We got 'em on the run. The marshal said he's sent to Cheyenne for an engineer. I don't want them pullin' anything on us."

"You got the lookouts on top?"

"Yeah, two. Tim's gettin' nervous, though."

The second guard looked around the car. "I ain't feelin' none too easy about this, either."

Dawson grunted a noncommittal reply, then turned back to the first guard. "Shut her up," he growled, indicating the still sobbing woman. Obeying orders, the guard walked back to where the woman stood and stared at her for a moment before he reached out and backhanded her into unconsciousness.

Rosa felt the bile rise in her throat. She choked it down.

Dawson opened a window and bellowed out one word. "Marshal!"

Rosa held her breath and waited for Kase to answer.

"I'm still here, Dawson," Kase called back.

Moments before, when the sound of a gunshot rent the air, Kase had been hard put to keep from rushing the train. Now, as he waited for Dawson to respond to his shout, he glanced at the men beside him. Zach chewed his tobacco as he stared off in the direction of Cheyenne. His face an emotionless mask, he held his rifle at the ready. As smooth and unruffled as he was when he held a winning hand, Slick Knox worked a toothpick between his teeth. The stout Irish barkeep was sweating profusely, his thick neck creased by the starched celluloid collar that seemed to have grown tighter in the last few moments. John Tuttle, wearing a jacket one of the men had loaned him, looked about to vomit onto the slush at their feet.

Kase knew he could count on Zach. As for the others, he was afraid to hazard a guess as to how they might react in a crisis. Even as Kase measured the men's worth, Bart Dawson's voice drew his attention.

"We're sick of waitin', Marshal."

"It'll take time to get an engineer out here from Cheyenne." Kase's even tone belied the nervous tension that was eating at him. "We're working on it."

"You damn well better be," Dawson warned.

Kase tensed when he heard a woman on the train scream. He felt Zach step closer. The scout put a restraining hand on his shoulder. When two more shots rang out, Zach's fingers bit into Kase.

The sound of a hollow thud alerted them to movement on the platform. Kase shook off Zach's hold and stepped forward, careful to keep close to the station wall. Slowly, carefully, he looked around the corner of the building and saw a man's body sprawled lifeless on the wood-plank loading dock beside the train. A vibrant bloodstain bloomed across the man's shirt-front, the crimson a shock of color against the brown tweed of the dead man's suit.

"That's just a warning, Marshal. If you don't want more dead men littering your station, you best hurry it up."

"Dammit, Dawson," Kase called out, "it's going to take some time!"

"Yeah? Well, jest be sure you ain't usin' the time to get any big ideas about comin' in after us. We won't stop to think about puttin' the rest of these folks outta their misery."

Hard-pressed to contain his outrage, Kase did not deign to reply. He motioned Zach forward. The scout stared at the fallen man as he whispered to Kase, "We can wait 'em out. Try and stall 'em for a few hours, but Dawson sounds as jumpy as a flea on a dead dog."

"No way I'm putting an engineer on that train," Kase affirmed. "No way in hell."

"You may not have to worry about it. If the folks that run the line come in from Cheyenne, you may not have a say." Zach looked out toward the horizon. "With the sky as gray as it is, there ain't more'n a few hours of good daylight left. If we could hold off till dark—"

"We'd stand a better chance of boarding," Kase finished for him.

"Jest what I was thinkin'."

"Think it can be done?" Kase asked, his eyes searching the frosted windows for any sign of Rose.

"Anythin' can be done if you put your mind to it." Zach spit an amber stream of tobacco across the slush-coated ground.

"Keep reminding me."

When Bart Dawson and his henchman dragged the lifeless man's body down the aisle past her, Rosa started shaking. When they fired two shots into the body and shoved it out of the car, she was certain her tremors would never cease. Now, three hours later, she discovered that all visible trembling had subsided, but not her overwhelming fear of the men who held her hostage. Rosa was certain of one thing; she was enough of a coward to do anything the men asked. For that reason, she thanked God they had not paid any more attention to her. As the afternoon passed, Bart Dawson had been too preoccupied with his plans to notice her. He spent the day roving from car to car, occasionally stopping to talk to the ever-changing guards he left with the passengers.

Rosa hated Bart Dawson, and it was a new feeling for her; she could not remember ever having hated anyone in her life. The other guards were nothing more than faceless entities to her—puppets that did Dawson's bidding—but each of them represented a threat that was so vile she could not put the thought into words.

The hysterical woman passenger who had witnessed not only her own husband's death but the subsequent mutilation of his body, had become a mindless, helpless heap in the rear of the passenger car. Slouched in her seat, Rosa had long since given up any hope of offering the woman comfort. Around her, the male passengers sat as rigid as she, some staring into space, their thoughts centered on their own predicament, others ever watchful of their captors.

It had been hours since Dawson had exchanged words with Kase. Long, silent hours that passed as slowly as a hard winter. Rosa's tailbone ached from sitting, her bladder felt near to bursting, but she refused to ask—as some of the men had—for the privilege of using the toilet. The temperature in the car had dropped rapidly. As her breath fogged the chilly air, Rosa was thankful she had worn her heavy winter coat and the shawl that was still tied around her head. She suspected the shapelessness of her bulky coat turned aside the men's attention. Staring at the empty seat before her, Rosa wondered what, if anything, was happening outside. By now Kase and the men must have assumed that the robbers had killed the dead passenger outright. If so, they were aware of the dangers they faced. Suddenly, but not surprisingly, Rosa found herself grateful for Kase's ability with a gun.

*

Chapter
Seventeen

*

During the course of the afternoon, the number of men in Busted Heel had swollen to over thirty. A marshal with a posse of some fifteen riders arrived from Cheyenne escorting a Union Pacific official and engineer; Quentin preceded them with eight of his best hands. Eight of the nine full-time male residents of Busted Heel—the one exception being the laundryman, Yee—remained in force to lend Kase whatever support he needed. John Tuttle was good for little except to relate his part in the morning's affair.

Rosa's restaurant was in the building closest to the station, so it had been commandeered as headquarters for the lawmen. Inside the small building, the scent of hot coffee overrode the smell of damp wool and nervous men. Al-Ray's, like every other establishment in town except the Yee family laundry, had shut down for the day. Alice Wilkie moved among the men in Rosa's, passing out sandwiches and turning a blind eye to Flossie and the girls, who insisted upon helping. They distributed more smiles and encouragement than food.

Unable to sit idle in the café, Kase refused to leave the rear of the station. He was slouched against the wall, staring at the train through the gathering dusk when he heard the whisk of satin behind him. He cursed silently. All he needed now was the distraction of one of the girls, especially Mira and her unwanted attention. Before he could turn around, he caught a whiff of Flossie's overwhelming perfume.

"How ya doin', Kase?" She touched his sleeve reassuringly.

He tried to smile and shook his head. "Fine, Floss. Fine as can be."

"She'll be all right." Floss sounded surer than Kase felt.

"Yeah?"

She nodded. "Know how I know?"

He shook his head.

"Well, the way I figure it, there has to be a reason the good Lord led that girl all the way from Italy to this Podunk town, and I don't think the reason is so's she can end up comin' to harm in a stupid situation like this."

Kase stared hard at nothing. Would Rose survive the day? He could not accept any other possible outcome, and swore to himself that he would do everything in his power to rescue her. He wished for an instant that he could see the future as he had seen his past in his dream. Once more he heard the haunting voice that had been so familiar and yet so strange: *Look to the sacred center of yourself. Do not look to the past or to the future.*

Hesitant to deny the wisdom of the haunting reminder, Kase stared at the deserted platform and wondered exactly what might come of this fiasco and why Rose had to be involved. He knew one thing for certain; he'd see her safe or die trying.

He turned to Floss again. "Thanks," he said, struggling to smile. "That's what I needed to hear."

"What are you plannin'?"

"The Union Pacific official from Cheyenne and Marshal Olson have put themselves in charge. They refuse to meet the gang's demands. They're working out some way to board the train as soon as it gets dark enough. They figure the guards on top won't be able to see who's coming up on them." His gaze shifted toward the horizon as he measured the growing darkness. The temperature had dropped as the purple haze of twilight deepened the color of the sky. The few stars that were now visible stood out crisp and clear in the cold, dry air.

"You just take care, Kase," Floss advised, keeping her tone light.

"You bet."

"Speakin' of bets," she said, "I won two dollars from that old coot, Zach. He told me earlier that you and Rosa plan to be married."

"Yeah." He shoved his hands in his pockets and shifted his weight as he fought to keep himself warm. "Yeah, we are."

Trying to recapture the euphoric happiness he had experienced just that morning, Kase stared up at the stars and made a silent vow: Everything's going to be all right, Rose. I promise.

Marshal Glenn Olson was a head shorter than Kase. A new Stetson covered his balding pate, but it did little to shadow his worried brown eyes. Kase watched as Olson and Quentin approached the station. Both men walked with purpose. Earlier, each had offered myriad suggestions for the expulsion of the outlaws. Their footsteps were punctuated by the metallic jingle of Olson's spurs.

"My men are ready," he whispered to Kase.

"I don't mind telling you I think your idea smells as bad as a dead mule at forty paces," Quentin grumbled.

"There's not a damn thing I can do about that, is there, Rawlins? The railroad representative said that under no circumstances are we to let that locomotive roll an inch out of this town with those killers aboard. Give 'em one train and there's no telling what kind of notion another gang'll come up with."

Kase pushed away from the wall as Zach appeared silently behind the other two men. In a low tone that brooked no argument, Kase asked Olson, "How can you guarantee the safety of the hostages?"

Olson turned away and signaled a group of men waiting beside Slick's barbershop. They moved forward under the cover of growing darkness.

"I can't guarantee it, Marshal. But I'm sure as hell going to try to see they all get out of this safely. I've got my crack shots picked out to board the train. The rest of us will be waiting outside."

Kase rested his hand on his holstered Colt. "I want to be among the men who go aboard." There was no way he would wait outside when there was a chance to board the train and see Rose to safety himself. No way in hell.

Olson's sigh was audible, his tone emphatic. "Listen, Storm, I heard all about your fiancée being aboard. Under the circumstances, I—"

Quentin added his assurance. "He's the best shot here, Olson. Hands down. There's not a man among that crew you brought in from Cheyenne who can hold a candle to Kase. If anyone can get aboard and fire without hitting one of the hostages, it's him."

"Well . . ." Olson sounded skeptical.

"There's no use arguing," Kase said. "I'm going."

"It's your neck," Olson said. "Let's go over it one more time."

It took the men who were to board the train an hour to work their way along the tracks in either direction and then double back out of sight of Dawson's guards. Concealed by darkness, careful not to make a sound, the eight men chosen along with Kase crept stealthily toward the cars assigned to them. Blood pulsed through his veins with a thunderous, repetitive beat that echoed in his ears as Kase became physically aware of his situation and surroundings. He had gone from cold to hot until he had begun to sweat; his heavy coat was an irritation he longed to shed.

Aware of every breath he took, every sound he made as he moved over the uneven ground, Kase felt the hair at the base of his neck prickle. Instantly the image of a coyote he had once cornered came to mind. The animal's hackles had stood on end, and its teeth were bared in a vicious snarl.

He had only one goal as he edged close to the train: He planned to hold Rose safely in his arms before the hour was up.

"Hey, 'breed!" Dawson barked into the darkness.

From beneath lowered lashes, Rosa watched the man pace back and forth in a tight space between the first row of seats and the doorway, hating the way the man used the word *'breed* whenever he addressed Kase. She held her breath and waited to hear Kase respond.

She did not recognize the voice of the man who answered the summons.

"Where's that half-breed marshal?" Dawson yelled back. His question echoed Rosa's own thoughts.

"He ain't here. He's eatin' supper."

Eating supper? *Eating supper*? Rosa frowned. While she sat hostage in a cold, half-dark passenger car, her tailbone aching, the muscles in her neck screaming with tension, her bladder nearly bursting, Kase Storm was having *supper*?

"You tol' me an hour ago the engineer would be here before dark. We're damn sick of waitin'. In fact, we're so sick of waitin' we thought we'd hurry things along by relievin' ourselves of some of this unwanted baggage in here."

Dawson stomped to the rear of the car and paced the narrow aisle. He turned to the guard and said, "Pick out one of these men and take him to the door and shoot him. Maybe that'll make 'em sit up and take notice."

One of the hostages, the conductor, jumped to his feet with a roar and leapt toward Bart Dawson. He caught the outlaw unaware and nearly succeeded in resting the gun away before the startled guard aimed and fired.

The gunshot in the closed car reverberated with thunderous sound. Unlike the woman in the rear of the car, Rosa did not scream. Instead, she clamped her hands over her ears and ducked down in her seat.

The conductor's body hit the floor with a morbidly final sound. Rosa squeezed her eyes shut against the reality of what had just occurred not three feet from her. The outlaws moved quickly, Dawson snapping out commands as the guard dragged the conductor's body down the aisle toward the door.

"Toss him out," Dawson said. "We'll give 'em five minutes; then we shoot another one."

The rear door of the car was flung back on its hinges, and Rosa heard another member of the gang run in. The man's voice sounded much like Bart Dawson's but it pulsed with irritation.

"What in the hell is goin' on, Bart?"

"Tom had to shoot him. He tried to take my gun," Bart snapped. "Get back to the other car."

"I'm sick of this shit," the newcomer growled. "I'm takin' my share and movin' on out."

"Like hell you are, Charlie. You're goin' no place. We're all in this together."

"Thanks to you. Listenin' to you is how we got ourselves into this mess in the first place. Ike's sick of it, too. We want out of here."

"What about the gold shipment? There's damn near more than we can carry out on foot, and there's a town full of men just itchin' for you to try it."

"Gold ain't gonna do us much good if we're dead. Ike and me's cold and hungry. We're gettin' out of here."

Rosa peered over the edge of her seat and caught her breath when she saw Bart cast a frantic glance around the interior of the car.

"You plannin' on just walkin' to Mexico?" he asked the man named Charlie.

"We'll take our chances. There's bound to be a house nearby, maybe on the outskirts of town—"

"Hell, there ain't even much of what you could call a town." Bart Dawson visibly stalled as his eyes roamed over the subdued hostages. He paused, staring for a moment at the glassy-eyed woman who sat staring forward in shock in the rear seat. The jaunty hat Rosa had so admired now hung pitifully askew. The outlaw leader turned on his heel and began to stalk down the aisle. Rosa faced forward again and slid low in her seat. She felt rather than saw Bart Dawson stop beside her.

"Get up. It's time to play my ace in the hole."

Rosa shuddered and stared down at the fingers she held clenched tightly together in her lap.

Kase stood beside the passenger car. He was so close he could press his cheek against the cold finish of the outside wall. The other men were in place, dark shadows against a moonless skyline. He listened for the soft whistle that would tell him it was time to climb aboard.

Inside the passenger car, two men were shouting at each other. He could barely make out the words, but he was certain they were fighting about the gunshot that had just ripped through the car. As he strained closer to hear what the men were saying, the sound of a low, slow whistle drifted on the night air. He hoped the guards were too preoccupied to realize it was far too late in the year to be hearing birdsong.

His hands gripped the cold metal ladder on the side of the car. Gingerly he climbed aboard and waited, standing on the coupler between two cars. Just as he was about to climb onto the deck at the front of the passenger car, he heard the door on the other side of the wall bang open.

The sound of Bart Dawson's voice shattered the night. "I got a woman right here who won't live to see the dawn if you don't get six horses to me fast. We ain't waitin' on no engineer."

"It'll take a minute."

Kase cursed Olson for stalling. Why couldn't the man have told Dawson he would comply immediately? Edging closer to the door, Kase stayed well behind the side of the car. He was no more than two feet from Dawson; only the rear wall of the car separated them. His heart pounded as he wondered whether the woman Dawson held in the doorway was his Rose.

The slight sound of metal against metal sounded above him on the baggage car. It was followed by a groan, and then ominous silence. He assumed the guard on the roof of the car had been overtaken. He strained to hear more.

"Get the horses we asked for. Have the marshal bring 'em right up to the other side of the train, the side away from the depot."

"He's on the way," Olson lied.

There had to be at least one other man, if not two, in the passenger car with Dawson, Kase reckoned. The rest were scattered about the cars both inside and on top. He held his breath and counted to ten, waiting for something to happen that would give him the chance to rush Dawson.

Suddenly a shot rang out from somewhere near the engine. Kase stiffened and then quickly relaxed, ready to move. One hand on the boarding rail, he swung around the end of the car, and let his momentum carry him toward the open door. A glimpse of Dawson standing in the doorway holding Rose before him was all he saw before he slammed into them both. The gun in Bart Dawson's hand discharged into the roof of the car as he fell backwards. Fighting to catch his balance, he let go of Rosa.

Kase grasped the sleeve of Rose's coat, yanked her up, and threw her past him out the open doorway. He did not look back to see how she fared, but kept his attention pinned on Bart Dawson. Kase sidestepped and ducked, whirled, and then kicked the gun out of Dawson's hand. A guard near the rear door took aim, fired, and missed as Kase lunged out of the line of fire.

One of the hostages crept down the aisle behind the guard and with his hands clenched together, brought his arms up and hit the guard from behind. Another shot went wild as the guard fell to the floor. Nearly every man in the car was on his feet, some rushing toward the door, others helping to subdue the downed guard.

Kase straightened, his gun on Bart Dawson.

"It's over, Dawson," he said, afraid to take his eyes off the man long enough to see what had become of Rose.

"You think so, Marshal?" Dawson squinted up at Kase with unmasked hatred in his eyes. "You killed my brother. Ain't none of us gonna forget it."

"I don't imagine any of you will have much time on your hands from here on out."

Before Dawson could answer, even before Kase could react, the front connecting door flew open. A wild-eyed gunman paused long enough to take aim. Kase swerved, ready to fire, but Dawson lunged to his feet with a roar and barreled into him. He grabbed Kase in a fierce bear hug, intending to use him as a shield. The outlaw's shot hit Kase low in the back, but propelled by pain and rage, Kase swerved and spun Dawson into the line of fire. The man's second shot entered through the back and pierced Bart Dawson's heart.

A third shot echoed through the car as one of the former hostages in the rear, using the gun Kase had kicked out of Dawson's hand, opened fire on the final intruder. The outlaw fell forward over Kase and Dawson.

Finally, as the echoing sound of gunshots pulsed into silence, everything went still.

When the sound of gunfire ceased, Rosa stared in horror at the crumpled body of the conductor, which lay beside her on the platform. She felt as if every bone in her body had been jarred out of place when she hit the ground, but as she dragged herself to her feet and gauged the distance she'd fallen when Kase had thrown her out of the car, she decided nothing was broken. The shooting spree inside the car seemed to have ended. Cautiously she stepped forward intending to board, willing to face Dawson again if need be, to learn what had become of Kase.

"Wait here." A hand on her sleeve held her back. She recognized Zach Elliot's voice.

"But Kase—"

"Stay put."

The man's sharp tone brooked no argument, so she waited

silently until he was aboard. Then Rosa used the metal stairs.

Oblivious to the many men who streamed in both doors, Rosa sought Kase. At first she was unable to locate him in the confusion. The last of the former hostages was filing out the rear door, carefully stepping around a fallen man Rosa recognized as Charlie Dawson. An older man dressed in a heavy fleece-lined jacket with a badge pinned to the lapel stood over the fallen outlaw. It wasn't until she stepped farther into the car that she saw Zach Elliot kneeling over Kase, who was stretched out in the aisle.

Her heart in her throat, she stepped forward cautiously. She reached out to steady herself with a hand on Zach's shoulder. He turned at her touch, his face grim.

"Kase's been hit. Took a bullet in the back."

"*Dio.*" As she whispered the word, she had a fleeting vision of Giovanni's crudely marked grave as it must be now—covered with snow. Her mind rebelled even as it formed the thought. Not Kase. Please, God, not Kase.

"Give me your scarf." Zach reached out for her shawl. For a moment she stood frozen with fear. He touched her skirt. "Ma'am?"

She removed her hat, jerked the shawl off, and handed it to him. He balled the wool and gently slid it beneath Kase, then rose to his feet.

"Stay with him. I'm gonna see what's keeping help."

Rosa stared down at the blood-smeared streak on the floor, shoved aside her fear, and reached out to brace herself on the armrest of a seat as she lowered herself to the floor. Mimicking Zach's movements, she touched the wadded shawl to be sure it was secure beneath Kase. It was already wet to the touch.

The noise around them receded as the men dragged the Dawsons out of the car. Even in the dimness of the flickering lamplight, she could see that the usual deep color had drained from Kase's face. His eyes were closed tight against the pain, his breathing shallow. She reached out and smoothed a hand over his brow. He felt so clammy, so cold to the touch, that she jerked her hand away. Quickly Rosa slipped off her coat and covered him to the chin. She leaned over and brushed a feather-light kiss against his lips.

"I'm not dead yet," he whispered. "You can do better than that."

"Kase?"

"What?"

"You are all right?" She felt stupid the moment she said the words, but she needed to have his reassurance.

His voice was so weak she had to lean close to hear him. "I've been better."

"Zach is bringing help."

"I'm not going anyplace."

Kneeling on the hard floor, squeezed in beside him in the aisle of the railroad car, Rosa crushed his fingers between her own. It was all she could do, and somehow she hoped that if she clung hard enough, she could keep him from slipping away from her.

Seconds passed like hours. Finally she heard a commotion behind her. Quentin Rawlins's booming voice filled the car as he shouted directions to the men with him.

"Some of you go around and come in the opposite door. We'll lift him out and carry him to Flossie's."

Suddenly the car was full of grim-faced men intent on getting Kase to more comfortable quarters.

"Here, Rosa," Quentin said as he held his hand out to her. "Let us take him now."

She nearly refused, but Quentin stood his ground, his hand extended, until she took it and let him pull her to her feet. Kase gave her other hand a squeeze before she let him go.

"Take care, Signor Quentin," she whispered.

"I will."

Somehow she stumbled out of the railroad car on her own. Dazed, Rosa stepped out into the night, unaware of the activity around her, oblivious to the cold.

She heard Chicago Sue call her name just before Flossie Gibbs hurried forward and threw her arm about Rosa's shoulders. "My God, girl, I thought they'd never get you out of there."

Dazed, Rosa blinked and said, "Kase has been hurt."

Chicago sobbed and Flossie shushed her before she said to Rose, "I know, honey, but he's in good hands. Let's get in out of the cold. They're takin' him home."

"But—"

"Come on. Let's get you in and warm so you can take care of Kase when he gets there."

Flossie held Rosa close and Chicago led the way as they wove through the confusion on the platform. Men were everywhere, some laying out the bodies of the dead outlaws while others stood by with guns leveled on the four prisoners who were still alive. All of them were shouting, their voices carrying on the night air. Rosa let Floss lead her toward the hospitality parlor. The three women fought against the wind that whistled down Main Street.

After Rosa visited the outhouse, Floss ushered her through the parlor and up the stairs. Chicago Sue lit the lamps in Kase's room, her audible, heart-wrenching sobs doing little to secure the tenuous grip Rosa held on her shattered nerves. They were in the room just long enough for Rosa to turn back the spread on Kase's bed and take a sip of the hot coffee Flossie pressed into her hands. She tasted it, then paused to listen to the sound of Quentin's voice as it echoed in the stairwell. All three women crowded into the hallway to wait.

Quentin and Zach carried Kase on a narrow plank, trying hard not to upset it and send him tumbling back down the stairs. When Quentin insisted they could tip the makeshift stretcher slightly and wedge it through the doorway into the upstairs hallway, Zach refused to try. Finally, the bearers negotiated the opening and then moved along to Kase's room.

Rosa silently watched them shift Kase gingerly from the doorway to the bed. Carefully she lifted her coat off him and found Kase nude to the waist, a bandage wrapped tightly about his midsection. A spot of blood had already penetrated the bandage. Zach stripped off his boots and then covered him with a blanket, ignoring Quentin's argument as to how to go about doing so.

"How is he?" she asked.

"Passed out. Probably best, after the way we thumped him down the street." Zach paused long enough to glower at Quentin.

"He's here, isn't he?" Quentin countered.

"Barely." Zach grumbled.

"*Basta*. Stop." Rosa put a halt to their bickering and pushed the men out of the way. "A doctor?" She glanced over her shoulder as she reached out to touch Kase.

"There's one on the way. Olson sent for him before it got

dark, just in case. I didn't think Kase'd be the one needing him, though." Quentin looked thoughtful. "I'll go wait outside."

With a lingering look at the young man lying face down on the bed, Zach Elliot turned away. He paused before the door and with a shattered expression that said more than words ever could, he told Rosa, "I'll be downstairs if you need me."

"*Grazie*, Signor Zach."

As the door closed softly behind him, Rosa turned her attention to Kase.

"Rose?"

The barely whispered word startled her so that she jumped. Quickly, she knelt beside the bed and took his hand.

"*Sì*. I am here."

He opened his eyes and found her watching him intently. Her frightened expression troubled Kase more than his own pain. He hadn't seen her so defeated since the day he told her that her husband had died.

"I'm going to be all right, Rose." His hand slid across the sheets as he reached for her.

Tears welled up in her topaz eyes and began to spill over her lashes.

"Really," he whispered. "Don't cry."

"I'm not crying," she insisted even as tears continued to course down her cheeks.

"Do something for me," he whispered. "Lie down beside me."

"But—"

"Please?"

Brushing at her tears, Rosa glanced once at the closed door and then stood and walked around the bed. With the utmost care, she gingerly climbed onto the bed and eased herself down beside him. Kase did not move, nor did he speak, but the sight of his slow, lazy smile tore at her heartstrings. Her tears began to flow again.

She lay beside him for what seemed an eternity, listening for the sound of footsteps that would herald the doctor's arrival. As Kase remained silent, barely breathing, she sensed that he was hoarding his strength, fighting to remain conscious, yet unwilling to move or speak lest he weaken himself further. She kept her eye on the makeshift bandage tied about his waist. There was no sign of blood other than the dollar-sized spot that had shown through it when the men carried him in. Unwilling to think beyond this moment in time, she called to mind the night before. It seemed a lifetime ago that they were lying side by side in Quentin's guest room, chatting easily about their future together.

It was so quiet in the room—so peaceful compared to the riotous last few minutes and the wearing hours she'd been held hostage on the train—that Rosa found it impossible to keep her eyes open. Just for a moment, she thought, just for a second, I will close my eyes. Clutching Kase's hand in her own, she closed her eyes against the light.

The kitchen in the hospitality parlor was overwarm, the stove in the corner pulsating visibly with heat. Adding wood to the fire was the only outlet for nervous tension, and so Rosa watched in silence as Quentin and Zach alternately fed the oven from the wood box beside the stove.

She stared at the sandwich on the plate before her, certain that even one bite would choke her. Ignoring the food, she glanced at Quentin, Zach, and Flossie who were all seated at the long, oil-cloth-covered table in the center of the room. Until a few minutes earlier, Floss had tried to keep the conversation flowing among them, but she had finally given up the effort. The men stared down into their coffee cups, their attention tuned to any sound that might alert them to the doctor's footsteps on the stairs.

The man had been closeted with Kase for well over an hour. Rosa had been reluctant to leave his side, but the doctor had insisted on it. Between Floss and Zach Elliot's urging, she was finally convinced it would be best to wait in the kitchen.

The sounds in the house were routine, and because they were, Rosa found them maddening. Doors slammed, the girls whispered. While Kase was lying wounded at the mercy of the man attending him, business went on as usual in the upstairs rooms, and she found herself upset by it. Floss had tried to make light of the situation, for indeed, her business was booming.

"Things like this gets 'em all riled up," she said, trying to explain. "Give a man a good fight, a little bloodlettin', and there's nothin' more that he wants afterward than a good woman. Or a good cigar," she added with a laugh.

Rosa's dark expression had quickly squelched the other woman's laughter.

She jumped when Zach stretched out in his chair and his foot hit the table leg nearest her.

"Sorry," he growled before he turned to Quentin. "How many of them Dawsons are left after tonight?"

"Charlie and Bart are dead. Ike was wounded. The three men with 'em have a few scratches; one took it in the arm. They surrendered easily enough once the shooting started. Olson rounded them up and took them all back to Cheyenne."

Before he could add more, the doctor appeared in the doorway and everyone at the table looked up expectantly. There was a momentary pause before Floss shook herself into action. She stood and motioned the doctor toward the chair closest to Rosa's. As Floss hurried to pour the man a cup of coffee, he settled into the chair and set his medical bag beside him on the floor.

Rosa studied the man who was about to tell her whether Kase would live or die. She fought to remember his name and as she stared hard at the faded blue eyes behind the round wire-framed spectacles, it came to her—Dr. Richard Earhart. He was wearing a crumpled wool suit of a nondescript brown that looked as if he might have slept in it. His hands and nails were clean, his shirt a bright white, even if it was not ironed. If she had been in a better mood, his wild mane of frizzy brown hair would have made her smile. He appeared to be in his late forties, but his mild manner and self-assurance made him seem older somehow.

He took a sip of coffee before he straightened and looked around the table again. Zach slouched lower, as if he were trying to avoid the man's pronouncement. Quentin was suddenly alert and attentive; he leaned forward with both arms on the table. Flossie stood by the stove; sweat beaded her upper lip and brow.

Rosa could do little but stare and press her clenched hands together below the table.

"I won't hide the truth from any of you," Dr. Earhart began, "but I want you to remember that things could be worse."

A distinct ringing began in Rosa's ears and for a moment she was afraid she was about to faint. She took a deep breath and tried to relax, but her heart was beating so rapidly she thought it might burst. She tried to concentrate on the man's words.

"The bullet entered very close to the spine." The doctor leaned forward to emphasize his point. "Very close. Had it crushed the vertebrae, injury to the spinal column would have been permanent."

The words meant nothing to her. She glanced at Zach who immediately straightened and explained. "He said the bullet missed Kase's spine." He pantomimed a long column with his hand and pointed at his back. "The spine is all right."

Rosa nodded and turned back to the doctor.

"It doesn't look like any vertebrae were severed." He turned to Rosa. "No bones broken," he clarified with a shake of his head. "But for some reason he doesn't seem to have movement in his legs."

Zach touched Rosa's shoulder. "He said—"

"I understand," Rosa whispered.

"Dammit," Quentin muttered. "Why not?"

Flossie moved away from the stove and sat down heavily in the remaining chair. She fanned herself with her hand.

Dr. Earhart took another long sip of coffee and then tried to explain. "I don't know why, unless there is such trauma near the spine that it will take time to heal. There's no reason he can't move, no physical reason that I can see. He still has some sensation, and he's fully capable of—of controlling his bodily functions."

"You mean he just thinks he can't move?" Quentin sounded incredulous.

The doctor nodded.

"That don't sound like Kase to me," Zach frowned. "Ain't no way that boy would be layin' up there limp as a lizard if he could move. You sayin' Kase is a liar?"

Earhart shook his head. "Not at all. What I'm saying is that his body has suffered a tremendous shock. His mind may be totally convinced that he is paralyzed. When his mind accepts the fact he isn't, he should recover completely."

"What if he's really hurt? Maybe whatever moves his legs is bruised?" Flossie tried to sort it all out.

Silent, Rosa listened to the exchange. Not all of it was understandable, but she did know that Kase could not move his legs and that he was unable to walk. It was just too soon, she told herself. How could he walk yet, after what he had been through?

The doctor's answer to Flossie was blunt. "There's not much chance of that, as I said. I don't really know why he says he can't move. Everything else seems fine."

"So you say he ain't lyin', just that he's crazy?" Zach was still trying to sort it all out.

Quentin stood up. His dour expression matched his tone. "Maybe we need another doctor."

Richard Earhart placed his cup in the saucer. "By all means. Call in someone else." He picked up his bag and pushed back his chair as he stood. "I've done all I can. The bullet is out, and as far as I can see, his spine is intact. Have him rest quietly until he feels he can be up and about. He's out now, and I've left laundanum in case he has any pain."

"Can he be moved?" Quentin asked.

The doctor paused for a moment as he considered the question. "I think so, in a day or two. Just move him slowly and carefully."

Rosa, Zach, and Floss sat in silence, staring down at the patterned tablecloth, as the man quit the room accompanied by Quentin.

"I'll have to wire his folks," Zach said to no one in particular.

Flossie shook her head. "I'm for callin' in a new doctor."

"Don't you worry none on that score. Caleb Storm'll bring in the best money can buy or I ain't a one-eyed bastard."

Numb, Rosa tried to stand. Zach stood and in an uncommon show of gentlemanly manners, pulled her chair out for her. "I want to look at him again," she said to Floss.

The madam stood and took Rosa by the elbow. She leaned close and said, "Listen, honey, if you'd like to stay the night with Kase, you go right on up and do it. I don't see how it can do any harm now, not with you two bein' engaged and all."

Rosa glanced at Zach, who nodded his assent. "Try and get some sleep."

She turned and took each of their hands in her own. "*Grazie, mi amici. Molti grazie.*"

*

Chapter
Eighteen

*

The guest room at Mountain Shadows was simply but comfortably furnished with a golden bird's-eye maple bedroom set. The sleigh bed, so named for its curved headboard and footboard, was the widest bed Kase had ever slept in. The length of it even accommodated his height. A dresser with an oval beveled mirror stood opposite the bed. A matching commode with a towel bar stood beside the bed, and near the door, a tall chiffonier completed the group. Two armless chairs graced the room. Part of a parlor set, the chairs were tufted in a gold brocaded plush that complemented the light wood furniture.

Kase Storm's dark mood was not the fault of the cheery second-story room with a view of the Rockies. Hard as he might, he tried to keep his eyes off of the reflection of himself in the mirror across the room. For two weeks now he had been lying in bed, forced to stare either at himself or out the window. During that time he had become more than a man who was unable to walk. He had become a prisoner of his own making. Too proud to be carried down the stairs, he refused to leave the room. Quentin Rawlins had been courtesy itself, determined that Kase should have every comfort.

It had been Quentin who insisted Kase be moved to Mountain Shadows as soon as the doctor gave permission. Three days after the shooting he was wrapped in blankets, stretched out upon a makeshift bed in the back of a flatbed wagon and driven out to the ranch. Rose had been at his side then, as she had every moment since his accident. Consideration for Rose had been part of the reason behind Quentin's insistence that Kase be moved out of Flossie's.

He gazed at himself in the mirror and then looked away. It was not hard to remember the discussion he had had with Quentin the day he was carried into this room and Rose was finally persuaded to rest.

Quentin had been fidgeting about the room, shifting the draperies, fluffing the pillows, until Kase irritably told him to stop. "You remind me of an old woman," Kase had grumbled.

"Well, I'm just glad to have you here. It's best for Rosa, you know, to have her out of Flossie's," Quentin admitted.

"You care a lot about her, don't you?"

"Yeah. I do."

Quentin had paused and quickly dropped his gaze. Too quickly. A sudden thought struck Kase. "You're against her marrying me, aren't you?"

"I hope I didn't give you that impression, Kase."

"But it's true, isn't it? I didn't realize what was wrong until now, or maybe I didn't want to see the truth. You weren't surprised or enthusiastic when I told you about our engagement. You don't think she should marry me."

"I have to admit I had my objections at first, but she loves you so much she won't be happy without you. I just hope you've thought about what marrying you will mean to her."

"I had hoped it would mean she'd be happy. But now?" Kase shrugged and plucked at the bedspread. "Now we have even less on our side."

"It would have been tough before you were . . ."

Kase had watched Quentin struggle to put his disabling condition into words. The man could not bring himself to say the word "paralyzed," and so he omitted it altogether.

"But don't get me wrong. You know I'd give you the shirt off my back."

"I've got all the shirts I need, Quentin. In your own way you consider me a friend, but even if I could still walk, you wouldn't think me good enough for Rose. I'd be better off marrying someone with mixed blood, or a pure-blooded Indian. Or how about a Mexican? Would a Mexican girl do?"

"Kase—"

Abruptly Kase admitted, "You'll be happy to know I've decided not to marry Rose."

Rawlins had managed to look genuinely dismayed. "But she's in love with you! She's got her heart set on it."

"She'll have to get it unset."

Quentin shook his head. "Rosa Audi? You tried to change her mind about living in Busted Heel, and a lot of good it did. This is going to hurt her, Kase."

"Rose is like a cat. She'll land on her feet. Besides, you'll be around to pick her up. Won't you?"

"Your parents will be here in a couple of weeks."

Kase had felt his heart lurch. "What?"

"I wired them. They're on their way." Quentin turned and started to leave the room. "Maybe they can talk some sense into you."

"Quentin, wait," Kase had called out just as the door was about to close.

Rawlins paused in the open doorway.

"Don't say anything to them about Rose and me."

"Won't they wonder who she is? I can't exactly lock her out of here."

"I'll take care of them."

With a final meaningful stare, Quentin had said, "I bet you will."

Kase put the memory aside, closed his eyes, and tried to sleep. He wished he wasn't beholden to Quentin, wished he could refuse the man's hospitality, get up and walk away. But until Caleb and Analisa arrived, there was not much he could do.

They were due to be here in a few hours. Zach was ready and waiting in town to bring them out to the ranch. As much as he looked forward to seeing them again, Kase dreaded the coming reunion. How was he to apologize for everything he had said to them? He had been selfishly cruel and unfeeling toward them both, and now he found himself needing them more than ever. He wouldn't have blamed them if they had refused to come to Wyoming, but as always, they would stand by him.

He didn't deserve them. Either of them. But he hoped that after they arrived he would find the right words to let them know how much he loved them both. And, he thought hopefully, maybe their presence would keep him from dwelling on Rose.

Analisa Van Meeteren Storm paused outside her son's bedroom door and drew a long, steadying breath. She reached out for the knob, saw how badly her hand was shaking, and pulled it back. She pressed her palms together. Her fingers were icy cold. She pressed her hands against her cheeks and took another deep breath.

Analisa was not sure what she would find on the other side of the door. Dear Zach, on the way out from town, had told them about the shooting. When they arrived, Quentin had assured them that Kase was still strong, although bedridden. He expressed some concern for her son's spirits, but said his health was as good as could be expected.

She wished she could breeze through the door as if the confrontation that had caused Kase to leave home had never happened. But her feelings ran too deep to make light of the issue. She could not hide her emotions as so many women did. For the first time in her life, Analisa was hesitant to be with her son.

How would he respond? What did he think of her after what he had learned in Boston? She had been spared any memory of the rape she had suffered that had resulted in his birth, but she had been foolish to hope to hide the facts from him for so many years. Kase was intelligent and sensitive. He had been so all of his life. She should have known that the questions he persisted in asking about his real father would not easily be brushed aside.

And now, because she had tried to shield him from the truth, he had left home, taken a job as marshal, and as a result, lay paralyzed in the bed beyond the door.

Listening intently, she did not hear a sound coming from the room. She reached out again, her hand not much steadier than before, and silently turned the knob.

Kase was sound asleep. Analisa tiptoed across the room and stood beside the bed staring down at him. Except for the shadows beneath his eyes he looked much the same as he had when he left Boston. For a moment he frowned in his sleep; then his facial features relaxed. He had looked the same as when he was a child.

Even in sleep he was not at peace.

Life in the East had been a struggle for him, much more so than when they had all lived in the Dakotas where a half-breed, though not fully accepted, was not viewed as an oddity the way Kase and Caleb had been in Boston. When Kase was a little boy she wanted to keep him safely hidden away from the world in their little sod house on the prairie. But even then she knew in her heart that her plan was not a realistic one. When Caleb came to them he had opened the door to a world Analisa might have never known. He had loved Kase and called him his own.

Caleb was her strength. She would have chosen him over a hundred men. A thousand. Just as Kase was a part of her soul, Caleb was her life.

Kase frowned again and shifted uncomfortably. Unable to resist touching him any longer, Analisa carefully sat on the bed and smoothed his hair back off his forehead. She palmed his cheek and watched as his eyes opened and the slow light of recognition dawned in them.

He stared at her for a moment and started to speak, then stopped. Analisa smiled down at him.

He lifted her hand to his lips and softly kissed her palm and placed it against his cheek again. His eyes filled with tears.

Analisa continued to smile through tears of her own as she bent to embrace him. She cradled her son, helped him to sit upright, and then gently rocked him in her arms.

Time passed slowly as mother and son nurtured each other in a way they had not done in years. Finally Kase raised his head and brushed away his tears, embarrassed by such a show of raw emotion.

"Mama?"

"*Ja?*"

"*Ik hou van jou,*" he said in Dutch. "I love you."

"*Ik hou van jou,*" she whispered back.

He continued speaking softly in her native language. "I'm so sorry, Mama."

"Don't speak of it."

"No, I must. I hurt you and I hurt Caleb. I said many things that were cruel and unjust. I was only thinking of myself—"

"Of your own hurt. Which I understand. We did not want you to know the truth, but in that we were wrong."

He reclined against the pillow but held her hands, rubbing

the backs of them with his thumbs. "I probably would have done the same thing in your place."

Analisa felt relief at his admission. "Can you put the past behind you now? *Laat het gaan*?"

Kase nodded. "I'm trying to let it go."

"Good. It is the only way." She hugged him again and wiped her eyes.

He studied her carefully. Aside from soft lines about her eyes and mouth, she had not changed for as long as he could remember. His mother was a beautiful woman, one any man would be proud to have on his arm. Her blond hair was upswept in a sophisticated new style that was unlike her. Her dress was tastefully impeccable, a two-piece aqua silk, fitted and gathered at the back into a cascade of ruffles. Although Analisa was an accomplished seamstress in her own right, Caleb insisted she buy the very best clothes in Boston and New York. They attended so many receptions in Washington that she obliged him.

In a characteristic movement, she reached up and swept her hand along her neckline to make certain her hair was still in place. He watched her as she seemed to struggle with a decision.

"Caleb wants to see you," she said, her eyes full of hope for reconciliation.

"I don't know why. I said some pretty rough things to him."

"May I get him?"

Kase nodded. "Of course. I've missed him. I've missed you both."

Her smile was as radiant as the sun as she stood and went to get his stepfather.

Just as Analisa had done before him, Caleb entered the room alone. But unlike his wife, he did not need to hesitate outside the door. There was much he needed to say to his stepson and the sooner said the better.

The sight of Kase in bed, the knowledge that the young man could not stand to greet him, shook Caleb to the core. He hid his concern and crossed the room, a warm smile on his face.

"Kase."

Kase turned away from the window and watched Caleb Storm walk confidently to his bedside. He reached out and the two shook hands formally until Kase tugged him forward and they embraced. With much back-slapping and bear-hugging, the two were reunited, but both knew there was still much to be said.

Caleb rose abruptly, wiped his eyes as he turned away from Kase, and pulled a chair up close to the bedside. He sat down heavily and let out a sigh of relief. "Do you know how glad I am to see you?"

Kase smiled. "I think so. I feel the same way about you."

"I wish we were all together under other circumstances."

"Yeah." Kase shrugged. "I was all ready to go back to Boston soon to apologize to you and Mama." He would not allow himself to think of Rose and their plans.

"I've got a few apologies of my own saved up."

"They won't match mine, but you go first."

Both men smiled.

"Kase, we only did what we thought was right. I was trying to protect your mother."

"I know that now," Kase admitted, "and I wish to God I hadn't goaded you into telling me the truth. But I'm glad it's out in the open."

"We are, too. I just hope you haven't agonized over this all these months."

Kase refused to lie. "It haunted me for quite a while. I wondered if I was becoming like him, if I was capable of committing the type of crimes he did, but I learned the hard way that I don't enjoy killing. Even if the man deserves it."

"You aren't the first man to discover that." Caleb looked down at Kase's immobile legs. Had he refused to fire on the gunman who had brought him down? Was that why he had been wounded? "Self-defense is another matter, though."

"Before my time as marshal was through I had to kill again. We had quite a bit of excitement here for Busted Heel."

"So I heard from Zach."

"I think all I ended up inheriting from"—he paused, carefully choosing his words—"from that man is a hell of a temper and the tendency to carry a grudge."

Caleb laughed. "Don't forget you got some of that temper from your mother."

Kase glanced up at his reflection in the mirror and collected his courage. "What I said about you and Mother—"

"You said it in anger. The world had just been knocked out from under you."

"That's no excuse. I can't imagine her with anyone but you."

Caleb smiled a faraway smile and agreed. "Nor can I imagine what my life would have been without her."

"Do you forgive me?"

Caleb reached out toward the man he considered his son and shook his hand.

A thin layer of bright white snow crusted the ground but quickly turned to mud-brown slush beneath the red wheels of the buggy. From where she sat snuggled amid the blankets Zach Elliot had provided for the long ride to Mountain Shadows in the hired carriage, Rosa stared out at the endless miles of rolling plains backdropped by snow-blanketed mountains. The sky stretched out in every direction, a pure ceiling of blue unrelieved by even a wisp of a cloud. Although the sun was shining, the air was so thick with cold that Zach claimed he could cut it with a knife.

When Quentin Rawlins insisted Kase be taken to Mountain Shadows, Zach had driven her out to the ranch as often as weather would permit. Rosa had spent the first five days and nights caring for Kase, unwilling to leave his side. Then, as he slowly began to recover, his confinement did little to ease his ill humor. Although Quentin extended an invitation for her to stay on, Kase had insisted she return to town and the restaurant. Quentin's housekeeper would see to his needs, he said. His parents would arrive soon enough, and there was no longer any reason for Rosa to hover over him. She had finally agreed when she realized that should Kase be bedridden long, they would need the income from the restaurant to support them both.

As the buggy jostled over the familiar rutted road toward the ranch, Rosa thought about the night Kase had driven her to the barbecue over this same route. It seemed a lifetime ago. The frustrated, angry man lying in bed in Quentin's guest room reminded her little of the man who had whirled her through the steps of the waltz and out into the autumn night. She frowned and tried to put such thoughts aside. Time would heal his wound and his anxiety. She tried to understand the fear and confusion he felt as he faced an uncertain future.

Zach flicked the reins and grumbled, "Colder than hell out here."

Rosa smiled to herself. She had come to know the crotchety old man well during the past two weeks. His loyalty to Kase ran deep; indeed, he treated the younger man like a son. She recalled his kindness just yesterday when he returned the shawl she'd given him to use as a makeshift bandage for Kase. Rosa had all but forgotten it until Zach handed it back to her all laundered and folded. "Took it to Yee," he had said offhandedly before he offered his thanks.

On their trips back and forth to Mountain Shadows, Rosa and Zach had continually ignored the obvious question. Rosa refused to give up hope that Kase would walk again; Zach talked about the things she and Kase could do and places they might go once they were married. On bad days, she wondered if Zach was keeping up a pretense of belief in Kase's recovery for her sake, but she was too afraid to ask.

They soon arrived at Mountain Shadows, and Zach drew the buggy to a halt before the wide veranda. He helped Rosa down and then climbed back aboard to take the carriage to the stable area. Rosa shivered from the cold that cut through her heavy coat as she crossed the porch. The door opened to her knock, but instead of Quentin's usual warm welcome, Rosa found herself staring up at a statuesque blond woman.

"You must be Rosa," the woman said, her words laced with a heavy accent. "Come in. Come in and warm up."

"*Grazie*," Rosa said as she stepped past the woman into the well-heated entry hall. Quentin's home always smelled of firewood and spices.

"I have heard many good things about you."

Rosa slipped off her hat, coat, and scarf and took a long look at the woman who greeted her with such familiarity. She was tall, her height accented by the crown of shining braids that encircled her head. Any woman would envy the woman's radiant complexion; it reminded Rosa of the blushing pink of the roses in Zia Rina's spring garden. Her gown was of taffeta plaid in blue and brown; the waistline dipped in front to a point that emphasized her slimness. The stranger did nothing to hide her commanding height. Instead, she stood straight and proud. And smiling.

Rosa suddenly remembered her manners. "I beg pardon, *signora*." She hesitated for a moment.

"I'm sorry!" The woman blushed. "I forget we have not met. Quentin has said so much about you, I feel already I know you."

Quentin must have sent for this woman to care for Kase. Rosa felt a deep, sinking sensation. The striking blond was at least forty years old, Rosa guessed, but still so very beautiful, so aristocratic, that she reminded Rosa of a young version of the contessa. Still, there was something familiar about the woman's eyes.

"I am Analisa Storm. Kase's mother."

Rosa could think of nothing to say. Sudden insecurity coursed through her, and she reached up to pat her hair into place. As usual, her thick hair was slipping from the pins, and the bun atop her head was slightly askew. She blinked, swallowed, and tried to find her tongue. Never, ever, had she imagined that anyone's mother, especially Kase's, might look like royalty. Rosa felt like a little brown mouse beside her fiancé's mother.

Still, she tried to smile. "*Sono molto lieta di fare la sua conoscenza.*"

When Analisa Storm nodded with an expression of incomprehension fleeting across her perfect features, Rosa flushed red. In her startled confusion, her English had momentarily left her. "*Scusi.*" She continued to blush. "I said I am very pleased to meet you."

"I am pleased to meet you, too," Analisa said with a relieved smile. "Come, Kase is waiting."

As they neared the stairs, a man who reminded Rosa very much of Kase came from the kitchen bearing a tray laden with dishes. Analisa's smile brightened at the sight of him, and Rosa was again arrested by her beauty. She watched as the two exchanged smiles before the man's attention shifted to her.

"You must be Rose," he said, echoing his wife's greeting. "Just in time to cajole Kase into eating. I seem to be at a loss in that department. I'm Caleb Storm."

"I am Rosa Audi," she said, unable to stop staring at him. Although he and Kase were alike in many ways, from the deep blue-black hair and warm nutmeg skin tones to the sky-blue eyes, their basic facial structure was far different. Caleb Storm's features were not so starkly chiseled as his son's. His hair waved with a hint of curl while Kase's was perfectly straight. Caleb's lips were thinner, his nose shorter and narrower, where his son's was full. Although Caleb Storm's lips were far less intriguing, they seemed to curve more readily into a smile. As she looked from Caleb to Analisa and back again, Rosa knew where Kase had inherited his own striking, exotic looks.

As they climbed the stairs, Analisa chatted about the cold weather and told Rosa that Quentin had gone into Cheyenne for three days. When they reached the door to Kase's room, Analisa paused and Rosa waited as the other woman drew herself up even straighter, as if steeling herself to enter the room. A bright smile replaced the fleeting concern that darkened the woman's blue eyes.

"Look, Kase. See who is here," Analisa announced with a flourish as she led Rosa and Caleb into the room.

He had been staring out the window, and as the others entered, Kase swung his gaze toward the door. He smiled, but when his eyes met hers, Rosa became all too aware of the concern shadowed there. She took a deep breath and stepped close to the bed.

"You look well today," Rosa told him.

"You think so?" He arched a brow.

"I think so," she said.

Caleb set the tray on a bedside table before he moved to join his wife at the foot of their son's bed. Rosa envied the easy way the man slipped his arm about Analisa's waist and drew her to him. She could feel the concern they tried to hide from their son.

"Sit down," Kase invited, indicating the chair beside the bed.

Used to sitting perched on the edge of his bed, Rosa realized that with his parents in the room, propriety dictated she keep her distance.

"Quentin and Kase have told us all about you, Rosa," Caleb said. "He says you're the best cook in the States, and that you own your own café."

Rosa smiled, pleased with their compliments. "Everyone

here likes my Italian food. I will bring you something special when I come again."

Analisa smiled and leaned against her husband. "I will look forward to it. I'm glad that Kase has found such a good friend. Quentin said you have spent many hours caring for our son. For this I am thankful."

"It is nothing," Rosa assured them and turned to Kase. He was staring down at his folded hands. *Friend*? Had he not told his parents that they were to be married?

As if he sensed the mounting tension, Caleb Storm stepped away from his wife and moved toward the door. "I'm sure you two would like to visit without us old folks standing around. See if you can get him to eat something, Miss Audi"—he nodded toward the tray—"before it all gets cold."

Analisa stopped beside the chair and extended an invitation for Rosa to join her later for tea downstairs. Rosa watched the woman go, the soft rustle of Analisa's Scotch plaid dress the only sound in the room as she swept past her husband. Caleb paused in the doorway as if he was about to say more, then turned and walked away.

Rosa wasted no time in moving to sit beside Kase. She reached out for his hands and leaned forward to kiss him. He did not protest, but neither did he respond when she pressed her lips against his. Rosa pulled back, pretending not to have noticed his lack of interest, but an overwhelming sadness swept through her.

Unable to meet his eyes, she reached for the tray and carefully balanced it until he took it from her and set it on his lap. She removed a plate that covered a steaming bowl of chicken noodle soup, unwrapped a hunk of warm bread, and poured him a glass of milk from an earthenware pitcher.

Today, instead of his usual request that she share his meal, he said nothing as he began with the soup. Kase paused to blow on each spoonful to cool it while Rosa related the events of the past two days. There was not much to tell. G.W. was down with a cough and so had not pestered her for two days. Rosa missed the child sorely. Al-Ray's was now selling Christmas candies, and even though the holiday was still a month away, Flossie had decided to have a gala party.

"I have promised to make bagna calda," Rosa informed him and went on to tell him in detail about the traditional Piedmontese dish consisting of raw vegetables dipped in a sauce made of anchovies and garlic. "By then you will be better and we will go together."

The moment the words had been issued, Rosa knew she had made a grave error. Kase put down his spoon and looked at her. His eyes were shadowed with anger as he frowned.

With a hard edge to his tone he said, "Look, Rose, it's been two weeks and my wound is healing *nicely*, as the doctor puts it, but I still haven't recovered any movement in my legs. I couldn't get out of this bed if I had to, so I wish you'd quit talking as if it's a possibility."

"But the doctor said there is no reason why you cannot walk. There is no reason why you will not get better."

"Don't you think that if I could, I would?" He no longer tried to hide his simmering anger.

Nor did she hide hers. "*Sì*, but I think you maybe give up."

He hit the bed with his fist and nearly upset the tray. Rosa reached out to keep it from overturning. "I'm not giving up, I'm trying to be realistic."

It was her turn to frown. "I do not understand."

He sighed and looked away, his attention focused on the wintry scene outside the window. "I think it would be better if you stopped coming out here, Rose."

She felt her heart skip a beat and thought surely she had mistaken the meaning of his words. When he failed to look at her, she knew she had not. Hadn't they pledged their love to each other? Didn't the fact that they were to marry mean that no matter what the future held, they would face it together?

"Better for who?" She held her trembling fingers together in her lap.

"Better for both of us."

"You did not tell them about us." She nodded toward the door.

"No."

Her intuition had been correct. He had not told his parents of their engagement. Now she understood why.

"You do not love me."

His reaction to her words was swift. His eyes blazed as he stared back. He started to speak, then stopped. She saw his shoulders slump as he let out a long, slow breath. The passionate anger in his eyes dimmed. Kase shook his head and, without voicing the word "no," said, "I think it's best we forget about getting married."

Rosa blinked back her tears. As always, whenever she felt her temper snap, hot tears of anger betrayed her. She leaned close to Kase, afraid she might forget herself and begin shouting, afraid her voice would carry through the open door and down the stairs. "I think you are crazy, Kase Storm. I think it is not fair that you sit here and decide what is better for Rosa. It is *better* not to come here. It is *better* not to marry. You do not know what is better for me."

He answered with cold finality. "I know what's best for me. My parents are here now. They can see to whatever I need. They want to take me back to Boston to see a specialist, and under the circumstances, I can't very well argue, can I?"

"But I can take care for you. I have the restaurant." She watched his lips curve into a mocking half-smile.

"You plan to slave over that oven day and night to make enough to support both of us? I have money of my own, Rose, and plenty of it. I didn't need the damned job as marshal of Busted Heel, and if I'd had any sense, I'd never have come here at all."

He might as well have hit her. "And so you would not have met me, either," she added.

"Look, you're too much of a woman to waste your life with half a man. I had my doubts about asking you to marry me, and things were a lot different then."

"Doubts?" She shook her head in disbelief.

"Yeah, doubts. I should never have asked you to marry me. Things would have been hard enough on you, married to a half-breed, without this—"

"Don't say such things."

"I won't have you married to a cripple, too. I'm sorry, Rose, but the wedding's off."

"But I do not care that you don't walk. I still love you." She tried to accept the fact that his expression had closed down. He was staring at her as coldly as if she were a stranger. His frosty glare reminded her of the way he had looked when they first met.

His voice was low, barely audible, when he turned to stare out the window. "I'd like you to leave now, Rose. If you think about what I've said, you'll realize I'm right."

"I did not know you were a coward." Slowly, with as much dignity as she could muster, Rosa stood. She balled her fists and hid them in the folds of her skirt as she stood staring down at him, trembling from head to toe. He would not look at her.

Furious, too angry to cry in front of him, she turned away and stalked toward the door. Before she stepped into the hall, she paused to look back. It was hard to imagine that the strong, finely honed body that nearly filled the wide bed was disabled in any way. She could not bear to go without trying again.

"I am going because you say to, but you are a fool, Kase Storm. When you change your mind, I will come again."

As she stared at his profile, he continued to ignore her.

Unable to bear any more, she turned on her heel and left the room, but not without slamming the door behind her. Halfway down the stairs, Rosa felt her strength give way and she crumpled where she stood, lowering herself with one hand on the banister. Cradling her head in her arms, she sobbed against her knees.

"Rosa?"

Rosa did not have to look up to know when Analisa Storm sat beside her. The woman did not hesitate to wrap her arm around Rosa's heaving shoulders and draw her near. Rosa was thankful that Analisa allowed her to sob out her sorrow and frustration without asking any questions as she held her close.

When the soft, ragged sound of Rosa's sobs reached him, Kase damned himself for the harsh way he had dealt with her. He set the tray on the bed beside him and threw back the covers, intent on going to her, before reality came crashing down around him and he remembered he could not walk.

When his own eyes misted, he cursed his weakness and stared out at the snowscape.

He had to let her go.

For a solid week he had sought an alternative, but he had been unable to come up with one. There was no easy way, except to tell her good-bye. He had had hours to come to his decision and he hoped that once Rose was over the shock and rejection, his practical girl would understand the reason behind his rejection. By then he would be back in Boston and out of her life forever.

His Rose. Would he ever learn not to think of her as *his* Rose?

As he listened to the sound of her hollow sobs and shared her pain, he wished he could have been gentler—but he was certain that had he shown the least vulnerability, she would never have left him. What kind of life would she have had with a cripple? Certainly not the life she deserved, not after all she had already been through.

He leaned back against the headboard and stared up at the patterned ceiling, willing himself not to hear the muffled sound of her crying in the stairwell, cursing the tears that dampened his own cheeks.

"What's all the caterwaulin' for?" Zach asked from the foot of the stairs.

Rosa sniffed and looked up, then rapidly palmed the tears from her cheeks. What had she been thinking of to let go and show such weakness before these people?

"Are you all right now?" Analisa asked softly.

The concern in her voice was nearly Rosa's undoing, "*Sì*. I am good."

"Well?" Zach stood firm and stared up at them, his good eye nearly squinted shut as he frowned.

"Rose is a little upset, Zach," Analisa explained. "We will have a strong cup of tea and she will be better."

"Looks to me like she needs a hell of a lot more'n a cup of tea. What's wrong with Kase?"

"Nothing," Analisa assured him. He instantly looked relieved. "He is tired of being inside, I think."

"Bored, more'n likely. I'll go up and bend his ear so's you two can jaw over that tea."

"Thank you, Zach." Analisa stood and helped Rosa rise.

Rosa shook her head. "I want to go home. No tea."

"Please, stay," Analisa insisted. "I think we must talk."

With a heavy, heartfelt sigh, she followed Kase's mother down the stairs.

"You take some store in makin' widow women cry?"

There was no mistaking Zach Elliot's dry tone. Kase was glad he had gotten hold of his emotions before the scout crept up on him unannounced.

"What are you talking about?" Kase feigned ignorance.

"Just what I said. You had that gal spoutin' like a waterin' can a minute ago, and even if you don't think I got a right to it, I want to know the reason why."

"You're right. You don't have a right to it."

Zach walked to the window and leaned against the sill. He slouched with his hands in his pockets, his hat pushed back onto the crown of his head. "That ain't good enough."

Kase stared at him stonily and wished he would leave. "I told her the wedding's off."

"Jest like that. You got any particular reason, or are you jest feelin' ornery?"

"I've got a reason." Kase stared at his legs. "Two of them." He thought he heard Zach mumble, "Shit."

"Feelin' a bit sorry for yourself today, boy?"

"Not as sorry as I have been. I feel as if I finally did something worthwhile."

"Like lettin' that gal go away thinkin' you don't care anymore."

Kase shook his head. "No. Like letting her go so she'll have some chance at happiness with a man who's whole."

"Pretty damn noble of ya."

Kase ignored the cutting tone of Zach's remark.

"Pretty damn ignorant, too."

"That all depends on your point of view, I guess," Kase countered.

"Was a time I thought your word meant somethin'." Zach frowned and shook his head sadly.

"What's that supposed to mean?"

"You asked that girl to marry you. Ain't no way you should get out of it unless she decides it ain't a good idea."

"Things have changed. I've changed my mind."

"I don't mean to stick my nose in your business—"

"Nothing ever stopped you before," Kase reminded him.

"—but did you ever stop to think she might be carryin' your kid?"

Kase felt the color drain from his face. "Did I ever give you reason to think I slept with her?"

"No. But I been puttin' two and two together. An' I ain't so old as I can't remember what it feels like to be young and in love. The more I think back on it, the more I realize how careful you was not to let me see who was in your room the mornin' the Dawsons came to town an' shot out Miz Rosa's window."

"Get out of here."

"Think about it," Zach advised.

Kase watched Zach stalk from the room with his familiar carefree stride and wished like hell that he could follow the old man out the door.

"You say Kase asked you to marry him?" Analisa's eyes were bright with tears as she listened to Rosa talk about her relationship to Kase.

Rosa nodded. "*Sì*. The day before he was hurt. Since then, he has changed. He is no longer in love with me, I think. Today he said he does not want to see me again."

Analisa sighed and pushed her cup away, the tea now cold and forgotten. It was not like her son to be cruel. She knew that his impatience with her and Caleb over the last three days was only due to his inability to be up and about. She felt herself frown and reached up to rub her forehead with her fingertips.

The girl across the table from her looked as despondent as she herself felt. Back in Boston she could not leave soon enough to be at Kase's side, but now that she and Caleb were here, Analisa felt at a loss as to how to deal with her son's paralysis. Seeing Kase and Rosa together, Analisa had known at once he cared more for the diminutive Italian than he had let on.

She was not disappointed with his choice. The girl was obviously in love with Kase, her tortured expression told Analisa more than words could say. As she watched Rosa stare listlessly into space, Analisa could not deny the earthy beauty cloaked in innocence that the girl possessed. She wished she could reassure Rosa that all would be well. Instead, she felt unsure, unwilling to make promises that she could not keep.

"Kase is stubborn. More even than me," Analisa tried to explain, "and I have a head as hard as a brick, Caleb always says."

There was a glimmer of a smile in Rosa's eyes. "I, too."

"I think that Kase is very confused, Rosa. He does not know if he will walk again." Analisa tried to push aside the fear she held that, indeed, her son might never recover. "It could be because of this that he does not wish to hold you to the promise to be wed."

"But I love him still. I do not care if he can walk or no. I do not care even if he has a head or no. I love him. I will take care for him."

Analisa offered the only plan she could devise this quickly. "Maybe it is best that you give him time alone. Do you think so? Maybe he will be so lonely for you that he will change his mind. He will miss you and soon regret his words."

"But he says he will go with you to Boston, *signora*. And I think Boston is very far away." A tear trickled down her cheek and Rosa wiped it away.

Analisa took a deep breath and wished Caleb would join her. She could have used some help in handling this new and confounding situation. Why was it she never felt any older? Certainly she did not feel old enough to have a son full grown, let alone a son who had left the care of his dejected fiancée up to her. Yes, Caleb's presence would be most welcome, but she knew he was in the parlor enjoying the roaring fire and a new book.

Analisa drummed her fingers on the dining table and made an abrupt decision. "We will not leave for three weeks. It is nearly Christmas, and Quentin has invited us to stay. Yes"— she nodded, more and more certain as her ideas began to take shape—"we will stay. You will go to town and wait. Kase will soon come to miss you and send for you once he realizes that he cannot live without you." She smiled brightly. "Then you will see. We will have a wedding after all, and you will be one of the family."

There, Analisa thought. It all sounded so final, so sure. Things would work out. Hadn't her own life been like one of the fairy tales she had told Kase as a child? Life was good. Kase would be well. He and Rosa would marry. She had decided, and so it would be.

Still, as she watched the small golden-eyed girl don her heavy winter coat and cover her luxuriant dark hair with a black wool scarf, Analisa felt a deep sense of foreboding that she might be wrong.

*

Chapter
Nineteen

*

The wind blew fiercely against the window of Kase's room, but he noticed neither the sound nor the chill that seeped in through the minuscule cracks around the sill. Lately he had taken to sitting in the straight-backed chair near the window and staring out at the mountains for long hours at a time. The silent snow-covered giants—massive upheavals from the belly of the earth—were somehow soothing. He had made a habit of marking time by watching the sunlight shift and play across the face of the mountains until evening, when it slipped behind them.

For the past two weeks the sun had continued to rise and set just as it always had, but nothing had been the same since Rose slammed out of his room. He should have been happy. His wish had been granted; she had given him up without a fight. But the cold finality of her departure from his life was not an easy reality to face in the cold light of each new dawn. Not a morning passed that he did not wonder where she was or what she was doing, and in a secret corner of his heart Kase found himself wishing she would come to see him again.

Just once more, he told himself. If I could see her just once more. But then he would realize the futility of his wish. He refused to condemn her to life with a cripple. Every day he tried to move his legs, tried to pull himself to the edge of the bed in the hope that he might be able to inch his legs toward the side and somehow stand, but his lifeless limbs kept him immobile. There was no way he could protect her if he had to, no way he could do anything but be a burden on her. Rose deserved a better bargain. It was far better this way.

Still, he wondered if she thought of him every waking moment and in her dreams, as he thought of her.

Kase pulled out his watch and checked the time. It was nearly two o'clock. He pocketed the timepiece and straightened his cuffs. Dressing had been his latest accomplishment. His mother had insisted on helping him dress, and even he had to admit that he felt better dressed and seated in a chair than he had lying in bed in a nightshirt. Just as he had long ago given up lying in bed all day, he had given up feeling sorry for himself; now he felt nothing.

The door opened and he glanced up to find Caleb standing on the threshold smiling at him.

"I brought up the paper."

"Come in," Kase invited as he turned his attention away from the window. "I was just beginning to wonder when you'd be in." His stepfather had taken to spending the afternoon in his room, content to talk, or to read silently if Kase was not in the mood for conversation. Kase was grateful for the company and thankful that Caleb could sense his varying moods.

"Anything worth reading?" Kase asked. He watched Caleb's expression sober.

"Not really. I was hoping to find news of the impending legislation that would change the terms of the Dawes Act." Although no longer an active agent for the Bureau of Indian Affairs, Caleb kept up on legislation that concerned the Indians.

"The one that spells out general allotment of reservation lands?"

"Exactly. There's a move in Congress to allot to the Sioux whatever reservation land is left *after* they negotiate cession of any surplus lands."

Kase knew what such cuts would mean. "And naturally the Sioux would lose more of their allotted reservation land." His expression darkened as he remembered the living conditions of the people at Pine Ridge. "Conditions are already deplorable there. Hasn't the government taken enough?"

"If you don't mind my asking, son, when did you get to be

such an authority on affairs at the reservation?" Caleb drew up a chair and straddled it.

Kase took a deep breath before he answered. He had waited for an opportunity to tell Caleb what he had experienced at Pine Ridge, but until now the time had not presented itself.

"I went up to Pine Ridge about two months ago." Kase waited for a comment from Caleb, but when none came, he continued. "There was a lot I had to come to terms with, and at first I didn't know how to go about it. I went up to the reservation searching for the man who fathered me. I found out he's dead. Has been for years. But I met someone who helped."

"Care to tell me about it?"

"There's not much to tell, not much I could put into words anyway. I went to see a shaman, Running Elk."

Caleb nodded. "He is supposedly a very powerful man."

"Running Elk helped me see inside myself, if you can understand that. I'm not even sure that I do. He sent me on a vision quest, though I'm not certain if what I had was a vision or a hallucination. It helped settled my concern about any traits I might have inherited from the man named Red Dog."

Caleb was visibly relieved. "I'm glad to hear it. I guess I have myself to blame for letting your training go by the wayside. I should have taught you myself, sent you on your quest when you were younger."

"That wouldn't have been very practical in Boston."

"I don't think it matters where you go to find yourself."

"Do you think there's a way to see into the future as well as the past?" Kase asked.

"There's no harm in trying to see what lies ahead. I'm not sure how to tell you to go about it, though." Caleb suddenly smiled. "I'm sure Aunt Ruth would be happy to read her astrological charts for you."

They both laughed, knowing full well that whether he requested it or not, Ruth Storm was probably going to advise him of his predicted future. Kase wished she could guarantee that he was doing the right thing by shutting Rose out of his life. What if he did walk again someday? What if he lost her because he was too impatient to wait until all hope was exhausted? He glanced out the window and watched as shadows from passing clouds moved over the face of the land

and undulated across the peaks and valleys of the mountain-sides.

Caleb broke the silence. "Zach stopped by a few minutes ago. He'll be up to see you as soon as your mother stops filling him with appelflappen. He said your friend Flossie is having a Christmas party. If you'd like, we'll drive you into town and we can all go together. It might be fun."

"No!" Kase answered sharply. "No, I don't think so," he said more gently. Attending another one of Flossie's parties would only remind him of the first time he and Rose had made love after the birthday celebration. Besides, he thought, Rose was sure to be there. It was too soon to see her again. He was still far too vulnerable to her.

"We'll be leaving for Boston the week after Christmas," Caleb said. "Are you looking forward to going home?"

Kase paused to think about his answer. Home? He had never thought of Boston as home. Now, at the thought of leaving Rose behind, the thought of returning to Boston made him sad. Still, he did look forward to seeing his sister, Annameike, as he called her, once again. He would miss sharing their traditional Christmas celebration with her.

As if Caleb had read his mind he said, "Annika said to tell you that we will all have to celebrate Christmas again with her and Aunt Ruth when we get home."

Kase smiled as he thought of his aunt Ruth, who was Caleb's stepmother. Absentminded and a bit eccentric, Ruth kept them all laughing. She nearly created a whirlwind as she bustled about the mansion.

"Your mother and I have high hopes that the doctors in Boston will be able to help you walk again."

"I know. I just hope you don't have those hopes set too high," Kase warned.

Caleb took a deep breath and tapped the folded newspaper against his knee. "Kase, I know it's none of my business, but I was wondering if you ever intend to see Rosa again?"

"You're right. It's none of your business."

"It's pretty obvious that she cares for you."

Kase arched a brow, his voice cynical. "Yeah? How long do you think she'd love living with someone who can't even put his own pants on?"

Caleb did not hesitate to answer. "If she loved you? Forever."

"Really? I don't think so."

"So you're shutting her out of your life because you can't walk?"

"That and other obvious reasons."

They stared at each other in silence. Kase wrestled with a question that had long been on his mind.

"If you had to do it all over, would you marry Mother again?"

Caleb frowned. "I told you the other day that she is my life. If you're wondering if I think it was fair of me to subject her to life with a half-breed, yes, even then I would do it again, not because I'm the world's most selfish bastard, but because your mother loves me as much as I love her. We never doubt that in each other. That love makes us stronger than any prejudice or hardship we have to face. And we've always faced them together."

Caleb stood up and walked across the room. He paused momentarily to toss another log on the fire before he left. "Does that answer your question?"

Kase turned his head and watched the light and shadows play across the land. "Yeah. Yeah, it does. But it doesn't change my mind."

"I mean it, Rosie gal. You just close this place on up and come over for dinner with me and the girls tonight. Paddie's droppin' in and so's Slick. Prob'ly won't be more than half a dozen cowboys in tonight, bein' as how it's Christmas Eve."

Rosa shook her head. For a good fifteen minutes she had tried to convince Flossie that Christmas Eve meant little to her except that it was the night before a holy day. In Italy the family had always celebrated the legend of the old crone, the Bifana, on January 6. The children were told of the old woman dressed in black who passed by their homes and left surprises for those who were good.

Flossie was adamant and not about to budge when Quentin strode across the sidewalk and opened the front door. Cold air swept in behind him. He pulled off his hat and smoothed his hair into place. Rosa's heart began to pound. Did he bring news of Kase?

"Hello, Rosa. Floss. What's the gossip today?"

"No gossip, Quentin. I'm just tryin' to talk a little sense into this gal. She's fixed us all up with a heap o' food for the holidays and now she's refusin' to come over and eat with us."

"I certainly hope she doesn't, because then she won't be able to come out the ranch and have dinner with us."

Rosa's mind spun out of control. She had not heard from Analisa except for a short note delivered a week ago that advised her to wait a while longer before she returned to Mountain Shadows for a visit. Now that Analisa had sent for her she was suddenly nervous.

"But—"

Quentin shot a glance at Floss. She waited as anxiously for his response as Rosa did. "Analisa sent me to fetch you, Rose. She said it's Christmas and that you and Kase should be together."

"And Kase?" Rosa asked.

The big man shrugged. "I don't know what he's thinkin' anymore."

Rosa turned to Floss and grabbed the woman's hands. "What should I do, *signora*?"

Flossie's eyes searched Rosa's for a moment before she squeezed her fingers and urged, "Don't keep your ride waitin'. You hurry on now and dress, and I'll keep Quentin company."

Suddenly brimming with hope, Rosa reached out for Flossie and gave the woman an exuberant hug. She swung around and set her skirt twirling, then called out over her shoulder to Quentin. "*Un momento*, Signor Quentin, and I will be ready."

The sleigh ride out to the ranch stretched Rosa's patience to the limit. The minutes crawled by as Quentin insisted on chatting amiably all the way. Although she nodded at all the right times, she had no idea what he was talking about. Her imagination had taken possession of her mind.

Wrapped warmly in her cocoon of woolen blankets, her ears and mouth muffled against the cold by her shawl, Rosa tried to foresee the scene that would unfold once she was face to face with Kase again.

He would be stronger, more like the Kase she had known before the shooting. He would tell her how much he had missed her, what a fool he had been, and how he could not live without her. If he cared even half as much for her as she did for him, he would have suffered through the long weeks of separation.

She shifted on the seat, afraid of wrinkling her black velvet dress. Flossie had altered it so that she no longer felt lost in the voluminous layers of heavy velvet. It had been cleaned and pressed and was ready for just the moment when she would see Kase Storm again.

Aware of an abrupt halt in Quentin's stream of conversation, Rosa looked around and discovered that he had drawn the sled up beside his porch and was waiting for her to comment.

"Are you ready to go in?"

Rosa glanced up at the second-story window of Kase's room and took a deep breath. The moment she had been awaiting was at hand. She smiled behind the shawl. Her eyes were bright, her heart fighting to keep up a steady rhythm without skipping beats. It would be wonderful just to see Kase again. She had missed him terribly and had wondered when he would ask Analisa to send for her again, and now the time had come. Christmas was a time of love, of giving. Perhaps he had waited until today to see her so as to make their reconciliation that much sweeter.

Greetings were exchanged all around in the entry hall. Festive garlands of pine adorned every available surface and twined around the banister. The rich smell of cinnamon, nutmeg, and cloves spiced the air and added to the warmth in the room. Analisa and Caleb did not hesitate to welcome Rosa with familiarity, bestowing hugs and smiles that she knew were genuine. Analisa looked regal in a deep burgundy satin that enhanced her upswept golden hair. As Rosa let Caleb help her out of her coat, she wondered if the severe black of her gown would inject a note of sadness into the happy holiday gathering. Then she recalled Flossie's compliment. Her friend had assured her that the dark gown, which now fit perfectly, lent sophistication to her youthful beauty. She clung to the hope that Floss was correct as she smoothed the fitted bodice and straightened the waistline.

Instead of her usual, unmanageable hairstyle, she had chosen to wear her hair in a crown of braids, as Analisa had done on the day they met. It was a style she had often worn in

Corio, but felt far too plain for America. Having seen how elegant the simple style looked on Analisa, Rosa had hoped to achieve the same effect.

"I have brought food," she announced, remembering Quentin, who stood just inside the door laden with covered plates. "Crostoli. My little friend in Busted Heel says they are cookies." She shrugged, unsure if G.W.'s comparison was correct. "And I have also brought fresh bread with herbs and some tortellini."

"How wonderful, Rosa. You should not have gone to so much trouble for us," Analisa said graciously.

"Is not trouble for me," Rosa assured them with a smile and shake of her head. She could not keep her glance from straying to the parlor beyond the wide archway. Was Kase willing to leave his room yet?

Caleb sensed her impatience to see his stepson. "Would you like to go up to see Kase? Anja has everything nearly ready, but take your time. We'll eat in an hour."

Rosa turned to Analisa. "Kase is not eating with us?"

The woman's smile dimmed, and she looked at her husband for support. Caleb answered, "I'm afraid not, Rosa. He still hasn't been downstairs. His stubborn pride won't allow him to let us carry him down, and he refuses to let us celebrate up there with him."

"Then I will eat in his room." It seemed a simple enough solution until she watched them all exchange worried glances. "Is a problem?"

"Analisa didn't tell him we invited you," Caleb said softly, his voice apologetic. "We wanted to surprise him. We thought you might be able to entice him to come downstairs."

"I see," Rosa said. Suddenly the bountiful fullness of the day diminished. Kase had not sent for her. He did not even know she was joining the family. Everyone seemed to be waiting expectantly for her to do something, say anything to relieve the tension in the room.

"I will go up and surprise him, then," she said, mustering her spirit and donning a wide if tremulous smile.

She lifted her skirt and carefully held it aside as she walked up the steps. Rosa could feel everyone in the hallway below watching her ascend the stairs, and for a moment she felt like a condemned prisoner walking toward her fate. She shook herself mentally and called to mind the scene she had envisioned in the sleigh. In a few moments she would be laughing at her fear.

Below her in the entry hall, Analisa Storm leaned back against her husband and called upon his steady strength. "I hope I have done the right thing," she whispered.

"I do, too," Caleb said. "I hate to see her hurt, but I know how our son is once he's made up his mind."

"Kase?"

Rosa stood just inside the door. Her gaze going directly to the bed, she found Kase missing. Then she heard a sound and turned to find him sitting near the fireplace in a straight-backed chair.

When she entered the room on the soft hush of velvet over rustling petticoats, Kase thought he had conjured her up. When she spoke his name aloud with the accent and inflection he knew so well, he was certain the vision was real, but he could not speak. He must have made some sound, for he watched her turn wide, startled eyes in his direction. She paused like a sparrow about to take wing before she crossed the room and stood close enough for him to become enveloped by the scent of her, a delicious, tempting scent that he could almost have sworn was vanilla.

"Hello." Her voice cracked on the word and she was unable to say more.

"*Buon giorno.*"

"You speak good Italian," Rosa said, longing to throw herself into his arms.

He let himself feast on the sight of her. The once oversized, baggy dress now fit her with maddening perfection showing off her full breasts and narrow waist. Zach's words came back to haunt him and he stared hard at her. She looked thinner than when he'd seen her last. "I haven't had much practice lately, though. You look"—he stopped short of saying *ravishing*—"nice."

Nervously she ran her hands down the front of he skirt. "*Grazie*. Signora Flossie haltered my dress."

Kase knew there was no use fighting the smile her innocently mistaken disclosure inspired.

Rosa's heart tripped as she watched the familiar light

blossom in his eyes and his sensual lips turn upward as he smiled.

"I think you mean she *altered* it for you. A halter is something a horse wears, Rose." There, he thought. He had said her name aloud and nothing much had happened. Nothing except that the blood was surging through him in a way it had not in weeks. He still wanted her. Even his body was betraying him.

He did not ask her to sit down, but she sat in a chair across from him and stared at him for a moment, trying to gauge the extent of his recovery. He had regained his color; he had even smiled at her mistake.

"You, too, look nice," she said, her words halting and suddenly awkward. "I am glad to see you are not in bed."

He refrained from making a comment she knew she would not understand. "I'm feeling better every day. Still not walking, as you can see. But Caleb and Quentin insist on moving me around the room, so to keep them from nagging, I let them. It doesn't seem to be doing much good, but then, it doesn't hurt either."

She nodded, hating his casual, offhand tone, wishing he would ask her to move closer, to sit beside him.

He stared back, wishing she would pull her chair closer to him.

They talked of Busted Heel. Kase asked after everyone he could think of, which was everyone in town, and Rosa told him all she knew. Things were slow now that the snow had come. Even the farmers from outlying homesteads had given up coming into town. Slick, Paddie, Flossie, and the girls kept her busy cooking for them. Floss had once again asked her to move in and cook for her exclusively now that winter had diminished the restaurant trade. Rosa told him she still refused.

"Stubborn as ever," he said softly.

As you are, she wanted to respond, but she bit her tongue. "A person should take care for themselves."

"Independent."

"*Sì*. Independent."

If it had not been awkward to do so, Kase would have been content to sit and stare, to memorize every detail of her features, from the way her lashes curled upward at the tips to the way her full lower lip tempted him to kiss it. Her eyes shone like two huge, evenly matched topazes beneath her fine, arched brows. He knew without touching her that her skin was as smooth as satin and as warm as the velvet she wore.

"I brought you some cookies," she said, trying to break the spell his lazy gaze had cast over her.

"Thank you. I can't wait to try them."

"Your father said you will take dinner here. I will eat with you."

"I don't want you to miss the fun downstairs."

"You have no wish to join them?"

He shook his head. "No. I'm getting used to it here. It's a good place to think." He watched her stiffen and straighten on the chair.

"You think of me?"

"Sometimes," he lied. He could not tell her she was never out of his thoughts.

She tried to read the truth in his azure eyes, but his feelings were shuttered away. With every passing second, Rosa fought to ignore the tension building between them. It did no good for her to look away from his eyes, for everything about him made her want him more. The brilliant white shirt he was wearing only accentuated his smooth copper skin. His dark hair was neatly combed into place, no longer subjected to the wind that continually tossed the wayward, endearing lock over his forehead. The eyes, the nose, the lips she had come to love had not changed. It was the shuttered expression his features assumed—the cold, unswerving aloofness so reminiscent of the way he looked at her when they first met—that she could no longer stand.

She should never have come back.

Abruptly Rosa stood. "I still love you," she blurted out.

"Rose, listen—"

She cut the space between them in two. "To give up is the coward's way."

"Rose, stop."

She refused to beg, but she knew that if she had the least hope it would work, she was not too proud to try. This was her last chance. Soon he might be gone. She remembered what Flossie had said earlier: *Some men are too proud to bend.* Rosa leaned down, braced her hands on his shoulders, and pressed her lips against his.

Kase let her kiss him, but he steeled himself against the inevitable reaction. He kept his hands clamped around the edge of the chair seat, afraid to touch her, afraid of crushing her to him, of pouring out words of love.

When she did not end the kiss, but demanded more of him—deepened the pressure on his lips and played her tongue against the seam of his mouth—Kase felt his body come alive with sensations he had denied himself for far too long. The blood pulsed in his veins and surged into his loins with every heartbeat as his desire and need for Rose heightened. He fought against overwhelming need, refused to take advantage of her willingness when he knew it would only lead to pain.

Rosa let go of his shoulders and cradled his face between her palms. Now that she had tasted his lips, there was no turning back. She would make him love her, make him see that they belonged together forever. Under her unrelenting assault, his lips parted and she groaned with the pleasure of success as she slipped her tongue into the warm recesses of his mouth. Their tongues met and parted time after time as Kase and Rosa reveled in the reunion of senses.

His willpower crumbled as easily as dry leaves turned to dust underfoot. Kase enfolded her in his arms until he crushed her against him and she was lying across his lap.

Rosa melted into his embrace, her heart singing with joy. Kase loved her still. Just as she could not keep herself from loving him, he could not resist the temptation she offered. Aware of her position, she became suddenly wary, afraid of causing him pain or further injury, but when he pressed her closer and reached out to shift her against him until she was more comfortable, she felt the proof of his desire burgeoning beneath the pin-striped wool of his pants.

She slipped her arms about his neck and clung to him, afraid to speak for fear she might break the spell of love that bound them together. She knew that as long as she lived—whether she convinced him they belonged together or not—she would never forget this moment or the overwhelming desire and love that welled within her.

Kase knew he should stop himself, knew he should end the kiss and put aside the temptation she presented, but he could not stop himself any more than a starving man who had been invited to a banquet would deny himself food.

He groaned, half in protest, half in pleasure, when he felt her fingers loosen his waistband and then move down to free the buttons along the front of his pants. His throbbing member came to attention upon release and he heard her gasp when her warm fingertips tentatively touched his smooth, hard flesh.

She clung to him, eyes closed, lips seeking, as he held her there in his arms. Finally resigned to the fact that things had gone too far to be halted, Kase reached out and grasped her ankle, then ran his hand slowly along the gentle curve of her leg and up over the satin smoothness of her thigh until he reached the moist heated nest at the apex of her thighs.

Rosa was afraid to open her eyes for fear of finding that all she was experiencing was a dream, afraid that any moment he would reject her love again. Cradled in Kase's strong embrace, she willed herself to relax and enjoy the sensations that were building inside her. She dared not think about his family gathered downstairs, or what Analisa or Caleb would say should they walk in and find her on his lap. It was as it had always been with this man; she could deny him nothing.

As he slipped his fingers inside her, Rosa hoped he was preparing the way for his own more intimate entrance. She clung to his neck and pulled herself closer to the throbbing shaft imprisoned between them. His fingers moved faster, his touch became more demanding as he sought to bring her to fulfillment without him.

Rosa groaned and wriggled closer to him. She heard him sigh. When he slowed his ministrations and began to work her pantalets down around her hips and past her thighs, she hid her smile against his lips. Soon now they would be one.

She pulled away and hid her face against his neck. Her breathing was rapid, as ragged as his own. She ran one hand down the front of his shirt. Lower, ever lower, her fingers explored until she came in contact with his shaft again. Rosa took full advantage of his silent consent. With trembling hands, she enfolded his pulsing, hardened member.

When he groaned aloud and breathed her name against her ear, tears welled behind her lowered lids. It was the sweetest sound she had ever heard.

"Please, Kase," she pleaded softly. "Please love me."

He carefully raised her heavy skirt until it was gathered about her waist. His hands steady and sure, Kase grasped Rosa by the hips and helped her stand. He turned her until she faced him, then urged her forward, until she straddled him. He closed his eyes as Rosa gently lowered herself, easing him into her honeyed inner depths. He pressed her down until he was sheathed fully inside, then clasped her to him, afraid to move, afraid that he would reach his peak before she had even neared her own.

Rosa kissed him again. As her body quivered in readiness, her mind reeled with the knowledge of what she had done. What they were doing. She turned the thoughts aside and ached for more, longing for the completion she craved, yet savoring every moment. As Kase sat immobile, encased inside her, Rosa realized that he was unable to move and bring her to climax. With her arms locked about his neck, she drew herself upward along his length and heard him catch his breath before she lowered herself again. Two, three, four more times she rose up and thrust downward until she heard his strangled cry.

White heat shot through Rosa as Kase grasped her hips hard, held her immobile and poured himself into her. When she started to cry out in ecstasy, he silenced her with his lips. Still, his precaution could not quell the explosion of release that tore through her.

Kase kissed her slowly, lingeringly, until the inner throbbing subsided. Rosa pulled back and rested her head against his broad shoulder. She gazed up into the crystal blue eyes that stared down into hers, drank in the sight and smell of him, then wet her lips with her tongue and smiled tremulously.

Kase thought she had never looked so beautiful as she did lying satiated and content in his arms.

Chapter Twenty

He released her abruptly and in the most even, unfeeling tone he could manage said, "There's water in the basin. You'll want to wash up before you go downstairs."

Rosa pushed away from Kase and stared at him in disbelief. "But—"

He steeled himself against the slowly building anguish he saw gathering in her eyes. "I'd help you up"—he said coldly—"but as you know, I can't move."

She held her breath, her shock a viable thing he could almost feel. Kase began to hate himself for what he had to do.

"I don't understand," she whispered.

"This changes nothing, Rose."

"You said that I must have a whole man. What we have just done proves to me that you are still a man. There is no need for you to go away."

"There's still the fact that I can't walk. I can't do even the simplest things for myself. I can't work; I couldn't protect you if I had to. You might think this is enough for now, but I don't want to be around when you start hating me for the limitations I'd put on your life."

"I care nothing for these things. They do not matter to me."

"They matter to me. Would you please get up now?"

"Have you not enough love to trust me? I will never stop loving you."

"That's easy for you to say now. I've made up my mind."

"You are a *maiale*, a pig. You think only of yourself."

"Think what you want. Just get out and leave me alone."

She slapped him as hard as she could. "I hate you."

His expression was emotionless. "Good."

Humiliated, Rosa pushed herself up and away from him, then whirled around so as not to have to suffer the look on his face. The hem of her skirt dropped into place; then she nearly tripped over her pantalets as they tangled around her ankles. Her face aflame, Rosa bent and quickly pulled them up. Refusing to face him, she walked to the far side of the room and paused before the washstand.

He watched her walk away before he fastened the front of his trousers. Kase cleared his throat and finger-combed his hair into place. He longed to go to Rosa and hold her, to reassure her that it was best they parted this way—but if he could walk, if he could go to her, there would be no need to hurt her so.

Rosa found herself shaking. She tried to still the shudders that quaked through her, but found it impossible. She could feel him staring at her. Was he looking at her with disgust?

She refused to wash in front of him. There was no way she would humiliate herself any more than she had already. Determined to get out of the room while she still had the strength to do so, Rosa took a deep breath and whirled around.

Kase watched her straighten, tried to gauge her feelings when she turned toward him. His cool rejection had extinguished the glow in her eyes. Not only had the color in her cheeks flared but so had her anger. She was furious.

Good, he thought. Rose was a survivor. Her temper would see her through the next few hours and, he hoped, through the pain she would experience once the numbness left her. He only hoped it would be as easy for him.

With a sure, even stride, she walked to the door. For a moment he thought she might leave him without a word, but then he waited, certain that Rose would insist on having the last word. She proved him correct when she paused with her hand on the doorknob and glared at him.

It was a far different ending from the one she had envisioned on the ride out to the ranch. She watched Kase sit as still as a stone, his hands once again grasping the chair seat. She gave him one final chance to open his heart and his arms to her, but all he did was stare stonily.

"*Ciao*, Kase Storm," Rosa whispered.

Kase watched in silence until Rose was out of the room. Then, with a shaking hand, he lifted the crystal decanter of brandy from the table beside him and poured himself an overflowing glassful.

Rosa found the door to Caleb and Analisa's room open, so she slipped inside and helped herself to the water pitcher and basin. Once she had sponged away all traces of her encounter with Kase Storm, she pressed a cool, damp cloth against her brow. She stared at her reflection in the mirror above the chiffonier and wondered how she would ever muster the courage to go downstairs and eat dinner. The thought of food made her want to retch.

She was numb. Her feelings had flown along with her self-respect. She had tried and failed, and in doing so had made herself a fool in her own eyes. Moving without thought, she rinsed the washcloth clean, then carried the water basin across the room and set it on the floor while she raised the window. A blast of cold air swirled into the room, hitting her like a slap in the face. She shivered and quickly tossed the water outside, where it landed on the snow-covered porch roof below the window.

She shut out the cold, replaced the bowl and washcloth, and returned to peer into the mirror. The unrelieved black dress was a fitting choice, considering the circumstances; she felt as if someone had just died. Had her wearing black on such a festive day caused her ill luck? Had she gotten up on the left side of the bed? Rosa shrugged, pushed aside the superstitious thoughts that reminded her of Zia Rina, and continued to scrutinize her appearance. Her hair was still tightly wound in the coronet of braids. The cold air had added a spot of color to her pale complexion. She ignored the disbelief in her eyes and the way her lips trembled, and wondered if she would ever look at herself again without seeing an incredibly foolish woman.

Kase did not want her. Nothing she said or did could change the glaring realization she had faced a few moments ago. She had humiliated herself beyond redemption with a man she loved more than life itself. Her rage had peaked. Now she felt nothing.

Without looking back at the mirror, Rosa left the room and

went downstairs to join the others. Determined that they would never know the pain she was experiencing, she swore somehow to survive dinner as she had survived every other crisis she had faced. When she was back at the restaurant, secure in the privacy of her own room, then perhaps she might cry and purge herself of Kase Storm. Until then, she refused to let anyone see how very much he had hurt her.

"Rosa, come in. Join us," Analisa said when she noticed the girl standing uncertainly in the doorway.

They had gathered in the parlor—Quentin, Caleb, Analisa and Zach—to await the outcome of Rosa's visit with Kase. Now, as they stood expectantly waiting for her to make some comment, Analisa's heart went out to her. She wondered if Caleb was aware of the ashen pallor of the young woman's skin or the vacant expression in her eyes. Immediately, Analisa went to Rosa and led her into the parlor.

"Does he want to come down for dinner?" Quentin stood, obviously expecting the answer to be affirmative, ready to go up and help Caleb carry Kase downstairs.

Rosa paused momentarily before she shook her head. Analisa was afraid the girl was about to faint, but then she heard Rosa speak in a voice barely above a whisper. "No. He does not want to come down."

"I think we ought to bring him down here anyway," Quentin insisted. "I hate to think of him sitting up there all alone on Christmas Eve. What do you think, Caleb?"

Caleb glanced at Analisa and then shook his head. His face was grim, but his tone was sure. "I know Kase. He won't change his mind, and he wouldn't take kindly to our going against his wishes." He turned back to Analisa, glanced at Rosa, and with a reassuring nod added, "I think we should go on in and eat."

The table was spread with a veritable Christmas feast. Gilt-edged Haviland china sparkled on an Irish lace tablecloth. Ruby wineglasses added festive holiday color that complemented sprigs of pine spread about the tabletop. Roast goose, stuffing, potatoes, gravy, glazed carrots, Rosa's tortellini, fresh bread, jams and jellies. Quentin said the blessing, and the serving dishes were passed around the table. Analisa tried to ignore the sadness that lingered on the air. Despite the festive table setting, the delicious food, and good friends gathered together, she missed Kase and his teasing smile. She missed Annika, who should have been with them. Analisa looked around the table and told herself that this crisis would soon pass. Far worse things had happened in her life. She had a loving husband, a beautiful daughter, and a son who had survived a near fatal shooting. She had much to be thankful for. Why, then, did she feel such loss?

She watched Rosa toy with her food. The girl had taken little enough, but even the small portions proved to be too much. Caleb and Quentin tried to include Rosa in their conversation, but she failed to respond with more than monosyllabic answers. Zach was intent on his food. Although he still wore his fringed buckskin jacket, he had donned a new striped shirt for the occasion, and the usual stubble of a beard was missing. Analisa watched the old man, wondering if he knew how to deal with her son. The scout knew Kase as well as or better than anyone—and he had befriended Rosa. If he had any notion of what was happening between the two, Analisa could not tell.

When a heavy object hit the second floor just over their heads, everyone at the table started and looked up. Analisa began to rise, then abruptly sat back down. Rosa closed her eyes for an instant. Caleb frowned. The noise did not repeat itself.

"I'd better go up," Caleb said after a long, silent pause.

Analisa shook her head. "No. Leave him be. If he needs us he will call."

Rosa took a hearty drink of wine and turned to Quentin. Seated as he was at the head of the table, he reminded her of a king reigning over a royal banquet, for he made quite an imposing figure in his formal black suit and starched white shirt, his graying hair slicked down and shining.

She gathered her courage and took a deep breath. "Signor Quentin, you said once if ever I want your help, I must only ask for it."

"And I meant it. Are you thinking of expanding the business?"

"No"—she shook her head—"I want to sell."

Zach stopped chewing long enough to raise his head and stare at her.

"Sell?" Quentin frowned.

"Are you sure, Rosa? Isn't this a little sudden?" Caleb asked. He was so quick to furrow his brow that he reminded Rosa of Kase. She fought back an overwhelming urge to cry.

Instead, she shook her head and rapidly blinked back tears. "I want to sell Rosa's. I am leaving Wyoming."

Analisa could not keep the sadness from her voice. "Oh, Rosa. Think more about this."

Rose turned to her, her features set with determination. "I want to go."

Caleb stared at the girl and said softly, "Will you go back to Italy, Rosa?"

She shook her head emphatically. "No. Not Italy. I will go to California. There are many Italians there."

Quentin offered a solution. "How about if I give you the money to go to California, Rosa? You can see how you like it before you sell out. Then, if you don't want to come back here, you can deed over the place to me."

"I do not wish to come back. I leave for good."

Caleb, obviously upset, put his napkin beside his plate. "Listen, Rosa, I think you're being much too hasty about this. Why don't you wait a while longer?"

Analisa watched as Rosa turned to Caleb. Bright spots of color stained the girl's ivory cheeks. "I have waited. I have thought. I want to leave."

Zach leaned back and hooked an arm around the back of his chair. "Rosa's ain't a restaurant without a cook."

"He's got a point there, Rosa. If I buy your place, how am I supposed to run it?"

Analisa thought the girl was going to cry. She tried to intercede. "Rosa is just tired. She has been under a strain, like the rest of us."

Rosa shook her head. "I am not tired." She turned to Quentin and offered, "I will make promise, *signore*. You will not pay for the restaurant until I go to California and find another Italian who will come here to cook. Maybe it is better for a husband and wife to come to Busted Heel to run Rosa's. I will do this for you, and you will buy the café. Yes?"

"Of course." Quentin nodded, but he did not smile.

"*Va bene*. This is good."

Analisa felt more despondent with every passing moment.

Had she been wrong to hope for a reconciliation? Had she been responsible for Rosa's high hopes and subsequent disappointment? She glanced across the table at Caleb and found him watching her intently. As always, he was attuned to her feelings. She read the expression in his eyes, knew that her husband wished he could fix everything the way he had done when Kase was a child. She found herself smiling in response despite her anxiety. He returned her smile with one of his own. The gesture made her feel more secure, but she was far from convinced that things would ever be right again.

When Kase looked up through a drunken haze and saw Zach Elliot push open the door to his room, he was thankful that it was his old mentor and not his mother.

"You look like one hell of a mess," Zach said.

Kase tried not to slur his words. "I can always count on you to tell me the truth."

Zach walked over to where Kase sat sprawled on the floor, leaning back against the bed for support. The brandy decanter, empty now, sat on the floor between his legs. The top had rolled across the room and rested against the dresser. His glass had been abandoned an hour ago. Amber stains spotted his shirtfront, his hair dangled in his eyes. As Zach Elliot stood staring down at him, Kase felt the heat of embarrassment stain his cheeks.

"Never knew an Indian that could hold his liquor."

"Shut up, Zach."

"Get up and make me."

Kase stared at the other man's worn, mud-spattered boots and thought it quite remarkable how such details seemed overwhelmingly important when a man was drunk. "Go away."

Zach left Kase on the floor and sauntered over to the chair near the fire. "Nothing I hate more'n seein' a man at rock bottom."

"Yeah, well, this is it."

"I know, I been there."

Kase turned bleary eyes to Zach.

Without invitation, Zach began to explain. "Back in the late sixties, the year I was down in Texas, just after the war, I didn't never want to see the light o' day again. Tried to drown myself in a vat o' whiskey."

Zach stopped talking and leaned forward, forearms resting on his knees. Kase waited for him to continue, but the man infuriated him by remaining silent. Kase tried to focus, but instead of seeing Zach, he imagined himself and Rose using the chair as they had earlier.

He shook his head to dispel the memory and immediately regretted such a brain-jarring action. "You might as well finish it. What in the hell happened to you?"

"Found my kid dead. Wife butchered."

Kase snorted. "Indians, no doubt."

"My wife and kid *were* Indians. It were comancheros that killed 'em."

"I'm sorry."

Zach stretched. "No need for you to be sorry for me, boy. I did a fine job of bein' sorry for myself, jest like you are now. Then I got up and went on with my life."

"You're still expecting me to get up and walk just like the rest of them down there. Well, I hate to disappoint you."

"You don't know unless you try," Zach said softly.

Kase batted the decanter away, and the heavy cut-crystal piece slid across the hardwood floor until it bumped into the wall. He turned on Zach. "That's what you think, is it? That I haven't tried? How in the hell do you think I ended up down here? And this isn't the first time." He looked up, unable to stop the increasingly familiar fear and despair that swept through him. "I hate this. I hate what I've become. Hell, Zach, I've tried. I wake up in the middle of the night and try to walk. I pull myself as far as the edge of the bed. Sometimes I try to stand, but my legs just won't hold me. Then I ask myself if I want my mother to find me on the floor when she comes in of a morning. It happened once, you know, and I don't ever want to see that look on her face again. This is killing her, Zach."

Zach leaned forward, his elbows on his knees and looked Kase square in the eyes. "It ain't your ma I'm seein' sprawled drunk on the floor, boy. Seems to me it ain't killin' her as much as it is you." He leaned back again and said smugly, "You and that little Eye-talian girl downstairs."

"Leave her out of this."

"You won't have to worry about her anymore." Zach

shrugged. "Not with you goin' off to Boston and her leavin' Busted Heel for good."

Kase braced a hand against the floor as the room began to spin. "What are you talking about?"

"She's leavin'. Said so at the table. Quentin's buying her out. Probably givin' her twice what the place is worth, but after lookin' at her face when she asked if he'd help her, well, hell, I'da given her anything I had—if I had anything."

"How can she sell the business?" Kase scoffed in disbelief. "She *is* the business."

"Goin' to California. Said she'll send back some Eye-talians who can cook."

Kase shook his head, certain he'd heard wrong. "What in the hell does she plan on doing in California?"

Zach didn't answer.

"Well?" Kase prodded.

"What the hell do you care?"

The overwhelming certainty that he knew what was best for Rose hit him in much the same way it had the very first time he saw her. His mind drifted back to the day when he walked into his office and saw her hanging half off the chair, clinging to the bars of the jail cell. He smiled at nothing and shook his head.

Zach's gravelly voice interrupted his drunken musing. "She'll do just fine. Miz Rosa seems the type to land on her feet."

"Yeah." Somehow the thought did little to reassure Kase Storm.

"Yeah," Zach went on as if he were talking to himself, "she'll probably end up with some handsome Eye-talian fella that'll know how to treat her. Keep her locked up, a passel of kids runnin' at her heels. Probably the best thing for her."

Kase felt his anger rise within him. "Where is she now?"

"Shoot, she left an hour ago. Quentin drove her back."

Kase felt himself list to the left and tried to straighten up. His eyes focused again and he recognized the booted feet beside his legs. Zach was standing over him again.

"I'll put you back in bed." The old man's voice was low and filled with pity.

Whether the pity was feigned or not, it was more than Kase

could stand. "Keep your hands off me, you old coot. Just get out."

Zach ignored him and stooped over, hefting the heavier man with a grunt until he had Kase on the edge of the bed. "Ya big oaf, like t'kill me," he grumbled.

Kase wavered back and forth until he nearly toppled onto the floor again. Zach shoved him, and he sprawled on his back. Staring at the ceiling, he listened to Zach's footsteps as the man crossed the room.

The footsteps halted and Kase heard Zach open the door.

"If you have any notion of ever gettin' up and walkin', I think you come to that place in time."

As Zach Elliot closed the door, Kase Storm closed his eyes, but he could not shut out the spinning in his head or the tightening sensation around his heart.

A cozy fire crackled in the massive stone fireplace in the parlor at Mountain Shadows. As Analisa carried a tray laden with a silver coffee service and a plate of cookies into the room, Caleb stood to relieve her of the burden. He set the tray on a table drawn up before the settee, and Analisa poured the aromatic coffee into china cups. She handed the first cup to Kase, who sat alone on the settee. It was the day after Christmas, and his bout with self-pity had ended. He had even requested that Caleb and Quentin carry him downstairs for dinner. When he told Quentin he wanted time to speak to his parents alone, Rawlins had suggested they take their after-dinner coffee in the parlor.

Analisa served Caleb and herself and then sat down beside Kase on the settee, where she and her husband waited expectantly to hear what their son had to say.

"I'm staying here," Kase said without preamble.

Analisa looked to her husband for comment, but Caleb waited for Kase to explain.

"Quentin said he would put up with me a few more weeks, and Zach promised to help out. The doctor here says there is no evident medical reason why I can't walk, and if he's right, then I'd just be wasting your time and money going to Boston."

"You know that we can well afford any expense," Caleb began.

"I know that," Kase agreed, "but I want to try to get over this on my own before I give up and go to Boston."

Caleb looked at his wife, who gave him a nod of encouragement. "Did Rosa's announcement that she's leaving have anything to do with your decision?"

"Of course. But I don't want her to know anything about this. There's no need to get her hopes up, because there's no guarantee that I'll ever walk again. I want everything between us to stay just as it is for now."

"What if she leaves for San Francisco before you show any progress? Will you chance losing her?" Caleb asked.

"As far as I'm concerned, I've already lost her. That's the way I want it until I can go to her on my own two feet. If I succeed after she leaves, then I'll just have to go after her."

"And if she meets someone else?" Analisa could not hide her worry.

"That's a chance I'll just have to take. After what I've put her through, I'll be lucky if she'll have me. I want your word that you won't tell her that I'm staying. If I haven't made any progress in two to three weeks, I'll meet you in Boston." If there was no sign of progress, no hope of him ever walking again, Kase knew he would not care where he lived. "Quentin has agreed to stall Rose on the sale of the restaurant. That will give me a little more time before she leaves. Zach has agreed to take over as acting marshal."

"It sounds as if you've already thought this all through," Caleb said.

"I have. I woke up in the middle of the night with one hell of a hangover and nothing to do but think."

"We will stay to help—" Analisa began.

"Anja—" Caleb warned.

Kase interrupted them both. "This is something I have to do alone. You need to get home to Ruth and Annika. There's no telling what the two of them have gotten into." They all laughed, reminded of Caleb's stepmother, the self-proclaimed astrologer and the young beauty at home alone together in Boston.

"We'll go into town and get our tickets tomorrow," Caleb decided.

Kase looked at his mother and could almost see her mind at

work. "Mother, promise me you won't say anything to Rose when you go into Busted Heel."

"Kase—"

"Promise me."

"*Ik beloof je*. I promise."

Kase concentrated on the cup and saucer in his hand. "Good. I'll wire you in two to three weeks. *Ik beloof ja*." He smiled.

Silver dollar–sized flakes of snow drifted lazily to the ground on a windless morning two days after Christmas. Unable to stand the silence in the empty restaurant, Rosa tied on her scarf and donned her coat, trudged through the snow to the Davis shack, and asked permission to take G.W. and Martha home with her. Zetta readily complied, thankful for some reprieve from the two small children now that a new baby had joined them in such close quarters.

It did not take the children long to tire of playing underfoot, so Rosa decided to let them help her make some bicciolani di vercelli, the sweet spiced cookies Zia Rina always made at Christmastime. She pulled two chairs up to the worktable in the kitchen and had the children stand on them. They laughed and chattered as Rosa opened tins and pulled ingredients off the shelves. She let them sift the flour, and within moments she realized the idea had been a mistake. By the time they were finished, there was more flour on G.W. and Martha than in the bowl. As she scooped more flour out of the tin, Rosa shook her head and finally laughed for the first time in two days. There was no possible way she could scold the children for having such innocent fun. They were dusted with the powdery flour, their dark eyes and hair stood out in stark relief.

"Here," she said, breaking two eggs into the flour and sugar mixture in the bowl, "see if you can stir without making the mix fall out from the bowl."

She dampened a dish towel as they worked and was busy wiping flour off Martha's cheeks when Flossie opened the back door. Floss was bundled against the falling snow, a dark wool cape pulled tight across her overabundant bosom. The cold had heightened the color of her heavily rouged cheeks until they shone like polished red apples.

"Howdy, Rosie gal. I came to see how you're doin', but it

looks like you have your hands full." Flossie eyed the children as if she was not quite sure whether she should stay and witness the destruction of the kitchen.

"*Benvenuto*, Signora Flossie. Come. I will pour you coffee. We will talk."

Floss removed her cape and gloves and shook the snow from her hair. They sat at one end of the worktable so that Rosa could watch the children and occasionally add another ingredient to the cookie mixture.

"You plan on servin' those when they're finished?" Flossie asked skeptically.

Aware that G.W. was listening to her every word, Rosa assured her friend, "Of course, *signora*. These will be the best bicciolani ever."

G.W. smiled with satisfaction as his sister sneaked a lump of dough into her mouth.

Flossie's face mirrored the seriousness of her next question. "Are you of a different mind today, Rosa, or are you still set on leaving Busted Heel?"

Rosa tried not to show her sadness as she thought of leaving her dear friend behind. "Yes, *signora*. I must." There was no way she could remain and not be reminded of Kase everywhere she went.

"I sure wish you'd reconsider. If it's money you need, I'll give you whatever you want."

Rosa shook her head and blinked back tears. "No, *signora*, it is not money I need. In San Francisco there are many Italians. I will live among my own people. It will be easier."

"When you goin' away, Miz Rosa?" G.W.'s eyes were wide with disbelief.

"Not for many days," Rosa said. She had agreed to stay until the end of January. Quentin had asked her to wait until he sold a lot in Cheyenne. Until then, he had said, his funds were tied up.

Over cups of steaming coffee the two women spoke of the weather, of Paddie O'Hallohan's cough, of the latest news in the *Cheyenne Leader*. Flossie did not ask after Kase, and Rosa refused to bring up his name. The past was best forgotten.

A knock on the door of the restaurant summoned Rosa to the other room. She recognized Analisa and Caleb Storm at once and unlocked the door, ushering them inside. She was reminded once more what a striking couple they made, he tall and dark, a contrast to the glowing golden blond woman who looked like a queen, cloaked as she was in a rich sable coat.

Rosa immediately feared for Kase, then reminded herself that she no longer cared. But she could hide neither her concern nor the hope that he might have come to his senses. "Welcome, Signora, Signor Storm. Kase is well?"

They exchanged a glance that Rosa could not read, and then Analisa assured her, "He is as he always is—stubborn. But he is fine."

"I see." Rosa smiled, trying to assure them that she was over him. "Come in, then. I am happy to see you."

"We have been meaning to come in before this, but it's hard to get away from the ranch. Quentin is too kind a host." Caleb took off his hat and gloves and looked around the room. "You have a nice place here, Rosa."

"*Grazie, signore.*"

"It is so warm," Analisa added. "I am cold from the ride to town."

"You must stay and have coffee," Rosa said as she led them toward the kitchen. "You must meet my friend."

As soon as the words were out she prayed that Analisa and Caleb would not shun Flossie Gibbs when they were introduced to her. If it came to that, she would have to send them away, for Flossie had proven her friendship on more than one occasion and Rosa refused to see the woman hurt. She soon discovered she had worried unnecessarily, for when Analisa and Caleb entered the small back room they had only smiles and kind greetings for both Flossie and the children.

"What's this?" Caleb asked. "Cookie-baking day?" Making himself at home, he shrugged out of his coat and casually tossed it on the cot in the corner. "Hello"—he stood beside Martha and bent to inspect the dough balls she was forming— "I'm Caleb. Who are you?"

"Martha Washington Davis," the little girl lisped.

Caleb arched a brow as he addressed G.W. "And I suppose this is George Washington Davis?"

G.W. beamed, obviously delighted that the big man knew him. "Yes, suh. I am."

Rosa introduced Flossie, who stood up and prepared to leave.

At the mention of the other woman's name, Analisa Storm reached out and took Flossie Gibbs's hand and smiled. "I am so happy to meet you at last, Miss Gibbs. Kase speaks of you often and with much affection."

The madam beamed and Rosa wanted to hug Analisa for her sincere gesture of kindness, but at the mention of Kase's name, Floss's eyes filled with unshed tears. "If I'd ever had a son, I'd want one just like him," she said as she wiped away a stray tear. "We all miss him like the dickens. Still got his things up there in his room."

Caleb and Analisa exchanged a look of puzzlement and then Caleb laughed. "His room? We just assumed he had a place in the jailhouse."

Flossie turned beet red and shrugged before she sat back down. "Guess he didn't tell ya everything. He was rentin' a room from me over to the hospitality parlor." She suddenly flushed and cleared her throat before she took a sip of coffee.

Rosa wondered what was suddenly so amusing. Caleb Storm seemed unable to stop chuckling.

"Hospitality parlor." Analisa mused over the title. "It is a nice name for a rooming house, is it not, Caleb?"

Caleb winked at Flossie. It was Rosa's turn to flush. It seemed that Kase had told Caleb more about Flossie Gibbs than he had told his mother.

Caleb carried in two more chairs while Rosa served up two more cups of coffee and added more flour to the now useless cookie dough. The children were still interested and busy, rolling, patting and shaping the dough, and so Rosa let them play while the adults talked. Soon Flossie announced it was time for her to return home. Caleb offered to walk her back, but she insisted he stay where it was warm.

Once Floss had departed, Caleb said softly, "We came to tell you good-bye, Rosa." He took his wife's hand in his own and pressed it reassuringly. "We just came in today to see about tickets and to arrange for the trip to Boston."

And so the time had come. Rosa was grateful to them for warning her. She would not be anywhere near the front window tomorrow; she could not risk seeing them heading toward the station with Kase.

"We welcome you to stay with us in Boston if you ever wish

to visit," Analisa added. "Our Annika would be happy to show you the city."

Caleb pulled a folded square of paper from his pocket. "Here's our address."

"*Grazie. Molti grazie.*" It was all she could manage with her heart in her throat.

Caleb stood and collected their coats. He held Analisa's fur as she slipped it on. The deep sable created a startling contrast against her golden hair. Rosa watched them as they prepared to leave. There was nothing more she could do or say. She warned the children to stand still and not to make a mess while she walked her guests to the door.

"Safe journey," she bade the Storms. "I wish you well."

They walked through the dining room in silence. Analisa stayed behind with Rosa while Caleb stepped outside to untie the horses and brush the snow off the seat of the sleigh. The moment Rosa had dreaded was at hand.

Analisa reached out and took Rosa's hand in hers. For a moment she seemed to wrestle with her thoughts before she spoke softly, her accent heavily laced with Dutch. "Many times, Rosa, when things seem to be the worst, life brings to you a special gift. Never forget this in the days to come."

Rosa thought of all Analisa Storm had been through in the early years of her life. She remembered the story Kase had told her about his mother's rape, her family's murder, his own birth. Indeed, when Analisa's life must have seemed not worth living, she was given the gift of a son. Rosa tried to smile. If Analisa had survived so much tragedy, surely she could survive a broken heart.

"*Sì, signora.* I will remember." Rosa hugged Analisa and then stepped away. "*Ciao.*"

Analisa nodded. Her blue eyes glistened with unshed tears as she stepped outside. Rosa stood in the doorway and watched until the sleigh disappeared down Main Street.

*

Chapter
Twenty-One

*

The days passed slowly—frigid days with few hours of sunlight and many long, empty hours of darkness. Rosa kept the restaurant open, but heavy snow and fierce winds prevented most of the inhabitants of outlying ranches from coming into town. Paddie had a fierce cold for weeks. Afraid that he might develop pneumonia, Floss and Rosa combined forces to make certain he stayed in bed. Rosa hung a wreath of garlic about his neck and poured gallons of chicken soup down the little man while Flossie kept his bar open and liquor flowing for the few men who ventured into town every night. The two women talked of cutting a door through the wall of the Ruffled Garter into Rosa's, certain that it would be more convenient than having customers of both places face the cold walk back and forth. Flossie thought the idea a good one for Paddie, but not so good for Rosa. She worried that the proper ladies who ate in the café would not relish being in a room that opened into a saloon. Rosa finally agreed. She would leave the decision up to the new owner.

Two weeks earlier Zach Elliot had disappeared, so Slick Knox took over as acting marshal. Zach finally came to town once to let Rosa know he was working for Quentin and that she could send for him if she needed anything. She did not mention Kase, nor did he. She had hoped Kase's friend would return to tell her good-bye before she left for California, but now that her last full day in town had arrived, it was not likely that he would reappear.

Dawn imbued the frosted land with sparkling colors. Rosa drank in the scene from the wide front window of the café and considered it a parting gift from nature. When the sun was well up, she had a cup of coffee and then began packing a basket with baked goods she had made the day before. There was something for everyone—nut bread for the Davises, bicciollani for the Yees. Slick Knox favored her wheat bread and so she had made him two large loaves. There were two more for the Wilkies. Paddie would have a huge pan of rice pudding; for John Tuttle and the girls at Flossie's—more bicciollani.

She had decided to present Flossie with one of the crocheted doilies her *zia* had made, along with a bottle of the fine cabernet she had ordered from New York. Colorful grosgrain ribbons adorned each lovingly tied package.

Delivering the parting gifts proved harder than she had imagined. At each stop her friends alternately begged her not to leave and then—once they were convinced she would not change her mind—wished her a good journey. By the time she completed her rounds, Rosa had repeated her plans so often that she was tired of hearing the details: Quentin would come by in the morning to escort her as far as Cheyenne; yes, she would take the train directly to San Francisco; no, she had no one to meet her there, but she would locate the Italian quarter and find a place to stay; yes, she would write to them all. It was as hard leaving the people she had grown so close to as it had been to leave her family.

An early dinner with Flossie and the girls in the hospitality parlor kitchen was a subdued affair. Even Mira, who had never been as cordial to Rosa as the others, seemed genuinely sad to see her leave Busted Heel.

"Now we'll have to resort to eating Bertha Matheson's cookin' again," Flossie admitted through tears. "An' besides tastin' terrible, it's a pain in the neck to buy. I have to send Slick or Paddie by for my order. The hypocrite'll take my money, but she don't want me to be seen orderin' from her."

Rosa tried to smile as she reached out to pat Flossie's hand. "It will be only until I send someone to cook. Soon the restaurant will be open again."

A tear streaked Floss's powdered cheek. "Aw, Rosie gal, it'll be different without you here."

When the meal ended and Rosa announced it was time for her to leave, they all lined up in the front parlor to bid her farewell. Chicago Sue, her round china-doll eyes brimming with tears, hugged Rosa and sobbed until Flossie announced that the girl was ruining both her eyes and the front of her red satin gown. Ever cool, Mira didn't shed a tear, but she took Rosa's hand and wished her well. Satin, her plump cheeks ruddy with embarrassment, presented Rosa with a fine lace-edged handkerchief that had been doused with perfume. Felicity, with the bouncing black hair Rosa so admired, gave her a swift, tight hug and warned her against taking up with strangers on the train.

Finally it was time to bid Flossie farewell. The buxom redhead wiped her eyes on her own kerchief time and again as she stood with an arm about Rosa. "If that cussed mule Zach were here, he'd say I was spoutin' like a watering can." Flossie laughed through her tears.

"And so you are, my friend. Maybe you will come to San Francisco to visit me?" Rosa's expression was hopeful.

"You better believe it. I always wanted to see the place. Why"—Floss began to brighten—"I sometimes think I'd like to spend my old age in a warmer climate. Why not?" She shrugged, smiling once more. "Plan on it, Rosie gal. I'll be there before you know it."

"I will write to you as soon as I am there."

"You better," Flossie admonished. "And I'll let you know how everybody around these parts is gettin' along."

The time had come to end the farewells. Rosa gave them all a last look, a smile, and then kissed Flossie Gibbs on her rouged and powdered cheek.

"*Ciao, signora.*" When Rosa stepped out of the door, she was hit by a cold blast of wind. Quickly she wiped the tears from her cheeks before they had a chance to freeze.

The black velvet dress had been relegated to the very bottom of her trunk. Too practical to toss it out entirely, Rosa decided to take it with her, although the sight of the dress she had worn on Christmas Eve still conjured up far too much pain. Also packed safely away were her candlesticks and handmade cloths and runners—and one brittle, dried red rose from the bouquet Kase had given her. Determined to carry no reminders of him, she had nearly thrown it away, but then changed her mind. It was only a small token of what they had shared in happier times, so she decided to keep it a while longer.

The dishes and cooking utensils she would definitely leave behind; she considered them part of the place now. For a moment she wondered what kind of position she would find for herself in San Francisco. Maybe she would teach English, she thought, or perhaps find a job in a big hotel like the Inner Ocean in Cheyenne. Surely San Francisco had far bigger, grander places where she might find work.

When everything was safely packed away in her trunk, Rosa glanced around the kitchen to be certain she had not forgotten anything. Except for the pots, pans, and food tins on the shelves, the walls looked as bare and forlorn as they had on the day she moved in. The photographs of her mother and father no longer hung on the wall above her cot, nor did any of her clothing. There was a fire in the stove, but nothing simmering on top, no warm loaves of bread in readiness for tomorrow, no hint of cinnamon or other spices on the air. Her sauce pots were all clean and empty, hanging on the wall near the worktable.

She fed more wood into the stove and then took her last bottle of cabernet off of the shelf. Along with matches, an empty glass, and a candle, Rosa carried the wine into the darkened dining room and sat down alone at one of the tables. Earlier she had pulled the café curtains closed, hoping to discourage any last-minute visitors or customers who were not aware that the place was closed.

As Rosa lit the candle and poured herself a glass of wine, she paused to look around and think that this really was the perfect way to end her time in Busted Heel, for this was where it had all started. This was the place Giovanni had chosen to make their home. It was here, in the café, that she had begun her new life of independence. And here, she remembered, Kase Storm had walked in unexpectedly and kissed her for the first time.

Kase. She allowed herself to think of him for one moment, long enough to wonder how he fared in Boston, whether he was happy—or if he would ever be happy again.

The pins slipped easily from her hair, and she shook it free until it rippled down around her back. Rosa sighed and took a sip of wine, then stared into the candle's steady flame, thinking of how tomorrow she would board the train and head farther west, farther from Crotte than she ever imagined possible. Guido would be furious when he received her letter that announced her move to San Francisco. She had yet to receive any letters from home and wondered if she was out of their thoughts as well as their lives.

After another sip of wine she began counting the time since she arrived in Busted Heel. Only seven short months, yet they seemed to hold a lifetime of learning.

Halting footsteps scraped against the wooden sidewalk outside, and Rosa paused in her introspection to wonder if another stumbling drunk from Paddie's had lost his way. Her gaze flickered to the doorknob. Even though she tried to remember, she still had the bad habit of forgetting to lock both doors. Tonight she was certain that she had secured the front and back entries. Almost certain.

The shuffling stopped. She waited—listened—held her breath. Then, when there was no further sound from outside, she breathed a slow sigh of relief.

When something bumped against the door, she started and held her breath. Beyond the glow of the single candle, the room was swathed in darkness. Rosa stared hard at the place where she knew the doorknob to be, but could not see it. Slowly, silently, she stood, intent on moving across the room to bar the door.

She tried to call out, to tell whoever was on the other side that the place was closed, but the words stuck in her throat. All that came out was a croaking "Is closed."

Memories came flooding back. There was the reminder to lock the door Kase had issued so effectively the first night she had stayed alone here. Then, all too vividly, she recalled the day Bert Dawson had tried to assault her in this very room. Rosa found her mouth gone suddenly dry as her heart began to pound. She took two more steps toward the door.

It swung open before she could reach it and she stopped, arrested by the sight of the tall, dark shape of a man silhouetted against the star-spattered sky behind him. The man's height was exaggerated by the tall-crowned hat he wore. Whoever it was stood head and shoulders taller than any of the men she knew in Busted Heel. It was not the diminutive Paddie or the

lanky Slick. As he stepped closer, the candlelight further
defined his shape, and that of the bundle he held in his arms.
Whatever he carried he held dear, for he cradled the bulky
object as a mother would a babe.

Was her mind playing tricks on her? Had she wanted to see
Kase Storm again so badly that she was ready to claim that this
apparition in her doorway might be him? She licked her lips
and hoped that she could find her voice. "What do you want?"
The words came out in a hush that was barely a whisper.

"I want to know if you'll still have me."

There was no denying the deep, resonant timbre of Kase
Storm's voice. He took a slow, steady step forward and then
halted again.

Rosa could not move, nor could she speak. Her legs were
trembling so fiercely she thought she might collapse. She
reached out and braced herself with one hand on the back of a
nearby chair.

"Rose?"

She stared, speechless. Then she crossed herself. She
offered up a swift, silent prayer to San Genesio and swore that
if he removed this apparition, she would never sin again.

He took two more steps forward.

Frigid air swept in through the open door and set the
tablecloths fluttering. It guttered the candle flame, engulfing
them in darkness.

Shuffling sounds told her that he had stepped closer. One,
two, three more steps. She could hear his soft, steady breathing, then heard him move again.

A chair scraped somewhere nearby and then clattered to the
floor with a loud bang.

"Damn!" he cursed softly.

His frustrated curse jolted Rosa out of her shock. She
extended her arms and felt the air, stepping carefully in his
direction.

"Do not move," she said, at last able to think, to act.

"Don't worry," he assured her. "The last thing I intend to do
is fall."

The heavy wool of his coat was the first thing she grasped as
she reached out for him in the darkness. It was only natural
then to clutch his upper sleeves and hold on. The bundle in his
arms prevented her from stepping any closer. She made certain

he was steady on his feet, hoped she was steady on hers, and then breathed a sigh of relief.

"This isn't exactly the way I planned this scene," he said.

Even in the darkness, Rosa could hear the old familiar smile in his voice. It was a tone he had not used since the shooting. She swallowed and waited for him to explain.

"I wanted you to be able to witness the big surprise, but here we are in the dark. I guess that's not all that bad either." She felt him shrug.

"You are not in Boston." Her hands tightened on his sleeves.

"No. I'm not in Boston," he said softly. "I'm standing in the middle of a restaurant, in the dark, hoping I'm not about to break my damn-fool neck. Do you think you could let go long enough to light the candle?" he teased.

"Do you think you will not break any more of the furniture?" she countered.

"I'll try not to."

She let go and felt her way around him and closed the door. Then Rosa worked her way back to the table where she had left the candle. Her hands were shaking so hard it took her three tries to light a match, but finally the candle flared to life. She whirled around and found that he had not been a dream, nor was he an apparition. Kase Storm was standing in the middle of her café holding in his arms something wrapped in what appeared to be a linen dish towel. Rosa ignored the curious object and drank in the sight of him standing on his own feet.

Her hair swirled about her as she shook her head in disbelief. "How?"

He reached out and ran his fingers through the glossy fall of ebony. "God, you're beautiful."

Rosa reached out, her fingers hungry for the feel of him, and touched his cheek. "You are beautiful, too," she said.

They did not move. Rosa was afraid that he might disappear, Kase refused to rush the moment, and so they stood in silence, each engrossed with the other. He continued to stroke her hair. Rosa reached up and brushed the wayward lock of hair back off his brow and watched it fall back out of place. She fought to still her beating heart, fought to keep her emotions in check until she learned what he wanted, why he had come, and how he had regained his health.

Someone rode a horse down Main Street and the distraction broke the spell that surrounded them. Kase looked around the room. "May I sit down?"

Rosa pressed her palms against her flaming cheeks. "*Testa quadra.*" Blockhead. She whispered the curse under her breath. She had forgotten that he might be in pain. Quickly she pulled out a chair and held it while he set his bundle on the table and then slowly sat down.

Hastily she moved the candle to his table and then pulled out a chair for herself.

"Sit by me," he said softly.

She complied and pulled her chair up directly beside him. "Talk," she said.

He took off his hat and gloves and ran a hand through his hair. Even in the candlelight she could see his eyes sparkling with anticipation.

"First, Rose, I have to apologize. And I have to tell you that if you cannot forgive me for the way I treated you that I will understand." He took her cold hands and held them between his warm ones. "I'm so sorry, Rose. Truly, truly sorry."

She bit her trembling lips together and swallowed a sob. All she could manage was a nod.

"After you left my room on Christmas Eve, I proceeded to drink myself into oblivion. But the problem was that there wasn't enough liquor in Wyoming to make me forget what I'd done to you. Or to myself. When Zach told me you were leaving Busted Heel for good, something snapped inside me." He shrugged and squeezed her hands. "When I woke up from my stupor—with the worst hangover I've ever had, by the way—I was determined not to let you leave me."

"But you did not send for me again. It has been over a month."

"I put a condition on it. Since everyone but me was convinced there was no real reason why I couldn't walk, I told myself I was going to walk again, or crawl on my hands and knees and beg you to forgive me, if that's what it took to have you back. I sent my mother and Caleb home without me, made them promise not to tell you that I had changed my mind about leaving and that I was determined to get back on my feet. When I was finally regaining some feeling in my legs, Zach moved out to Mountain Shadows so he could help me daily."

"And so you walked again:"

"It wasn't all that simple. I had to spend a lot of time convincing myself there was nothing stopping me. Then I had Quentin and Zach half drag me around until I began to retrain myself to move. As time went on, whatever the problem was seemed to leave me."

Although he claimed it was not, it almost sounded too simple. She was still shaking, clinging to his hands, but she needed to have him answer one question more. "Will it come again?"

"My paralysis? My parents contacted a doctor in Boston who tried to explain it to them and then they wrote to tell me all he had said. I guess after I was wounded, somewhere in the back of my mind I was convinced I couldn't walk, and so I stayed paralyzed. As I fought to regain movement, it became easier and easier, until now the symptoms are gone. Now all I have to do is regain my strength."

Even more puzzled by his explanation, she frowned.

Kase smiled. "In a word, no. It won't come again."

"Zach helped you?"

He nodded. "That's why he hasn't been to town. I was afraid he'd let it slip somehow. I didn't want you to find out about this, in case I failed. He's been so damn smug about it all. I knew if he had the chance to place any bets about us getting back together, he'd be doing it. He drove me into town tonight."

"But I have a ticket." She glanced around the room, her eyes wide, uncertain. "I have sold the *caffè* to Signor Quentin. I—"

"Do you still love me, Rose? Can you still love me after everything I've put you through?"

How could I not? she wondered, but she asked him, "Why did you not come before this? Why did you make me wait until the last day? Tomorrow I am to leave."

"We were snowed in up at Mountain Shadows for nearly a week. I thought I was going to lose my mind before it cleared up enough for us to get into town. Zach tried to reassure me he'd drive me clear to San Francisco if he had to, but it didn't do much for my temper."

Rosa smiled. It wasn't hard for her to imagine the two of them arguing.

He leaned close, staring at her intently as his fingers began to rub the vulnerable spot on the inside of her wrist. "Will you have me back?"

For a fleeting second she wanted the satisfaction of saying no. No, because he had caused her such unrelieved pain; no, because she had nearly left behind all she had built. But as she stared into his eyes—eyes shining with love that he could not deny any more than she could deny her love for him—Rosa knew what her answer would be. It was the only answer she could give.

"I love you still," she whispered. "I will always love you, Kase Storm."

He reached toward her, and she flew out of her chair and into his arms. Bundled against him, she pressed as close as the bulk of his heavy coat would allow and wound her arms about his neck.

"God, I've missed you, Rose," he breathed against her lips. "More than you'll ever know."

His mouth came down on hers and he pressed her back as his lips and tongue made demands on her that she happily met and returned. His breath was warm, his skin still slightly chilled from the outdoors. An indefinable scent lingered on the air about him. Rosa pressed closer, eager to be as near him as possible. The kiss deepened until, breathless and panting, she pulled back.

"I think that before the night is over I will know how much you have missed me," she said.

He squeezed her tight. "You had better believe it." Then he straightened as he suddenly remembered the bundle on the table. "I almost forgot. I brought you a gift."

"Yes?"

"Yes. Close your eyes."

She did as he asked and felt him shift in the chair as he reached across her. Something brushed against her cheek and she suddenly caught an all too familiar scent drifting on the air.

She opened her eyes. The dish towel was gone, but in its place was a bouquet of deep red roses.

"For you," he said with as much of a bow as he could manage with her on his lap.

Gathering the roses in her arms, she dipped her head and drank in the scent of them. She realized their subtle fragrance had teased her since the moment he walked in the door.

"I'm afraid hothouse roses aren't as fragrant as the others."

"Roses in the month of January are *miracoloso*," she informed him, crushing the flowers between them as she leaned forward to kiss him again.

Kase stiffened when they heard a slight rattle against the front window. "Shh," he whispered. "Did you hear that?"

"*Sì*. What is—"

He put his hand across her lips.

This time he whispered against her ear. "Don't say anything."

Eyes wide, she nodded in understanding and he pulled his hand away.

Kase leaned close again. "I have a feeling it's either Zach or Flossie—or both of them—trying to see in."

Rosa tried to stifle a giggle.

He continued in a low voice. "Before I came over here we stopped at the hospitality parlor to surprise Floss and let her know I'd be staying in my old room tonight. Zach was taking bets from everybody as to whether or not you'd have me back."

She let go of him and slid off his lap, then tiptoed to the table where she had left her glass. She drank the last drops of wine and then smiled mischievously.

"What are you doing?" he whispered.

She held a finger to her lips silencing him before she winked and then drew back her arm and threw the wineglass at the side wall. "*Basta!*" she shouted. Rosa returned to his side and whispered, "They must not think that you are having the good luck yet. This will make the betting higher."

Footsteps faded on the walk outside as Kase stood to take her into his arms.

"And now?" she asked.

"Now I guess we had better decide what we're going to do next."

"I have, as you say in America, a very good idea."

"I have a feeling we both have the same idea."

"*Sì*."

"Will you marry me?"

"Now?"

"Tomorrow."

Rosa shrugged. "Tomorrow I was going to California—"

He squeezed her and glowered with feigned anger.

She shrugged. "But I think maybe tomorrow I marry."

"As long as it's me you're marrying," he warned.

"But of course." She smiled.

"About tonight . . ." He was not sure how to approach the subject of accommodations for the night. Kase held Rose close, tantalized by the fresh honeyed scent of her, and knew that leaving her for even a few hours would be hell after all the time they had been apart. He was determined, though, after all she had been through, to let her set the terms.

"Tonight I will sleep in your arms."

"You know, it's kind of strange, but suddenly I'm pretty tired." A slow, provocative half-smile teased his lips. "What do you say we go over to my room? Flossie said she'd leave the outside door to the second floor unlocked, and with all this snow the town's deserted."

"Suddenly I, too, am very tired. You will wait and I will get my coat."

"I'll wait," Kase said as he watched her cradle the flowers against her breast and savor the scent of them once more before she laid them on the table and left to collect her wrap.

A sound in the doorway between the two rooms caused him to look up. Rosa stood staring at him, her golden brown eyes shining in the candlelight, her expression radiant and alive with love and promise as she tied her scarf about her head and donned her jaunty Stetson. When she gathered up the roses and then placed her hand in his, Kase felt his heart swell with pride and happiness. He thought of his mother and Caleb and the years of happiness they had shared and knew that he and his Rose would know the same happiness. As he gazed down on her he could not resist teasing her once more. He reached out and toyed with one of the rose petals.

"Was my proposal romantic enough for you?"

Rosa arched a brow as she tried to look speculative. "If you were Italian I would say it was not so good . . ."

He put his hands on his hips and tried to look offended.

"But for an American"—she shrugged and then laughed—"is all right. We will go to Flossie's now and when we are in your room, I will let you try again."

"Until I get it right?"

"*Sì*, until you get it right."

Leaning close to her ear he whispered, "We have other things to practice, too."

"Many, many hours of practice," she said seriously.

Kase's laughter was a lighthearted, happy sound that filled Rosa with joy. He put on his gloves and hat. Rosa picked up the candle. Kase put an arm about her shoulders as they made their way through the darkness together.

If you enjoyed this book, take advantage of this special offer. Subscribe now and...

GET A *FREE*

NO OBLIGATION (a $3.95 value)

If you enjoy reading the very best historical romances, you'll want to subscribe to the True Value Historical Romance Home Subscription Service. Now that you have read one of the best historical romances around today, we're sure you'll want more of the same fiery passion, intimate romance and historical settings that set these books apart from all others.

Each month the editors of True Value will select the four very best historical romance novels from America's leading publishers of romantic fiction. Arrangements have been made for you to preview them in your home Free for 10 days. And with the first four books you receive, we'll send you a FREE book as our introductory gift. No obligation.

free home delivery

We will send you the four best and newest historical romances as soon as they are published to preview Free for 10 days. If for any reason you decide not to keep them, just return them and owe nothing. But if you like them as much as we think you will, you'll pay *just* $3.50 each and save at least $.45 each off the cover price. (Your savings are a minimum of $1.80 a month. There is *no* postage and handling – or other hidden charges. There are no minimum number of books to buy and you may cancel at any time.

HISTORICAL ROMANCE –

—send in the coupon below—

To get your FREE historical romance and start saving, fill out the coupon below and mail it today. As soon as we receive it we'll send you your FREE book along with your first month's selections.

Mail to: 10346-B
True Value Home Subscription Services, Inc.
P.O. Box 5235
120 Brighton Road
Clifton, New Jersey 07015-5235

YES! I want to start previewing the very best historical romances being published today. Send me my FREE book along with the first month's selections. I understand that I may look them over FREE for 10 days. If I'm not absolutely delighted I may return them and owe nothing. Otherwise I will pay the low price of just $3.50 each; a total of $14.00 (at least a $15.80 value) and save at least $1.80. Then each month I will receive four brand new novels to preview as soon as they are published for the same low price. I can always return a shipment and I may cancel this subscription at any time with no obligation to buy even a single book. In any event the FREE book is mine to keep regardless.

Name _____

Address _____ Apt. _____

City _____ State _____ Zip _____

Signature _____
                    (if under 18 parent or guardian must sign)
Terms and prices subject to change.